BIRTH OF A LOST NATION . . .

The young man was dressed only in walking shorts and soft bush shoes. "Friends," he said, "we are gathered here tonight to found a new nation."

He paused to let the idea sink in. "You know our situation. We fervently hope to be rescued. I will even go so far as to say that I think we will be rescued . . . eventually.

"It might be tomorrow . . . it might be our descendants a thousand years from now. But when the main body of our great race reestablishes contact with us, it is up to us whether they find a civilized society, or flea-bitten animals without language, without art—with the light of reason grown dim. Or no survivors at all, nothing but bones picked clean!"

"Heinlein has produced another ingenious piece of scientific imagination."
—*Saturday Review*

Tunnel
IN THE
Sky

Robert A. Heinlein

A Del Rey Book

BALLANTINE BOOKS • NEW YORK

A Del Rey Book
Published by Ballantine Books

Library of Congress Catalog Card Number: 55-10142

ISBN 0-345-26065-1-150

This edition published by arrangement with
Charles Scribner's Sons

Manufactured in the United States of America

First Ballantine Books Edition: March 1977

Cover art by Darrell Sweet

For **Jeannie** and **Bibs**

Contents

1

The Marching Hordes

THE BULLETIN BOARD OUTSIDE LECTURE HALL 1712-A of Patrick Henry High School showed a flashing red light. Rod Walker pushed his way into a knot of students and tried to see what the special notice had to say. He received an elbow in the stomach, accompanied by: "Hey! Quit shoving!"

"Sorry. Take it easy, Jimmy." Rod locked the elbow in a bone breaker but put no pressure on, craned his neck to look over Jimmy Throxton's head. "What's on the board?"

"No class today."

"Why not?"

A voice near the board answered him. "Because tomorrow it's 'Hail, Caesar, we who are about to die—'"

"So?" Rod felt his stomach tighten as it always did before an examination. Someone moved aside and he managed to read the notice:

PATRICK HENRY HIGH SCHOOL
Department of Social Studies

SPECIAL NOTICE to all students Course 410
(elective senior seminar) *Advanced Survival,*
instr. Dr. Matson, 1712-A MWF
1. There will be no class Friday the 14th.
2. *Twenty-Four Hour Notice* is hereby given of final examination in Solo Survival. Students will present themselves for physical check at 0900 Saturday in the dispensary of Templeton Gate and will start passing through the gate at 1000, using three-minute intervals by lot.

1

3. *TEST CONDITIONS:*
   (a) ANY planet, ANY climate, ANY terrain;
   (b) NO rules, ALL weapons, ANY equipment;
   (c) TEAMING IS PERMITTED but teams will not be allowed to pass through the gate in company;
   (d) TEST DURATION is not less than forty-eight hours, not more than ten days.
4. Dr. Matson will be available for advice and consultation until 1700 Friday.
5. Test may be postponed only on recommendation of examining physician, but any student may withdraw from the course without administrative penalty up until 1000 Saturday.
6. Good luck and long life to you all!

                                   (s)   **B. P. Matson, Sc.D.**

Approved:
   J. R. ROERICH, *for the Board*

Rod Walker reread the notice slowly, while trying to quiet the quiver in his nerves. He checked off the test conditions—why, those were not "conditions" but a total lack of conditions, no limits of any sort! They could dump you through the gate and the next instant you might be facing a polar bear at forty below—or wrestling an octopus deep in warm salt water.

Or, he added, faced up to some three-headed horror on a planet you had never heard of.

He heard a soprano voice complaining, " 'Twenty-four hour notice!' Why, it's less than twenty hours now. That's not fair."

Another girl answered, "What's the difference? I wish we were starting this minute. I won't get a wink of sleep tonight."

"If we are supposed to have twenty-four hours to get ready, then we ought to have them. Fair is fair."

Another student, a tall, husky Zulu girl, chuckled softly. "Go on in. Tell the Deacon that."

Rod backed out of the press, taking Jimmy Throxton with him. He felt that he knew what "Deacon" Matson would say . . . something about the irrelevancy of fairness to survival. He chewed over the bait in paragraph five; nobody would say boo if he dropped the course.

2

After all, "Advanced Survival" was properly a college course; he would graduate without it.

But he knew down deep that if he lost his nerve now, he would never take the course later.

Jimmy said nervously, "What d'you think of it, Rod?"

"All right, I guess. But I'd like to know whether or not to wear my long-handled underwear. Do you suppose the Deacon would give us a hint?"

"Him? Not him! He thinks a broken leg is the height of humor. That man would eat his own grandmother—without salt."

"Oh, come now! He'd use salt. Say, Jim? You saw what it said about teaming."

"Yeah . . . what about it?" Jimmy's eyes shifted away.

Rod felt a moment's irritation. He was making a suggestion as delicate as a proposal of marriage, an offer to put his own life in the same basket with Jimmy's. The greatest risk in a solo test was that a fellow just had to sleep sometime . . . but a team could split it up and stand watch over each other.

Jimmy must know that Rod was better than he was, with any weapon or bare hands; the proposition was to his advantage. Yet here he was hesitating as if he thought Rod might handicap him. "What's the matter, Jim?" Rod said bleakly. "Figure you're safer going it alone?"

"Uh, no, not exactly."

"You mean you'd rather not team with *me?*"

"No, no, I didn't mean that!"

"Then what did you mean?"

"I meant—Look, Rod, I surely do thank you. I won't forget it. But that notice said something else, too."

"What?"

"I said we could dump this durned course and still graduate. And I just happened to remember that I don't need it for the retail clothing business."

"Huh? I thought you had ambitions to become a wide-angled lawyer?"

"So exotic jurisprudence loses its brightest jewel . . . so what do I care? It will make my old man very happy

3

to learn that I've decided to stick with the family business."

"You mean you're scared."

"Well, that's one way of putting it. Aren't you?"

Rod took a deep breath. "Yes. I'm scared."

"Good! Now let's both give a classic demonstration of how to survive and stay alive by marching down to the Registrar's office and bravely signing our names to withdrawal slips."

"Uh, no. You go ahead."

"You mean you're sticking?"

"I guess so."

"Look, Rod, have you looked over the statistics on last year's classes?"

"No. And I don't want to. So long." Rod turned sharply and headed for the classroom door, leaving Jimmy to stare after him with a troubled look.

The lecture room was occupied by a dozen or so of the seminar's students. Doctor Matson, the "Deacon," was squatting tailor-fashion on one corner of his desk and holding forth informally. He was a small man and spare, with a leathery face, a patch over one eye, and most of three fingers missing from his left hand. On his chest were miniature ribbons, marking service in three famous first expeditions; one carried a tiny diamond cluster that showed him to be the last living member of that group.

Rod slipped into the second row. The Deacon's eye flicked at him as he went on talking. "I don't understand the complaints," he said jovially. "The test conditions say 'all weapons' so you can protect yourself any way you like . . . from a slingshot to a cobalt bomb. I think final examination should be bare hands, not so much as a nail file. But the Board of Education doesn't agree, so we do it this sissy way instead." He shrugged and grinned.

"Uh, Doctor, I take it then that the Board knows that we are going to run into dangerous animals?"

"Eh? You surely will! The most dangerous animal known."

"Doctor, if you mean that literally—"

"Oh, I do, I do!"

"Then I take it that we are either being sent to

4

Mithra and will have to watch out for snow apes, or we are going to stay on Terra and be dumped where we can expect leopards. Am I right?"

The Deacon shook his head despairingly. "My boy, you had better cancel and take this course over. Those dumb brutes aren't dangerous."

"But Jasper says, in *Predators and Prey,* that the two trickiest, most dangerous—"

"Jasper's maiden aunt! I'm talking about the *real* King of the Beasts, the only animal that is always dangerous, even when not hungry. The two-legged brute. Take a look around you!"

The instructor leaned forward. "I've said this nineteen dozen times but you still don't believe it. Man is the one animal that can't be tamed. He goes along for years as peaceful as a cow, when it suits him. Then when it suits him not to be, he makes a leopard look like a tabby cat. Which goes double for the female of the species. Take another look around you. All friends. We've been on group-survival field tests together; we can depend on each other. So? Read about the Donner Party, or the First Venus Expedition. Anyhow, the test area will have several other classes in it, all strangers to you." Doctor Matson fixed his eye on Rod. "I hate to see some of you take this test, I really do. Some of you are city dwellers by nature; I'm afraid I have not managed to get it through your heads that there are no policemen where you are going. Nor will I be around to give you a hand if you make some silly mistake."

His eye moved on; Rod wondered if the Deacon meant him. Sometimes he felt that the Deacon took delight in rawhiding him. But Rod knew that it was serious; the course was required for all the Outlands professions for the good reason that the Outlands were places where you were smart—or you were dead. Rod had chosen to take this course before entering college because he hoped that it would help him to get a scholarship—but that did not mean that he thought it was just a formality.

He looked around, wondering who would be willing to team with him now that Jimmy had dropped out. There was a couple in front of him, Bob Baxter and Carmen Garcia. He checked them off, as they undoubtedly would team together; they planned to become medical missionaries and intended to marry as soon as they could.

How about Johann Braun? He would make a real partner, all right—strong, fast on his feet, and smart. But Rod did not trust him, nor did he think that Braun would want him. He began to see that he might have made a mistake in not cultivating other friends in the class besides Jimmy.

That big Zulu girl, Caroline something-unpronounceable. Strong as an ox and absolutely fearless. But it would not do to team with a girl; girls were likely to mistake a cold business deal for a romantic gambit. His eyes moved on until at last he was forced to conclude that there was no one there to whom he wished to suggest partnership.

"Prof, how about a hint? Should we take suntan oil? Or chilblain lotion?"

Matson grinned and drawled, "Son, I'll tell you every bit that I know. This test area was picked by a teacher in Europe . . . and I picked one for his class. But I don't know what it is any more than you do. Send me a post card."

"But—" The boy who had spoken stopped. Then he suddenly stood up. "Prof, this isn't a fair test. I'm checking out."

"What's unfair about it? Not that we meant to make it fair."

"Well, you could dump us any place—"

"That's right."

"—the back side of the Moon, in vacuum up to our chins. Or onto a chlorine planet. Or the middle of an ocean. I don't know whether to take a space suit, or a canoe. So the deuce with it. Real life isn't like that."

"It isn't, eh?" Matson said softly. "That's what Jonah said when the whale swallowed him." He added, "But I will give you some hints. We mean this test to be passed by anyone bright enough to deserve it. So we won't let you walk into a poisonous atmosphere, or a vacuum, without a mask. If you are dumped into water, land won't be too far to swim. And so on. While I don't know where you are going, I did see the list of test areas for this year's classes. A smart man can survive in any

6

of them. You ought to realize, son, that the Board of Education would have nothing to gain by killing off all its candidates for the key professions."

The student sat down again as suddenly as he had stood up. The instructor said, "Change your mind again?"

"Uh, yes, sir. If it's a fair test, I'll take it."

Matson shook his head. "You've already flunked it. You're excused. Don't bother the Registrar; I'll notify him."

The boy started to protest; Matson inclined his head toward the door. "Out!" There was an embarrassed silence while he left the room, then Matson said briskly, "This is a class in applied philosophy and I am sole judge of who is ready and who is not. Anybody who thinks of the world in terms of what it 'ought' to be, rather than what it is, isn't ready for final examination. You've got to relax and roll with the punch . . . not get yourself all worn out with adrenalin exhaustion at the slings and arrows of outrageous fortune. Any more questions?"

There were a few more but it became evident that Matson either truthfully did not know the nature of the test area, or was guarding the knowledge; his answers gained them nothing. He refused to advise as to weapons, saying simply that the school armorer would be at the gate ready to issue all usual weapons, while any unusual ones were up to the individual. "Remember, though, your best weapon is between your ears and under your scalp—provided it's loaded."

The group started to drift away; Rod got up to leave. Matson caught his eye and said, "Walker, are you planning to take the test?"

"Why, yes, of course, sir."

"Come here a moment." He led him into his office, closed the door and sat down. He looked up at Rod, fiddled with a paperweight on his desk and said slowly, "Rod, you're a good boy . . . but sometimes that isn't enough."

Rod said nothing.

"Tell me," Matson continued, "why you want to take this test?"

"Sir?"

" 'Sir' yourself," Matson answered grumpily. "Answer my question."

Rod stared, knowing that he had gone over this with Matson before he was accepted for the course. But he explained again his ambition to study for an Outlands profession. "So I have to qualify in survival. I couldn't even get a degree in colonial administration without it, much less any of the planetography or planetology specialties."

"Want to be an explorer, huh?"

"Yes, sir."

"Like me."

"Yes, sir. Like you."

"Hmm . . . would you believe me if I told you that it was the worst mistake I ever made?"

"Huh? No, sir!"

"I didn't think you would. Son, the cutest trick of all is how to know *then* what you know *now*. No way to, of course. But I'm telling you straight: I think you've been born into the wrong age."

"Sir?"

"I think you are a romantic. Now this is a very romantic age, so there is no room in it for romantics; it calls for practical men. A hundred years ago you would have made a banker or lawyer or professor and you could have worked out your romanticism by reading fanciful tales and dreaming about what you might have been if you hadn't had the misfortune to be born into a humdrum period. But this happens to be a period when adventure and romance are a part of daily existence. Naturally it takes very practical people to cope with it."

Rod was beginning to get annoyed. "What's the matter with *me?*"

"Nothing. I like you. I don't want to see you get hurt. But you are 'way too emotional, too sentimental to be a real survivor type."

Matson pushed a hand toward him. "Now keep your shirt on. I know you can make fire by rubbing a couple of dry words together. I'm well aware that you won merit badges in practically everything. I'm sure you can devise a water filter with your bare hands and know which side of the tree the moss grows on. But I'm not sure that you can beware of the Truce of the Bear."

8

" 'The Truce of the Bear?' "

"Never mind. Son, I think you ought to cancel this course. If you must, you can repeat it in college."

Rod looked stubborn. Matson sighed. "I could drop you. Perhaps I should."

"But *why,* sir?"

"That's the point. I couldn't give a reason. On the record, you're as promising a student as I have ever had." He stood up and put out his hand. "Good luck. And remember—when it gets down to fundamentals, do what you have to do and shed no tears."

Rod should have gone straight home. His family lived in an out-county of Greater New York City, located on the Grand Canyon plateau through Hoboken Gate. But his commuting route required him to change at Emigrants' Gap and he found himself unable to resist stopping to rubberneck.

When he stepped out of the tube from school he should have turned right, taken the rotary lift to the level above, and stepped through to Arizona Strip. But he was thinking about supplies, equipment, and weapons for tomorrow's examination; his steps automatically bore left, he got on the slideway leading to the great hall of the planetary gates.

He told himself that he would watch for only ten minutes; he would not be late for dinner. He picked his way through the crowd and entered the great hall—not onto the emigration floor itself, but onto the spectator's balcony facing the gates. This was the new gate house he was in, the one opened for traffic in '68; the original Emigrants' Gap, now used for Terran traffic and trade with Luna, stood on the Jersey Flats a few kilometers east alongside the pile that powered it.

The balcony faced the six gates. It could seat eighty-six hundred people but was half filled and crowded only in the center. It was here, of course, that Rod wished to sit so that he might see through all six gates. He wormed his way down the middle aisle, squatted by the railing, then spotted someone leaving a front row seat. Rod grabbed it, earning a dirty look from a man who had started for it from the other aisle.

Rod fed coins into the arm of the seat; it opened out,

he sat down and looked around. He was opposite the replica Statue of Liberty, twin to the one that had stood for a century where now was Bedloe Crater. Her torch reached to the distant ceiling; on both her right and her left three great gates let emigrants into the outer worlds.

Rod did not glance at the statue; he looked at the gates. It was late afternoon and heavily overcast at east coast North America, but gate one was open to some planetary spot having glaring noonday sun; Rod could catch glimpses through it of men dressed in shorts and sun hats and nothing else. Gate number two had a pressure lock rigged over it; it carried a big skull & crossbones sign and the symbol for chlorine. A red light burned over it. While he watched, the red light flickered out and a blue light replaced it; the door slowly opened and a traveling capsule for a chlorine-breather crawled out. Waiting to meet it were eight humans in diplomatic full dress. One carried a gold baton.

Rod considered spending another half pluton to find out who the important visitor was, but his attention was diverted to gate five. An auxiliary gate had been set up on the floor, facing gate five and almost under the balcony. Two high steel fences joined the two gates, forming with them an alley as wide as the gates and as long as the space between, about fifteen meters by seventy-five. This pen was packed with humanity moving from the temporary gate toward and through gate five—and onto some planet light-years away. They poured out of nowhere, for the floor back of the auxiliary gate was bare, hurried like cattle between the two fences, spilled through gate five and were gone. A squad of brawny Mongol policemen, each armed with a staff as tall as himself, was spread out along each fence. They were using their staves to hurry the emigrants and they were not being gentle. Almost underneath Rod one of them prodded an old coolie so hard that he stumbled and fell. The man had been carrying his belongings, his equipment for a new world, in two bundles supported from a pole balanced on his right shoulder.

The old coolie fell to his skinny knees, tried to get up, fell flat. Rod thought sure he would be trampled, but somehow he was on his feet again—minus his baggage.

He tried to hold his place in the torrent and recover his possessions, but the guard prodded him again and he was forced to move on barehanded. Rod lost sight of him before he had moved five meters.

There were local police outside the fence but they did not interfere. This narrow stretch between the two gates was, for the time, extraterritorial; the local police had no jurisdiction. But one of them did seem annoyed at the brutality shown the old man; he put his face to the steel mesh and called out something in lingua terra. The Mongol cop answered savagely in the same simple language, telling the North American what he could do about it, then went back to shoving and shouting and prodding still more briskly.

The crowd streaming through the pen were Asiatics—Japanese, Indonesians, Siamese, some East Indians, a few Eurasians, but predominantly South Chinese. To Rod they all looked much alike—tiny women with babies on hip or back, or often one on back and one in arms, endless runny-nosed and shaven-headed children, fathers with household goods in enormous back packs or pushed ahead on barrows. There were a few dispirited ponies dragging two-wheeled carts much too big for them but most of the torrent had only that which they could carry.

Rod had heard an old story which asserted that if all the Chinese on Terra were marched four abreast past a given point the column would never pass that point, as more Chinese would be born fast enough to replace those who had marched past. Rod had taken his slide rule and applied arithmetic to check it—to find, of course, that the story was nonsense; even if one ignored deaths, while counting all births, the last Chinese would pass the reviewing stand in less than four years. Nevertheless, while watching this mob being herded like brutes into a slaughterhouse, Rod felt that the old canard was true even though its mathematics was faulty. There seemed to be no end to them.

He decided to risk that half pluton to find out what was going on. He slid the coin into a slot in the chair's speaker; the voice of the commentator reached his ears: "—the visiting minister. The prince royal was met by officials of the Terran Corporation including the Director General himself and now is being escorted to the locks of the Ratoonian enclave. After the television reception tonight staff level conversations will start. A spokesman close to the Director General has pointed out that, in view of the impossibility of conflict of interest between oxygen types such as ourselves and the Ratoonians, any outcome of the conference must be to our advantage, the question being to what extent.

"If you will turn your attention again to gate five, we will repeat what we said earlier: gate five is on forty-eight hour loan to the Australasian Republic. The temporary gate you see erected below is hyperfolded to a point in central Australia in the Arunta Desert, where this emigration has been mounting in a great encampment for the past several weeks. His Serene Majesty Chairman Fung Chee Mu of the Australasian Republic has informed the Corporation that his government intends to move in excess of two million people in forty-eight hours, a truly impressive figure, more than forty thousand each hour. The target figure for this year for all planetary emigration gates taken together—Emigrants' Gap, Peter the Great, and Witwatersrand Gates —is only seventy million emigrants or an average of eight thousand per hour. This movement proposes a rate five times as great using only *one* gate!"

The commentator continued: "Yet when we watch the speed, efficiency and the, uh—*forthrightness* with which they are carrying out this evolution it seems likely that they will achieve their goal. Our own figures show them to be slightly ahead of quota for the first nine hours. During those same nine hours there have been one hundred seven births and eighty-two deaths among the emigrants, the high death rate, of course, being incident to the temporary hazards of the emigration.

"The planet of destination, GO-8703-IV, to be called henceforth 'Heavenly Mountains' according to Chairman Fung, is classed as a bounty planet and no attempt had been made to colonize it. The Corporation has been assured that the colonists are volunteers." It seemed to Rod that the announcer's tone was ironical. "This is understandable when one considers the phenomenal population pressure of the Australasian Republic. A brief historical rundown may be in order. After the re-

12

moval of the remnants of the former Australian population to New Zealand, pursuant to the Peiping Peace Treaty, the first amazing effort of the new government was the creation of the great inland sea of—"

Rod muted the speaker and looked back at the floor below. He did not care to hear school-book figures on how the Australian Desert had been made to blossom like the rose . . . and nevertheless had been converted into a slum with more people in it than all of North America. Something new was happening at gate four—

Gate four had been occupied by a moving cargo belt when he had come in; now the belt had crawled away and lost itself in the bowels of the terminal and an emigration party was lining up to go through.

This was no poverty-stricken band of refugees chivvied along by police; here each family had its own wagon . . . long, sweeping, boat-tight Conestogas drawn by three-pair teams and housed in sturdy glass canvas . . . square and businesslike Studebakers with steel bodies, high mudcutter wheels, and pulled by one or two-pair teams. The draft animals were Morgans and lordly Clydesdales and jug-headed Missouri mules with strong shoulders and shrewd, suspicious eyes. Dogs trotted between wheels, wagons were piled high with household goods and implements and children, poultry protested the indignities of fate in cages tied on behind, and a little Shetland pony, riderless but carrying his saddle and just a bit too tall to run underneath with the dogs, stayed close to the tailgate of one family's rig.

Rod wondered at the absence of cattle and stepped up the speaker again. But the announcer was still droning about the fertility of Australasians; he muted it again and watched. Wagons had moved onto the floor and taken up tight echelon position close to the gate, ready to move, with the tail of the train somewhere out of sight below. The gate was not yet ready and drivers were getting down and gathering at the Salvation Army booth under the skirts of the Goddess of Liberty, for a cup of coffee and some banter. It occurred to Rod that there probably was no coffee where they were going and might not be for years, since Terra never exported food —on the contrary, food and fissionable metals were almost the only permissible imports; until an Outland

13

colony produced a surplus of one or the other it could expect precious little help from Terra.

It was extremely expensive in terms of uranium to keep an interstellar gate open and the people in this wagon train could expect to be out of commercial touch with Earth until such a time as they had developed surpluses valuable enough in trade to warrant reopening the gate at regular intervals. Until that time they were on their own and must make do with what they could take with them . . . which made horses more practical than helicopters, picks and shovels more useful than bulldozers. Machinery gets out of order and requires a complex technology to keep it going—but good old "hayburners" keep right on breeding, cropping grass, and pulling loads.

Deacon Matson had told the survival class that the real hardhips of primitive Outlands were not the lack of plumbing, heating, power, light, nor weather conditioning, but the shortage of simple things like coffee and tobacco.

Rod did not smoke and coffee he could take or let alone; he could not imagine getting fretful over its absence. He scrunched down in his seat, trying to see through the gate to guess the cause of the holdup. He could not see well, as the arching canvas of a prairie schooner blocked his view, but it did seem that the gate operator had a phase error; it looked as if the sky was where the ground ought to be. The extradimensional distortions necessary to match places on two planets many light-years apart were not simply a matter of expenditure of enormous quantities of energy; they were precision problems fussy beyond belief, involving high mathematics and high art—the math was done by machine but the gate operator always had to adjust the last couple of decimal places by prayer and intuition.

In addition to the dozen-odd proper motions of each of the planets involved, motions which could usually be added and canceled out, there was also the rotation of each planet. The problem was to make the last hyperfold so that the two planets were internally tangent at the points selected as gates, with their axes parallel and their rotations in the *same* direction. Theoretically it was possible to match two points in contra-rotation,

14

twisting the insubstantial fabric of space-time in exact step with "real" motions; practically such a solution was not only terribly wasteful of energy but almost unworkable—the ground surface beyond the gate tended to skid away like a slidewalk and tilt at odd angles.

Rod did not have the mathematics to appreciate the difficulties. Being only about to finish high school his training had gone no farther than tensor calculus, statistical mechanics, simple transfinities, generalized geometries of six dimensions, and, on the practical side, analysis for electronics, primary cybernetics and robotics, and basic design of analog computers; he had had no advanced mathematics as yet. He was not aware of his ignorance and simply concluded that the gate operator must be thumb-fingered. He looked back at the emigrant party.

The drivers were still gathered at the booth, drinking coffee and munching doughnuts. Most of the men were growing beards; Rod concluded from the beavers that the party had been training for several months. The captain of the party sported a little goatee, mustaches, and rather long hair, but it seemed to Rod that he could not be many years older than Rod himself. He was a professional, of course, required to hold a degree in Outlands arts—hunting, scouting, jackleg mechanics, gunsmithing, farming, first aid, group psychology, survival group tactics, law, and a dozen other things the race has found indispensable when stripped for action.

This captain's mount was a Palomino mare, lovely as a sunrise, and the captain was dressed as a California don of an earlier century—possibly as a compliment to his horse. A warning light flashed at the gate's annunciator panel and he swung into saddle, still eating a doughnut, and cantered down the wagons for a final inspection, riding toward Rod. His back was straight, his seat deep and easy, his bearing confident. Carried low on a fancy belt he wore two razor guns, each in a silver-chased holster that matched the ornate silver of his bridle and saddle.

Rod held his breath until the captain passed out of sight under the balcony, then sighed and considered studying to be like him, rather than for one of the more intellectual Outlands professions. He did not know just

15

what he did want to be . . . except that he meant to get off Earth as soon as he possibly could and get out there where things were going on!

Which reminded him that the first hurdle was tomorrow; in a few days he would either be eligible to matriculate for whatever it was he decided on, or he would be—but no use worrying about *that*. He remembered uneasily that it was getting late and he had not even decided on equipment, nor picked his weapons. This party captain carried razor guns; should he carry one? No, this party would fight as a unit, if it had to fight. Its leader carried that type of weapon to enforce his authority—not for solo survival. Well, what should he take?

A siren sounded and the drivers returned to their wagons. The captain came back at a brisk trot. "Reins up!" he called out. "Reeeeeeiiiins UP!" He took station by the gate, facing the head of the train; the mare stood quivering and tending to dance.

The Salvation Army lassie came out from behind her counter carrying a baby girl. She called to the party captain but her voice did not carry to the balcony.

The captain's voice did carry. "Number four! Doyle! Come get your child!" A red-headed man with a spade beard climbed down from the fourth wagon and sheepishly reclaimed the youngster to a chorus of cheers and cat calls. He passed the baby up to his wife, who upped its skirt and commenced paddling its bottom. Doyle climbed to his seat and took his reins.

"Call off!" the captain sang out.

"One."

"Tuh!"

"Three!"

"*Foah!*"

"*Five!*"

The count passed under the balcony, passed down the chute out of hearing. In a few moment it came back, running down this time, ending with a shouted *"ONE!"* The captain held up his right arm and watched the lights of the order panel.

A light turned green. He brought his arm down smartly with a shout of "Roll 'em! *Ho!*" The Palomino took off like a race horse, cut under the nose of the nigh lead horse of the first team, and shot through the gate.

Whips cracked. Rod could hear shouts of "Git, Molly! Git, Ned!" and "No, no, you jugheads!" The train begin to roll. By the time the last one on the floor was through the gate and the much larger number which had been in the chute below had begun to show it was rolling at a gallop, with the drivers bracing their feet wide and their wives riding the brakes. Rod tried to count them, made it possibly sixty-three wagons as the last one rumbled through the gate . . . and was gone, already half a galaxy away.

He sighed and sat back with a warm feeling sharpened with undefined sorrow. Then he stepped up the speaker volume: "—onto New Canaan, the premium planet described by the great Langford as 'The rose without thorns.' These colonists have paid a premium of sixteen thousand four hundred per person—not counting exempt or co-opted members—for the privilege of seeking their fortunes and protecting their posterity by moving to New Canaan. The machines predict that the premium will increase for another twenty-eight years; therefore, if you are considering giving your children the priceless boon of citizenship on New Canaan, the time to act is now. For a beautiful projection reel showing this planet send one pluton to 'Information, Box One, Emigrants' Gap, New Jersey County, Greater New York.' For a complete descriptive listing of all planets now open plus a special list of those to be opened in the near future add another half pluton. Those seeing this broadcast in person may obtain these at the information booth in the foyer outside the great hall."

Rod did not listen. He had long since sent for every free item and most of the non-free ones issued by the Commission for Emigration and Trade. Just now he was wondering why the gate to New Canaan had not relaxed.

He found out at once. Stock barricades rose up out of the floor, forming a fenced passage from gate four to the chute under him. Then a herd of cattle filled the gate and came flooding toward him, bawling and snorting. They were prime Hereford steers, destined to become tender steaks and delicious roasts for a rich but

17

slightly hungry Earth. After them and among them rode New Canaan cowpunchers armed with long goads with which they urged the beasts to greater speed—the undesirability of running weight off the animals was offset by the extreme cost of keeping the gate open, a cost which had to be charged against the cattle.

Rod discovered that the speaker had shut itself off; the half hour he had paid for was finished. He sat up with sudden guilt, realizing that he would have to hurry or he would be late for supper. He rushed out, stepping on feet and mumbling apologies, and caught the slideway to Hoboken Gate.

This gate, being merely for Terra-surface commuting, was permanently dilated and required no operator, since the two points brought into coincidence were joined by a rigid frame, the solid Earth. Rod showed his commuter's ticket to the electronic monitor and stepped through to Arizona, in company with a crowd of neighbors.

"The (almost) solid Earth—" The gate robot took into account tidal distortions but could not anticipate minor seismic variables. As Rod stepped through he felt his feet quiver as if to a small earthquake, then the *terra* was again *firma*. But he was still in an airlock at sea-level pressure. The radiation from massed bodies triggered the mechanism, the lock closed and air pressure dropped. Rod yawned heavily to adjust to the pressure of Grand Canyon plateau, North Rim, less than three quarters that of New Jersey. But despite the fact that he made the change twice a day he found himself rubbing his right ear to get rid of an earache.

The lock opened, he stepped out. Having come two thousand miles in a split second he now had ten minutes by slide tube and a fifteen minute walk to get home. He decided to dogtrot and be on time after all. He might have made it if there had not been several thousand other people trying to use the same facilities.

2

The Fifth Way

ROCKET SHIPS DID NOT CONQUER SPACE; THEY MERELY challenged it. A rocket leaving Earth at seven miles per second is terribly slow for the vast reaches beyond. Only the Moon is reasonably near—four days, more or less. Mars is thirty-seven weeks away, Saturn a dreary six years, Pluto an impossible half century, by the elliptical orbits possible to rockets.

Ortega's torch ships brought the Solar System within reach. Based on mass conversion, Einstein's deathless $e = Mc^2$, they could boost for the entire trip at any acceleration the pilot could stand. At an easy one gravity the inner planets were only hours from Earth, far Pluto only eighteen days. It was a change like that from horseback to jet plane.

The shortcoming of this brave new toy was that there was not much anywhere to go. The Solar System, from a human standpoint, is made up of remarkably unattractive real estate—save for lovely Terra herself, lush and green and beautiful. The steel-limbed Jovians enjoy gravity 2.5 times ours and their poisonous air at inhuman pressure keeps them in health. Martians prosper in near vacuum, the rock lizards of Luna do not breathe at all. But these planets are not for men.

Men prosper on an oxygen planet close enough to a G-type star for the weather to cycle around the freezing point of water . . . that is to say, on Earth.

When you are already there why go anywhere? The reason was babies, too many babies. Malthus pointed it out long ago; food increases by aritmetical progression, people increase by geometrical progression. By World War I half the world lived on the edge of starvation;

by World War II Earth's population was increasing by 55,000 people *every day;* before World War III, as early as 1954, the increase had jumped to 100,000 mouths and stomachs per day, 35,000,000 additional people each year . . . and the population of Terra had climbed well beyond that which its farm lands could support.

The hydrogen, germ, and nerve gas horrors that followed were not truly political. The true meaning was more that of beggars fighting over a crust of bread.

The author of *Gulliver's Travels* sardonically proposed that Irish babies be fattened for English tables; other students urged less drastic ways of curbing population—none of which made the slightest difference. Life, *all* life, has the twin drives to survive and to reproduce. Intelligence is an aimless byproduct except as it serves these basic drives.

But intelligence *can* be made to serve the mindless demands of life. Our Galaxy contains in excess of one hundred thousand Earth-type planets, each as warm and motherly to men as sweet Terra. Ortega's torch ships could reach the stars. Mankind could colonize, even as the hungry millions of Europe had crossed the Atlantic and raised more babies in the New World.

Some did . . . hundreds of thousands. But the entire race, working as a team, cannot build and launch a hundred ships a day, each fit for a thousand colonists, and keep it up day after day, year after year, time without end. Even with the hands and the will (which the race never had) there is not that much steel, aluminum, and uranium in Earth's crust. There is not one hundredth of the necessary amount.

But intelligence can find solutions where there are none. Psychologists once locked an ape in a room, for which they had arranged only four ways of escaping. Then they spied on him to see which of the four he would find.

The ape escaped a fifth way.

Dr. Jesse Evelyn Ramsbotham had not been trying to solve the baby problem; he had been trying to build a time machine. He had two reasons: first, because time machines are an impossibility; second, because his hands would sweat and he would stammer whenever in the presence of a nubile female. He was not aware that the first reason was compensation for the second, in fact he was not aware of the second reason—it was a subject his conscious mind avoided.

It is useless to speculate as to the course of history had Jesse Evelyn Ramsbotham's parents had the good sense to name their son Bill instead of loading him with two girlish names. He might have become an All-American halfback and ended up selling bonds and adding his quota of babies to a sum already disastrous. Instead he became a mathematical physicist.

Progress in physics is achieved by denying the obvious and accepting the impossible. Any nineteenth century physicist could have given unassailable reasons why atom bombs were impossible if his reason were not affronted at the question; any twentieth century physicist could explain why time travel was incompatible with the real world of space-time. But Ramsbotham began fiddling with the three greatest Einsteinian equations, the two relativity equations for distance and duration and the mass-conversion equation; each contained the velocity of light. "Velocity" is first derivative, the differential of distance with respect to time; he converted those equations into differential equations, then played games with them. He would feed the results to the Rakitiac computer, remote successor to Univac, Eniac and Maniac. While he was doing these things his hands never sweated nor did he stammer, except when he was forced to deal with the young lady who was chief programmer for the giant computer.

His first model produced a time-stasis or low-entropy field no bigger than a football—but a lighted cigarette placed inside with full power setting was still burning a week later. Ramsbotham picked up the cigarette, resumed smoking and thought about it.

Next he tried a day-old chick, with colleagues to witness. Three months later the chick was unaged and no hungrier than chicks usually are. He reversed the phase relation and cut in power for the shortest time he could manage with his bread-boarded hook-up.

In less than a second the newly-hatched chick was long dead, starved and decayed.

He was aware that he had simply changed the slope

21

of a curve, but he was convinced that he was on the track of true time travel. He never did find it, although once he thought that he had—he repeated by request his demonstration with a chick for some of his colleagues; that night two of them picked the lock on his lab, let the little thing out and replaced it with an egg. Ramsbotham might have been permanently convinced that he had found time travel and then spent the rest of his life in a blind alley had they not cracked the egg and showed him that it was hard-boiled.

But he did not give up. He made a larger model and tried to arrange a dilation, or anomaly (he did not call it a "Gate") which would let him get in and out of the field himself.

When he threw on power, the space between the curving magnetodes of his rig no longer showed the wall beyond, but a steaming jungle. He jumped to the conclusion that this must be a forest of the Carboniferous Period. It had often occurred to him that the difference between space and time might simply be human prejudice, but this was not one of the times; he believed what he wanted to believe.

He hurriedly got a pistol and with much bravery and no sense crawled between the magnetodes.

Ten minutes later he was arrested for waving firearms around in Rio de Janeiro's civic botanical gardens. A lack of the Portuguese language increased both his difficulties and the length of time he spent in a tropical pokey, but three days later through the help of the North American consul he was on his way home. He thought and filled notebooks with equations and question marks on the whole trip.

The short cut to the stars had been found.

Ramsbotham's discoveries eliminated the basic cause of war and solved the problem of what to do with all those dimpled babies. A hundred thousand planets were no farther away than the other side of the street. Virgin continents, raw wilderness, fecund jungles, killing deserts, frozen tundras, and implacable mountains lay just beyond the city gates, and the human race was again going out where the street lights do not shine, out where there was no friendly cop on the corner nor indeed a

22

corner, out where there were no well-hung, tender steaks, no boneless hams, no packaged, processed foods suitable for delicate minds and pampered bodies. The biped omnivore again had need of his biting, tearing, animal teeth, for the race was spilling out (as it had so often before) to kill or be killed, eat or be eaten.

But the human race's one great talent is survival. The race, as always, adjusted to conditions, and the most urbanized, mechanized, and civilized, most upholstered and luxurious culture in all history trained its best children, its potential leaders, in primitive pioneer survival —man naked against nature.

Rod Walker knew about Dr. J. E. Ramsbotham, just as he knew about Einstein, Newton, and Columbus, but he thought about Ramsbotham no oftener than he thought about Columbus. These were figures in books, each larger than life and stuffed with straw, not real. He used the Ramsbotham Gate between Jersey and the Arizona Strip without thinking of its inventor the same way his ancestors used elevators without thinking of the name "Otis." If he thought about the miracle at all, it was a half-formed irritation that the Arizona side of Hoboken Gate was so far from his parents' home. It was known as Kaibab Gate on this side and was seven miles north of the Walker residence.

At the time the house had been built the location was at the extreme limit of tube delivery and other city utilities. Being an old house, its living room was above ground, with only bedrooms, pantry, and bombproof buried. The living room had formerly stuck nakedly above ground, an ellipsoid monocoque shell, but, as Greater New York spread, the neighborhood had been zoned for underground apartments and construction above ground which would interfere with semblance of virgin forest had been forbidden.

The Walkers had gone along to the extent of covering the living room with soil and planting it with casual native foliage, but they had refused to cover up their view window. It was the chief charm of the house, as it looked out at the great canyon. The community corporation had tried to coerce them into covering it up and had offered to replace it with a simulacrum window

23

such as the underground apartments used, with a relayed view of the canyon. But Rod's father was a stubborn man and maintained that with weather, women, and wine there was nothing "just as good." His window was still intact.

Rod found the family sitting in front of the window, watching a storm work its way up the canyon—his mother, his father, and, to his great surprise, his sister. Helen was ten years older than he and an assault captain in the Amazons; she was seldom home.

The warmth of his greeting was not influenced by his realization that her arrival would probably cause his own lateness to pass with little comment. "Sis! Hey, this is *swell*—I thought you were on Thule."

"I was . . . until a few hours ago." Rod tried to shake hands; his sister gathered him in a bear hug and bussed him on the mouth, squeezing him against the raised ornaments of her chrome corselet. She was still in uniform, a fact that caused him to think that she had just arrived—on her rare visits home she usually went slopping around in an old bathrobe and go-ahead slippers, her hair caught up in a knot. Now she was still in dress armor and kilt and had dumped her side arms, gauntlets, and plumed helmet on the floor.

She looked him over proudly. "My, but you've grown! You're almost as tall as I am."

"I'm taller."

"Want to bet? No, don't try to wiggle away from me; I'll twist your arm. Slip off your shoes and stand back to back."

"Sit down, children," their father said mildly. "Rod, why were you late?"

"Uh . . ." He had worked out a diversion involving telling about the examination coming up, but he did not use it as his sister intervened.

"Don't heckle him, Pater. Ask for excuses and you'll get them. I learned that when I was a sublieutenant."

"Quiet, daughter. I can raise him without your help."

Rod was surprised by his father's edgy answer, was more surprised by Helen's answer: "So? Really?" Her tone was odd.

Rod saw his mother raise a hand, seem about to speak, then close her mouth. She looked upset. His

24

sister and father looked at each other; neither spoke. Rod looked from one to the other, said slowly, "Say, what's all this?"

His father glanced at him. "Nothing. We'll say no more about it. Dinner is waiting. Coming, dear?" He turned to his wife, handed her up from her chair, offered her his arm.

"Just a minute," Rod said insistently. "I was late because I was hanging around the Gap."

"Very well. You know better, but I said we would say no more about it." He turned toward the lift.

"But I wanted to tell you something else, Dad. I won't be home for the next week or so."

"Very well—*eh?* What did you say?"

"I'll be away for a while, sir. Maybe ten days or a bit longer."

His father looked perplexed, then shook his head. "Whatever your plans are, you will have to change them. I can't let you go away at this time."

"But, Dad—"

"I'm sorry, but that is definite."

"But, Dad, I *have* to!"

"No."

Rod looked frustrated. His sister said suddenly, "Pater, wouldn't it be well to find out why he wants to be away?"

"Now, daughter—"

"Dad, I'm taking my solo survival, starting tomorrow morning!"

Mrs. Walker gasped, then began to weep. Her husband said, "There, there, my dear!" then turned to his son and said harshly, "You've upset your mother."

"But, Dad, I . . ." Rod shut up, thinking bitterly that no one seemed to give a hoot about *his* end of it. After all, *he* was the one who was going to have to sink or swim. A lot they knew or—

"You see, Pater," his sister was saying. "He does have to be away. He has no choice, because—"

"I see nothing of the sort! Rod, I meant to speak about this earlier, but I had not realized that your test would take place so soon. When I signed permission for you to take that course, I had, I must admit, a mental reservation. I felt that the experience would be valuable

25

later . . . when and if you took the course in college. But I never intended to let you come up against the final test while still in high school. You are too young."

Rod was shocked speechless. But his sister again spoke for him. "Fiddlesticks!"

"Eh? Now, daughter, please remember that—"

"Repeat fiddlesticks! Any girl in my company has been up against things as rough and many of them are not much older than Buddy. What are you trying to do, Pater? Break his nerve?"

"You have no reason to . . . I think we had best discuss this later."

"I think that is a good idea." Captain Walker took her brother's arm and they followed their parents down to the refectory. Dinner was on the table, still warm in its delivery containers; they took their places, standing, and Mr. Walker solemnly lighted the Peace Lamp. The family was evangelical Monist by inheritance, each of Rod's grandfathers having been converted in the second great wave of proselyting that swept out of Persia in the last decade of the previous century, and Rod's father took seriously his duties as family priest.

As the ritual proceeded Rod made his responses automatically, his mind on this new problem. His sister chimed in heartily but his mother's answers could hardly be heard.

Nevertheless the warm symbolism had its effect; Rod felt himself calming down. By the time his father intoned the last "—one Principle, one family, one flesh!" he felt like eating. He sat down and took the cover off his plate.

A yeast cutlet, molded to look like a chop and stripped with real bacon, a big baked potato, and a grilled green lobia garnished with baby's buttons . . . Rod's mouth watered as he reached for the catsup.

He noticed that Mother was not eating much, which surprised him. Dad was not eating much either but Dad often just picked at his food . . . he became aware with sudden warm pity that Dad was thinner and greyer than ever. How old was Dad?

His attention was diverted by a story his sister was telling: "—and so the Commandant told me I would have to clamp down. And I said to her, 'Ma'am, girls

26

will be girls. If I have to bust a petty officer everytime one of them does something like that, pretty soon I won't have anything but privates. And Sergeant Dvorak is the best gunner I have.' "

"Just a second," her father interrupted. "I thought you said 'Kelly,' not 'Dvorak.' "

"I did and she did. Pretending to misunderstand which sergeant she meant was my secret weapon—for I had Dvorak cold for the same offense, and Tiny Dvorak (she's bigger than I am) is the Squadron's white hope for the annual corps-wide competition for best trooper. Of course, losing her stripes would put her, and us, out of the running.

"So I straightened out the 'mix up' in my best wide-eyed, thick-headed manner, let the old gal sit for a moment trying not to bite her nails, then told her that I had both women confined to barracks until that gang of college boys was through installing the new 'scope, and sang her a song about how the quality of mercy is not strained, it droppeth as the gentle rain from heaven, and made myself responsible for seeing to it that she was not again embarrassed by scandalous—her word, not mine —scandalous incidents . . . especially when she was showing quadrant commanders around.

"So she grumpily allowed as how the company commander was responsible for her company and she would hold me to it and now would I get out and let her work on the quarterly training report in peace? So I threw her my best parade ground salute and got out so fast I left a hole in the air."

"I wonder," Mr. Walker said judicially, "if you should oppose your commanding officer in such matters? After all, she is older and presumably wiser than you are."

Helen made a little pile of the last of her baby's buttons, scooped them up and swallowed them. "Fiddlesticks squared and cubed. Pardon me, Pater, but if you had any military service you would know better. I am as tough as blazes to my girls myself . . . and it just makes them boast about how they've got the worst fire-eater in twenty planets. But if they're in trouble higher up, I've got to take care of my kids. There always comes a day when there is something sticky up ahead

27

and I have to stand up and walk toward it. And it will be all right because I'll have Kelly on my right flank and Dvorak on my left and each of them trying to take care of Maw Walker all by her ownself. I know what I'm doing. 'Walker's Werewolves' are a team."

Mrs. Walker shivered. "Gracious, darling, I wish you had never taken up a calling so . . . well, so *dangerous*."

Helen shrugged. "The death rate is the same for us as for anybody . . . one person, one death, sooner or later. What would you want, Mum? With eighteen million more women than men on this continent did you want me to sit and knit until my knight comes riding? Out where I operate, there are more men than women; I'll wing one yet, old and ugly as I am."

Rod asked curiously, "Sis, would you really give up your commission to get married?"

"Would I! I won't even count his arms and legs. If he is still warm and can nod his head, he's had it. My target is six babies and a farm."

Rod looked her over. "I'd say your chances are good. You're quite pretty even if your ankles are thick."

"Thanks, pardner. Thank you too much. What's for dessert, Mum?"

"I didn't look. Will you open it, dear?"

Dessert turned out to be iced mangorines, which pleased Rod. His sister went on talking. "The Service isn't a bad shake, on active duty. It's garrison duty that wears. My kids get fat and sloppy and restless and start fighting with each other from sheer boredom. For my choice, barracks casualties are more to be dreaded than combat. I'm hoping that our squadron will be tagged to take part in the pacification of Byer's Planet."

Mr. Walker looked at his wife, then at his daughter. "You have upset your mother again, my dear. Quite a bit of this talk has hardly been appropriate under the Light of Peace."

"I was asked questions, I answered."

"Well, perhaps so."

Helen glanced up. "Isn't it time to turn it out, anyway? We all seem to have finished eating."

"Why, if you like. Though it is hardly reverent to hurry."

"The Principle knows we haven't all eternity." She

28

turned to Rod. "How about making yourself scarce, mate? I want to make palaver with the folks."

"Gee, Sis, you act as if I was—"

"Get lost, Buddy. I'll see you later."

Rod left, feeling affronted. He saw Helen blow out the pax lamp as he did so.

He was still making lists when his sister came to his room. "Hi, kid."

"Oh. Hello, Sis."

"What are you doing? Figuring what to take on your solo?"

"Sort of."

"Mind if I get comfortable?" She brushed articles from his bed and sprawled on it. "We'll go into that later."

Rod thought it over. "Does that mean Dad won't object?"

"Yes. I pounded his head until he saw the light. But, as I said, we'll go into that later. I've got something to tell you, youngster."

"Such as?"

"The first thing is this. Our parents are not as stupid as you probably think they are. Fact is, they are pretty bright."

"I never said they were stupid!" Rod answered, uncomfortably aware of what his thoughts had been.

"No. But I heard what went on before dinner and so did you. Dad was throwing his weight around and not listening. But, Buddy, it has probably never occurred to you that it is hard work to be a parent, maybe the hardest job of all—particularly when you have no talent for it, which Dad hasn't. He knows it and works hard at it and is conscientious. Mostly he does mighty well. Sometimes he slips, like tonight. But, what you did not know is this: Dad is going to die."

"*What?*" Rod looked stricken. "I didn't know he was ill!"

"You weren't meant to know. Now climb down off the ceiling; there is a way out. Dad is terribly ill, and he would die in a few weeks at the most—unless something drastic is done. But something is going to be. So relax."

29

She explained the situation bluntly: Mr. Walker was suffering from a degenerative disease under which he was slowly starving to death. His condition was incurable by current medical art; he might linger on, growing weaker each day, for weeks or months—but he would certainly die soon.

Rod leaned his head on his hands and chastised himself. Dad dying . . . and he hadn't *even noticed*. They had kept it from him, like a baby, and he had been too stupid to see it.

His sister touched his shoulder. "Cut it out. If there is anything stupider than flogging yourself over something you can't help, I've yet to meet it. Anyhow, we are doing something about it."

"What? I thought you said nothing could be done?"

"Shut up and let your mind coast. The folks are going to make a Ramsbotham jump, five hundred to one, twenty years for two weeks. They've already signed a contract with Entropy, Incorporated. Dad has resigned from General Synthetics and is closing up his affairs; they'll kiss the world good-by this coming Wednesday—which is why he was being stern about your plans to be away at that time. You're the apple of his eye—Heaven knows why."

Rod tried to sort out too many new ideas at once. A time jump . . . of course! It would let Dad stay alive another twenty years. But— "Say, Sis, this doesn't get them anything! Sure, it's twenty years but it will be just two weeks to them . . . and Dad will be as sick as ever. I know what I'm talking about; they did the same thing for Hank Robbin's great grandfather and he died anyhow, right after they took him out of the stasis. Hank told me."

Captain Walker shrugged. "Probably a hopeless case to start with. But Dad's specialist, Dr. Hensley, says that he is morally certain that Dad's case is not hopeless . . . twenty years from now. I don't know anything about metabolic medicine, but Hensley says that they are on the verge and that twenty years from now they ought to be able to patch Dad up as easily they can graft on a new leg today."

"You really think so?"

"How should I know? In things like this you hire the

30

best expert you can, then follow his advice. The point is, if we don't do it, Dad is finished. So we do it."

"Yeah. Sure, sure, we've got to."

She eyed him closely and added, "All right. Now do you want to talk with them about it?"

"Huh?" He was startled by the shift. "Why? Are they waiting for me?"

"No. I persuaded them that it was best to keep it from you until it happened. Then I came straight in and told you. Now you can do as you please—pretend you don't know, or go have Mum cry over you, and listen to a lot of last-minute, man-to-man advice from Dad that you will never take. About midnight, with your nerves frazzled, you can get back to your preparations for your survival test. Play it your own way—but I've rigged it so you can avoid that, if you want to. Easier on everybody. Myself, I like a cat's way of saying good-by.'"

Rod's mind was in a turmoil. Not to say good-by seemed unnatural, ungrateful, untrue to family sentiment—but the prospect of saying good-by seemed almost unbearably embarrassing. "What's that about a cat?"

"When a cat greets you, he makes a big operation of it, bumping, stropping your legs, buzzing like mischief. But when he leaves, he just walks off and never looks back. Cats are smart."

"Well . . ."

"I suggest," she added, "that you remember that they are doing this for their convenience, not yours."

"But Dad has to—"

"Surely, Dad must, if he is to get well." She considered pointing out that the enormous expense of the time jump would leave Rod practically penniless; she decided that this was better left undiscussed. "But Mum does not have to."

"But she has to go with Dad!"

"So? Use arithmetic. She prefers leaving you alone for twenty years in order to be with Dad for two weeks. Or turn it around: she prefers having you orphaned to having herself widowed for the same length of time."

"I don't think that's quite fair to Mum," Rod answered slowly.

31

"I wasn't criticizing. She's making the right decision. Nevertheless, they both have a strong feeling of guilt about you and—"

"About *me?*"

"About you. I don't figure into it. If you insist on saying good-by, their guilt will come out as self-justification and self-righteousness and they will find ways to take it out on you and everybody will have a bad time. I don't want that. You are all my family."

"Uh, maybe you know best."

"I didn't get straight A's in emotional logic and military leadership for nothing. Man is not a rational animal; he is a rationalizing animal. Now let's see what you plan to take with you."

She looked over his lists and equipment, then whistled softly. "Whew! Rod, I never saw so much plunder. You won't be able to move. Who are you? Tweedledum preparing for battle, or the White Knight?"

"Well, I was going to thin it down," he answered uncomfortably.

"I should think so!"

"Uh, Sis, what sort of gun should I carry?"

"Huh? Why the deuce do you want a gun?"

"Why, for what I might run into, of course. Wild animals and things. Deacon Matson practically said that we could expect dangerous animals."

"I doubt if he advised you to carry a gun. From his reputation, Dr. Matson is a practical man. See here, infant, on this tour you are the rabbit, trying to escape the fox. You aren't the fox."

"What do you mean?"

"Your only purpose is to stay alive. Not to be brave, not to fight, not to dominate the wilds—but just stay breathing. One time in a hundred a gun might save your life; the other ninety-nine it will just tempt you into folly. Oh, no doubt Matson would take one, and I would, too. But we are salted; we know when not to use one. But consider this. That test area is going to be crawling with trigger-happy young squirts. If one shoots you, it won't matter that you have a gun, too—because you will be dead. But if you carry a gun, it makes you feel cocky; you won't take proper cover. If you don't have one, then you'll *know* that you are the rabbit. You'll be careful."

"Did you take a gun on your solo test?"

"I did. And I lost it the first day. Which saved my life."

"How?"

"Because when I was caught without one I ran away from a Bessmer's griffin instead of trying to shoot it. You savvy Bessmer's griffin?"

"Uh, Spica V?"

"Spica IV. I don't know how much outer zoology they are teaching you kids these days—from the ignoramuses we get for recruits I've reached the conclusion that this new-fangled 'functional education' has abolished studying in favor of developing their cute little personalities. Why, I had one girl who wanted to— never mind; the thing about the griffin is that it does not really have vital organs. Its nervous system is decentralized, even its assimilation system. To kill it quickly you would have to grind it into hamburger. Shooting merely tickles it. But I did not know that; if I had had my gun I would have found out the hard way. As it was, it treed me for three days, which did my figure good and gave me time to think over the philosophy, ethics, and pragmatics of self-preservation."

Rod did not argue, but he still had a conviction that a gun was a handy thing to have around. It made him feel good, taller, stronger and more confident, to have one slapping against his thigh. He didn't have to use it—not unless he just had to. And he knew enough to take cover; nobody in the class could do a silent sneak the way he could. While Sis was a good soldier, still she didn't know everything and—

But Sis was still talking. "I know how good a gun feels. It makes you bright-eyed and bushy-tailed, three meters tall and covered with hair. You're ready for anything and kind of hoping you'll find it. Which is exactly what is dangerous about it—because you aren't anything of the sort. You are a feeble, hairless embryo, remarkably easy to kill. You could carry an assault gun with two thousand meters precision range and isotope charges that will blow up a hill, but you still would not have eyes in the back of your head like a janus bird,

33

nor be able to see in the dark like the Thetis pygmies. Death can cuddle up behind you while you are drawing a bead on something in front."

"But, Sis, your own company carries guns."

"Guns, radar, bombs, black scopes, gas, warpers, and some things which we light-heartedly hope are secret. What of it? You aren't going to storm a city. Buddy, sometimes I send a girl out on an infiltration patrol, object: information—go out, find out, come back alive. How do you suppose I equip her?"

"Uh—"

"Never mind. In the first place I don't pick an eager young recruit; I send some unkillable old-timer. She peels down to her underwear, darkens her skin if it is not dark, and goes out bare-handed and bare-footed, without so much as a fly swatter. I have yet to lose a scout that way. Helpless and unprotected you do grow eyes in the back of your head, and your nerve ends reach out and feel everything around you. I learned that when I was a brash young j.o., from a salty trooper old enough to be my mother."

Impressed, Rod said slowly, "Deacon Matson told us he would make us take this test bare-handed, if he could."

"Dr. Matson is a man of sense."

"Well, what would *you* take?"

"Test conditions again?"

Rod stated them. Captain Walker frowned. "Mmm . . . not much to go on. Two to ten days probably means about five. The climate won't be hopelessly extreme. I suppose you own a Baby Bunting?"

"No, but I've got a combat parka suit. I thought I would carry it, then if the test area turned out not to be cold, I'd leave it at the gate. I'd hate to lose it; it weighs only half a kilo and cost quite a bit."

"Don't worry about that. There is no point in being the best dressed ghost in Limbo. Okay, besides your parka I would make it four kilos of rations, five of water, two kilos of sundries like pills and matches, all in a vest pack . . . and a knife."

"That isn't much for five days, much less ten."

"It is all you can carry and still be light on your feet. Let's see your knife, dear."

Rod had several knives, but one was "his" knife, a lovely all-purpose one with a 21-cm. molysteel blade and a fine balance. He handed it to his sister, who cradled it lightly. "Nice!" she said, and glanced around the room.

"Over there by the outflow."

"I see." She whipped it past her ear, let fly, and the blade sank into the target, sung and quivered. She reached down and drew another from her boot top. "This is a good one, too." She threw and it bit into the target a blade's width from the first.

She retrieved both knives, stood balancing them, one on each hand. She flipped her own so that the grip was toward Rod. "This is my pet, 'Lady Macbeth.' I carried her on my own solo, Buddy. I want you to carry her on yours."

"You want to trade knives? All right." Rod felt a sharp twinge at parting with "Colonel Bowie" and a feeling of dismay that some other knife might let him down. But it was not an offer that he could refuse, not from Sis.

"My very dear! I wouldn't deprive you of your own knife, not on your solo. I want you to carry both, Buddy. You won't starve nor die of thirst, but a spare knife may be worth its weight in thorium."

"Gee, Sis! But I shouldn't take your knife, either—you said you were expecting active duty. I can carry a spare of my own."

"I won't need it. My girls haven't let me use a knife in years. I want you to have Lady Macbeth on your test." She removed the scabbard from her boot top, sheathed the blade, and handed it to him. "Wear it in good health, brother."

3

Through the Tunnel

ROD ARRIVED AT TEMPLETON GATE THE NEXT MORNING feeling not his best. He had intended to get a good night's sleep in preparation for his ordeal, but his sister's arrival in conjunction with overwhelming changes in his family had defeated his intention. As with most children Rod had taken his family and home for granted; he had not thought about them much, nor placed a conscious value on them, any more than a fish treasures water. They simply were.

Now suddenly they were not.

Helen and he had talked late. She had begun to have strong misgivings about her decision to let him know of the change on the eve of his test. She had weighed it, decided that it was the "right" thing to do, then had learned the ages-old sour truth that right and wrong can sometimes be determined only through hindsight. It had not been fair, she later concluded, to load anything else on his mind just before his test. But it had not seemed fair, either, to let him leave without knowing . . . to return to an empty house.

The decision was necessarily hers; she had been his guardian since earlier that same day. The papers had been signed and sealed; the court had given approval. Now she found with a sigh that being a "parent" was not unalloyed pleasure; it was more like the soul-searching that had gone into her first duty as member of a court martial.

When she saw that her "baby" was not quieting, she had insisted that he go to bed anyhow, then had given him a long back rub, combining it with hypnotic instructions to sleep, then had gone quietly away when he seemed asleep.

But Rod had not been asleep; he had simply wanted to be alone. His mind raced like an engine with no load for the best part of an hour, niggling uselessly at the matter of his father's illness, wondering what it was going to be like to greet them again after twenty years —why, he would be almost as old as Mum!—switching over to useless mental preparations for unknown test conditions.

At last he realized that he had to sleep—forced himself to run through mental relaxing exercises, emptying his mind and hypnotizing himself. It took longer than ever before but finally he entered a great, golden, warm cloud and was asleep.

His bed mechanism had to call him twice. He woke bleary-eyed and was still so after a needle shower. He looked in a mirror, decided that shaving did not matter where he was going and anyhow he was late—then decided to shave after all . . . being painfully shy about his sparse young growth.

Mum was not up, but she hardly ever got up as early as that. Dad rarely ate breakfast these days . . . Rod recalled why with a twinge. But he had expected Sis to show up. Glumly he opened his tray and discovered that Mum had forgotten to dial an order, something that had not happened twice in his memory. He placed his order and waited for service—another ten minutes lost.

Helen showed up as he was leaving, dressing surprisingly in a dress. "Good morning."

"Hi, Sis. Say, you'll have to order your own tucker. Mother didn't and I didn't know what you wanted."

"Oh, I had breakfast hours ago. I was waiting to see you off."

"Oh. Well, so long. I've got to run, I'm late."

"I won't hold you up." She came over and embraced him. "Take it easy, mate. That's the important thing. More people have died from worry than ever bled to death. And if you do have to strike, strike low."

"Uh, I'll remember."

"See that you do. I'm going to get my leave extended

37

today so that I'll be here when you come back." She kissed him. "Now run."

Dr. Matson was sitting at a desk outside the dispensary at Templeton Gate, checking names on his roll. He looked up as Rod arrived. "Why, hello, Walker. I thought maybe you had decided to be smart."

"I'm sorry I'm late, sir. Things happened."

"Don't fret about it. Knew a man once who didn't get shot at sunrise because he overslept the appointment."

"Really? Who was he?"

"Young fellow I used to know. Myself."

"Hunh? You really did, sir? You mean you were——"

"Not a word of truth in it. Good stories are rarely true. Get on in there and take your physical, before you get the docs irritated."

They thumped him and x-rayed him and made a wavy pattern from his brain and did all the indignities that examining physicians do. The senior examiner listened to his heart and felt his moist hand. "Scared, son?"

"Of course I am!" Rod blurted.

"Of course you are. If you weren't, I wouldn't pass you. What's that bandage on your leg?"

"Uh——" The bandage concealed Helen's knife "Lady Macbeth." Rod sleepishly admitted the fact.

"Take it off."

"Sir?"

"I've known candidates to pull dodges like that to cover up a disqualification. So let's have a look."

Rod started removing it; the physician let him continue until he was sure that it was a cache for a weapon and not a wound dressing. "Get your clothes on. Report to your instructor."

Rod put on his vest pack of rations and sundries, fastened his canteen under it. It was a belt canteen of flexible synthetic divided into half-litre pockets. The weight was taken by shoulder straps and a tube ran up the left suspender, ending in a nipple near his mouth so that he might drink without taking it off. He planned, if possible, to stretch his meager supply through the whole test, avoiding the hazards of contaminated water and the greater hazards of the water hole—assuming that fresh water could be found at all.

He wrapped twenty meters of line, light, strong, and thin, around his waist. Shorts, overshirt, trousers, and boot moccasins completed his costume; he belted "Colonel Bowie" on outside. Dressed, he looked fleshier than he was; only his knife showed. He carried his parka suit over his left arm. It was an efficient garment, hooded, with built-in boots and gloves, and with pressure seams to let him use bare hands when necessary, but it was much too warm to wear until he needed it. Rod had learned early in the game that Eskimos don't dare to sweat.

Dr. Matson was outside the dispensary door. "The late Mr. Walker," he commented, then glanced at the bulkiness of Rod's torso. "Body armor, son?"

"No, sir. Just a vest pack."

"How much penalty you carrying?"

"Eleven kilograms. Mostly water and rations."

"Mmm . . . well, it will get heavier before it gets lighter. No Handy-Dandy Young Pioneer's Kit? No collapsible patent wigwam?"

Rod blushed. "No, sir."

"You can leave that snow suit. I'll mail it to your home."

"Uh, thank you, sir." Rod passed it over, adding, "I wasn't sure I'd need it, but I brought it along, just in case."

"You did need it."

"Sir?"

"I've already flunked five for showing up without their snuggies . . . and four for showing up *with* vacuum suits. Both ways for being stupid. They ought to know that the Board would not dump them into vacuum or chlorine or such without specifying space suits in the test notice. We're looking for graduates, not casualties. On the other hand, cold weather is within the limits of useful test conditions."

Rod glanced at the suit he had passed over. "You're sure I won't need it, sir?"

"Quite. Except that you would have flunked if you hadn't fetched it. Now bear a hand and draw whatever pig shooter you favor; the armorer is anxious to close up shop. What gun have you picked?"

Rod gulped. "Uh, I was thinking about not taking one, Deacon—I mean 'Doctor.'"

"You can call me 'Deacon' to my face—ten days from now. But this notion of yours interests me. How did you reach that conclusion?"

"Uh, why, you see, sir . . . well, my sister suggested it."

"So? I must meet your sister. What's her name?"

"Assault Captain Helen Walker," Rod said proudly, "Corps of Amazons."

Matson wrote it down. "Get on in there. They are ready for the drawing."

Rod hesitated. "Sir," he said with sudden misgiving, "if I did carry a gun, what sort would you advise?"

Matson looked disgusted. "I spend a year trying to spoon-feed you kids with stuff I learned the hard way. Comes examination and you ask me to slip you the answers. I can no more answer that than I would have been justified yesterday in telling you to bring a snow suit."

"Sorry, sir."

"No reason why you shouldn't ask; it's just that I won't answer. Let's change the subject. This sister of yours . . . she must be quite a girl."

"Oh, she is, sir."

"Mmm . . . maybe if I had met a girl like that I wouldn't be a cranky old bachelor now. Get in there and draw your number. Number one goes through in six minutes."

"Yes, Doctor." His way led him past the school armorer, who had set up a booth outside the door. The old chap was wiping off a noiseless Summerfield. Rod caught his eye. "Howdy, Guns."

"Hi, Jack. Kind of late, aren't you? What'll it be?"

Rod's eye ran over the rows of beautiful weapons. Maybe just a little needle gun with poisoned pellets . . . He wouldn't have to *use* it . . .

Then he realized that Dr. Matson had answered his question, with a very broad hint. "Uh, I'm already heeled, Guns. Thanks."

"Okay. Well, good luck, and hurry back."

"Thanks a lot." He went into the gate room.

The seminar had numbered more than fifty students;

40

there were about twenty waiting to take the examination. He started to look around, was stopped by a gate attendant who called out, "Over here! Draw your number."

The lots were capsules in a bowl. Rod reached in, drew one out, and broke it open. "Number seven."

"Lucky seven! Congratulations. Your name, please."

Rod gave his name and turned away, looking for a seat, since it appeared that he had twenty minutes or so to wait. He walked back, staring with interest at what his schoolmates deemed appropriate for survival, any and all conditions.

Johann Braun was seated with empty seats on each side of him. The reason for the empty seats crouched at his feet—a big, lean, heavily-muscled boxer dog with unfriendly eyes. Slung over Braun's shoulder was a General Electric Thunderbolt, a shoulder model with telescopic sights and cone-of-fire control; its power pack Braun wore as a back pack. At his belt were binoculars, knife, first aid kit, and three pouches.

Rod stopped and admired the gun, wondering how much the lovely thing cost. The dog raised his head and growled.

Braun put a hand on the dog's head. "Keep your distance," he warned. "Thor is a one-man dog."

Rod gave back a pace. "Yo, you are certainly equipped."

The big blond youth gave a satisfied smile. "Thor and I are going to live off the country."

"You don't need him, with that cannon."

"Oh, yes, I do. Thor's my burglar alarm. With him at my side I can sleep sound. You'd be surprised at the things he can do. Thor's smarter than most people."

"Shouldn't wonder."

"The Deacon gave me some guff that the two of us made a team and should go through separately. I explained to him that Thor would tear the joint apart if they tried to separate us." Braun caressed the dog's ears. "I'd rather team with Thor than with a platoon of Combat Pioneers."

"Say, Yo, how about letting me try that stinger? After we come out, I mean."

"I don't mind. It really is a honey. You can pick off

41

a sparrow in the air easily as you can drop a moose at a thousand meters. Say, you're making Thor nervous. See you later."

Rod took the hint, moved on and sat down. He looked around, having in mind that he might still arrange a survival team. Near the shuttered arch of the gateway there was a priest with a boy kneeling in front of him, with four others waiting.

The boy who had been receiving the blessing stood up—and Rod stood up hastily. "Hey! *Jimmy!*"

Jimmy Throxton looked around, caught his eye and grinned, hurried over. "Rod!" he said, "I thought you had ducked out on me. Look, you haven't teamed?"

"No."

"Still want to?"

"Huh? Sure."

"Swell! I can declare the team as I go through as long as you don't have number two. You don't, do you?"

"No."

"Good! Because I'm—"

"NUMBER ONE!" the gate attendant called out. " 'Throxton, James.' "

Jimmy Throxton looked startled. "Oh, gee!" He hitched at his gun belt and turned quickly away, then called over his shoulder, "See you on the other side!" He trotted toward the gate, now unshuttered.

Rod called out, "Hey, Jimmy! How are we going to find—" But it was too late. Well, if Jimmy had sense enough to drive nails, he would keep an eye on the exit.

"Number two! Mshiyeni, Caroline." Across the room the big Zulu girl who had occurred to Rod as a possible team mate got up and headed for the gate. She was dressed simply in shirt and shorts, with her feet and legs and hands bare. She did not appear to be armed but she was carrying an overnight bag.

Someone called out, "Hey, Carol! What you got in the trunk?"

She threw him a grin. "Rocks."

"Ham sandwiches, I'll bet. Save me one."

"I'll save you a rock, sweetheart."

42

Too soon the attendant called out, "Number seven—Walker, Roderick L."

Rod went quickly to the gate. The attendant shoved a paper into his hand, then shook hands. "Good luck, kid. Keep your eyes open." He gave Rod a slap on the back that urged him through the opening, dilated to man size.

Rod found himself on the other side and, to his surprise, still indoors. But that shock was not as great as immediate unsteadiness and nausea; the gravity acceleration was much less than earth-normal.

He fought to keep from throwing up and tried to figure things out. Where was he? On Luna? On one of Jupiter's moons? Or somewhere 'way out there?

The Moon, most likely—Luna. Many of the longer jumps were relayed through Luna because of the danger of mixing with a primary, particularly with binaries. But surely they weren't going to leave him here; Matson had promised them no airless test areas.

On the floor lay an open valise; he recognized it absent-mindedly as the one Caroline had been carrying. At last he remembered to look at the paper he had been handed.

It read:

SOLO SURVIVAL TEST—Recall Instructions

1. You must pass through the door ahead in the three minutes allowed you before another candidate is started through. An overlapping delay will disqualify you.
2. Recall will be by standard visual and sound signals. You are warned that the area remains hazardous even after recall is sounded.
3. The exit gate will not be the entrance gate. Exit may be as much as twenty kilometers in the direction of sunrise.
4. There is no truce zone outside the gate. Test starts at once. Watch out for stobor. Good luck!

—B. P. M.

Rod was still gulping at low gravity and staring at the paper when a door opened at the far end of the long, narrow room he was in. A man shouted, "Hurry up! You'll lose your place."

Rod tried to hurry, staggered and then recovered too much and almost fell. He had experienced low gravity on field trips and his family had once vacationed on Luna, but he was not used to it; with difficulty he managed to skate toward the far door.

Beyond the door was another gate room. The attendant glanced at the timer over the gate and said, "Twenty seconds. Give me that instruction sheet."

Rod hung onto it. "I'll use the twenty seconds."—*as much as twenty kilometers in the direction of sunrise.* A nominal eastward direction—call it "east." But what the deuce was, or were, "stobor"?

"Time! Through you go." The attendant snatched the paper, shutters rolled back, and Rod was shoved through a dilated gate.

He fell to his hands and knees; the gravity beyond was something close to earth-normal and the change had caught him unprepared. But he stayed down, held perfectly still and made no sound while he quickly looked around him. He was in a wide clearing covered with high grass and containing scattered trees and bushes; beyond was dense forest.

He twisted his neck in a hasty survey. Earth-type planet, near normal acceleration, probably a G-type sun in the sky . . . heavy vegetation, no fauna in sight—but that didn't mean anything; there might be hundreds within hearing. Even a stobor, whatever that was.

The gate was behind him, tall dark-green shutters which were in reality a long way off. They stood unsupported in the tall grass, an anomalism unrelated to the primitive scene. Rod considered wriggling around behind the gate, knowing that the tangency was one-sided and that he would be able to see through the locus from the other side, see anyone who came out without himself being seen.

Which reminded him that he himself could be seen from that exceptional point; he decided to move.

Where was Jimmy? Jimmy ought to be behind the gate, watching for him to come out . . . or watching from some other spy point. The only certain method of rendezvous was for Jimmy to have waited for Rod's appearance; Rod had no way to find him now.

Rod looked around more slowly and tried to spot anything that might give a hint as to Jimmy's whereabouts. Nothing . . . but when his scanning came back to the gate, the gate was no longer there.

Rod felt cold ripple of adrenalin shock trickle down his back and out his finger tips. He forced himself to quiet down and told himself that it was better this way. He had a theory to account for the disappearance of the gate; they were, he decided, refocusing it between each pair of students, scattering them possibly kilometers apart.

No, that could not be true—"twenty kilometers toward sunrise" had to relate to a small area.

Or did it? He reminded himself that the orientation given in the sheet handed him might not be that which appeared in some other student's instruction sheet. He relaxed to the fact that he did not really know anything . . . he did not know where he was, nor where Jimmy was, nor any other member of the class, he did not know what he might find here, save that it was a place where a man might stay alive if he were smart—and lucky.

Just now his business was to stay alive, for a period that he might as well figure as ten Earth days. He wiped Jimmy Throxton out of his mind, wiped out everything but the necessity of remaining unceasingly alert to all of his surroundings. He noted wind direction as shown by grass plumes and started crawling cautiously down wind.

The decision to go down wind had been difficult. To go up wind had been his first thought, that being the natural direction for a stalk. But his sister's advice had already paid off; he felt naked and helpless without a gun and it had reminded him that he was not the hunter. His scent would carry in any case; if he went down wind he stood a chance of seeing what might be stalking him, while his unguarded rear would be comparatively safe.

Something ahead in the grass!

He froze and watched. It had been the tiniest movement; he waited. There it was again, moving slowly from right to left across his front. It looked like a dark spike

45

with a tuft of hair on the tip, a tail possibly, carried aloft.

He never saw what manner of creature owned the tail, if it was a tail. It stopped suddenly at a point Rod judged to be directly down wind, then moved off rapidly and he lost sight of it. He waited a few minutes, then resumed crawling.

It was extremely hot work and sweat poured down him and soaked his overshirt and trousers. He began to want a drink very badly-but reminded himself that five litres of water would not last long if he started drinking the first hour of the test. The sky was overcast with high cirrus haze, but the primary or "sun"—he decided to call it the Sun—seemed to burn through fiercely. It was low in the sky behind him; he wondered what it would be like overhead? Kill a man, maybe. Oh, well, it would be cooler in that forest ahead, or at least not be the same chance of sunstroke.

There was lower ground ahead of him and hawklike birds were circling above the spot, round and round. He held still and watched. Brothers, he said softly, if you are behaving like vultures back home, there is something dead ahead of me and you are waiting to make sure it stays dead before you drop in for lunch. If so, I had better swing wide, for it is bound to attract other things . . . some of which I might not want to meet.

He started easing to the right, quartering the light breeze. It took him onto higher ground and close to a rock outcropping. Rod decided to spy out what was in the lower place below, making use of cover to let him reach an overhanging rock.

It looked mightily like a man on the ground and a child near him. Rod reached, fumbled in his vest pack, got out a tiny 8-power monocular, took a better look. The man was Johann Braun, the "child" was his boxer dog. There was no doubt but that they were dead, for Braun was lying like a tossed rag doll, with his head twisted around and one leg bent under. His throat and the side of his head were a dark red stain.

While Rod watched, a doglike creature trotted out, sniffed at the boxer, and began tearing at it . . . then the first of the buzzard creatures landed to join the feast. Rod took the glass from his eye, feeling queasy. Old Yo had not lasted long—jumped by a "stobor" maybe—and his smart dog had not saved him. Too bad! But it did prove that there were carnivores around and it behooved him to be careful if he did not want to have jackals and vultures arguing over the leavings!

He remembered something and put the glass back to his eye. Yo's proud Thunderbolt gun was nowhere in sight and the corpse was not wearing the power pack that energized it. Rod gave a low whistle in his mind and thought. The only animal who would bother to steal a gun ran around on two legs. Rod reminded himself that a Thunderbolt could kill at almost any line-of-sight range—and now somebody had it who obviously took advantage of the absence of law and order in a survival test area.

Well, the only thing to do was not to be in line of sight. He backed off the rock and slid into the bushes.

The forest had appeared to be two kilometers away, or less, when he had started. He was close to it when he became uncomfortably aware that sunset was almost upon him. He became less cautious, more hurried, as he planned to spend the night in a tree. This called for light to climb by, since he relished a night on the ground inside the forest still less than he liked the idea of crouching helpless in the grass.

It had not taken all day to crawl this far. Although it had been morning when he had left Templeton Gate the time of day there had nothing to do with the time of day here. He had been shoved through into late afternoon; it was dusk when he reached the tall trees.

So dusky that he decided that he must accept a calculated risk for what he must do. He stopped at the edge of the forest, still in the high grass, and dug into his pack for his climbers. His sister had caused him to leave behind most of the gadgets, gimmicks, and special-purpose devices that he had considered bringing; she had not argued at these. They were climbing spikes of a style basically old, but refined, made small and light—the pair weighed less than a tenth of a kilogram—and made foldable and compact, from a titanium alloy, hard and strong.

He unfolded them, snapped them under his arches and around his shins, and locked them in place. Then he eyed the tree he had picked, a tall giant deep enough in the mass to allow the possibility of crossing to another tree if the odds made a back-door departure safer and having a trunk which, in spite of its height, he felt sure he could get his arms around.

Having picked his route, he straightened up and at a fast dogtrot headed for the nearest tree. He went past it, cut left for another tree, passed it and cut right toward the tree he wanted. He was about fifteen meters from it when something charged him.

He closed the gap with instantaneous apportation which would have done credit to a Ramsbotham hyperfold. He reached the first branch, ten meters above ground, in what amounted to levitation. From there on he climbed more conventionally, digging the spurs into the tree's smooth bark and setting his feet more comfortably on branches when they began to be close enough together to form a ladder.

About twenty meters above ground he stopped and looked down. The branches interfered and it was darker under the trees than it had been out in the open; nevertheless he could see, prowling around the tree, the denizen that had favored him with attention.

Rod tried to get a better view, but the light was failing rapidly. But it looked like . . . well, if he had not been certain that he was on some uncolonized planet 'way out behind and beyond, he would have said that it was a *lion*.

Except that it looked eight times as big as any lion ought to look.

He hoped that, whatever it was, it could not climb trees. Oh, quit fretting, Rod!—if it had been able to climb you would have been lunch meat five minutes ago. Get busy and rig a place to sleep before it gets pitch dark. He moved up the tree, keeping an eye out for the spot he needed.

He found it presently, just as he was beginning to think that he would have to go farther down. He needed two stout branches far enough apart and near enough the same level to let him stretch a hammock. Having found such, he worked quickly to beat the failing light. From a pocket of his vest pack he took out his hammock, a web strong as spider silk and almost as thin and light. Using the line around his waist he stretched it, made sure his lashings would hold and then started to get into it.

A double-jointed acrobat with prehensile toes might have found it easy; a slack-wire artist would simply have walked into it and sat down. But Rod found that he needed sky hooks. He almost fell out of the tree.

The hammock was a practical piece of equipment and Rod had slept in it before. His sister had approved it, remarking that it was a better model than the field hammock they gave her girls. "Just don't sit up in your sleep."

"I won't," Rod had assured her. "Anyway, I always fasten the chest belt."

But he had never slung it in this fashion. There was nothing to stand on under the hammock, no tree limb above it close enough to let him chin himself into it. After several awkward and breath-catching attempts he began to wonder whether he should perch like a bird the rest of the night, or drape himself in the notch of a limb. He did not consider spending the night on the ground—not with that *thing* prowling around.

There was another limb higher up almost directly over the hammock. Maybe if he tossed the end of his line over it and used it to steady himself . . .

He tried it. But it was almost pitch dark now; the only reason he did not lose his line was that one end was bent to the hammock. At last he gave up and made one more attempt to crawl into the hammock by main force and extreme care. Bracing both hands wide on each side of the head rope he scooted his feet out slowly and cautiously. Presently he had his legs inside the hammock, then his buttocks. From there on it was a matter of keeping his center of gravity low and making no sudden moves while he insinuated his body farther down into the cocoon.

At last he could feel himself fully and firmly supported. He took a deep breath, sighed, and let himself relax. It was the first time he had felt either safe or comfortable since passing through the gate.

After a few minute of delicious rest Rod located the nipple of his canteen and allowed himself two swallows of water, after which he prepared supper. This consisted in digging out a quarter-kilo brick of field ration, eleven hundred calories of yeast protein, fat, starch, and glucose, plus trace requirements. The label on it, invisible in the dark, certified that it was "tasty, tempting and pleasing in texture," whereas chewing an old shoe would have attracted a gourmet quite as much.

But real hunger gave Rod the best of sauces. He did not let any crumb escape and ended by licking the wrapper. He thought about opening another one, quelled the longing, allowed himself one more mouthful of water, then pulled the insect hood of the hammock down over his face and fastened it under the chest belt. He was immune to most insect-carried Terran diseases and was comfortably aware that humans were not subject to most Outlands diseases, but he did not want the night fliers to use his face as a drinking fountain, nor even as a parade ground.

He was too hot even in his light clothing. He considered shucking down to his shorts; this planet, or this part of this planet, seemed quite tropical. But it was awkward; tonight he must stay as he was, even if it meant wasting a day's ration of water in sweat. He wondered what planet this was, then tried to peer through the roof of the forest to see if he could recognize stars. But either the trees were impenetrable or the sky was overcast; he could see nothing. He attempted to draw everything out of his mind and sleep.

Ten minutes later he was wider awake than ever. Busy with his hammock, busy with his dinner, he had not paid attention to distant sounds; now he became aware of all the voices of the night. Insects buzzed and sang and strummed, foliage rustled and whispered, something coughed below him. The cough was answered by insane laughter that ran raggedly up, then down, and died in asthmatic choking.

Rod hoped that it was a bird.

He found himself straining to hear every sound, near and far, holding his breath. He told himself angrily to stop it; he was safe from at least nine-tenths of potential enemies. Even a snake, if this place ran to such, would be unlikely to crawl out to the hammock, still less likely to attack—if he held still. Snakes, button-brained as they were, showed little interest in anything too big to

50

swallow. The chances of anything big enough to hurt him—and interested in hurting him—being in this tree-top were slim. So forget those funny noises, pal, and go to sleep. After all, they're no more important than traffic noises in a city.

He reminded himself of the Deacon's lecture on alarm and could not see sky; he floated in a leafy cloud. The traced to the body's coming too urgently to battle sta-tions, remaining too long at full alert. Or, as his sister had put it, more people worry themselves to death than bleed to death. He set himself conscientiously to running through the mental routines intended to produce sleep.

He almost made it. The sound that pulled him out of warm drowsiness came from far away; involuntarily he roused himself to hear it. It sounded almost human . . . no, it *was* human—the terrible sound of a grown man crying with heartbreak, the deep, retching, bass sobs that tear the chest.

Rod wondered what he ought to do. It was none of his business and everyone there was on his own—but it went against the grain to hear such agony from a fellow human and ignore it. Should he climb down and feel his way through the dark to wherever the poor wretch was? Stumbling into tree roots, he reminded himself, and falling into holes and maybe walking straight into the jaws of something hungry and big.

Well, should he? Did he have any right *not* to?

It was solved for him by the sobs being answered by more sobs, this time closer and much louder. This new voice did not sound human, much as it was like the first, and it scared him almost out of his hammock. The chest strap saved him.

The second voice was joined by a third, farther away. In a few moments the peace of the night had changed to sobbing, howling ululation of mass fear and agony and defeat unbearable. Rod knew now that this was nothing human, nor anything he had ever heard, or heard of, before. He suddenly had a deep conviction that these were the stobor he had been warned to avoid.

But what were they? How was he to avoid them? The one closest seemed to be higher up than he was and no farther than the next tree . . . good grief, it might even be *this* tree!

51

When you meet a stobor in the dark what do you do? Spit in its face? Or ask it to waltz?

One thing was certain: anything that made that much noise in the jungle was not afraid of anything; therefore it behooved him to be afraid of it. But, there being nothing he could do, Rod lay quiet, his fear evidenced only by tense muscles, gooseflesh, and cold sweat. The hellish concert continued with the "stobor" closest to him sounding almost in his pocket. It seemed to have moved closer.

With just a bit more prodding Rod would have been ready to sprout wings and fly. Only at home on the North American continent of Terra had he ever spent a night alone in the wilderness. There the hazards were known and minor . . . a few predictable bears, an occasional lazy rattlesnake, dangers easily avoided.

But how could he guard against the utterly unknown? That stobor—he decided that he might as well call it that—that stobor might be moving toward him now, sizing him up with night eyes, deciding whether to drag him home, or eat him where it killed him.

Should he move? And maybe move right into the fangs of the stobor? Or should he wait, helpless, for the stobor to pounce? It was possible that the stobor could not attack him in the tree. But it was equally possible that stobor were completely arboreal and his one chance lay in climbing down quickly and spending the night on the ground.

What was a stobor? How did it fight? Where and when was it dangerous? The Deacon evidently expected the class to know what to do about them. Maybe they had studied the stobor those days he was out of school right after New Year's? Or maybe he had just plain forgotten . . . and would pay for it with his skin. Rod was good at Outlands zoology—but there was just too much to learn it all. Why, the zoology of Terra alone used to give oldstyle zoologists more than they could handle; how could they expect him to soak up all there was to learn about dozens of planets?

It wasn't *fair!*

When Rod heard himself think that ancient and useless protest he had a sudden vision of the Deacon's kindly, cynical smile. He heard his dry drawl: Fair? You expected this to be *fair,* son? This is not a game. I tried to tell you that you were a city boy, too soft and stupid for this. You would not listen.

He felt a gust of anger at his instructor; it drove fear out of his mind. Jimmy was right; the Deacon would eat his own grandmother! A cold, heartless fish!

All right, what would the Deacon do?

Again he heard his teacher's voice inside his head, an answer Matson had once given to a question put by another classmate: "There wasn't anything I could do, so I took a nap."

Rod squirmed around, rested his hand on "Colonel Bowie" and tried to take a nap. The unholy chorus made it almost impossible, but he did decide that the stobor in his tree—or was it the next tree?—did not seem to be coming closer. Not that it could come much closer without breathing on his neck, but at least it did not seem disposed to attack.

After a long time he fell into restless sleep, sleep that was no improvement, for he dreamed that he had a ring of sobbing, ululating stobor around him, staring at him, waiting for him to move. But he was trussed up tight and could not move.

The worst of it was that every time he turned his head to see what a stobor looked like it would fade back into the dark, giving him just a hint of red eyes, long teeth.

He woke with an icy shock, tried to sit up, found himself restrained by his chest strap, forced himself to lie back. What was it? What had happened?

In his suddenly-awakened state it took time to realize what had happened: the noise had stopped. He could not hear the cry of a single stobor, near or far. Rod found it more disturbing than their clamor, since a noisy stobor advertised its location whereas a silent one could be anywhere—why, the nearest one could now be sitting on the branch behind his head. He twisted his head around, pulled the insect netting off his face to see better. But it was too dark; stobor might be queued up three abreast for all he could tell.

Nevertheless the silence was a great relief. Rod felt himself relax as he listened to the other night sounds, noises that seemed almost friendly after that devils' choir. He decided that it must be almost morning and that we would do well to stay awake.

Presently he was asleep.

He awoke with the certainty that someone was looking at him. When he realized where he was and that it was still dark, he decided that it was a dream. He stirred, looked around, and tried to go back to sleep.

Something *was* looking at him!

His eyes, made sensitive by darkness, saw the thing as a vague shape on the branch at his foot. Black on black, he could not make out its outline—but two faintly luminous eyes stared unwinkingly back into his.

"—nothing I could do, so I took a nap." Rod did not take a nap. For a time measured in eons he and the thing in the tree locked eyes. Rod tightened his grip on his knife and held still, tried to quell the noise of his pounding heart, tried to figure out how he could fight back from a hammock. The beast did not move, made no sound; it simply stared and seemed prepared to do it all night.

When the ordeal had gone on so long that Rod felt a mounting impulse to shout and get it over, the creature moved with light scratching sounds toward the trunk and was gone. Rod could feel the branch shift; he judged that the beast must weigh as much as he did.

Again he resolved to stay awake. Wasn't it getting less dark? He tried to tell himself so, but he still could not see his own fingers. He decided to count to ten thousand and bring on the dawn.

Something large went down the tree very fast, followed at once by another, and still a third. They did not stop at Rod's bedroom but went straight down the trunk. Rod put his knife back and uttered, "Noisy neighbors! You'd think this was Emigrants' Gap." He waited but the frantic procession never came back.

He was awakened by sunlight in his face. It made him sneeze; he tried to sit up, was caught by his safety belt, became wide awake and regretted it. His nose was stopped up, his eyes burned, his mouth tasted like a ditch, his teeth were slimy, and his back ached. When he moved to ease it he found that his legs ached, too—

and his arms—and his head. His neck refused to turn to the right.

Nevertheless he felt happy that the long night was gone. His surroundings were no longer terrifying, but almost idyllic. So high up that he could not see the ground he was still well below the roof of the jungle and could not see sky; he floated in a leafy cloud. The morning ray that brushed his face was alone, so thoroughly did trees shut out the sky.

This reminded him that he had to mark the direction of sunrise. Hmmm . . . not too simple. Would he be able to see the sun from the floor of the jungle? Maybe he should climb down quickly, get out in the open, and mark the direction while the sun was still low. But he noticed that the shaft which had wakened him was framed by a limb notch of another forest giant about fifteen meters away. Very well, that tree was "east" of his tree; he could line them up again when he reached the ground.

Getting out of his hammock was almost as hard as getting in; sore muscles resented the effort. At last he was balanced precariously on one limb. He crawled to the trunk, pulled himself painfully erect and, steadied by the trunk, took half-hearted setting-up exercises to work the knots out. Everything loosened up but his neck, which still had a crick like a toothache.

He ate and drank sitting on the limb with his back to the trunk. He kept no special lookout, rationalizing that night feeders would be bedded down and day feeders would hardly be prowling the tree tops—not big ones, anyway; they would be on the ground, stalking herbivores. The truth was that his green hide-away looked too peaceful to be dangerous.

He continued to sit after he finished eating, considered drinking more of his precious water, even considered crawling back into his hammock. Despite the longest night he had ever had he was bone tired and the day was already hot and sleepy and humid; why not stretch out? His only purpose was to survive; how better than by sleeping and thereby saving food and water?

He might have done so had he known what time it was. His watch told him that it was five minutes before twelve, but he could not make up his mind whether that was noon on Sunday or midnight coming into Monday. He was sure that this planet spun much more slowly than did Mother Earth; the night before had been at least as long as a full Earth day.

Therefore the test had been going on at least twenty-six hours and possibly thirty-eight—and recall could be any time after forty-eight hours. Why, it might be today, before sunset, and here he was in fine shape, still alive, still with food and water he could trust.

He felt good about it. What did a stobor have that a man did not have more of and better? Aside from a loud voice, he added.

But the exit gate might be as much as twenty kilometers "east" of where he had come in; therefore it behooved him to reach quickly a point ten kilometers east of where he had come in; he would lay money that that would land him within a kilometer or two of the exit. Move along, hole up, and wait—why, he might sleep at home tonight, after a hot bath!

He started unlashing his hammock while reminding himself that he must keep track of hours between sunrise and sunset today in order to estimate the length of the local day. Then he thought no more about it as he had trouble folding the hammock. It had to be packed carefully to fit into a pocket of his vest pack. The filmy stuff should have been spread on a table, but where he was the largest, flattest area was the palm of his hand.

But he got it done, lumpy but packed, and started down. He paused on the lowest branch, looked around. The oversized and hungry thing that had chased him up the tree did not seem to be around, but the undergrowth was too dense for him to be sure. He made a note that he must, all day long and every day, keep a climbable tree in mind not too far away; a few seconds woolgathering might use up his luck.

Okay, now for orientation— Let's see, there was the tree he had used to mark "east." Or was it? Could it be that one over there? He realized that he did not know and swore at himself for not checking it by compass. The truth was that he had forgotten that he was carrying a compass. He got it out now, but it told him nothing, since east by compass bore no necessary relation to direction of sunrise on this planet. The rays of the primary did not penetrate where he was; the forest was bathed by a dim religious light unmarked by shadows.

Well, the clearing could not be far away. He would just have to check. He descended by climbing spurs, dropped to spongy ground, and headed the way it should be. He counted his paces while keeping an eye peeled for hostiles.

One hundred paces later he turned back, retracing his own spoor. He found "his" tree; this time he examined it. There was where he had come down; he could see his prints. Which side had he gone up? There should be spur marks.

He found them . . . and was amazed at his own feat; they started high as his head. "I must have hit that trunk like a cat!" But it showed the direction from which he had come; five minutes later he was at the edge of the open country he had crossed the day before.

The sun made shadows here, which straightened him out and he checked by compass. By luck, east was "east" and he need only follow his compass. It took him back into the forest.

He traveled standing up. The belly sneak which he had used the day before was not needed here; he depended on moving noiselessly, using cover, and keeping an eye out behind as well as in front. He zigzagged in order to stay close to trees neither too big nor too small but corrected his course frequently by compass.

One part of his mind counted paces. At fifteen hundred broken-country steps to a kilometer Rod figured that fifteen thousand should bring him to his best-guess location for the exit gate, where he planned to set up housekeeping until recall.

But, even with part of his mind counting paces and watching a compass and a much larger part watching for carnivores, snakes, and other hazards, Rod still could enjoy the day and place. He was over his jitters of the night before, feeling good and rather cocky. Even though he tried to be fully alert, the place did not feel dangerous now—stobor or no stobor.

It was, he decided, jungle of semi-rainforest type, not dense enough to require chopping one's way. It was interlaced with game paths but he avoided these on the assumption that carnivores might lie waiting for lunch to come down the path—Rod had no wish to volunteer.

The place seemed thick with game, mostly of antelope type in many sizes and shapes. They were hard to spot; they faded into the bush with natural camouflage, but the glimpses he got convinced him that they were plentiful. He avoided them as he was not hunting and was aware that even a vegetarian could be dangerous with hooves and horns in self or herd defense.

The world above was inhabited, too, with birds and climbers. He spotted families of what looked like monkeys and speculated that this world would probably have developed its own race of humanoids. He wondered again what planet it was? Terrestrial to several decimal places it certainly seemed to be—except for the inconveniently long day—and probably one just opened, or it would be swarming with colonists. It would be a premium planet certainly; that clearing he had come through yesterday would make good farm land once it was burned off. Maybe he would come back some day and help clean out the stobor.

In the meantime he watched where he put his hands and feet, never walked under a low branch without checking it, and tried to make his eyes and ears as efficient as a rabbit's. He understood now what his sister had meant about how being unarmed makes a person careful, and realized also how little chance he would have to use a gun if he let himself be surprised.

It was this hyperacuteness that made him decide that he was being stalked.

At first it was just uneasiness, then it became a conviction. Several times he waited by a tree, stood frozen and listened; twice he did a sneak through bushes and doubled back on his tracks. But whatever it was seemed as good as he was at silent movement and taking cover and (he had to admit) a notch better.

He thought about taking to the trees and outwaiting it. But his wish to reach his objective outweighed his caution; he convinced himself that he would be safer if he pushed on. He continued to pay special attention to his rear, but after a while he decided that he was no longer being followed.

When he had covered, by his estimate, four kilometers, he began to smell water. He came to a ravine which sliced across his route. Game tracks led him to think it might lead down to a watering place, just the sort of danger area he wished to avoid, so Rod crossed quickly and went down the shoulder of the ravine instead. It led to a bank overlooking water; he could hear the stream before he reached it.

He took to the bushes and moved on his belly to a point where he could peer out from cover. He was about ten meters higher than the water. The ground dropped off on his right as well as in front; there the ravine joined the stream and an eddy pool formed the watering place he had expected. No animals were in sight but there was plenty of sign; a mud flat was chewed with hoof marks.

But he had no intention of drinking where it was easy; it would be too easy to die there. What troubled him was that he must cross the stream to reach the probable recall area. It was a small river or wide brook, not too wide to swim, probably not too deep to wade if he picked his spot. But he would not do either one unless forced—and not then without testing the water by chucking a lure into it . . . a freshly killed animal. The streams near his home were safe, but a tropical stream must be assumed to have local versions of alligator, piranha, or even worse.

The stream was too wide to cross through the tree tops. He lay still and considered the problem, then decided that he would work his way upstream and hope that it would narrow, or split into two smaller streams which he could tackle one at a time.

It was the last thing he thought about for some time.

When Rod regained consciousness it was quickly; a jackal-like creature was sniffing at him. Rod lashed out with one hand and reached for his knife with the other. The dog brute backed away, snarling, then disappeared in the leaves.

His knife was gone! The realization brought him groggily alert; he sat up. It made his head swim and hurt. He felt it and his fingers came away bloody. Further gingerly investigation showed a big and very tender swelling on the back of his skull, hair matted with blood, and failed to tell him whether or not his skull was fractured. He gave no thanks that he had been left alive; he was sure that the blow had been intended to kill.

But not only his knife was gone. He was naked, save for his shorts. Gone were his precious water, his vest pack with rations and a dozen other invaluable articles —his antibiotics, his salt, his compass, his climbers, his matches, his hammock . . . everything.

His first feeling of sick dismay was replaced by anger. Losing food and gear was no more than to be expected, since he had been such a fool as to forget his rear while he looked at the stream—but taking the watch his father had given him, that was stealing; he would make somebody pay for that!

His anger made him feel better. It was not until then that he noticed that the bandage on his left shin was undisturbed.

He felt it. Sure enough! Whoever it was who had hijacked him had not considered a bandage worth stealing; Rod unwrapped it and cradled Lady Macbeth in his hand.

Somebody was going to be sorry.

4

Savage

ROD WALKER WAS CROUCHING ON A TREE LIMB. HE HAD not moved for two hours, he might not move for as long a time. In a clearing near him a small herd of yearling bachelor buck were cropping grass; if one came close enough Rod intended to dine on buck. He was very hungry.

He was thirsty, too, not having drunk that day. Besides that, he was slightly feverish. Three long, imperfectly healed scratches on his left arm accounted for the fever, but Rod paid fever and scratches no attention —he was alive; he planned to stay alive.

A buck moved closer to him; Rod became quiveringly alert. But the little buck tossed his head, looked at the branch, and moved away. He did not appear to see Rod; perhaps his mother had taught him to be careful of overhanging branches—or perhaps a hundred thousand generations of harsh survival had printed it in his genes.

Rod swore under his breath and lay still. One of them was bound to make a mistake eventually; then he would eat. It had been days since he had thought about anything but food . . . food and how to keep his skin intact, how to drink without laying himself open to ambush, how to sleep without waking up in a fellow-denizen's belly.

The healing wounds on his arm marked how expensive his tuition had been. He had let himself get too far from a tree once too often, had not even had time to draw his knife. Instead he had made an impossible leap and had chinned himself with the wounded arm. The thing that had clawed him he believed to be the same sort as the creature that had treed him the day of his arrival; furthermore he believed it to be a lion. He had a theory about that, but had not yet been able to act on it.

He was gaunt almost to emaciation and had lost track of time. He realized that the time limit of the survival test had probably—almost certainly—passed, but he did not know how long he had lain in the crotch of a tree, waiting for his arm to heal, nor exactly how long it had been since he had come down, forced by thirst and hunger. He supposed that the recall signal had probably been given during one of his unconscious periods, but he did not worry nor even think about it. He was no longer interested in survival tests; he was interested in survival.

Despite his weakened condition his chances were better now than when he had arrived. He was becoming sophisticated, no longer afraid of things he had been afraid of, most acutely wary of others which had seemed harmless. The creatures with the ungodly voices which he had dubbed "stobor" no longer fretted him; he had seen one, had disturbed it by accident in daylight and it had given voice. It was not as big as his hand, and reminded him of a horned lizard except that it had the habits of a tree toad. Its one talent was its voice; it could blow up a bladder at its neck to three times its own size, then give out with that amazing, frightening sob.

But that was all it could do.

Rod had guessed that it was a love call, then had filed the matter. He still called them "stobor."

He had learned about a forest vine much like a morning glory, but its leaves carried a sting worse than that of a nettle, toxic and producing numbness. Another vine had large grape-like fruits, deliciously tempting and pleasant to the palate; Rod had learned the hard way that they were a powerful purgative.

He knew, from his own narrow brushes and from kills left half-eaten on the ground, that there were carnivores around even though he had never had a good look at one. So far as he knew there were no carnivorous tree-climbers large enough to tackle a man, but he could not be certain; he slept with one eye open.

The behavior of this herd caused him to suspect that there must be carnivores that hunted as he was now hunting, even though he had had the good fortune not to tangle with one. The little buck had wandered all over the clearing, passed close by lesser trees, yet no one of them had grazed under the tree Rod was in.

Steady, boy . . . here comes one. Rod felt the grip of "Lady Macbeth," got ready to drop onto the graceful little creature as it passed under. But five meters away it hesitated, seemed to realize that it was straying from its mates, and started to turn.

Rod let fly.

He could hear the meaty *tunk!* as blade bit into muscle; he could see the hilt firm against the shoulder of the buck. He dropped to the ground, hit running and moved in to finish the kill.

The buck whipped its head up, turned and fled. Rod dived, did not touch it. When he rolled to his feet the clearing was empty. His mind was filled with bitter thoughts; he had promised himself never to throw his knife when there was any possibility of not being able to recover it, but he did not let regrets slow him; he got to work on the tracking problem.

Rod had been taught the first law of hunting sportsmanship, that a wounded animal must always be tracked down and finished, not left to suffer and die slowly. But there was no trace of "sportsmanship" in his present conduct; he undertook to track the buck because he intended to eat it, and—much more urgently—because he had to recover that knife in order to stay alive.

The buck had not bled at once and its tracks were mixed up with hundreds of other tracks. Rod returned three times to the clearing and started over before he picked up the first blood spoor. After that it was easier but he was far behind now and the stampeded buck moved much faster than he could track. His quarry stayed with the herd until it stopped in a new pasture a half kilometer away. Rod stopped still in cover and looked them over. His quarry did not seem to be among them.

But blood sign led in among them; he followed it and they stampeded again. He had trouble picking it up; when he did he found that it led into brush instead of following the herd. This made it easier and harder— easier because he no longer had to sort one spoor from many, harder because pushing through the brush was hard in itself and much more dangerous, since he must never forget that he himself was hunted as well as hunter, and lastly because the signs were so much harder to spot there. But it cheered him up, knowing that only a weakened animal would leave the herd and try to hide. He expected to find it down before long.

But the beast did not drop; it seemed to have a will to live as strong as his own. He followed it endlessly and was beginning to wonder what he would do if it grew dark before the buck gave up. He *had* to have that knife.

He suddenly saw that there were two spoors.

Something had stepped beside a fresh, split-hooved track of the little antelope; something had stepped on a drop of blood. Quivering, his subconscious "bush radar" at full power, Rod moved silently forward. He found new marks again . . . a man!

The print of a shod human foot—and so wild had he become that it gave him no feeling of relief; it made him more wary than ever.

Twenty minutes later he found them, the human and the buck. The buck was down, having died or perhaps been finished off by the second stalker. The human, whom Rod judged to be a boy somewhat younger and smaller than himself, was kneeling over it, slicing its belly open. Rod faded back into the bush. From there he watched and thought. The other hunter seemed much preoccupied with the kill . . . and that tree hung over the place where the butchering was going on—

A few minutes later Rod was again on a branch, without a knife but with a long thorn held in his teeth. He looked down, saw that his rival was almost under him, and transferred the thorn to his right hand. Then he waited.

The hunter below him laid the knife aside and bent to turn the carcass. Rod dropped.

He felt body armor which had been concealed by his victim's shirt. Instantly he transferred his attention to the bare neck, pushing the thorn firmly against vertebrae. "Hold still or you've had it!"

The body under him suddenly quit struggling.

"That's better," Rod said approvingly. "Cry pax?"

No answer. Rod jabbed the thorn again. "I'm not playing games," he said harshly. "I'm giving you one chance to stay alive. Cry pax and mean it, and we'll both eat. Give me any trouble and you'll never eat again. It doesn't make the least difference."

There was a moment's hesitation, then a muffled voice said, "Pax."

Keeping the thorn pressed against his prisoner's neck, Rod reached out for the knife which had been used to gut the buck. It was, he saw, his own Lady Macbeth. He sheathed it, felt around under the body he rested on, found another where he expected it, pulled it and kept it in his hand. He chucked away the thorn and stood up. "You can get up."

The youngster got up and faced him sullenly. "Give me my knife."

"Later . . . if you are a good boy."

"I said 'Pax.' "

"So you did. Turn around, I want to make sure you don't have a gun on you."

"I left—I've nothing but my knife. Give it to me."

"Left it where?"

The kid did not answer. Rod said, "Okay, turn around," and threatened with the borrowed knife. He was obeyed. Rod quickly patted all the likely hiding places, confirmed that the youngster was wearing armor under clothes and over the entire torso. Rod himself was dressed only in tan, scratches, torn and filthy shorts, and a few scars. "Don't you find that junk pretty hot in this weather?" he asked cheerfully. "Okay, you can turn around. Keep your distance."

The youngster turned around, still with a very sour expression. "What's your name, bud?"

"Uh, Jack."

"Jack what? Mine's Rod Walker."

"Jack Daudet."

"What school, Jack?"

"Ponce de Leon Institute."

"Mine's Patrick Henry High School."

"*Matson's* class?"

"The Deacon himself."

"I've heard of him." Jack seemed impressed.

"Who hasn't? Look, let's quit jawing; we'll have the whole county around our ears. Let's eat. You keep watch that way; I'll keep watch behind you."

"Then give me my knife. I need it to eat."

"Not so fast. I'll cut you off a hunk or two. Special Waldorf service."

Rod continued the incision Jack had started, carried it on up and laid the hide back from the right shoulder, hacked off a couple of large chunks of lean. He tossed one to Jack, hunkered down and gnawed his own piece while keeping sharp lookout. "You keeping your eyes peeled?" he asked.

"Sure."

Rod tore off a rubbery mouthful of warm meat. "Jack, how did they let a runt like you take the test? You aren't old enough."

"I'll bet I'm as old as you are!"

"I doubt it."

"Well . . . I'm qualified."

65

"You don't look it."

"I'm *here*, I'm alive."

Rod grinned. "You've made your point. I'll shut up." Once his portion was resting comfortably inside, Rod got up, split the skull and dug out the brains. "Want a handful?"

"Sure."

Rod passed over a fair division of the dessert. Jack accepted it, hesitated, then blurted out, "Want some salt?"

"*Salt!* You've got *salt?*"

Jack appeared to regret the indiscretion. "Some. Go easy on it."

Rod held out his handful. "Put some on. Whatever you can spare."

Jack produced a pocket shaker from between shirt and armor, sprinkled a little on Rod's portion, then shrugged and made it liberal. "Didn't you bring salt along?"

"Me?" Rod answered, tearing his eyes from the mouth-watering sight. "Oh, sure! But— Well, I had an accident." He decided that there was no use admitting that he had been caught off guard.

Jack put the shaker firmly out of sight. They munched quietly, each watching half their surroundings. After a while Rod said softly, "Jackal behind you, Jack."

"Nothing else?"

"No. But it's time we whacked up the meat and got out of here; we're attracting attention. How much can you use?"

"Uh, a haunch and a chunk of liver. I can't carry any more."

"And you can't eat more before it spoils, anyway." Rod started butchering the hind quarters. He cut a slice of hide from the belly, used it to sling his share around his neck. "Well, so long, kid. Here's your knife. Thanks for the salt."

"Oh, that's all right."

"Tasted mighty good. Well, keep your eyes open."

"Same to you. Good luck."

Rod stood still. Then he said almost reluctantly, "Uh, Jack, you wouldn't want to team up, would you?" He regretted it as soon as he said it, remembering how easily he had surprised the kid.

Jack chewed a lip. "Well . . . I don't know."

Rod felt affronted. "What's the matter? Afraid of me?" Didn't the kid see that Rod was doing him a favor?

"Oh, no! You're all right, I guess."

Rod had an unpleasant suspicion. "You think I'm trying to get a share of your salt, don't you?"

"Huh? Not at all. Look, I'll divvy some salt with you."

"I wouldn't touch it! I just thought—" Rod stopped. He had been thinking that they had both missed recall; it looked like a long pull.

"I didn't mean to make you mad, Rod. You're right. We ought to team."

"Don't put yourself out! I can get along."

"I'll bet you can. But let's team up. Is it a deal?"

"Well . . . Shake."

Once the contract was made Rod assumed leadership. There was no discussion; he simply did so and Jack let it stand. "You lead off," Rod ordered, "and I'll cover our rear."

"Okay. Where are we heading?"

"That high ground downstream. There are good trees there, better for all night than around here. I want us to have time to settle in before dark—so a quick sneak and no talking."

Jack hesitated. "Okay. Are you dead set on spending the night in a tree?"

Rod curled his lip. "Want to spend it on the ground? How did you stay alive this long?"

"I spent a couple of nights in trees," Jack answered mildly. "But I've got a better place now, maybe."

"Huh? What sort?"

"A sort of a cave."

Rod thought about it. Caves could be death traps. But the prospect of being able to stretch out swayed him. "Won't hurt to look, if it's not too far."

"It's not far."

5

The Nova

JACK'S HIDEAWAY WAS IN A BLUFF OVERLOOKING THE stream by which Rod had been robbed. At this point the bluffs walled a pocket valley and the stream meandered between low banks cut in an alluvial field between the bluffs. The cave was formed by an overhang of limestone which roofed a room water-carved from shale in one bluff. The wall below it was too sheer to climb; the overhanging limestone protected it above and the stream curved in sharply almost to the foot of the bluff. The only way to reach it was to descend the bluff farther upstream to the field edging the creek, then make a climbing traverse of the shale bank where it was somewhat less steep just upstream of the cave.

They slanted cautiously up the shale, squeezed under an overhang at the top, and stepped out on a hard slaty floor. The room was open on one side and fairly long and deep, but it squeezed in to a waist-high crawl space; only at the edge was there room to stand up. Jack grabbed some gravel, threw it into the dark hole, waited with knife ready. "Nobody home, I guess." They dropped to hands and knees, crawled inside. "How do you like it?"

"It's swell . . . provided we stand watches. Something could come up the way we did. You've been lucky."

"Maybe," Jack felt around in the gloom, dragged out dry branches of thorn bush, blocked the pathway, jamming them under the overhang. "That's my alarm."

"It wouldn't stop anything that got a whiff of you and really wanted to come in."

"No. But I would wake up and let it have some

rocks in the face. I keep a stack over there. I've got a couple of scare-flares, too."

"I thought— Didn't you say you had a gun?"

"I didn't say, but I do. But I don't believe in shooting when you can't see."

"It looks all right. In fact it looks good. I guess I did myself a favor when I teamed with you." Rod looked around. "You've had a *fire!*"

"I've risked it a couple of times, in daylight. I get so tired of raw meat."

Rod sighed deeply. "I know. Say, do you suppose?"

"It's almost dark. I've never lighted one when it could show. How about roast liver for breakfast, instead? With salt?"

Rod's mouth watered. "You're right, Jack. I do want to get a drink before it is too dark, though. How about coming along and we cover each other?"

"No need. There's a skin back there. Help yourself."

Rod congratulated himself on having teamed with a perfect housekeeper. The skin was of a small animal, not identifiable when distended with water. Jack had scraped the hide but it was uncured and decidedly unsavory. Rod was not aware that the water tasted bad; he drank deeply, wiped his mouth with his hand and felt at peace.

They did not sleep at once, but sat in the dark and compared notes. Jack's class had come through one day earlier, but with the same instructions. Jack agreed that recall was long overdue.

"I suppose I missed it while I was off my head," Rod commented. "I don't know how long I was foggy . . . I guess I didn't miss dying by much."

"That's not it, Rod."

"Why not?"

"I've been okay and keeping track of the time. There never was any recall."

"You're sure?"

"How could I miss? The siren can be heard for twenty kilometers, they use a smoke flare by day and a searchlight at night, and the law says they have to keep it up at least a week unless everybody returns . . . which certainly did not happen this time."

"Maybe we are out of range. Matter of fact—well, I don't know about you, but I'm lost. I admit it."

"I'm not. I'm about four kilometers from where they let my class through; I could show you the spot. Rod, let's face it; something has gone wrong. There is no way of telling how long we are going to be here." Jack added quietly, "That's why I thought it was a good idea to team."

Rod chewed it over, decided it was time to haul out his theory. "Me, too."

"Yes. Solo is actually safer, for a few days. But if we are stuck here indefinitely, then—"

"Not what I meant, Jack."

"Huh?"

"Do you know what planet this is?"

"No. I've thought about it, of course. It has to be one of the new list and it is compatible with—"

"I *know* what one it is."

"Huh? Which one?"

"It's Earth. Terra herself."

There was a long silence. At last Jack said, "Rod, are you all right? Are you still feverish?"

"I'm fine, now that I've got a full belly and a big drink of water. Look, Jack, I know it sounds silly, but you just listen and I'll add it up. We're on Earth and I think I know about where, too. I don't think they meant to sound recall; they meant us to figure out where we are . . . and walk out. It's a twist Deacon Matson would love."

"But—"

"Keep quiet, can't you? Yapping like a girl. Terrestrial planet, right?"

"Yes, but—"

"Stow it and let me talk. G-type star. Planetary rotation same as Earth."

"But it's not!"

"I made the same mistake. The first night I thought was a week long. But the truth was I was scared out of my skin and that made it seem endless. Now I know better. The rotation matches."

"No, it doesn't. My watch shows it to be about twenty-six hours."

"You had better have your watch fixed when we get back. You banged it against a tree or something."

"But— Oh, go ahead. Keep talking; it's your tape."

"You'll see. Flora compatible. Fauna compatible. I know how they did it and why and where they put us. It's an economy measure."

"A what?"

"Economy. Too many people complaining about school taxes being too high. Of course, keeping an interstellar gate open is expensive and uranium doesn't grow on trees. I see their point. But Deacon Matson says it is false economy. He says, sure, it's expensive— but that the only thing more expensive than a properly trained explorer or pioneer leader is an improperly trained dead one.

"He told us after class one day," Rod went on, "that the penny-pinchers wanted to run the practices and tests in selected areas on Earth, but the Deacon claims that the essence of survival in the Outlands is the skill to cope with the unknown. He said that if tests were held on Earth, the candidates would just study up on terrestrial environments. He said any Boy Scout could learn the six basic Earth environments and how to beat them out of books . . . but that it was criminal to call that survival training and then dump a man in an unEarthly environment on his first professional assignment. He said that it was as ridiculous as just teaching a kid to play chess and then send him him out to fight a duel."

"He's right," Jack answered. "Commander Benboe talks the same way."

"Sure he's right. He swore that if they went ahead with this policy this would be the last year he would teach. But they pulled a gimmick on him."

"How?"

"It's a good one. What the Deacon forgot is that any environment is as unknown as any other if you don't have the slightest idea where you are. So they rigged it so that we could not know. First they shot us to Luna; the Moon gates are always open and that doesn't cost anything extra. Of course that made us think we were in for a long jump. Besides, it confused us; we wouldn't know we were being dumped back into the gravity field

71

we had left—for that was what they did next; they shoved us back on Earth. Where? Africa, I'd say. I think they used the Luna Link to jump us to Witwatersrand Gate outside Johannesburg and there they were all set with a matched-in temporary link to drop us into the bush. Tshaka Memorial Park or some other primitive preserve, on a guess. Everything matches. A wide variety of antelope-type game, carnivores to feed on them —I've seen a couple of lions and—"

"You *have?*"

"Well, they will do for lions until I get a chance to skin one. But they threw in other dodges to confuse us, too. The sky would give the show away, particularly if we got a look at Luna. So they've hung an overcast over us. You can bet there are cloud generators not far away. Then they threw us one more curve. Were you warned against 'stobor'?"

"Yes."

"See any?"

"Well, I'm not sure what stobor are."

"Neither am I. Nor any of us, I'll bet. 'Stobor' is the bogeyman, chucked in to keep our pretty little heads busy. There aren't any 'stobor' on Terra so naturally we must be somewhere else. Even a suspicious character like me would be misled by that. In fact, I was. I even picked out something I didn't recognize and called it that, just as they meant me to do."

"You make it sound logical, Rod."

"Because it *is* logical. Once you realize that this is Earth—" He patted the floor of the cave. "—but that they have been trying to keep us from knowing it, everything falls into place. Now here is what we do. I was going to tackle it alone, as soon as I could—I haven't been able to move around much on account of this bad arm—but I decided to take you along, before you got hurt. Here's my plan. I think this is Africa, but it might be South America, or anywhere in the tropics. It does not matter, because we simply follow this creek downstream, keeping our eyes open because there really are hazards; you can get just as dead here as in the Outlands. It may take a week, or a month, but one day we'll come to a bridge. We'll follow the road it serves until somebody happens along. Once in town we'll check in with the authorities and get them to flip us home . . . and we get our solo test certificates. Simple."

"You make it sound too simple," Jack said slowly.

"Oh, we'll have our troubles. But we can do it, now that we know what to do. I didn't want to bring this up before, but do you have salt enough to cure a few kilos of meat? If we did not have to hunt every day, we could travel faster. Or maybe you brought some Kwik-Kure?"

"I did, but—"

"Good!"

"Wait a minute, Rod. That won't do."

"Huh? We're a team, aren't we?"

"Take it easy. Look, Rod, everything you said is logical, but—"

"No 'buts' about it."

"It's logical . . . but it's *all wrong!*"

"Huh? Now, listen, Jack—"

"*You* listen. You've done all the talking so far."

"But— Well, all right, say your say."

"You said that the sky would give it away, so they threw an overcast over the area."

"Yes. That's what they must have done, nights at least. They wouldn't risk natural weather; it might give the show away."

"What I'm trying to tell you is that it *did* give the show away. It hasn't been overcast every night, though maybe you were in deep forest and missed the few times it has been clear. But I've seen the night sky, Rod. I've seen stars."

"So? Well?"

"They aren't *our* stars, Rod. I'm sorry."

Rod chewed his lip. "You probably don't know southern constellations very well?" he suggested.

"I knew the Southern Cross before I could read. These aren't our stars, Rod; I know. There is a pentagon of bright stars above where the sun sets; there is nothing like that to be seen from Earth. And besides, anybody would recognize Luna, if it was there."

Rod tried to remember what phase the Moon should be in. He gave up, as he had only a vague notion of elapsed time. "Maybe the Moon was down?"

"Not a chance. I didn't see our Moon, Rod, but I

saw *moons* . . . two of them, little ones and moving fast, like the moons of Mars."

"You don't mean this is *Mars?*" Rod said scornfully.

"Think I'm crazy? Anyhow, the stars from Mars are exactly like the stars from Earth. Rod, what are we jawing about? It was beginning to clear when the sun went down; let's crawl out and have a look. Maybe you'll believe your eyes."

Rod shut up and followed Jack. From inside nothing was visible but dark trees across the stream, but from the edge of the shelf part of the sky could be seen. Rod looked up and blinked.

"Mind the edge," Jack warned softly.

Rod did not answer. Framed by the ledge above him and by tree tops across the stream was a pattern of six stars, a lopsided pentagon with a star in its center. The six stars were as bright and unmistakable as the seven stars of Earth's Big Dipper . . . nor did it take a degree in astrography to know that this constellation had never been seen from Terra.

Rod stared while the hard convictions he had formed fell in ruins. He felt lost and alone. The tree across the way seemed frightening. He turned to Jack, his cocky sophistication gone. "You've convinced me," he said dully. "What do we do now?"

Jack did not answer.

"Well?" Rod insisted. "No good standing here."

"Rod," Jack answered, "that star in the middle of the Pentagon—it wasn't there before."

"Huh? You probably don't remember."

"No, no, I'm sure! Rod, you know what? We're seeing a *nova.*"

Rod was unable to arouse the pure joy of scientific discovery; his mind was muddled with reorganizing his personal universe. A mere stellar explosion meant nothing. "Probably one of your moonlets."

"Not a chance. The moons are big enough to show disks. It's a nova; it has to be. What amazing luck to see one!"

"I don't see anything lucky about it," Rod answered moodily. "It doesn't mean anything to us. It's probably a hundred light-years away, maybe more."

"Yes, but doesn't it thrill you?"

"No." He stooped down and went inside. Jack took another look, then followed.

There was silence, moody on Rod's part. At last Jack said, "Think I'll turn in."

"I just can't see," Rod answered irrelevantly, "how I could be so wrong. It was a logical certainty."

"Forget it," Jack advised. "My analytics instructors says that all logic is mere tautology. She says it is impossible to learn anything through logic that you did not already know."

"Then what use is logic?" Rod demanded.

"Ask me an easy one. Look, partner, I'm dead for sleep; I want to turn in."

"All right. But, Jack, if this isn't Africa—and I've got to admit it isn't—what do we do? They've gone off and *left* us."

"Do? We do what we've been doing. Eat, sleep, stay alive. This is a listed planet; if we just keep breathing, someday somebody will show up. It might be just a power breakdown; they may pick us tomorrow."

"In that case, then—"

"In that case, let's shut up and go to sleep."

6

"I Think He Is Dead"

ROD WAS AWAKENED BY HEAVENLY ODORS. HE ROLLED over, blinked at light streaming under the overhang, managed by great effort to put himself back into the matrix of the day before. Jack, he saw, was squatting by a tiny fire on the edge of the shelf; the wonderful fragrance came from toasting liver.

Rod got to his knees, discovering that he was slightly stiff from having fought dream stobor in his sleep.

These nightmare stobor were bug-eyed monsters fit for a planet suddenly strange and threatening. Nevertheless he had had a fine night's sleep and his spirits could not be daunted in the presence of the tantalizing aroma drifting in.

Jack looked up. "I thought you were going to sleep all day. Brush your teeth, comb your hair, take a quick shower, and get on out here. Breakfast is ready." Jack looked him over again. "Better shave, too."

Rod grinned and ran his hand over his chin. "You're jealous of my manly beard, youngster. Wait a year or two and you'll find out what a nuisance it is. Shaving, the common cold, and taxes . . . my old man says those are the three eternal problems the race is never going to lick." Rod felt a twinge at the thought of his parents, a stirring of conscience that he had not thought of them in he could not remember how long. "Can I help, pal?"

"Sit down and grab the salt. This piece is for you."

"Let's split it."

"Eat and don't argue. I'll fix me some." Rod accepted the charred and smoky chunk, tossed it in his hands and blew on it. He looked around for salt. Jack was slicing a second piece; Rod's eyes passed over the operation—then whipped back.

The knife Jack was using was "Colonel Bowie."

The realization was accompanied by action; Rod's hand darted out and caught Jack's wrist in an anger-hard grip. "You stole my knife!"

Jack did not move. "Rod . . . have you gone crazy?"

"You slugged me and stole my knife."

Jack made no attempt to fight, nor even to struggle. "You aren't awake yet, Rod. Your knife is on your belt. This is another knife . . . mine."

Rod did not bother to look down. "The one I'm wearing is Lady Macbeth. I mean the knife you're using, Colonel Bowie—*my* knife."

"Let go my wrist."

"Drop it!"

"Rod . . . you can probably make me drop this knife. You're bigger and you've got the jump on me. But yesterday you teamed with me. You're busting that team right now. If you don't let go right away, the team is broken. Then you'll have to kill me . . . because if you

76

don't, I'll trail you. I'll keep on trailing you until I find you asleep. Then you've had it."

They faced each other across the little fire, eyes locked. Rod breathed hard and tried to think. The evidence was against Jack. But had this little runt tracked him, slugged him, stolen everything he had? It looked like it.

Yet it did not *feel* like it. He told himself that he could handle the kid if his story did not ring true. He let go Jack's wrist. "All right," he said angrily, "tell me how you got my knife."

Jack went on slicing liver. "It's not much of a story . . . and I don't know that it is *your* knife. But it was not mine to start with—you've seen mine. I use this one as a kitchen knife. Its balance is wrong."

"Colonel Bowie! Balanced wrong? That's the best throwing knife you ever saw!"

"Do you want to hear this? I ran across this hombre in the bush, just as the jackals were getting to him. I don't know what got him—stobor, maybe; he was pretty well clawed and half eaten. He wasn't one of my class, for his face wasn't marked and I could tell. He was carrying a Thunderbolt and—"

"Wait a minute. A Thunderbolt gun?"

"I said so, didn't I? I guess he tried to use it and had no luck. Anyhow, I took what I could use—this knife and a couple of other things; I'll show you. I left the Thunderbolt; the power pack was exhausted and it was junk."

"Jack, look at me. You're not lying?"

Jack shrugged. "I can take you to the spot. There might not be anything left of him, but the Thunderbolt ought to be there."

Rod stuck out his hand. "I'm sorry. I jumped to conclusions."

Jack looked at his hand, did not shake it. "I don't think you are much of a team mate. We had better call it quits." The knife flipped over, landed at Rod's toes. "Take your toadsticker and be on your way."

Rod did not pick up the knife. "Don't get sore, Jack. I made an honest mistake."

"It was a mistake, all right. You didn't trust me and I'm not likely to trust you again. You can't build a team on that." Jack hesitated. "Finish your breakfast and shove off. It's better than way."

"Jack, I truly am sorry. I apologize. But it was a mistake anybody could make—you haven't heard my side of the story."

"You didn't wait to hear *my* story!"

"So I was wrong, I *said* I was wrong." Rod hurriedly told how he had been stripped of his survival gear. "—so naturally, when I saw Colonel Bowie, I assumed that you must have jumped me. That's logical, isn't it?" Jack did not answer; Rod persisted: "Well? Isn't it?"

Jack said slowly, "You used 'logic' again. What you call 'logic.' Rod, you use the stuff the way some people use dope. Why don't you use your head, instead?"

Rod flushed and kept still. Jack went on, "If I had swiped your knife, would I have let you see it? For that matter, would I have teamed with you?"

"No, I guess not. Jack, I jumped at a conclusion and lost my temper."

"Commander Benboe says," Jack answered bleakly, "that losing your temper and jumping at conclusions is a one-way ticket to the cemetery."

Rod looked sheepish. "Deacon Matson talks the same way."

"Maybe they're right. So let's not do it again, huh? Every dog gets one bite, but only one."

Rod looked up, saw Jack's dirty paw stuck out at him. "You mean we're partners again?"

"Shake. I think we had better be; we don't have much choice." They solemnly shook hands. Then Rod picked up Colonel Bowie, looked at it longingly, and handed it hilt first to Jack.

"I guess it's yours, after all."

"Huh? Oh, no. I'm glad you've got it back."

"No," Rod insisted. "You came by it fair and square."

"Don't be silly, Rod. I've got 'Bluebeard'; that's the knife for me."

"It's yours. I've got Lady Macbeth."

Jack frowned. "We're partners, right?"

"Huh? Sure."

"So we share everything. Bluebeard belongs just as

much to you as to me. And Colonel Bowie belongs to both of us. But you are used to it, so it's best for the team for you to wear it. Does that appeal to your lop-sided sense of logic?"

"Well . . ."

"So shut up and eat your breakfast. Shall I toast you another slice? That one is cold."

Rod picked up the scorched chunk of liver, brushed dirt and ashes from it. "This is all right."

"Throw it in the stream and have a hot piece. Liver won't keep anyhow."

Comfortably stuffed, and warmed by companionship, Rod stretched out on the shelf after breakfast and stared at the sky. Jack put out the fire and tossed the remnants of their meal downstream. Something broke water and snapped at the liver even as it struck. Jack turned to Rod. "Well, what do we do today?"

"Mmm . . . what we've got on hand ought to be fit to eat tomorrow morning. We don't need to make a kill today."

"I hunt every second day, usually, since I found this place. Second-day meat is better than first, but by the third . . . phewy!"

"Sure. Well, what do you want to do?"

"Well, let's see. First I'd like to buy a tall, thick chocolate malted milk—or maybe a fruit salad. Both. I'd eat those—"

"Stop it, you're breaking my heart!"

"Then I'd have a hot bath and get all dressed up and flip out to Hollywood and see a couple of good shows. That superspectacle that Dirk Manleigh is starring in and then a good adventure show. After that I'd have another malted milk . . . strawberry, this time, and then—"

"*Shut up!*"

"You asked me what I wanted to do."

"Yes, but I expected you to stick to possibilities."

"Then why didn't you say so? Is that 'logical'? I thought you always used logic?"

"Say, lay off, will you? I apologized."

"Yeah, you apologized," Jack admitted darkly. "But I've got some mad I haven't used up yet."

"Well! Are you the sort of pal who keeps raking up the past?"

"Only when you least expect it. Seriously, Rod, I think we ought to hunt today."

"But you agreed we didn't need to. It's wrong, and dangerous besides, to make a kill you don't need."

"I think we ought to hunt people."

Rod pulled his ear. "Say that again."

"We ought to spend the day hunting people."

"Huh? Well, anything for fun I always say. What do we do when we find them? Scalp them, or just shout 'Beaver!'?"

"Scalping is more definite. Rod, how long will we be here?"

"Huh? All we know is that something has gone seriously cockeyed with the recall schedule. You say we've been here three weeks. I would say it was longer but you have kept a notch calendar and I haven't. Therefore . . ." He stopped.

"Therefore what?"

"Therefore nothing. They might have had some technical trouble, which they may clear up and recall us this morning. Deacon Matson and his fun-loving colleagues might have thought it was cute to double the period and not mention it. The Dalai Lama might have bombed the whiskers off the rest of the world and the Gates may be radioactive ruins. Or maybe the three-headed serpent men of the Lesser Magellanic Cloud have landed and have the situation well in hand—for them. When you haven't data, guessing is illogical. We might be here forever."

Jack nodded. "That's my point."

"Which point? We know we may be marooned; that's obvious."

"Rod, a two-man team is just right for a few weeks. But suppose this runs into months? Suppose one of us breaks a leg? Or even if we don't, how long is that thornbush alarm going to work? We ought to wall off that path and make this spot accessible only by rope ladder, with somebody here all the time to let the ladder down. We ought to locate a salt lick and think about curing hides and things like that—that water skin I made is getting high already. For a long pull we ought to have at least four people."

Rod scratched his gaunt ribs thoughtfully. "I know. I thought about it last night, after you jerked the rug out from under my optimistic theory. But I was waiting for you to bring it up."

"Why?"

"This is your cave. You've got all the fancy equipment, a gun and pills and other stuff I haven't seen. You've got salt. All I've got is a knife—two knives now, thanks to you. I'd look sweet suggesting that you share four ways."

"We're a team, Rod."

"Mmm . . . yes. And we both figure the team would be strengthened with a couple of recruits. Well, how many people are there out there?" He gestured at the wall of green across the creek.

"My class put through seventeen boys and eleven girls. Commander Benboe told us there would be four classes in the same test area."

"That's more than the Deacon bothered to tell us. However, my class put through about twenty."

Jack looked thoughtful. "Around a hundred people, probably."

"Not counting casualties."

"Not counting casualties. Maybe two-thirds boys, one-third girls. Plenty of choice, if we can find them."

"No girls on this team, Jack."

"What have you got against girls?"

"Me? Nothing at all. Girls are swell on picnics, they are just right on long winter evenings. I'm one of the most enthusiastic supporters of the female race. But for a hitch like this, they are pure poison."

Jack did not say anything. Rod went on, "Use your head, brother. You get some pretty little darling on this team and we'll have more grief inside than stobor, or such, can give us from outside. Quarrels and petty jealousies and maybe a couple of boys knifing each other. It will be tough enough without that trouble."

"Well," Jack answered thoughtfully, "suppose the first one we locate is a girl? What are you going to do? Tip your hat and say, 'It's a fine day, ma'am. Now drop dead and don't bother me.'?"

Rod drew a pentagon in the ashes, put a star in the middle, then rubbed it out. "I don't know," he said slowly. "Let's hope we get our team working before we meet any. And let's hope they set up their own teams."

"I think we ought to have a policy."

"I'm clean out of policies. You would just accuse me of trying to be logical. Got any ideas about how to find anybody?"

"Maybe. Somebody has been hunting upstream from here."

"So? Know who it is?"

"I've seen him only at a distance. Nobody from my class. Half a head shorter than you are, light hair, pink skin—and a bad sunburn. Sound familiar?"

"Could be anybody," Rod answered, thinking fretfully that the description did sound familiar. "Shall we see if we can pick up some sign of him?"

"I can put him in your lap. But I'm not sure we want him."

"Why not? If he's lasted this long, he must be competent."

"Frankly, I don't see how he has. He's noisy when he moves and he has been living in one tree for the past week."

"Not necessarily bad technique."

"It is when you drop your bones and leavings out of the tree. It was jackals sniffing around that tipped me off to where he was living."

"Hmm . . . well, if we don't like him, we don't have to invite him."

"True."

Before they set out Jack dug around in the gloomy cave and produced a climbing line. "Rod, could this be yours?"

Rod looked it over. "It's just like the one I had. Why?"

"I got it the way I got Colonel Bowie, off the casualty. If it is not yours, at least it is a replacement." Jack got another, wrapped it around and over body armor. Rod suspected that Jack had slept in the armor, but he said nothing. If Jack considered such marginal protection more important than agility, that was Jack's

82

business—each to his own methods, as the Deacon would say.

The tree stood in a semi-clearing but Jack brought Rod to it through bushes which came close to the trunk and made the final approach as a belly sneak. Jack pulled Rod's head over and whispered in his ear, "If we lie still for three or four hours, I'm betting that he will either come down or go up."

"Okay. You watch our rear."

For an hour nothing happened. Rod tried to ignore tiny flies that seemed to be all bite. Silently he shifted position to ward off stiffness and once had to kill a sneeze. At last he said, "Pssst!"

"Yeah, Rod?"

"Where those two big branches meet the trunk, could that be his nest?"

"Maybe."

"You see a hand sticking out?"

"Where? Uh, I think I see what you see. It might just be leaves."

"I think it's a hand and I think he is dead; it hasn't moved since we got here."

"Asleep?"

"Person asleep ordinarily doesn't hold still that long. I'm going up. Cover me. If that hand moves, yell."

"You ought not to risk it, Rod."

"You keep your eyes peeled." He crept forward.

The owner of the hand was Jimmy Throxton, as Rod had suspected since hearing the description. Jimmy was not dead, but he was unconscious and Rod could not rouse him.

Jim lay in an aerie half natural, half artificial; Rod could see that Jim had cut small branches and improved the triple crotch formed by two limbs and trunk. He lay cradled in this eagle's nest, one hand trailing out.

Getting him down was awkward; he weighed as much as Rod did. Rod put a sling under Jim's armpits and took a turn around a branch, checking the line by friction to lower him—but the hard part was getting Jim out of his musty bed without dropping him.

Halfway down the burden fouled and Jack had to

climb and free it. But with much sweat all three reached the ground and Jim was still breathing.

Rod had to carry him. Jack offered to take turns but the disparity in sizes was obvious; Rod said angrily for Jack to cover them, front, rear, all sides; Rod would be helpless if they had the luck to be surprised by one of the pseudo-lions.

The worst part was the climbing traverse over loose shale up to the cave. Rod was fagged from carrying the limp and heavy load more than a kilometer over rough ground; he had to rest before he could tackle it. When he did, Jack said anxiously, "Don't drop him in the drink! It won't be worthwhile fishing him out—I know."

"So do I. Don't give silly advice."

"Sorry."

Rod started up, as much worried for his own hide as for Jim's. He did not know what it was that lived in that stream; he did know that it was hungry. There was a bad time when he reached the spot where the jutting limestone made it necessary to stoop to reach the shelf. He got down as low as possible, attempted it, felt the burden on his back catch on the rock, started to slip.

Jack's hand steadied him and shoved him from behind. Then they were sprawled safe on the shelf and Rod gasped and tried to stop the trembling of his abused muscles.

They bedded Jimmy down and Jack took his pulse. "Fast and thready. I don't think he's going to make it."

"What medicines do you have?"

"Two of the neosulfas and verdomycin. But I don't know what to give him."

"Give him all three and pray."

"He might be allergic to one of them."

"He'll be more allergic to dying. I'll bet he's running six degrees of fever. Come on."

Rod supported Jim's shoulders, pinched his ear lobe, brought him partly out of coma. Between them they managed to get the capsules into Jim's mouth, got him to drink and wash them down. After that there was nothing they could do but let him rest.

They took turns watching him through the night. About dawn his fever broke, he roused and asked for water. Rod held him while Jack handled the waterskin. Jim drank deeply, then went back to sleep.

They never left him alone. Jack did the nursing and Rod hunted each day, trying to find items young and tender and suited to an invalid's palate. By the second day Jim, although weak and helpless, was able to talk without drifting off to sleep in the middle. Rod returned in the afternoon with the carcass of a small animal which seemed to be a clumsy cross between a cat and a rabbit. He encountered Jack heading down to fill the water skin. "Hi."

"Hi. I see you had luck. Say, Rod, go easy when you skin it. We need a new water bag. Is it cut much?"

"Not at all. I knocked it over with a rock."

"Good!"

"How's the patient?"

"Healthier by the minute. I'll be up shortly."

"Want me to cover you while you fill the skin?"

"I'll be careful. Go up to Jim."

Rod went up, laid his kill on the shelf, crawled inside. "Feeling better?"

"Swell. I'll wrestle you two falls out of three."

"Next week. Jack taking good care of you?"

"You bet. Say, Rod, I don't know how to thank you two. If it hadn't been for——"

"Then don't try. You don't owe me anything, ever. And Jack's my partner, so it's right with Jack."

"Jack is swell."

"Jack is a good boy. They don't come better. He and I really hit it off."

Jim looked surprised, opened his mouth, closed it suddenly. "What's the matter?" Rod asked. "Something bite you? Or are you feeling bad again?"

"What," Jim said slowly, "did you say about Jack?"

"Huh? I said they don't come any better. He and I team up like bacon and eggs. A number-one kid, that boy."

Jimmy Throxton looked at him. "Rod . . . were you born that stupid? Or did you have to study?"

"Huh?"

"Jack is a *girl.*"

7

"I Should Have Baked a Cake"

THERE FOLLOWED A LONG SILENCE. "WELL," SAID JIM, "close your mouth before something flies in."

"Jimmy, you're still out of your head."

"I may be out of my head, but not so I can't tell a girl from a boy. When that day comes, I won't be sick; I'll be dead."

"But . . ."

Jim shrugged. "Ask her."

A shallow fell across the opening; Rod turned and saw Jack scrambling up to the shelf. "Fresh water, Jimmy!"

"Thanks, kid." Jim added to Rod, "Go on, dopy!"

Jack looked from one to the other. "Why the tableau? What are you staring for, Rod?"

"Jack," he said slowly, "what is your name?"

"Huh? Jack Daudet. I told you that."

"No, no! What's your full name, your legal name?"

Jack looked from Rod to Jimmy's grinning face and back again. "My full name is . . . Jacqueline Marie Daudet—if it's any business of yours. Want to make something of it?"

Rod took a deep breath. "Jacqueline," he said carefully, "I didn't know. I—"

"You weren't supposed to."

"I— Look, if I've said anything to offend you, I surely didn't mean to."

"You haven't said anything to offend me, you big stupid dear. Except about your knife."

"I didn't mean that."

"You mean about girls being poison? Well, did it ever occur to you that maybe boys are pure poison, too?

Under these circumstances? No, of course it didn't. But I don't mind your knowing now . . . now that there are three of us."

"But, Jacqueline—"

"Call me 'Jack,' please." She twisted her shoulders uncomfortably. "Now that you know, I won't have to wear this beetle case any longer. Turn your backs, both of you."

"Uh . . ." Rod turned his back. Jimmy rolled over, eyes to the wall.

In a few moments Jacqueline said, "Okay." Rod turned around. In shirt and trousers, without torso armor, her shoulders seemed narrower and she herself was slender now and pleasantly curved. She was scratching her ribs. "I haven't been able to scratch properly since I met you, Rod Walker," she said accusingly. "Sometimes I almost died."

"I didn't make you wear it."

"Suppose I hadn't? Would you have teamed with me?"

"Uh . . . well, it's like this. I . . ." He stopped.

"You see?" She suddenly looked worried. "We're still partners?"

"Huh? Oh, sure, sure!"

"Then shake on it again. This time we shake with Jimmy, too. Right, Jim?"

"You bet, Jack."

They made a three-cornered handshake. Jack pressed her left hand over the combined fists and said solemnly, "All for one!"

Rod drew Colonel Bowie with his left hand, laid the flat of the blade on the stacked hands. "And one for all!"

"Plus sales tax," Jimmy added. "Do we get it notarized?"

Jacqueline's eyes were swimming with tears. "Jimmy Throxton," she said fiercely, "someday I am going to make you take life seriously!"

"I take life seriously," he objected. "I just don't want life to take me seriously. When you're on borrowed time, you can't afford not to laugh."

"We're all on borrowed time," Rod answered him. "Shut up, Jimmy. You talk too much."

87

"Look who's preaching! The Decibel Kid himself."

"Well . . . you ought not to make fun of Jacqueline. She's done a lot for you."

"She has indeed!"

"Then—"

"'Then' nothing!" Jacqueline said sharply. "My name is 'Jack,' Rod. Forget 'Jacqueline.' If either of you starts treating me with gallantry we'll have all those troubles you warned me about. 'Pure poison' was the expression you used, as I recall."

"But you can't reasonably expect—"

"Are you going to be 'logical' again? Let's be practical instead. Help me skin this beast and make a new water bag."

The following day Jimmy took over housekeeping and Jack and Rod started hunting together. Jim wanted to come along; he ran into a double veto. There was little advanage in hunting as a threesome whereas Jack and Rod paired off so well that a hunt was never hours of waiting, but merely a matter of finding game. Jack would drive and Rod would kill; they would pick their quarry from the fringe of a herd, Jack would sneak around and panic the animals, usually driving one into Rod's arms.

They still hunted with the knife, even though Jack's gun was a good choice for primitive survival, being an air gun that threw poisoned darts. Since the darts could be recovered and re-envenomed, it was a gun which would last almost indefinitely; she had chosen it for this reason over cartridge or energy guns.

Rod had admired it but decided against hunting with it. "The air pressure might bleed off and let you down."

"It never has. And you can pump it up again awfully fast."

"Mmm . . . yes. But if we use it, someday the last dart will be lost no matter how careful we are . . . and that might be the day we would need it bad. We may be here a long time, what do you say we save it?"

"You're the boss, Rod."

"No, I'm not. We all have equal say."

"Yes, you are. Jimmy and I agreed on that. Somebody has to boss."

Hunting took an hour or so every second day; they

spent most of daylight hours searching for another team mate, quartering the area and doing it systematically. Once they drove scavengers from a kill which seemed to have been butchered by knife; they followed a spoor from that and determined that it was a human spoor, but were forced by darkness to return to the cave. They tried to pick it up the next day, but it had rained hard in the night; they never found it.

Another time they found ashes of a fire, but Rod judged them to be at least two weeks old.

After a week of fruitless searching they returned one late afternoon. Jimmy looked up from the fire he had started. "How goes the census?"

"Don't ask," Rod answered, throwing himself down wearily. "What's for dinner?"

"Raw buck, roast buck, and burned buck. I tried baking some of it in wet clay. It didn't work out too well, but I've got some awfully good baked clay for dessert."

"Thanks. If that is the word."

"Jim," Jack said, "we ought to try to bake pots with that clay."

"I did. Big crack in my first effort. But I'll get the hang of it. Look, children," he went on, "has it ever occurred to your bright little minds that you might be going about this the wrong way?"

"What's wrong with it?" Rod demanded.

"Nothing . . . if it is exercise you are after. You are hurrying and scurrying over the countryside, getting in a sweat and nowhere else. Maybe it would be better to sit back and let them come to you."

"How?"

"Send up a smoke signal."

"We've discussed that. We don't want just anybody and we don't want to advertise where we live. We want people who will strengthen the team."

"That is what the engineers call a self-defeating criterion. The superior woodsman you want is just the laddy you will never find by hunting for him. *He* may find *you,* as you go tramping noisily through the brush, kicking rocks and stepping on twigs and scaring the birds. He may shadow you to see what you are up to. But *you* won't find *him.*"

"Rod, there is something to that," Jack said.

"We found *you* easily enough," Rod said to Jim. "Maybe you aren't the high type we need."

"I wasn't myself at the time," Jimmy answered blandly. "Wait till I get my strength back and my true nature will show. Ugh-Ugh, the ape man, that's me. Half Neanderthal and half sleek black leopard." He beat his chest and coughed.

"Are those the proportions? The Neanderthal strain seems dominant."

"Don't be disrespectful. Remember, you are my debtor."

"I think you read the backs of those cards. They are getting to be like waffles." When rescued, Jimmy had had on him a pack of playing cards, and had later explained that they were survival equipment.

"In the first place," he had said, "if I got lost I could sit down and play solitaire. Pretty soon somebody would come along and—"

"Tell you to play the black ten on the red jack. We've heard that one."

"Quiet, Rod. In the second place, Jack, I expected to team with old Stoneface here. I can always beat him at cribbage but he doesn't believe it. I figured that during the test I could win all his next year's allowance. Survival tactics."

Whatever his reasoning, Jimmy had had the cards. The three played a family game each evening at a million plutons a point. Jacqueline stayed more or less even but Rod owed Jimmy several hundred millions. They continued the discussion that evening over their game. Rod was still wary of advertising their hide-out.

"We might burn a smoke signal somewhere, though," he said thoughtfully. "Then keep watch from a safe spot. Cut 'em, Jim."

"Consider the relative risks—a five, just what I needed! If you put the fire far enough away to keep this place secret, then it means a trek back and forth at least twice a day. With all that running around you'll use up your luck; one day you won't come back. It's not that I'm fond of you, but it would bust up the game."

"Whose crib?"

"Jack's. But if we burn it close by and in sight, then

we sit up here safe and snug. I'll have my back to the wall facing the path, with Jack's *phht* gun in my lap. If an unfriendly face sticks up—*blooie!* Long pig for dinner. But if we like them, we cut them into the game."

"Your count."

"Fifteen-six, fifteen-twelve, a pair, six for jacks and the right jack. That's going to cost you another million, my friend."

"One of those jacks is a queen," Rod said darkly.

"Sure enough? You know, it's getting too dark to play. Want to concede?"

They adopted Jim's scheme. It gave more time for cribbage and ran Rod's debt up into billions. The signal fire was kept burning on the shelf at the downstream end, the prevailing wind being such that smoke usually did not blow back into the cave—when the wind did shift it was unbearable; they were forced to flee, eyes streaming.

This happened three times in four days. Their advertising had roused no customers and they were all getting tired of dragging up dead wood for fuel and green branches for smoke. The third time they fled from smoke Jimmy said, "Rod, I give up. You win. This is not the way to do it."

"No!"

"Huh? Have a heart, chum. I can't live on smoke— no vitamins. Let's run up a flag instead. I'll contribute my shirt."

Rod thought about it. "We'll do that."

"Hey, wait a minute. I was speaking rhetorically. I'm the delicate type. I sunburn easily."

"You can take it easy and work up a tan. We'll use your shirt as a signal flag. But we'll keep the fire going, too. Not up on the shelf, but down there—on that mud flat, maybe."

"And have the smoke blow right back into our summer cottage."

"Well, farther downstream. We'll make a bigger fire and a column of smoke that can be seen a long way. The flag we will put up right over the cave."

"Thereby inviting eviction proceedings from large, hairy individuals with no feeling for property rights."

"We took that chance when we decided to use a smoke signal. Let's get busy."

Rod picked a tall tree on the bluff above. He climbed to where the trunk had thinned down so much that it would hardly take his weight, then spent a tedious hour topping it with his knife. He tied the sleeves of Jim's shirt to it, then worked down, cutting foliage away as he went. Presently the branches became too large to handle with his knife, but the stripped main stem stuck up for several meters; the shirt could be seen for a long distance up and down stream. The shirt caught the wind and billowed; Rod eyed it, tired but satisfied—it was unquestionably a signal flag.

Jimmy and Jacqueline had built a new smudge farther downstream, carrying fire from the shelf for the purpose. Jacqueline still had a few matches and Jim had a pocket torch almost fully charged but the realization that they were marooned caused them to be miserly. Rod went down and joined them. The smoke was enormously greater now that they were not limited in space, and fuel was easier to fetch.

Rod looked them over. Jacqueline's face, sweaty and none too clean to start with, was now black with smoke, while Jimmy's pink skin showed the soot even more. "A couple of pyromaniacs."

"You ordered smoke," Jimmy told him. "I plan to make the burning of Rome look like a bonfire. Fetch me a violin and a toga."

"Violins weren't invented then. Nero played a lyre."

"Let's not be small. We're getting a nice mushroom cloud effect, don't you think?"

"Come on, Rod," Jacqueline urged, wiping her face without improving it. "It's fun!" She dipped a green branch in the stream, threw it on the pyre. A thick cloud of smoke and steam concealed her. "More dry wood, Jimmy."

"Coming!"

Rod joined in, soon was as dirty and scorched as the other two and having more fun than he had had since the test started. When the sun dropped below the tree tops they at last quit trying to make the fire bigger and better and smokier and reluctantly headed up to their cave. Only then did Rod realize that he had forgotten to remain alert.

Oh well, he assured himself, dangerous animals would avoid a fire.

While they ate they could see the dying fire still sending up smoke. After dinner Jimmy got out his cards, tried to riffle the limp mass. "Anyone interested in a friendly game? The customary small stakes."

"I'm too tired," Rod answered. "Just chalk up my usual losses."

"That's not a sporting attitude. Why, you won a game just last week. How about you, Jack?"

Jacqueline started to answer; Rod suddenly motioned for silence. "Sssh! I heard something."

The other two froze and silently got out their knives. Rod put Colonel Bowie in his teeth and crawled out to the edge. The pathway was clear and the thorn barricade was undisturbed. He leaned out and looked around, trying to locate the sound.

"Ahoy below!" a voice called out, not loudly. Rod felt himself tense. He glanced back, saw Jimmy moving diagonally over to cover the pathway. Jacqueline had her dart gun and was hurriedly pumping it up.

Rod answered, "Who's there?"

There was a short silence. Then the voice answered, "Bob Baxter and Carmen Garcia. Who are you?"

Rod sighed with relief. "Rod Walker, Jimmy Throxton. And one other, not our class . . . Jack Daudet."

Baxter seemed to think this over. "Uh, can we join you? For tonight, at least?"

"Sure!"

"How can we get down there? Carmen can't climb very well; she's got a bad foot."

"You're right above us?"

"I think so. I can't see you."

"Stay there. I'll come up." Rod turned, grinned at the others. "Company for dinner! Get a fire going, Jim."

Jimmy clucked mournfully. "And hardly a thing in the house. I should have baked a cake."

By the time they returned Jimmy had roast meat waiting. Carmen's semi-crippled condition had delayed them. It was just a sprained ankle but it caused her to crawl up the traverse-on her hands, and progress to that point had been slow and painful.

When she realized that the stranger in the party was another woman she burst into tears. Jackie glared at the males, for no cause that Rod could see, then led her into the remote corner of the cave where she herself slept. There they whispered while Bob Baxter compared notes with Rod and Jim.

Bob and Carmen had had no unusual trouble until Carmen had hurt her ankle two days earlier . . . except for the obvious fact that something had gone wrong and they were stranded. "I lost my grip," he admitted, "when I realized that they weren't picking us up. But Carmen snapped me out of it. Carmen is a very practical kid."

"Girls are always the practical ones," Jimmy agreed. "Now take me—I'm the poetical type."

"Blank verse, I'd say," Rod suggested.

"Jealousy ill becomes you, Rod. Bob, old bean, can I interest you in another slice? Rare, or well carbonized?"

"Either way. We haven't had much to eat the last couple of days. Boy, does this taste good!"

"My own sauce," Jimmy said modestly. "I raise my own herbs, you know. First you melt a lump of butter slowly in a pan, then you—"

"Shut up, Jimmy. Bob, do you and Carmen want to team with us? As I see it, we can't count on ever getting back. Therefore we ought to make plans for the future."

"I think you are right."

"Rod is always right," Jimmy agreed. " 'Plans for the future—' Hmm, yes . . . Bob, do you and Carmen play cribbage?"

"No."

"Never mind. I'll teach you."

8

"Fish, or Cut Bait"

THE DECISION TO KEEP ON BURNING THE SMOKE SIGNAL and thereby to call in as many recruits as possible was never voted on; it formed itself. The next morning Rod intended to bring the matter up but Jimmy and Bob rebuilt the smoke fire from its embers while down to fetch fresh water. Rod let the accomplished fact stand; two girls drifted in separately that day.

Nor was there any formal contract to team nor any selection of a team captain; Rod continued to direct operations and Bob Baxter accepted the arrangement. Rod did not think about it as he was too busy. The problems of food, shelter, and safety for their growing population left him no time to worry about it.

The arrival of Bob and Carmen cleaned out the larder, it was necessary to hunt the next day. Bob Baxter offered to go, but Rod decided to take Jackie as usual. "You rest today. Don't let Carmen put her weight on that bad ankle and don't let Jimmy go down alone to tend the fire. He thinks he is well again but he is not."

"I see that."

Jack and Rod went out, made their kill quickly. But Rod failed to kill clean and when Jacqueline moved in to help finish the thrashing, wounded buck she was kicked in the ribs. She insisted that she was not hurt; nevertheless her side was sore the following morning and Bob Baxter expressed the opinion that she had cracked a rib.

In the meantime two new mouths to feed had been added, just as Rod found himself with three on the sick list. But one of the new mouths was a big, grinning one belonging to Caroline Mshiyeni; Rod picked her as his hunting partner.

Jackie looked sour. She got Rod aside and whispered, "You haven't any reason to do this to me. I can hunt. My side is all right, just a little stiff."

"It is, huh? So it slows you down when I need you. I can't chance it, Jack."

She glanced at Caroline, stuck out her lip and looked stubborn. Rod said urgently, "Jack, remember what I said about petty jealousies? So help me, you make trouble and I'll paddle you."

"You aren't big enough!"

"I'll get help. Now, look—are we partners?"

"Well, I *thought* so."

"Then be one and don't cause trouble."

She shrugged. "All right. Don't rub it in—I'll stay home."

"I want you to do more than that. Take that old bandage of mine—it's around somewhere—and let Bob Baxter strap your ribs."

"No!"

"Then let Carmen do it. They're both quack doctors, sort of." He raised his voice. "Ready, Carol?"

"Quiverin' and bristlin'."

Rod told Caroline how he and Jacqueline hunted, explained what he expected of her. They located, and avoided, two family herds; old bulls were tough and poor eating and attempting to kill anything but the bull was foolishly dangerous. About noon they found a yearling herd upwind; they split and placed themselves cross wind for the kill. Rod waited for Caroline to flush the game, drive it to him.

He continued to wait. He was getting fidgets when Caroline showed up, moving silently. She motioned for him to follow. He did so, hard put to keep up with her and still move quietly. Presently she stopped; he caught up and saw that she had already made a kill. He looked at it and fought down the anger he felt.

Caroline spoke. "Nice tender one, I think. Suit you, Rod?"

He nodded. "Couldn't be better. A clean kill, too. Carol?"

"Huh?"

"I think you are better at this than I am."

"Oh, shucks, it was just luck." She grinned and looked sheepish.

"I don't believe in luck. Any time you want to lead the hunt, let me know. But be darn sure you let me know."

She looked at his unsmiling face, said slowly, "By any chance are you bawling me out?"

"You could call it that. I'm saying that any time you want to lead the hunt, you tell me. Don't switch in the middle. Don't ever. I mean it."

"What's the matter with you, Rod? Getting your feelings hurt just because I got there first—that's silly!"

Rod sighed. "Maybe that's it. Or maybe I don't like having a girl take the kill away from me. But I'm dead sure about one thing: I don't like having a partner on a hunt who can't be depended on. Too many ways to get hurt. I'd rather hunt alone."

"Maybe I'd rather hunt alone! I don't need any help."

"I'm sure you don't. Let's forget it, huh, and get this carcass back to camp."

Caroline did not say anything while they butchered. When they had the waste trimmed away and were ready to pack as much as possible back to the others Rod said, "You lead off. I'll watch behind."

"Rod?"

"Huh?"

"I'm sorry."

"What? Oh, forget it."

"I won't ever do it again. Look, I'll tell everybody you made the kill."

He stopped and put a hand on her arm. "Why tell anybody anything? It's nobody's business how we organize our hunt as long as we bring home the meat."

"You're still angry with me."

"I never was angry," he lied. "I just don't want us to get each other crossed up."

"Roddie, I'll never cross you up again! Promise."

Girls stayed in the majority to the end of the week. The cave, comfortable for three, adequate for twice that number, was crowded for the number that was daily accumulating. Rod decided to make it a girls' dormitory and moved the males out into the open on the field at the foot of the path up the shale. The spot was unprotected against weather and animals but it did guard the only access to the cave. Weather was no problem; protection against animals was set up as well as could be managed by organizing a night watch whose duty it was to keep fires burning between the bluff and the creek on the upstream side and in the bottleneck downstream.

Rod did not like the arrangements, but they were the best he could do at the time. He sent Bob Baxter and Roy Kilroy downstream to scout for caves and Caroline and Margery Chung upstream for the same purpose. Neither party was successful in the one-day limit he had imposed; the two girls brought back another straggler.

A group of four boys came in a week after Jim's shirt had been requisitioned; it brought the number up to twenty-five and shifted the balance to more boys than girls. The four newcomers could have been classed as men rather than boys, since they were two or three years older than the average. Three of the four classes in this survival-test area had been about to graduate from secondary schools; the fourth class, which included these four, came from Outlands Arts College of Teller University.

"Adult" is a slippery term. Some cultures have placed adult age as low as eleven years, others as high as thirty-five—and some have not recognized any such age as long as an ancestor remained alive. Rod did not think of these new arrivals as senior to him. There were already a few from Teller U. in the group, but Rod was only vaguely aware which ones they were—they fitted in. He was too busy with the snowballing problems of his growing colony to worry about their backgrounds on remote Terra.

The four were Jock McGowan, a brawny youth who seemed all hands and feet, his younger brother Bruce, and Chad Ames and Dick Burke. They had arrived late in the day and Rod had not had time to get acquainted, nor was there time the following morning, as a group of four girls and five boys poured in on them unexpectedly. This had increased his administrative problems almost to the breaking point; the cave would hardly sleep four more females. It was necessary to find, or build, more shelter.

Rod went over to the four young men lounging near the cooking fire. He squatted on his heels and asked, "Any of you know anything about building?"

He addressed them all, but the others waited for Jock McGowan to speak. "Some," Jock admitted. "I reckon I could build anything I wanted to."

"Nothing hard," Rod explained. "Just stone walls. Ever tried your hand at masonry?"

"Sure. What of it?"

"Well, here's the idea. We've got to have better living arrangements right away—we've got people pouring out of our ears. The first thing we are going to do is to throw a wall from the bluff to the creek across this flat area. After that we will build huts, but the first thing is a kraal to stop dangerous animals."

McGowan laughed. "That will be some wall. Have you seen this dingus that looks like an elongated cougar? One of those babies would go over your wall before you could say 'scat.' "

"I know about them," Rod admitted, "and I don't like them." He rubbed the long white scars on his left arm. "They probably could go over any wall we could build. So we'll rig a surprise for them." He picked up a twig and started drawing in the dirt. "We build the wall . . . and bring it around to here. Then, inside for about six meters, we set up sharpened poles. Anything comes over the wall splits its gut on the poles."

Jock McGowan looked at the diagram. "Futile."

"Silly," agreed his brother.

Rod flushed but answered, "Got a better idea?"

"That's beside the point."

"Well," Rod answered slowly, "unless somebody comes down with a better scheme, or unless we find really good caves, we've got to fortify this spot the best we can . . . so we'll do this. I'm going to set the girls to cutting and sharpening stakes. The rest of us will start on the wall. If we tear into it we ought to have a lot of it built before dark. Do you four want to work together? There will be one party collecting rock and an-

99

other digging clay and making clay mortar. Take your choice."

Again three of them waited. Jock McGowan lay back and laced his hands under his head. "Sorry. I've got a date to hunt today."

Rod felt himself turning red. "We don't need a kill today," he said carefully.

"Nobody asked you, youngster."

Rod felt the cold tenseness he always felt in a hunt. He was uncomfortably aware that an audience had gathered. He tried to keep his voice steady and said, "Maybe I've made a mistake. I—"

"You have."

"I thought you four had teamed with the rest of us. Well?"

"Maybe. Maybe not."

"You'll have to fish or cut bait. If you join, you work like anybody else. If not—well, you're welcome to breakfast and stop in again some time. But be on your way. I won't have you lounging around while everybody else is working."

Jock McGowan sucked his teeth, dug at a crevice with his tongue. His hands were still locked back of his head. "What you don't understand, sonny boy, is that nobody gives the McGowans orders. Nobody. Right, Bruce?" \

"Right, Jock."

"Right, Chad? Dick?"

The other two grunted approval. McGowan continued to stare up at the sky. "So," he said softly, "I go where I want to go and stay as long as I like. The question is not whether we are going to join up with you, but what ones I am going to let team with us. But not you, sonny boy; you are still wet behind your ears."

"Get up and get out of here!" Rod started to stand up. He was wearing Colonel Bowie, as always, but he did not reach for it. He began to straighten up from squatting.

Jock McGowan's eyes flicked toward his brother. Rod was hit low . . . and found himself flat on his face with his breath knocked out. He felt the sharp kiss of a knife against his ribs; he held still. Bruce called out, "How about it, Jock?"

Rod could not see Jock McGowan. But he heard him answer, "Just keep him there."

"Right, Jock."

Jock McGowan was wearing both gun and knife. Rod now heard him say, "Anybody want to dance? Any trouble out of the rest of you lugs?"

Rod still could not see Jock, but he could figure from the naked, startled expression of a dozen others that McGowan must have rolled to his feet and covered them with his gun. Everybody in camp carried knives; most had guns as well and Rod could see that Roy Kilroy was wearing his—although most guns were kept when not in use in the cave in a little arsenal which Carmen superintended.

But neither guns nor knives were of use; it had happened too fast, shifting from wordy wrangling to violence with no warning. Rod could see none of his special friends from where he was; those whom he could see did not seem disposed to risk death to rescue him.

Jock McGowan said briskly, "Chad—Dick—got 'em all covered?"

"Right, Skipper."

"Keep 'em that way while I take care of this cholo." His hairy legs appeared in front of Rod's face. "Pulled his teeth, Bruce?"

"Not yet."

"I'll do it. Roll over, sonny boy, and let me at your knife. Let him turn over, Bruce."

Bruce McGowan eased up on Rod and Jock bent down. As he reached for Rod's knife a tiny steel flower blossomed in Jock's side below his ribs. Rod heard nothing, not even the small sound it must have made when it struck. Jock straightened up with a shriek, clutched at his side.

Bruce yelled, "Jock! What's the matter?"

"They got me." He crumpled to the ground like loose clothing.

Rod still had a man with a knife on his back but the moment was enough; he rolled and grabbed in one violent movement and the situation was reversed, with Bruce's right wrist locked in Rod's fist, with Colonel Bowie threatening Bruce's face.

A loud contralto voice sang out, "Take it easy down there! We got you covered."

Rod glanced up. Caroline stood on the shelf at the top of the path to the cave,—with a rifle at her shoulder. At the downstream end of the shelf Jacqueline sat with her little dart gun in her lap; she was frantically pumping up again. She raised it, drew a bead on some one past Rod's shoulder.

Rod called out, "Don't shoot!" He looked around. "Drop it, you two!"

Chad Ames and Dick Burke dropped their guns. Rod added, "Roy! Grant Cowper! Gather up their toys. Get their knives, too." He turned back to Bruce McGowan, pricked him under the chin. "Let's have your knife." Bruce turned it loose; Rod took it and got to his feet.

Everyone who had been up in the cave was swarming down, Caroline in the lead. Jock McGowan was writhing on the ground, face turned blue and gasping in the sort of paralysis induced by the poison used on darts. Bob Baxter hurried up, glanced at him, then said to Rod, "I'll take care of that cut in your ribs in a moment." He bent over Jock McGowan.

Caroline said indignantly, "You aren't going to try to save him?"

"Of course."

"Why? Let's chuck him in the stream."

Baxter glanced at Rod. Rod felt a strong urge to order Caroline's suggestion carried out. But he answered, "Do what you can for him, Bob. Where's Jack? Jack—you've got antidote for your darts, haven't you? Get it."

Jacqueline looked scornfully at the figure on the ground. "What for? He's not hurt."

"Huh?"

"Just a pin prick. A practice dart—that's all I keep in Betsey. My hunting darts are put away so that nobody can hurt themselves—and I didn't have time to get them." She prodded Jock with a toe. "He's not poisoned. He's scaring himself to death."

Caroline chortled and waved the rifle she carried. "And this one is empty. Not even a good club."

Baxter said to Jackie, "Are you sure? The reactions look typical."

"Sure I'm sure! See the mark on the end sticking out? A target dart."

Baxter leaned over his patient, started slapping his face. "Snap out of it, McGowan! Stand up. I want to get that dart out of you."

McGowan groaned and managed to stand. Baxter took the dart between thumb and forefinger, jerked it free, Jock yelled. Baxter slapped him again. "Don't you faint on me," he growled. "You're lucky. Let it drain and you'll be all right." He turned to Rod. "You're next."

"Huh? There's nothing the matter with *me*."

"That stuff on your ribs is paint, I suppose." He looked around. "Carmen, get my kit."

"I brought it down."

"Good. Rod, sit down and lean forward. This is going to hurt a little."

It did hurt. Rod tried to chat to avoid showing that he minded it. "Carol," he asked, "I don't see how you and Jackie worked out a plan so fast. That was smooth."

"Huh? We didn't work out a plan; we both just did what we could and did it fast." She turned to Jacqueline and gave her a clap on the shoulder that nearly knocked her over. "This kid is solid, Roddie, solid!"

Jacqueline recovered, looked pleased and tried not to show it. "Aw, Carol!"

"Anyway I thank you both."

"A pleasure. I wish that pea shooter had been loaded. Rod, what are you going to do with them?"

"Well . . . ummph!"

"Whoops!" said Baxter, behind him. "I said it was going to hurt. I had better put one more clip in. I'd like to put a dressing on that, but we can't, so you lay off heavy work for a while and sleep on your stomach."

"Unh!" said Rod

"That's the last. You can get up now. Take it easy and give it a chance to scab."

"I still think," Caroline insisted, "that we ought to make them swim the creek. We could make bets on whether or not any of 'em make it across."

"Carol, you're uncivilized."

"I never claimed to be civilized. But I know which end wags and which end bites."

Rod ignored her and went to look at the prisoners. Roy Kilroy had caused them to lie down one on top of the other; it rendered them undignified and helpless. "Let them sit up."

Kilroy and Grant Cowper had been guarding them. Cowper said, "You heard the Captain. Sit up." They unsnarled and sat up, looking glum.

Rod looked at Jock McGowan. "What do you think we ought to do with you?"

McGowan said nothing. The puncture in his side was oozing blood and he was pale. Rod said slowly, "Some think we ought to chuck you in the stream. That's the same as condemning you to death—but if we are going to, we ought to shoot you or hang you. I don't favor letting anybody be eaten alive. Should we hang you?"

Bruce McGowan blurted out, "We haven't done anything!"

"No. But you sure tried. You aren't safe to have around other people."

Somebody called out, "Oh, let's shoot them and get it over with!" Rod ignored it. Grant Cowper came close to Rod and said, "We ought to vote on this. They ought to have a trial."

Rod shook his head. "No." He went on to the prisoners, "I don't favor punishing you—this is personal. But we can't risk having you around either." He turned to Cowper. "Give them their knives."

"Rod? You're not going to fight them?"

"Of course not." He turned back. "You can have your knives; we're keeping your guns. When we turn you loose, head downstream and keep going. Keep going for at least a week. If you ever show your faces again, you won't get a chance to explain. Understand me?"

Jock McGowan nodded. Dick Burke gulped and said, "But turning us out with just knives is the same as killing us."

"Nonsense! No guns. And remember, if you turn back this way, even to hunt, it's once too many. There may be somebody trailing you—with a gun."

"Loaded this time!" added Caroline. "Hey, Roddie, I want that job. Can I? Please?"

"Shut up, Carol. Roy, you and Grant start them on their way."

As exiles and guards, plus sightseers, moved off they ran into Jimmy Throxton coming back into camp. He stopped and stared. "What's the procession? Rod . . . what have you done to your ribs, boy? Scratching yourself again?"

Several people tried to tell him at once. He got the gist of it and shook his head mournfully. "And there I was, good as gold, looking for pretty rocks for our garden wall. Every time there's a party people forget to ask *me*. Discrimination."

"Stow it, Jim. It's not funny."

"That's what I said. It's discrimination."

Rod got the group started on the wall with an hour or more of daylight wasted. He tried to work on the wall despite Bob Baxter's medical orders, but found that he was not up to it; not only was his wound painful but also he felt shaky with reaction.

Grant Cowper looking him up during the noon break. "Skipper, can I talk with you? Privately?"

Rod moved aside with him. "What's on your mind?"

"Mmm . . . Rod, you were lucky this morning. You know that, don't you? No offense intended."

"Sure, I know. What about it?"

"Uh, do you know *why* you had trouble?"

"What? Of course I know—now. I trusted somebody when I should not have."

Cowper shook his head. "Not at all. Rod, what do you know about theory of government?"

Rod looked surprised. "I've had the usual civics courses. Why?"

"I doubt if I've mentioned it, but the course I'm majoring in at Teller U. is colonial administration. One thing we study is how authority comes about in human society and how it is maintained. I'm not criticizing . . . but to be blunt, you almost lost your life because you've never studied such things."

Rod felt annoyed. "What are you driving at?"

"Take it easy. But the fact remains that you didn't have any authority. McGowan knew it and wouldn't take orders. Everybody else knew it, too. When it came to a showdown, nobody knew whether to back you up or not. Because you don't have a milligram of real authority."

"Just a moment! Are you saying I'm not leader of this team?"

"You are *de facto* leader, no doubt about it. But you've never been elected to the job. That's your weakness."

Rod chewed this over. "I know," he said slowly. "It's just that we have been so confounded busy."

"Sure, I know. I'd be the last person to criticize. But a captain ought to be properly elected."

Rod sighed. "I meant to hold an election but I thought getting the wall built was more urgent. All right, let's call them together."

"Oh, you don't need to do it this minute."

"Why not? The sooner the better, apparently."

"Tonight, when it's too dark to work, is soon enough."

"Well . . . okay."

When they stopped for supper Rod announced that there woud be an organization and planning meeting. No one seemed surprised, although he himself had mentioned it to no one. He felt annoyed and had to remind himself that there was nothing secret about it; Grant had been under no obligation to keep it quiet. He set guards and fire tenders, then came back into the circle of firelight and called out, "Quiet, everybody! Let's get started. If you guys on watch can't hear, be sure to speak up." He hesitated. "We're going to hold an election. Somebody pointed out that I never have been elected captain of this survival team. Well, if any of you have your noses out of joint, I'm sorry. I was doing the best I could. But you are entitled to elect a captain. All right, any nominations?"

Jimmy Throxton shouted, "I nominate Rod Walker!"

Caroline's voice answered, "I second it! Move the nominations be closed."

Rod said hastily, "Carol, your motion is out of order."

"Why?"

Before he could answer Roy Kilroy spoke up. "Rod, can I have the floor a moment? Privileged question."

Rod turned, saw that Roy was squatting beside Grant Cowper. "Sure. State your question."

"Matter of procedure. The first thing is to elect a temporary chairman."

Rod thought quickly. "I guess you're right. Jimmy, your nomination is thrown out. Nominations for temporary chairman are in order."

"Rod Walker for temporary chairman!"

"Oh, shut up, Jimmy! I don't want to be temporary chairman."

Roy Kilroy was elected. He took the imaginary gavel and announcement, "The chair recognizes Brother Cowper for a statement of aims and purposes of this meeting."

Jimmy Throxton called out, "What do we want any speeches for? Let's elect Rod and go to bed. I'm tired —and I've got a two-hour watch coming up."

"Out of order. The chair recognizes Grant Cowper."

Cowper stood up. The firelight caught his handsome features and curly, short beard. Rod rubbed the scraggly growth on his own chin and wished that he looked like Cowper. The young man was dressed only in walking shorts and soft bush shoes but he carried himself with the easy dignity of a distinguished speaker before some important body. "Friends," he said, "brothers and sisters, we are gathered here tonight not to elect a survival-team captain, but to found a new nation."

He paused to let the idea sink in. "You know the situation we are in. We fervently hope to be rescued, none more so than I. I will even go so far as to say that I think we will be rescued . . . eventually. But we have no way of knowing, we have no data on which to base an intelligent guess, as to *when* we will be rescued.

"It might be tomorrow . . . it might be our descendants a thousand years from now." He said the last very solemnly.

"But when the main body of our great race re-establishes contact with us, it is up to us, this little group here tonight, whether they find a civilized society . . . or flea-bitten animals without language, without arts, with the light of reason grown dim . . . or no survivors at all, nothing but bones picked clean."

"Not mine!" called out Caroline. Kilroy gave her a dirty look and called for order.

"Not yours, Caroline," Cowper agreed gravely. "Nor mine. Not any of us. Because tonight we will take the step that will keep this colony alive. We are poor in things; we will make what we need. We are rich in knowledge; among us we hold the basic knowledge of our great race. We must preserve it . . . we *will!*"

Caroline cut through Cowper's dramatic pause with a stage whisper. "Talks pretty, doesn't he? Maybe I'll marry him."

He did not try to fit this heckling into his speech. "What is the prime knowledge acquired by our race? That without which the rest is useless? What flame must we guard like vestal virgins?"

Some one called out, "Fire." Cowper shook his head.

"Writing!"

"The decimal system."

"Atomics!"

"The wheel, of course."

"No, none of those. They are all important, but they are not the keystone. The greatest invention of mankind is government. It is also the hardest of all. More individualistic than cats, nevertheless we have learned to cooperate more efficiently than ants or bees or termites. Wilder, bloodier, and more deadly than sharks, we have learned to live together as peacefully as lambs. But these things are not easy. That is why that which we do tonight will decide our future . . . and perhaps the future of our children, our children's children, our descendants far into the womb of time. We are not picking a temporary survival leader; we are setting up a government. We must do it with care. We must pick a chief executive for our new nation, a mayor of our city-state. But we must draw up a constitution, sign articles binding us together. We must organize and plan."

"Hear, hear!"

"Bravo!"

"We must establish law, appoint judges, arrange for orderly administration of our code. Take for example, this morning—" Cowper turned to Rod and gave him a friendly smile. "Nothing personal, Rod, you understand that. I think you acted with wisdom and I was happy that you tempered justice with mercy. Yet no one could have criticized if you had yielded to your impulse and killed all four of those, uh . . . anti-social individuals. But justice should not be subject to the whims of a dictator. We can't stake our lives on your temper . . . good or bad. You see that, don't you?"

Rod did not answer. He felt that he was being accused of bad temper, of being a tyrant and dictator, of being a danger to the group. But he could not put his finger on it. Grant Cowper's remarks had been friendly . . . yet they felt intensely personal and critical.

Cowper insisted on an answer. "You do see that, Rod? Don't you? You don't want to continue to have absolute power over the lives and persons of our community? You don't want *that*? Do you?" He waited.

"Huh? Oh, yeah, sure! I mean, I agree with you."

"Good! I was sure you would understand. And I must say that *I* think you have done a very good job in getting us together. I don't agree with any who have criticized you. You were doing your best and we should let bygones be bygones." Cowper grinned that friendly grin and Rod felt as if he were being smothered with kisses.

Cowper turned to Kilroy. "That's all I have to say, Mr. Chairman." He flashed his grin and added as he sat down, "Sorry I talked so long, folks. I had to get it off my chest."

Kilroy clapped his hands once. "The chair will entertain nominations for— Hey, Grant, if we don't call it 'captain,' then what should we call it?"

"Mmm . . ." Cowper said judicially. " 'President' seems a little pompous. I think 'mayor' would be about right—mayor of our city-state, our village."

"The chair will entertain nominations for mayor."

"Hey!" demanded Jimmy Throxton. "Doesn't anybody else get to shoot off his face?"

"Out of order."

"No," Cowper objected, "I don't think you should rule Jimmy out of order, Roy. Anyone who has something to contribute should be encouraged to speak. We mustn't act hastily."

"Okay, Throxton, speak your piece."

"Oh, I didn't want to sound off. I just didn't like the squeeze play."

"All right, the chair stands corrected. Anybody else? If not, we will entertain——"

"One moment, Mr. Chairman!"

Rod saw that it was Arthur Nielsen, one of the Teller University group. He managed to look neat even in these circumstances but he had strayed into camp bereft of all equipment, without even a knife. He had been quite hungry.

Kilroy looked at him. "You want to talk, Waxie?"

"Nielsen is the name. Or Arthur. As you know. Yes."

"Okay. Keep it short."

"I shall keep it as short as circumstances permit. Fellow associates, we have here a unique opportunity, probably one which has not occurred before in history. As Cowper pointed out, we must proceed with care. But, already we have set out on the wrong foot. Our object should be to found the first truly scientific community. Yet what do I find? You are proposing to select an executive by counting noses! Leaders should not be chosen by popular whim; they should be determined by rigorous scientific criteria. Once selected, those leaders must have full scientific freedom to direct the bio-group in accordance with natural law, unhampered by such artificial anachronisms as statutes, constitutions, and courts of law. We have here an adequate supply of healthy females; we have the means to breed scientifically a new race, a super race, a race which, if I may say so——"

A handful of mud struck Nielsen in the chest; he stopped suddenly. "I saw who did that!" he said angrily. "Just the sort of nincompoop who always——"

"Order, order, please!" Kilroy shouted. "No mud-slinging, or I'll appoint a squad of sergeants-at-arms. Are you through, Waxie?"

"I was just getting started."

"Just a moment," put in Cowper. "Point of order Mr. Chairman. Arthur has a right to be heard. But I think he is speaking before the wrong body. We're going to have a constitutional committee, I'm sure. He should

110

present his arguments to them. Then, if we like them, we can adopt his ideas."

"You're right, Grant. Sit down, Waxie."

"Huh? I appeal!"

Roy Kilroy said briskly, "The chair has ruled this out of order at this time and the speaker has appealed to the house, a priority motion not debatable. All in favor of supporting the chair's ruling, which is for Waxie to shut up, make it known by saying 'Aye.' "

There was a shouted chorus of assent. "Opposed: 'No.' Sit down, Waxie."

Kilroy looked around. "Anybody else?"

"Yes."

"I can't see. Who is it?"

"Bill Kennedy, Ponce de Leon class. I don't agree with Nielsen except on one point: we are fiddling around with the wrong things. Sure, we need a group captain but, aside from whatever it takes to eat, we shouldn't think about anything but how to get back. I don't want a scientific society; I'd settle for a hot bath and decent food."

There was scattered applause. The chairman said, "I'd like a bath, too . . . and I'd fight anybody for a dish of cornflakes. But, Bill, how do you suggest that we go about it?"

"Huh? We set up a crash-priority project and build a gate. Everybody works on it."

There was silence, then several talked at once: "Crazy! No uranium."—"We might *find* uranium."—"Where do we get the tools? Shucks, I don't even have a screwdriver."—"But where are we?"—"It is just a matter of—"

"*Quiet!*" yelled Kilroy. "Bill, do you know how to build a gate?"

"No."

"I doubt if anybody does."

"That's a defeatist attitude. Surely some of you educated blokes from Teller have studied the subject. You should get together, pool what you know, and put us to work. Sure, it may take a long time. But that's what we ought to do."

Cowper said, "Just a minute, Roy. Bill, I don't dispute what you say; every idea should be explored. We're

111

bound to set up a planning committee. Maybe we had better elect a mayor, or a captain, or whatever you want to call him—and then dig into your scheme when we can discuss it in detail. I think it has merit and should be discussed at length. What do you think?"

"Why, sure, Grant. Let's get on with the election. I just didn't want that silly stuff about breeding a superman to be the last word."

"Mr. Chairman! I protest—"

"Shut up, Waxie. Are you ready with nominations for mayor? If there is no objection, the chair rules debate closed and will entertain nominations."

"I nominate Grant Cowper!"

"Second!"

"I second the nomination."

"Okay, I third it!"

"Let's make it unanimous! Question, question!"

Jimmy Throxton's voice cut through the shouting, "I NOMINATE ROD WALKER!"

Bob Baxter stood up. "Mr. Chairman?"

"Quiet, everybody. Mr. Baxter."

"I second Rod Walker."

"Okay. Two nominations, Grant Cowper and Rod Walker. Are there any more?"

There was a brief silence. Then Rod spoke up. "Just a second, Roy." He found that his voice was trembling and he took two deep breaths before he went on. "I don't want it. I've had all the grief I want for a while and I'd like a rest. Thanks anyhow, Bob. Thanks, Jimmy."

"Any further nominations?"

"Just a sec, Roy . . . point of personal privilege." Grant Cowper stood up. "Rod, I know how you feel. Nobody in his right mind seeks public office . . . except as a duty, willingness to serve. If you withdraw, I'm going to exercise the same privilege; I don't want the headaches any more than you do."

"Now wait a minute, Grant. You—"

"*You* wait a minute. I don't think either one of us should withdraw; we ought to perform any duty that is handed to us, just as we stand a night watch when it's our turn. But I think we ought to have more nominations." He looked around. "Since that mix-up this morn-

112

ing we have as many girls as men . . . yet both of the candidates are male. That's not right. Uh, Mr. Chairman, I nominate Caroline Mshiyeni."

"Huh? Hey, Grant, don't be silly. I'd look good as a lady mayoress, wouldn't I? Anyhow, I'm for Roddie."

"That's your privilege, Caroline. But you ought to let yourself be placed before the body, just like Rod and myself."

"Nobody's going to vote for *me!*"

"That's where you're wrong. I'm going to vote for you. But we still ought to have more candidates."

"Three nominations before the house," Kilroy announced. "Any more? If not, I declare the—"

"Mr. Chairman!"

"Huh? Okay, Waxie, you want to nominate somebody?"

"Yes."

"Who?"

"Me."

"You want to nominate *yourself?*"

"I certainly do. What's funny about that? I am running on a platform of strict scientific government. I want the rational minds in this group to have someone to vote for."

Kilroy looked puzzled. "I'm not sure that is correct parliamentary procedure. I'm afraid I'll have to over—"

"Never mind, never mind!" Caroline chortled. "*I* nominate him. But I'm going to vote for Roddie," she added.

Kilroy sighed. "Okay, four candidates. I guess we'll have to have a show of hands. We don't have anything for ballots."

Bob Baxter stood up. "Objection, Mr. Chairman. I call for a secret ballot. We can find some way to do it."

A way was found. Pebbles would signify Rod, a bare twig was a note for Cowper, a green leaf meant Caroline, while one of Jimmy's ceramic attempts was offered as a ballot box. "How about Nielsen?" Kilroy asked.

Jimmy spoke up. "Uh, maybe this would do: I made another pot the same time I made this one, only it busted. I'll get chunks of it and all the crackpots are votes for Waxie."

"Mr. Chairman, I resent the insinua—"

113

"Save it, Waxie. Pieces of baked clay for you, pebbles for Walker, twigs for Grant, leaves for Carol. Get your votes, folks, then file past and drop them in the ballot box. Shorty, you and Margery act as tellers."

The tellers solemnly counted the ballots by firelight. There were five votes for Rod, one for Nielsen, none for Caroline, and twenty-two for Cowper. Rod shook hands with Cowper and faded back into the darkness so that no one would see his face. Caroline looked at the results and said, "Hey, Grant! You promised to vote for me. What happened? Did you vote for yourself? Huh? How about that?"

Rod said nothing. He had voted for Cowper and was certain that the new mayor had not returned the compliment . . . he was sure who his five friends were. Dog take it!—he had seen it coming; why hadn't Grant let him bow out?

Grant ignored Caroline's comment. He briskly assumed the chair and said, "Thank you. Thank you all. I know you want to get to sleep, so I will limit myself tonight to appointing a few committees—"

Rod did not get to sleep at once. He told himself that there was no disgrace in losing an election—shucks, hadn't his old man lost the time he had run for community corporation board? He told himself, too, that trying to ride herd on those apes was enough to drive a man crazy and he was well out of it—he had never *wanted* the job! Nevertheless there was a lump in his middle and a deep sense of personal failure.

It seemed that he had just gone to sleep . . . his father was looking at him saying, "You know we are proud of you, son. Still, if you had had the foresight to—" when someone touched his arm.

He was awake, alert, and had Colonel Bowie out at once.

"Put away that toothpick," Jimmy whispered, "before you hurt somebody. Me, I mean."

"What's up?"

"I'm up, I've got the fire watch. You're about to be, because we are holding a session of the inner sanctum."

"Huh?"

"Shut up and come along. Keep quiet, people are asleep."

The inner sanctum turned out to be Jimmy, Caroline, Jacqueline, Bob Baxter, and Carmen Garcia. They gathered inside the ring of fire but as far from the sleepers as possible. Rod looked around at his friends. "What's this all about?"

"It's about this," Jimmy said seriously. "You're our Captain. And we like that election as much as I like a crooked deck of cards."

"That's right," agreed Caroline. "All that fancy talk!"

"Huh? Everybody got to talk. Everybody got to vote."

"Yes," agreed Baxter. "Yes . . . and no."

"It was all proper. I have no kick."

"I didn't expect you to kick, Rod. Nevertheless . . . well, I don't know how much politicking you've seen, Rod. I haven't seen much myself, except in church matters and we Quakers don't do things that way; we wait until the Spirit moves. But, despite all the rigamarole, that was a slick piece of railroading. This morning you would have been elected overwhelmingly; tonight you did not stand a chance."

"The point is," Jimmy put in, "do we stand for it?"

"What can we do?"

"What can we do? We don't have to stay here. We've still got our own group; we can walk out and find another place . . . a bigger cave maybe."

"Yes, sir!" agreed Caroline. "Right tonight."

Rod thought about it. The idea was tempting; they didn't need the others . . . guys like Nielsen—and Cowper. The discovery that his friends were loyal to him, loyal to the extent that they would consider exile rather than let him down choked him up. He turned to Jacqueline. "How about you, Jackie?"

"We're partners, Rod. Always."

"Bob—do you want to do this? You and Carmen?"

"Yes. Well . . ."

" 'Well' what?"

"Rod, we're sticking with you. This election is all very well—but you took us in when we needed it and teamed with us. We'll never forget it. Furthermore I think that you make a sounder team captain than Cowper is likely to make. But there is one thing."

"Yes."

"If you decide that we leave, Carmen and I will appreciate it if you put it off a day."

"Why?" demanded Caroline. "Now is the time."

"Well—they've set this up as a formal colony, a village with a mayor. Everybody knows that a regularly elected mayor can perform weddings."

"Oh!" said Caroline. "Pardon my big mouth."

"Carmen and I can take care of the religious end—it's not very complicated in our church. But, just in case we ever are rescued, we would like it better and our folks would like it if the civil requirements were all perfectly regular and legal. You see?"

Rod nodded. "I see."

"But if you say to leave tonight . . ."

"I don't," Rod answered with sudden decision. "We'll stay and get you two properly married. Then—"

"Then we all shove off in a shower of rice," Caroline finished.

"Then we'll see. Cowper may turn out to be a good mayor. We won't leave just because I lost an election." He looked around at their faces. "But . . . but I certainly do thank you. I—"

He could not go on. Carmen stepped forward and kissed him quickly. "Goodnight, Rod. Thanks."

9

"A Joyful Omen"

MAYOR COWPER GOT OFF TO A GOOD START. HE approved, took over, and embellished a suggestion that Carmen and Bob should have their own quarters. He suspended work on the wall and set the whole village to constructing a honeymoon cottage. Not until his deputy,

Roy Kilroy, reminded him did he send out hunting parties.

He worked hard himself, having set the wedding for that evening and having decreed that the building must be finished by sundown. Finished it was by vandalizing part of the wall to supply building stone when the supply ran short. Construction was necessarily simple since they had no tools, no mortar but clay mud, no way to cut timbers. It was a stone box as tall as a man and a couple of meters square, with a hole for a door. The roof was laid up from the heaviest poles that could be cut from a growth upstream of giant grass much like bamboo—the colonists simply called it "bamboo." This was thatched and plastered with mud; it sagged badly.

But it was a house and even had a door which could be closed—a woven grass mat stiffened with bamboo. It neither hinged nor locked but it filled the hole and could be held in place with a stone and a pole. The floor was clean sand covered with fresh broad leaves.

As a doghouse for a St. Bernard it would have been about right; as a dwelling for humans it was not much. But it was better than that which most human beings had enjoyed through the history and prehistory of the race. Bob and Carmen did not look at it critically.

When work was knocked off for lunch Rod self-consciously sat down near a group around Cowper. He had wrestled with his conscience for a long time in the night and had decided that the only thing to do was to eat sour grapes and pretend to like them. He could start by not avoiding Cowper.

Margery Chung was cook for the day; she cut Rod a chunk of scorched meat. He thanked her and started to gnaw it. Cowper was talking. Rod was not trying to overhear but there seemed to be no reason not to listen.

"—which is the only way we will get the necessary discipline into the group. I'm sure you agree." Cowper glanced up, caught Rod's eye, looked annoyed, then grinned. "Hello, Rod."

"Hi, Grant."

"Look, old man, we're having an executive committee meeting. Would you mind finding somewhere else to eat lunch?"

Rod stood up blushing. "Oh! Sure."

Cowper seemed to consider it. "Nothing private, of course—just getting things done. On second thought maybe you should sit in and give us your advice."

"Huh? Oh, no! I didn't know anything was going on." Rod started to move away.

Cowper did not insist. "Got to keep working, lots to do. See you later, then. Any time." He grinned and turned away.

Rod wandered off, feeling conspicuous. He heard himself hailed and turned gratefully, joined Jimmy Throxton. "Come outside the wall," Jimmy said quietly. "The Secret Six are having a picnic. Seen the happy couple?"

"You mean Carmen and Bob?"

"Know any other happy couples? Oh, there they are —staring hungrily at their future mansion. See you outside."

Rod went beyond the wall, found Jacqueline and Caroline sitting near the water and eating. From habit he glanced around, sizing up possible cover for carnivores and figuring escape routes back into the kraal, but his alertness was not conscious as there seemed no danger in the open so near other people. He joined the girls and sat down on a rock. "Hi, kids."

"Hello, Rod."

"H'lo, Roddie," Caroline seconded. " 'What news on the Rialto?"

"None, I guess. Say, did Grant appoint an executive committee last night?"

"He appointed about a thousand committees but no executive committee unless he did it after we adjourned. Why an executive committee? This gang needs one the way I need a bicycle."

"Who is on it, Rod?" asked Jacqueline.

Rod thought back and named the faces he had seen around Cowper. She looked thoughtful. "Those are his own special buddies from Teller U."

"Yes, I guess so."

"I don't like it," she answered.

"What's the harm?"

"Maybe none . . . maybe. It is about what we could expect. But I'd feel better if all the classes were on it, not just that older bunch. You know."

"Shucks, Jack, you've got to give him some leeway."

"I don't see why," put in Caroline. "That bunch you named are the same ones Hizzonor appointed as chairmen of the other committees. It's a tight little clique. You notice none of us unsavory characters got named to any important committee—I'm on waste disposal and camp sanitation, Jackie is on food preparation, and you aren't on any. You should have been on the constitution, codification, and organization committee, but he made himself chairman and left you out. Add it up."

Rod did not answer. Caroline went on, "I'll add it if you won't. First thing you know there will be a nominating committee. Then we'll find that only those of a certain age, say twenty-one, can hold office. Pretty soon that executive committee will turn into a senate (called something else, probably) with a veto that can be upset only by a three-quarters majority that we will never get. That's the way my Uncle Phil would have rigged it."

"Your Uncle Phil?"

"Boy, there was a politician! I never liked him—he had kissed so many babies his lips were puckered. I used to hide when he came into our house. But I'd like to put him up against Hizzonor. It'ud be a battle of dinosaurs. Look, Rod, they've got us roped and tied; I say we should fade out right after the wedding." She turned to Jacqueline. "Right, pardner?"

"Sure . . . if Rod says so."

"Well, I don't say so. Look, Carol, I don't like the situation. To tell the truth . . . well, I was pretty sour at being kicked out of the captaincy. But I can't let the rest of you pull out on that account. There aren't enough of us to form another colony, not safely."

"Why, Roddie, there are three times as many people still back in those trees as there are here in camp. This time we'll build up slowly and be choosy about whom we take. Six is a good start. We'll get by."

"Not six, Carol. Four."

"Huh? Six! We shook on it last night before Jimmy woke you."

Rod shook his head. "Carol, how can we expect Bob and Carmen to walk out . . . right after the rest have made them a wedding present of a house of their own?"

"Well . . . darn it, we'd build them another house!"

"They would go with us, Carol—but it's too much to ask."

"I think," Jacqueline said grudgingly, "that Rod has something, Carol."

The argument was ended by the appearance of Bob, Carmen, and Jimmy. They had been delayed, explained Jimmy, by the necessity of inspecting the house. "As if I didn't know every rock in it. Oh, my back!"

"I appreciate it, Jim," Carmen said softly. "I'll rub your back."

"Sold!" Jimmy lay face down.

"Hey!" protested Caroline. "I carried more rocks than he did. Mostly he stood around and bossed."

"Supervisory work is exceptionally tiring," Jimmy said smugly. "You get Bob to rub your back."

Neither got a back rub as Roy Kilroy called to them from the wall. "Hey! You down there—lunch hour is over. Let's get back to work."

"Sorry, Jimmy. Later." Carmen turned away.

Jimmy scrambled to his feet. "Bob, Carmen—don't go 'way yet. I want to say something."

They stopped. Rod waved to Kilroy. "With you in a moment!" He turned back to the others.

Jimmy seemed to have difficulty in choosing words. "Uh, Carmen . . . Bob. The future Baxters. You know we think a lot of you. We think it's swell that you are going to get married—every family ought to have a marriage. But . . . well, shopping isn't what it might be around here and we didn't know what to get you. So we talked it over and decided to give you this. It's from all of us. A wedding present." Jimmy jammed a hand in his pocket, hauled out his dirty, dog-eared playing cards and handed them to Carmen.

Bob Baxter looked startled. "Gosh, Jimmy, we can't take your cards—your *only* cards."

"I—we want you to have them."

"But—"

"Be quiet, Bob!" Carmen said and took the cards. "Thank you, Jimmy. Thank you very much. Thank you all." She looked around. "Our getting married isn't going to make any difference, you know. It's still one family. We'll expect you all . . . to come play cards . . .

at our house just as—" She stopped suddenly and started to cry, buried her head on Bob's shoulder. He patted it. Jimmy looked as if he wanted to cry and Rod felt nakedly embarrassed.

They started back, Carmen with an arm around Jimmy and the other around her betrothed. Rod hung back with the other two. "Did Jimmy," he whispered, "say anything to either of you about this?"

"No," Jacqueline answered.

"Not me," Caroline agreed. "I was going to give 'em my stew pan, but now I'll wait a day or two." Caroline's "bag of rocks" had turned out to contain an odd assortment for survival—among other things, a thin-page diary, a tiny mouth organ, and a half-litre sauce pan. She produced other unlikely but useful items from time to time. Why she had picked them and how she had managed to hang on to them after she discarded the bag were minor mysteries, but, as Deacon Matson had often told the class: "Each to his own methods. Survival is an art, not a science." It was undeniable that she had appeared at the cave healthy, well fed, and with her clothing surprisingly neat and clean in view of the month she had been on the land.

"They won't expect you to give up your stew pan, Caroline."

"I can't use it now that the crowd is so big, and they can set up housekeeping with it. Anyhow, I want to."

"I'm going to give her two needles and some thread. Bob made her leave her sewing kit behind in favor of medical supplies. But I'll wait a while, too."

"I haven't anything I can give them," Rod said miserably.

Jacqueline turned gentle eyes on him. "You can make them a water skin for their house, Rod," she said softly. "They would like that. We can use some of my Kwik-Kure so that it will last."

Rod cheered up at once. "Say, that's a swell idea!"

"We are gathered here," Grant Cowper said cheerfully, "to join these two people in the holy bonds of matrimony. I won't give the usual warning because we all know that no impediment exists to this union. In fact it is the finest thing that could happen to our little community, a joyful omen of things to come, a promise for the future, a guarantee that we are firmly resolved to keep the torch of civilization, now freshly lighted on this planet, forever burning in the future. It means that—"

Rod stopped listening. He was standing at the groom's right as best man. His duties had not been onerous but now he found that he had an overwhelming desire to sneeze. He worked his features around, then in desperation rubbed his upper lip violently and overcame it. He sighed silently and was glad for the first time that Grant Cowper had this responsibility. Grant seemed to know the right words and he did not.

The bride was attended by Caroline Mshiyeni. Both girls carried bouquets of a flame-colored wild bloom. Caroline was in shorts and shirt as usual and the bride was dressed in the conventional blue denim trousers and overshirt. Her hair was arranged *en brosse;* her scrubbed face shone in the firelight and she was radiantly beautiful.

"Who giveth this woman?"

Jimmy Throxton stepped forward and said hoarsely, "I do!"

"The ring, please."

Rod had it on his little finger; with considerable fumbling he got it off. It was a Ponce de Leon senior-class ring, borrowed from Bill Kennedy. He handed it to Cowper.

"Carmen Eleanora, do you take this man to be your lawfully wedded husband, to have and to hold, for better and for worse, in sickness and in health, till death do you part?"

"I do."

"Robert Edward, do you take this woman to be your lawfully wedded wife? Will you keep her and cherish her, cleaving unto her only, until death do you part?"

"I do. I mean, I will. Both."

"Take her hand in yours. Place the ring on her finger. Repeat after me—"

Rod's sneeze was coming back again; he missed part of it.

"—so, by authority vested in me as duly elected

Chief Magistrate of this sovereign community, I pronounce you man and wife! Kiss her, chum, before I beat you to it."

Carol and Jackie both were crying; Rod wondered what had gone wrong. He missed his turn at kissing the bride, but she turned to him presently, put an arm around his neck and kissed him. He found himself shaking hands with Bob very solemnly. "Well, I guess that does it. Don't forget you are supposed to carry her though the door."

"I won't forget."

"Well, you told me to remind you. Uh, may the Principle bless you both."

10

"I So Move"

THERE WAS NO MORE TALK OF LEAVING. EVEN CAROline dropped the subject.

But on other subjects talk was endless. Cowper held a town meeting every evening. These started with committee reports—the committee on food resources and natural conservation, the committees on artifacts and inventory, on waste disposal and camp sanitation, on exterior security, on human resources and labor allotment, on recruitment and immigration, on conservation of arts and sciences, on constitution, codification, and justice, on food preparation, on housing and city planning—

Cowper seemed to enjoy the endless talk and Rod was forced to admit that the others appeared to have a good time, too—he surprised himself by discovering that he too looked forward to the evenings. It was the village's social life, the only recreation. Each session produced wordy battles, personal remarks and caustic criticisms; what was lacking in the gentlemanly formality found in older congresses was made up in spice. Rod liked to sprawl on the ground with his ear near Jimmy Throxton and listen to Jimmy's slanderous asides about the intelligence, motives, and ancestry of each speaker. He waited for Caroline's disorderly heckling.

But Caroline was less inclined to heckle now; Cowper had appointed her Historian on discovering that she owned a diary and could take shorthand. "It is extremely important," he informed her in the presence of the village, "that we have a full record of these pioneer days for posterity. You've been writing in your diary every day?"

"Sure. That's what it's for."

"Good! From here on it will be an official account. I want you to record the important events of each day."

"All right. It doesn't make the tiniest bit of difference, I do anyhow."

"Yes, yes, but in greater detail. I want you to record our proceedings, too. Historians will treasure this document, Carol."

"I'll bet!"

Cowper seemed lost in thought. "How many blank leaves left in your diary?"

"Couple of hundred, maybe."

"Good! That solves a problem I had been wondering about. Uh, we will have to requisition half of that supply for official use—public notices, committee transactions, and the like. You know."

Caroline looked wide-eyed. "That's a lot of paper, isn't it? You had better send two or three big husky boys to carry it."

Cowper looked puzzled. "You're joking."

"Better make it *four* big huskies. I could probably manage three . . . and somebody is likely to get hurt."

"Now, see here, Caroline, it is just a temporary requisition, in the public interest. Long before you need all of your diary we will devise other writing materials."

"Go ahead and devise! That's *my* diary."

Caroline sat near Cowper, diary in her lap and style in her hand, taking notes. Each evening she opened proceedings by reading the minutes of the previous

124

meeting. Rod asked her if she took down the endless debates.

"Goodness no!"

"I wondered. It seemed to me that you would run out of paper. Your minutes are certainly complete."

She chuckled. "Roddie, want to know what I really write down? Promise not to tell."

"Of course I won't."

"When I 'read the minutes' I just reach back in my mind and recall what the gabble was the night before—I've got an awfully good memory. But what I actually dirty the paper with . . . well, here—" She took her diary from a pocket. "Here's last night: 'Hizzoner called us to disorder at half-past burping time. The committee on cats and dogs reported. No cats, no dogs. The shortage was discussed. We adjourned and went to sleep, those who weren't already.' "

Rod grinned. "A good thing Grant doesn't know shorthand."

"Of course, if anything *real* happens, I put it down. But not the talk, talk, talk."

Caroline was not adamant about not sharing her supply of paper when needed. A marriage certificate, drawn up in officialese by Howard Goldstein, a Teller law student, was prepared for the Baxters and signed by Cowper, the couple themselves, and Rod and Caroline as witnesses. Caroline decorated it with flowers and turtle doves before delivering it.

There were others who seemed to feel that the new government was long on talk and short on results. Among them was Bob Baxter, but the Quaker couple did not attend most of the meetings. But when Cowper had been in office a week, Shorty Dumont took the floor after the endless committee reports:

"Mr. Chairman!"

"Can you hold it, Shorty? I have announcements to make before we get on to new business."

"This is still about committee reports. When does the committee on our constitution report?"

"Why, I made the report myself."

"You said that a revised draft was being prepared and the report would be delayed. That's no report. What I want to know is: when do we get a permanent set-up? When do we stop floating in air, getting along from day to day on 'temporary executive notices'?"

Cowper flushed. "Do you object to my executive decisions?"

"Won't say that I do, won't say that I don't. But Rod was let out and you were put in on the argument that we needed constitutional government, not a dictatorship. That's why I voted for you. All right, where's our laws? When do we vote on them?"

"You must understand," Cowper answered carefully, "that drawing up a constitution is not done overnight. Many considerations are involved."

"Sure, sure—but it's time we had some notion of what sort of a constitution you are cooking up. How about a bill of rights? Have you drawn up one?"

"All in due time."

"Why wait? For a starter let's adopt the Virginia Bill of Rights as article one. I so move."

"You're out of order. Anyhow we don't even have a copy of it."

"Don't let that bother you; I know it by heart. You ready, Carol? Take this down . . ."

"Never mind," Caroline answered. "I know it, too. I'm writing it."

"You see? These things aren't any mystery, Grant; most of us could quote it. So let's quit stalling."

Somebody yelled, "Whoopee! That's telling him, Shorty. I second the motion."

Cowper shouted for order. He went on, "This is not the time nor the place. When the committee reports, you will find that all proper democratic freedoms and safeguards have been included—modified only by the stern necessities of our hazardous position." He flashed his smile. "Now let's get on with business. I have an announcement about hunting parties. Hereafter each hunting party will be expected to—"

Dumont was still standing. "I said no more stalling, Grant. You argued that what we needed was laws, not a captain's whim. You've been throwing your weight around quite a while now and I don't see any laws. What are your duties? How much authority do you have? Are you both the high and the low justice? Or do the rest of us have rights?"

"Shut up and sit down!"

"How long is your term of office?"

Cowper made an effort to control himself. "Shorty, if you have suggestions on such things, you must take them up with the committee."

"Oh, slush! Give me a straight answer."

"You are out of order."

"I am *not* out of order. I'm insisting that the committee on drawing up a constitution tell us what they are doing. I won't surrender the floor until I get an answer. This is a town meeting and I have as much right to talk as anybody."

Cowper turned red. "I wouldn't be too sure," he said ominously. "Just how old are you, Shorty?"

Dumont stared at him. "Oh, so *that's* it? And the cat is out of the bag!" He glanced around. "I see quite a few here who are younger than I am. See what he's driving at, folks? Second-class citizens. He's going to stick an age limit in that so-called constitution. Aren't you, Grant? Look me in the eye and deny it."

"Roy! Dave! Grab him and bring him to order."

Rod had been listening closely; the show was better than usual. Jimmy had been adding his usual flippant commentary. Now Jimmy whispered, "That tears it. Do we choose up sides or do we fade back and watch the fun?"

Before he could answer Shorty made it clear that he needed no immediate help. He set his feet wide and snapped, "Touch me and somebody gets hurt!" He did not reach for any weapon but his attitude showed that he was willing to fight.

He went on, "Grant, I've got one thing to say, then I'll shut up." He turned and spoke to all. "You can see that we don't have any rights and we don't know where we stand—but we are already organized like a strait-jacket. Committees for this, committees for that—and what good has it done? Are we better off than we were before all these half-baked committees were appointed? The wall is still unfinished, the camp is dirtier than ever, and nobody knows what he is supposed to do. Why, we even let the signal fire go out yesterday. When a roof leaks, you don't appoint a committee; you fix the leak. I say give the job back to Rod, get rid of these silly

127

committees, and get on with fixing the leaks. Anybody with me? Make some noise!"

They made plenty of noise. The shouts may have come from less than half but Cowper could see that he was losing his grip on them. Roy Kilroy dropped behind Shorty Dumont and looked questioningly at Cowper; Jimmy jabbed Rod in the ribs and whispered, "Get set, boy."

But Cowper shook his head at Roy. "Shorty," he said quietly, "are you through making your speech?"

"That wasn't a speech, that was a motion. And you had better not tell me it's out of order."

"I did not understand your motion. State it."

"You understood it. I'm moving that we get rid of you and put Rod back in."

Kilroy interrupted. "Hey, Grant, he can't do that. That's not according to—"

"Hold it, Roy. Shorty, your motion is not in order."

"I thought you would say that!"

"And it is really two motions. But I'm not going to bother with trifles. You say people don't like the way I'm doing things, so we'll find out." He went on briskly, "Is there a second to the motion?"

"Second!"

"I second it."

"Moved and seconded. The motion is to recall me and put Rod in office. Any remarks?"

A dozen people tried to speak. Rod got the floor by outshouting the others. "Mr. Chairman, *Mr. Chairman!* Privileged question!"

"The chair recognizes Rod Walker."

"Point of personal privilege. I have a statement to make."

"Well? Go ahead."

"Look, Grant, I didn't know Shorty planned to do this. Tell him, Shorty."

"That's right."

"Okay, okay," Cowper said sourly. "Any other remarks? Don't yell, just stick up your hands."

"I'm not through," insisted Rod.

"Well?"

"I not only did not know, I'm not for it. Shorty, I want you to withdraw your motion."

"No!"

"I think you should. Grant has only had a week; you can't expect miracles in that time—I *know;* I've had grief enough with this bunch of wild men. You may not like the things he's done—I don't myself, a lot of them. That's to be expected. But if you let that be an excuse to run him out of office, then sure as daylight this gang will break up."

"I'm not busting it up—he is! He may be older than I am but if he thinks that makes the least difference when it comes to having a say—well . . . he'd better think twice. I'm warning him. You hear that, Grant?"

"I heard it. You misunderstood me."

"Like fun I did!"

"Shorty," Rod persisted, "will you drop this idea? I'm asking you *please.*"

Shorty Dumont looked stubborn. Rod looked helplessly at Cowper, shrugged and sat down. Cowper turned away and growled, "Any more debate? You back there . . . Agnes? You've got the floor."

Jimmy whispered, "Why did you pull a stunt like that, Rod? Nobility doesn't suit you."

"I wasn't being noble. I knew what I was doing," Rod answered in low tones.

"You messed up your chances to be re-elected."

"Stow it." Rod listened; it appeared that Agnes Fries had more than one grievance. "Jim?"

"Huh?"

"Jump to your feet and move to adjourn."

"What? Ruin this when it's getting good? There is going to be some hair pulled . . . I hope."

"Don't argue; do it!—or I'll bang your heads together."

"Oh, all right. Spoilsport." Jimmy got reluctantly to his feet, took a breath and shouted, "I move we adjourn!"

Rod bounced to his feet. "SECOND THE MOTION!"

Cowper barely glanced at them. "Out of order. Sit down."

"It is *not* out of order," Rod said loudly. "A motion to adjourn is always in order, it takes precedence, and it cannot be debated. I call for the question."

"I never recognized you. This recall motion is going to be voted on if it is the last thing I do." Cowper's face was tense with anger. "Are you through, Agnes? Or do you want to discuss my table manners, too?"

"You *can't* refuse a motion to adjourn," Rod insisted "Question! Put the question."

Several took up the shout, drowning out Agnes Fries, preventing Cowper from recognizing another speaker. Boos and catcalls rounded out the tumult.

Cowper held up both hands for silence, then called out, "It has been moved and seconded that we adjourn. Those in favor say, 'Aye.'"

"*AYE!!*"

"Opposed?"

"No," said Jimmy.

"The meeting is adjourned." Cowper strode out of the circle of firelight.

Shorty Dumont came over, planted himself in front of Rod and looked up. "A fine sort of a pal you turned out to be!" He spat on the ground and stomped off.

"Yeah," agreed Jimmy, "what gives? Schizophrenia? Your nurse drop you on your head? That noble stuff in the right doses might have put us back in business. But you didn't know when to stop."

Jacqueline had approached while Jimmy was speaking. "I wasn't pulling any tricks," Rod insisted. "I meant what I said. Kick a captain out when he's had only a few days to show himself and you'll bust us up into a dozen little groups. *I* wouldn't be able to hold them together. Nobody could."

"Bosh! Jackie, tell the man."

She frowned. "Jimmy, you're sweet, but you're not bright."

"*Et tu,* Jackie?"

"Never mind, Jackie will take care of you. A good job, Rod. By tomorrow everybody will realize it. Some of them are a little stirred up tonight."

"What I don't see," Rod said thoughtfully, "is what got Shorty stirred up in the first place?"

"Hadn't you heard? Maybe it was while you were out hunting. I didn't see it, but he got into a row with Roy, then Grant bawled him out in front of everybody. I

130

think Shorty is self-conscious about his height," she said seriously. "He doesn't like to take orders."

"Does anybody?"

The next day Grant Cowper acted as if nothing had happened. But his manner had more of King Log and less of King Stork. Late in the afternoon he looked up Rod. "Walker? Can you spare me a few minutes?"

"Why not?"

"Let's go where we can talk." Grant led him to a spot out of earshot. They sat on the ground and Rod waited. Cowper seemed to have difficulty in finding words.

Finally he said, "Rod, I think I can depend on you." He threw in his grin, but it looked forced.

"Why?" asked Rod.

"Well . . . the way you behaved last night."

"So? Don't bank on it, I didn't do it for you." Rod paused, then added, "Let's get this straight. I don't like you."

For once Cowper did not grin. "That makes it mutual. I don't like you a little bit. But we've got to get along . . . and I think I can trust you."

"Maybe."

"I'll risk it."

"I agree with every one of Shorty's gripes. I just didn't agree with his solution."

Cowper gave a wry smile unlike his usual expression. For an instant Rod found himself almost liking him. "The sad part is that I agree with his gripes myself."

"Huh?"

"Rod, you probably think I'm a stupid jerk but the fact is I do know quite a bit about theory of government. The hard part is to apply it in a . . . a transitional period like this. We've got fifty people here and not a one with any practical experience in government—not even myself. But every single one considers himself an expert. Take that bill-of-rights motion; I couldn't let that stand. I know enough about such things to know that the rights and duties needed for a co-operative colony like this can't be taken over word for word from an agrarian democracy, and they are still different from those necessary for an industrial republic." He looked worried. "It is true that we had considered limiting the franchise."

"You do and they'll toss you in the creek!"

"I know. That's one reason why the law committee hasn't made a report. Another reason is—well, confound it, how can you work out things like a constitution when you practically haven't any writing paper? It's exasperating. But about the franchise: the oldest one of us is around twenty-two and the youngest is about sixteen. The worst of it is that the youngest are the most precocious, geniuses or near-geniuses." Cowper looked up. "I don't mean you."

"Oh, no," Rod said hastily. "I'm no genius!"

"You're not sixteen, either. These brilliant brats worry me. 'Bush lawyers,' every blessed one, with always a smart answer and no sense. We thought with an age limit—a reasonable one—the older heads could act as ballast while they grow up. But it won't work."

"No. It won't."

"But what am I to *do*? That order about hunting teams not being mixed—that wasn't aimed at teams like you and Carol, but she thought it was and gave me the very deuce. I was just trying to take care of these kids. Confound it, I wish they were all old enough to marry and settle down—the Baxters don't give me trouble."

"I wouldn't worry. In a year or so ninety per cent of the colony will be married."

"I hope so! Say . . . are *you* thinking about it?"

"Me?" Rod was startled. "Farthest thing from my mind."

"Um? I thought— Never mind; I didn't get you out here to ask about your private affairs. What Shorty had to say was hard to swallow—but I'm going to make some changes. I'm abolishing most of the committees."

"So?"

"Yes. Blast them, they don't *do* anything; they just produce reports. I'm going to make one girl boss cook —and one man boss hunter. I want you to be chief of police."

"Huh? Why in Ned do you want a chief of police?"

"Well . . . somebody has to see that orders are carried out. You know, camp sanitation and such. Somebody has to keep the signal smoking—we haven't accounted for thirty-seven people, aside from known dead. Somebody has to assign the night watch and check on it. The kids run hog wild if you don't watch them. You are the one to do it."

"Why?"

"Well . . . let's be practical, Rod. I've got a following and so have you. We'll have less trouble if everybody sees that we two stand together. It's for the good of the community."

Rod realized, as clearly as Grant did, that the group had to pull together. But Cowper was asking him to shore up his shaky administration, and Rod not only resented him but thought that Cowper was all talk and no results.

It was not just the unfinished wall, he told himself, but a dozen things. Somebody ought to search for a salt lick, every day. There ought to be a steady hunt for edible roots and berries and things, too—he, for one, was tired of an all-meat diet. Sure, you could stay healthy if you didn't stick just to lean meat, but who wanted to eat nothing but meat, maybe for a lifetime? And there were those stinking hides . . . Grant had ordered every kill skinned, brought back for use.

"What are you going to do with those green hides?" he asked suddenly.

"Huh? Why?"

"They stink. If you put me in charge, I'm going to chuck them in the creek."

"But we're going to need them. Half of us are in rags now."

"But we're not short on hides; tanning is what we need. Those hides won't sun-cure this weather."

"We haven't got tannin. Don't be silly, Rod."

"Then send somebody out to chew bark till they find some. You can't mistake the puckery taste. And get rid of those hides!"

"If I do, will you take the job?"

"Maybe. You said, 'See that orders are carried out.' Whose orders? Yours? Or Kilroy's?"

"Well, both. Roy is my deputy."

Rod shook his head. "No, thanks. You've got him, so

133

you don't need me. Too many generals, not enough privates."

"But, Rod, I *do* need you. Roy doesn't get along with the younger kids. He rubs them the wrong way."

"He rubs me the wrong way, too. Nothing doing, Grant. Besides, I don't like the title anyhow. It's silly."

"Pick your own. Captain of the Guard . . . City Manager. I don't care what you call it; I want you to take over the night guard and see that things run smoothly around camp—and keep an eye on the younger kids. You can do it and it's your duty."

"What will you be doing?"

"I've got to whip this code of laws into shape. I've got to think about long-range planning. Heavens, Rod, I've got a thousand things on my mind. I can't stop to settle a quarrel just because some kid has been teasing the cook. Shorty was right; we can't wait. When I give an order I want a law to back it and not have to take lip from some young snotty. But I can't do it all, I need help."

Cowper put it on grounds impossible to refuse, nevertheless . . . "What about Kilroy?"

"Eh? Confound it, Rod, you can't ask me to kick out somebody else to make room for *you*."

"I'm not *asking* for the job!" Rod hesitated. He needed to say that it was a matter of stubborn pride to him to back up the man who had beaten him, it was that more than any public-spiritedness. He could not phrase it, but he did know that Cowper and Kilroy were not the same case.

"I won't pull Kilroy's chestnuts out of the fire. Grant, I'll stooge for you; you were elected. But I won't stooge for a stooge."

"Rod, be reasonable! If you got an order from Roy, it would be *my* order. He would simply be carrying it out."

Rod stood up. "No deal."

Cowper got angrily to his feet and strode away.

There was no meeting that night, for the first time. Rod was about to visit the Baxters when Cowper called him aside. "You win. I've made Roy chief hunter."

"Huh?"

"You take over as City Manager, or Queen of the May, or whatever you like. Nobody has set the night watch. So get busy."

"Wait a minute! I never said I would take the job."

"You made it plain that the only thing in your way was Roy. Okay, you get your orders directly from me."

Rod hesitated. Cowper looked at him scornfully and said, "So you can't co-operate even when you have it all your own way?"

"Not that, but—"

"No 'buts.' Do you take the job? A straight answer: yes, or no."

"Uh . . . yes."

"Okay." Cowper frowned and added, "I almost wish you had turned it down."

"That makes two of us."

Rod started to set the guard and found that every boy he approached was convinced that he had had more than his share of watches. Since the exterior security committee had kept no records—indeed, had had no way to—it was impossible to find out who was right and who was shirking. "Stow it!" he told one. "Starting tomorrow we'll have an alphabetical list, straight rotation. I'll post it even if we have to scratch it on a rock." He began to realize that there was truth in what Grant had said about the difficulty of getting along without writing paper.

"Why don't you put your pal Baxter on watch?"

"Because the Mayor gave him two weeks honeymoon, as you know. Shut up the guff. Charlie will be your relief; make sure you know where he sleeps."

"I think I'll get married. I could use two weeks of loafing."

"I'll give you five to one you can't find a girl that far out of her mind. You're on from midnight to two."

Most of them accepted the inevitable once they were assured of a square deal in the future, but Peewee Schneider, barely sixteen and youngest in the community, stood on his "rights"—he had stood a watch the night before, he did not rate another for at least three nights, and nobody could most colorfully make him.

Rod told Peewee that he would either stand his watch, or Rod would slap his ears loose—and then he would still stand his watch. To which he added that if he heard Peewee use that sort of language around camp again he would wash Peewee's mouth out with soap.

Schneider shifted the argument. "Yah! Where are you going to find soap?"

"Until we get some, I'll use sand. You spread that word, Peewee: no more rough language around camp. We're going to be civilized if it kills us. Four to six, then, and show Kenny where you sleep." As he left Rod made a mental note that they should collect wood ashes and fat; while he had only a vague idea of how to make soap probably someone knew how . . . and soap was needed for other purposes than curbing foul-mouthed pip-squeaks. He had felt a yearning lately to be able to stand upwind of himself . . . he had long ago thrown away his socks.

Rod got little sleep. Everytime he woke he got up and inspected the guard, and twice he was awakened by watchmen who thought they saw something prowling outside the circle of firelight. Rod was not sure, although it did seem once that he could make out a large, long shape drifting past in the darkness. He stayed up a while each time, another gun in case the prowler risked the wall or the fires in the gap. He felt great temptation to shoot at the prowling shadows, but suppressed it. To carry the attack to the enemy would be to squander their scanty ammunition without making a dent in the dangerous beasts around them. There were prowlers every night; they had to live with it.

He was tired and cranky the next morning and wanted to slip away after breakfast and grab a nap in the cave. He had not slept after four in the morning, but had checked on Peewee Schneider at frequent intervals. But there was too much to do; he promised himself a nap later and sought out Cowper instead. "Two or three things on my mind, Grant."

"Spill it."

"Any reason not to put girls on watch?"

"Eh? I don't think it's a good idea."

"Why not? These girls don't scream at a mouse. Every one of them stayed alive by her own efforts at least a month before she joined up here. Ever seen Caroline in action?"

"Mmm . . . no."

"You should. It's a treat. Sudden death in both hands, and eyes in the back of her head. If she were on watch, I would sleep easy. How many men do we have now?"

"Uh, twenty-seven, with the three that came in yesterday."

"All right, out of twenty-seven who doesn't stand watch?"

"Why, everybody takes his turn."

"You?"

"Eh? Isn't that carrying it pretty far? I don't expect *you* to take a watch; you run it and check on the others."

"That's two off. Roy Kilroy?"

"Uh, look, Rod, you had better figure that he is a department head as chief hunter and therefore exempt. You know why—no use looking for trouble."

"I know, all right. Bob Baxter is off duty, too."

"Until next week."

"But this is this week. The committee cut the watch down to one at a time; I'm going to boost it to two again. Besides that I want a sergeant of the guard each night. He will be on all night and sleep all next day . . . then I don't want to put him on for a couple of days. You see where that leaves me? I need twelve watch-standers every night; I have less than twenty to draw from."

Cowper looked worried. "The committee didn't think we had to have more than one guard at a time."

"Committee be hanged!" Rod scratched his scars and thought about shapes in the dark. "Do you want me to run this the way I think it has to be run? Or shall I just go through the motions?"

"Well . . ."

"One man alone either gets jittery and starts seeing shadows—or he dopes off and is useless. I had to wake one last night—I won't tell you who; I scared him out of his pants; he won't do it again. I say we need a real guard, strong enough in case of trouble to handle things while the camp has time to wake up. But if you want it your way, why not relieve me and put somebody else in?"

"No, no, you keep it. Do what you think necessary."

"Okay, I'm putting the girls on. Bob and Carmen, too. And *you*."

"Huh?"

"And me. And Roy Kilroy. Everybody. That's the only way you will get people to serve without griping; that way you will convince them that it is serious, a first obligation, even ahead of hunting."

Cowper picked at a hangnail, "Do you honestly think I should stand watch? And you?"

"I do. It would boost morale seven hundred per cent. Besides that, it would be a good thing, uh, politically."

Cowper glanced up, did not smile. "You've convinced me. Let me know when it's my turn."

"Another thing. Last night there was barely wood to keep two fires going."

"Your problem. Use anybody not on the day's hunting or cooking details."

"I will. You'll hear some beefs. Boss, those were minor items; now I come to the major one. Last night I took a fresh look at this spot. I don't like it, not as a permanent camp. We've been lucky."

"Eh? Why?"

"This place is almost undefendable. We've got a stretch over fifty meters long between shale and water on the upstream side. Downstream isn't bad, because we build a fire in the bottleneck. But upstream we have walled off less than half and we need a lot more stakes behind the wall. Look," Rod added, pointing, "you could drive an army through there—and last night I had only two little bitty fires. We ought to finish that wall."

"We will."

"But we ought to make a real drive to find a better place. This is makeshift at best. Before you took over I was trying to find more caves—but I didn't have time to explore very far. Ever been to Mesa Verde?"

"In Colorado? No."

"Cliff dwellings, you've seen pictures. Maybe somewhere up or down stream—more likely down—we will find pockets like those at Mesa Verde where we can build homes for the whole colony. You ought to send a team out for two weeks or more, searching. I volunteer for it."

"Maybe. But you can't go; I need you."

"In a week I'll have this guard duty lined up so that it will run itself. Bob Baxter can relieve me; they respect him. Uh . . ." He thought for a moment. Jackie? Jimmy? "I'll team with Carol."

"Rod, I told you I want you here. But are you and Caroline planning to marry?"

"Huh? What gave you that notion?"

"Then you can't team with her in any case. We are trying to re-introduce amenities around here."

"Now see here, Cowper!"

"Forget it."

"Unh . . . all right. But the first thing—the very first —is to finish that wall. I want to put everybody to work right away."

"Mmm . . ." Cowper said. "I'm sorry. You can't."

"Why not?"

"Because we are going to build a house today. Bill Kennedy and Sue Briggs are getting married tonight."

"Huh? I hadn't heard."

"I guess you are the first to hear. They told me about it privately, at breakfast."

Rod was not surprised, as Bill and Sue preferred each other's company. "Look, do they have to get married tonight? That wall is urgent, Grant; I'm telling you."

"Don't be so intense, Rod. You can get along a night or two with bigger fires. Remember, there are human values more important than material values."

11

The Beach of Bones

"*July 29*—BILL AND SUE GOT MARRIED TONIGHT.
Hizzoner never looked lovelier. He made a mighty pretty
service out of it—I cried and so did the other girls. If
that boy could *do* the way he can talk! I played Men-
delssohn's Wedding March on my harmonica with tears
running down my nose and gumming up the reeds—
that's a touch I wanted to put into darling Carmen's
wedding but I couldn't resist being bridesmaid. The
groom got stuck carrying his lady fair over the threshold of their 'house'—if I may call it that—and had to
put her down and shove her in ahead of him. The ceiling is lower than it ought to be which is why he got
stuck, because we ran out of rock and Roddie raised
Cain when we started to use part of the wall. Hizzoner
was leading the assault on the wall and both of them
got red in the face and shouted at each other. But Hizzoner backed down after Roddie got him aside and said
something—Bill was pretty sore at Roddie but Bob
sweet-talked him and offered to swap houses and Roddie promised Bill that we would take the roof off and
bring the walls up higher as soon as the wall is finished.
That might not be as soon as he thinks, though—
usable rock is getting hard to find. I've broken all my
nails trying to pry out pieces we could use. But I agree
with Roddie that we ought to finish that wall and I
sleep a lot sounder now that he is running the watch
and I'll sleep sounder yet when that wall is tight and the
pin-cushion back of it finished. Of course we girls sleep
down at the safe end but who wants to wake up and
find a couple of our boys missing? It is not as if we had
them to spare, bless their silly little hearts. Nothing like

a man around the house, Mother always said, to give a home that lived-in look.

"*July 30*—I'm not going to write in this unless something happens. Hizzoner talks about making papyrus like the Egyptians but I'll believe it when I see it.

"*Aug 5*—I was sergeant of the guard last night and Roddie was awake practically all night. I turned in after breakfast and slept until late afternoon—when I woke up there was Roddie, red-eyed and cross, yelling for more rocks and more firewood. Sometimes Roddie is a little hard to take.

"*Aug 9*—the salt lick Alice found is closer than the one Shorty found last week, but not as good.

"*Aug 14*—Jackie finally made up her mind to marry Jim and I think Roddie is flabbergasted—but I could have told him a month ago. Roddie is stupid about such things. I see another house & wall crisis coming and Roddie will get a split personality because he will want Jimmy and Jacqueline to have a house right away and the only decent stone within reach is built into the wall.

"*Aug 15*—Jimmy and Jackie, Agnes and Curt, were married today in a beautiful double ceremony. The Throxtons have the Baxter house temporarily and the Pulvermachers have the Kennedy's doll house while we partition the cave into two sets of married quarters and a storeroom.

"*Sep 1*—the roots I dug up didn't poison me, so I served a mess of them tonight. The shield from power pack of that Thunderbolt gun we salvaged—Johann's, it must have been—made a big enough boiler to cook a little helping for everybody. The taste was odd, maybe because Agnes had been making soap in it—it wasn't very good soap, either. I'm going to call these things yams because they look like yams although they taste more like parsnips. There are a lot of them around. Tomorrow I'm going to try boiling them with greens, a strip of side meat, and plenty of salt. Yum, yum! I'm going to bake them in ashes, too.

"*Sep 16*—Chad Ames and Dick Burke showed up with their tails tucked in; Hizzoner got soft-hearted and let them stay. They say Jock McGowan is crazy. I can believe it.

"*Sep 28*—Philip Schneider died today, hunting. Roy carried him in, but he was badly clawed and lost a lot of blood and was D.O.A. Roy resigned as boss hunter and Hizzoner appointed Cliff. Roy is broken up about it and nobody blames him. The Lord giveth and the Lord taketh away. Blessed be the Name of the Lord.

"*Oct 7*—I've decided to marry M.

"*Oct 10*—seems I was mistaken—M. is going to marry Margery Chung. Well, they are nice kids and if we ever get out of this I'll be glad I'm single since I want to buck for a commission in the Amazons. Note: be a little more standoffish, Caroline. Well, *try!*

"*Oct 20*—Carmen????

"*Oct 21*—Yes.

"*Nov 1*—well Glory be! I'm the new *City Manager*. Little Carol, the girl with two left feet. Just a couple of weeks, temporary and acting while Roddie is away, but say 'sir' when you speak to me. Hizzoner finally let Roddie make the down-river survey he has been yipping about, accompanying it with a slough of advice and injunctions that Roddie will pay no attention to once he is out of sight—if I know Roddie. It's a two-man team and Roddie picked Roy as his teamer. They left this morning.

"*Nov 5*—being City Manager is not all marshmallow sundae. I wish Roddie would get back.

"*Nov 11*—Hizzoner wants me to copy off in here the 'report of the artifacts committee'! Mick Mahmud has been keeping it in his head which strikes me as a good place. But Hizzoner has been very jumpy since Roddie and Roy left, so I guess I will humor him—here it is:

"12 spare knives (besides one each for everybody)

"53 firearms and guns of other sorts—but only about half of them with even one charge left.

"6 Testaments

"2 Peace of the Flame

"1 Koran

"1 Book of Mormon

"1 Oxford Book of English Verse, Centennial Edition

"1 steel bow and 3 hunting arrows

"1 boiler made from a wave shield and quite a bit of metal and plastic junk (worth its weight in uranium, I admit) from the Thunderbolt Jackie salvaged.

"1 stew pan (Carmen's)

"1 pack playing cards with the nine of hearts missing

"13 matches, any number of pocket flamers no longer working, and 27 burning glasses

"1 small hand ax

"565 meters climbing line, some of it chopped up for other uses

"91 fishhooks (and no fish fit to eat!)

"61 pocket compasses, some of them broken

"19 watches that still run (4 of them adjusted to our day)

"2 bars of scented soap that Theo has been hoarding

"2 boxes Kwik-Kure and part of a box of Tan-Fast

"Several kilos of oddments that I suppose we will find a use for but I won't list. Mick has a mind like a pack rat.

"Lots of things we have made and can make more of —pots, bows and arrows, hide scrapers, a stone-age mortar & pestle we can grind seeds on if you don't mind grit in your teeth, etc. Hizzoner says the Oxford Verse is the most valuable thing we have and I agree, but not for his reasons. He wants me to cover all the margins with shorthand, recording all special knowledge that any of us have—everything from math to pig-raising. Cliff says go ahead as long as we don't deface the verses. I don't see when I'm going to find time. I've hardly been out of the settlement since Roddie left and sleep is something I just hear about.

"*Nov 13*—only two more days. 'For this relief, much thanks . . .'

"*Nov 16*—I didn't think they would be on time.

"*Nov 21*—We finally adopted our constitution and basic code today, the first town meeting we've had in weeks. It covers the flyleaves of two Testaments, Bob's and Georgia's. If anybody wants to refer to it, which I doubt, that's where to look.

"*Nov 29*—Jimmy says old Rod is too tough to kill. I hope he's right. Why, oh, why didn't I twist Hizzoner's arm and make him let me go?

"*Dec 15*—there's no use kidding ourselves any longer.

"*Dec 21*—the Throxtons and Baxters and myself and Grant gathered privately in the Baxter house tonight and Grant recited the service for the dead. Bob said a prayer for both of them and then we sat quietly for a long time, Quaker fashion. Roddie always reminded me of my brother Rickie, so I privately asked Mother to take care of him, and Roy, too—Mother had a lap big enough for three, any time.

"Grant hasn't made a public announcement; officially they are just 'overdue.'

"*Dec 25*—Christmas"

Rod and Roy traveled light and fast downstream, taking turns leading and covering. Each carried a few kilos of salt meat but they expected to eat off the land. In addition to game they now knew of many edible fruits and berries and nuts; the forest was a free cafeteria to those who knew it. They carried no water since they expected to follow the stream. But they continued to treat the water with respect; in addition to ichthyosaurs that sometimes pulled down a drinking buck there were bloodthirsty little fish that took very small bites—but they traveled in schools and could strip an animal to bones in minutes.

Rod carried both Lady Macbeth and Colonel Bowie; Roy Kilroy carried his Occam's Razor and a knife borrowed from Carmen Baxter. Roy had a climbing rope wrapped around his waist. Each had a hand gun strapped to his hip but these were for extremity; one gun had only three charges. But Roy carried Jacqueline Throxton's air pistol, with freshly envenomed darts; they expected it to save hours of hunting, save time for travel.

Three days downstream they found a small cave, found living in it a forlorn colony of five girls. They powwowed, then headed on down as the girls started upstream to find the settlement. The girls had told them of a place farther down where the creek could be crossed. They found it, a wide rocky shallows with natural stepping stones . . . then wasted two days on the far side before crossing back.

By the seventh morning they had found no cave other than one the girls had occupied. Rod said to Roy, "Today makes a week. Grant said to be back in two weeks."

"That's what the man said. Yes, sir!"

"No results."

"Nope. None."

"We ought to start back."

Roy did not answer. Rod said querulously, "Well, what do you think?"

Kilroy was lying down, watching the local equivalent of an ant. He seemed in no hurry to do anything else. Finally he answered, "Rod, you are bossing this party. Upstream, downstream—just tell me."

"Oh, go soak your head."

"On the other hand, a bush lawyer like Shorty might question Grant's authority to tell us to return at a given time. He might use words like 'free citizen' and 'sovereign autonomy.' Maybe he's got something—this neighborhood looks awfully far 'West of the Pecos.'"

"Well . . . we could stretch it a day, at least. We won't be taking that side trip going back."

"Obviously. Now, if I were leading the party—but I'm not."

"Cut the double talk! I asked for advice."

"Well, I say we are here to find caves, not to keep a schedule."

Rod quit frowning. "Up off your belly. Let's go."

They headed downstream.

The terrain changed from forest valley to canyon country as the stream cut through a plateau. Game became harder to find and they used some of their salt meat. Two days later they came to the first of a series of bluffs carved eons earlier into convolutions, pockets, blank dark eyes. "This looks like it."

"Yes," agreed Roy. He looked around. "It might be even better farther down."

"It might be."

They went on.

In time the stream widened out, there were no more caves, and the canyons gave way to a broad savannah, treeless except along the banks of the river. Rod sniffed. "I smell salt."

"You ought to. There's ocean over there somewhere."

"I don't think so." They went on.

They avoided the high grass, kept always near the trees. The colonists had listed more than a dozen predators large enough to endanger a man, from a leonine creature twice as long as the biggest African lion down to a vicious little scaly thing which was dangerous if cornered. It was generally agreed that the leonine monster was the "stobor" they had been warned against, although a minority favored a smaller carnivore which was faster, trickier, and more likely to attack a man.

One carnivore was not considered for the honor. It was no larger than a jack rabbit, had an oversize head, a big jaw, front legs larger than hind, and no tail. It was known as "dopy joe" from the silly golliwog expression it had and its clumsy, slow movements when disturbed. It was believed to live by waiting at burrows of field rodents for supper to come out. Its skin cured readily and made a good water bag. Grassy fields such as this savannah often were thick with them.

They camped in a grove of trees by the water. Rod said, "Shall I waste a match, or do it the hard way?"

146

"Suit yourself. I'll knock over something for dinner."

"Watch yourself. Don't go into the grass."

"I'll work the edges. Cautious Kilroy they call me, around the insurance companies."

Rod counted his three matches, hoping there would be four, then started making fire by friction. He had just succeeded, delayed by moss that was not as dry as it should have been, when Roy returned and dropped a small carcass. "The durnedest thing happened."

The kill was a dopy joe; Rod looked at it with distaste. "Was that the best you could do? They taste like kerosene."

"Wait till I tell you. I wasn't hunting him; he was hunting *me*."

"Don't kid me!"

"Truth. I had to kill him to keep him from snapping my ankles. So I brought him in."

Rod looked at the small creature. "Never heard the like. Must be insanity in his family."

"Probably." Roy started skinning it.

Next morning they reached the sea, a glassy body untouched by tide, unruffled by wind. It was extremely briny and its shore was crusted with salt. They concluded that it was probably a dead sea, not a true ocean. But their attention was not held by the body of water. Stretching away along the shore apparently to the horizon were millions on heaping millions of whitened bones. Rod stared. "Where did they all come from?"

Roy whistled softly. "Search me. But if we could sell them at five pence a metric ton, we'd be millionaires."

"Billionaires, you mean."

"Let's not be fussy." They walked out along the beach, forgetting to be cautious, held by the amazing sight. There were ancient bones, cracked by sun and sea, new bones with gristle clinging, big bones of the giant antelope the colonists never hunted, tiny bones of little buck no larger than terriers, bones without number of all sorts. But there were no carcasses.

They inspected the shore for a couple of kilometers, awed by the mystery. When they turned they knew that they were turning back not just to camp but to head home. This was as far as they could go.

On the trip out they had not explored the caves. On

their way back Rod decided that they should try to pick the best place for the colony, figuring game, water supply, and most importantly, shelter and ease of defense.

They were searching a series of arched galleries water-carved in sandstone cliff. The shelf of the lowest gallery was six or seven meters above the sloping stand of soil below. The canyon dropped rapidly here; Rod could visualize a flume from upstream, bringing running water right to the caves . . . not right away, but when they had time to devise tools and cope with the problems. Someday, someday—but in the meantime here was plenty of room for the colony in a spot which almost defended itself. Not to mention, he added, being in out of the rain.

Roy was the better Alpinist; he inched up, flat to the rock, reached the shelf and threw down his line to Rod —snaked him up quickly. Rod got an arm over the edge, scrambled to his knees, stood up—and gasped, "What the deuce!"

"That," said Roy, "is why I kept quiet. I thought you would think I was crazy."

"I think we both are." Rod stared around. Filling the depth of the gallery, not seen from below, was terrace on terrace of cliff dwellings.

They were not inhabited, nor had they ever been by men. Openings which must have been doors were no higher than a man's knee, not wide enough for shoulders. But it was clear that they were dwellings, not merely formations carved by water. There were series of rooms arranged in half a dozen low stories from floor to ceiling of the gallery. The material was a concrete of dried mud, an adobe, used with wood.

But there was nothing to suggest what had built them. Roy started to stick his head into an opening; Rod shouted, "Hey! Don't do that!"

"Why not? It's abandoned."

"You don't know what might be inside. Snakes, maybe."

"There are no snakes. Nobody's ever seen one."

"No . . . but take it easy."

"I wish I had a torch light."

"I wish I had eight beautiful dancing girls and a

148

Cadillac copter. Be careful. I don't want to walk back alone."

They lunched in the gallery and considered the matter. "Of course they were intelligent," Roy declared. "We may find them elsewhere. Maybe really civilized now—these look like ancient ruins."

"Not necessarily intelligent," Rod argued. "Bees make more complicated homes."

"Bees don't combine mud and wood the way these people did. Look at that lintel."

"Birds do. I'll concede that they were bird-brained, no more."

"Rod, you won't look at the evidence."

"Where are their artifacts? Show me one ash tray marked 'Made in Jersey City.' "

"I might find some if you weren't so jumpy."

"All in time. Anyhow, the fact that *they* found it safe shows that we can live here."

"Maybe. What killed them? Or why did they go away?"

They searched two galleries after lunch, found more dwellings. The dwellers had apparently formed a very large community. The fourth gallery they explored was almost empty, containing a beginning of a hive in one corner. Rod looked it over. "We can use this. It may not be the best, but we can move the gang in and then find the best at our leisure."

"We're heading back?"

"Uh, in the morning. This is a good place to sleep and tomorrow we'll travel from 'can' to 'can't'—I wonder what's up there?" Rod was looking at a secondary shelf inside the main arch.

Roy eyed it. "I'll let you know in a moment."

"Don't bother. It's almost straight up. We'll build ladders for spots like that."

"My mother was a human fly, my father was a mountain goat. Watch me."

The shelf was not much higher than his head. Roy had a hand over—when a piece of rock crumbled away. He did not fall far.

Rod ran to him. "You all right, boy?"

Roy grunted, "I guess so," then started to get up. He yelped.

"What's the matter?"

"My right leg. I think . . . ow! I think it's broken."

Rod examined the break, then went down to cut splints. With a piece of the line Roy carried, used economically, for he needed most of it as a ladder, he bound the leg, padding it with leaves. It was a simple break of the tibia, with no danger of infection.

They argued the whole time. "Of course you will," Roy was saying. "Leave me a fresh kill and what salt meat there is. You can figure some way to leave water."

"Come back and find your chawed bones!"

"Not at all. Nothing can get at me. If you hustle, you can make it in three days."

"Four, or five more likely. Six days to lead a party back. Then you want to go back in a stretcher? How would you like to be helpless when a stobor jumps us?"

"But I wouldn't go back. The gang would be moving down here."

"Suppose they do? Eleven days, more likely twelve— Roy, you didn't just bang your shin; you banged your head, too."

The stay in the gallery while Roy's leg repaired was not difficult nor dangerous; it was merely tedious. Rod would have liked to explore all the caves, but the first time he was away longer than Roy thought necessary to make a kill Rod returned to find his patient almost hysterical. He had let his imagination run away, visioning Rod as dead and thinking about his own death, helpless, while he starved or died of thirst. After that Rod left him only to gather food and water. The gallery was safe from all dangers; no watch was necessary, fire was needed only for cooking. The weather was getting warmer and the daily rains dropped off.

They discussed everything from girls to what the colony needed, what could have caused the disaster that had stranded them, what they would have to eat if they could have what they wanted, and back to girls again. They did not discuss the possibility of rescue; they took it for granted that they were there to stay. They slept much of the time and often did nothing, in animal-like torpor.

Roy wanted to start back as soon as Rod removed

the splints, but it took him only seconds to discover that he no longer knew how to walk. He exercised for days, then grew sulky when Rod still insisted that he was not able to travel; the accumulated irritations of invalidism spewed out in the only quarrel they had on the trip.

Rod grew as angry as he was, threw Roy's climbing rope at him and shouted, "Go ahead! See how far you get on that gimp leg!"

Five minutes later Rod was arranging a sling, half dragging Roy, white and trembling and thoroughly subdued, back up onto the shelf. Thereafter they spent ten days getting Roy's muscles into shape, then started back.

Shorty Dumont was the first one they ran into as they approached the settlement. His jaw dropped and he looked scared, then he ran to greet them, ran back to alert those in camp. "Hey, everybody! They're *back!*"

Caroline heard the shout, outdistanced the others in great flying leaps, kissed and hugged them both. "Hi, Carol," Rod said. "What are you bawling about?"

"Oh, Roddie, you bad, *bad* boy!"

12

"It Won't Work, Rod"

IN THE MIDST OF JUBILATION ROD HAD TIME TO NOTICE many changes. There were more than a dozen new buildings, including two long shedlike affairs of bamboo and mud. One new hut was of sunbaked brick; it had windows. Where the cooking fire had been was a barbecue pit and by it a Dutch oven. Near it a stream of water spilled out of bamboo pipe, splashed through a rawhide net, fell into a rock bowl, and was led away to the creek . . . he hardly knew whether to be pleased or irked at this anticipation of his own notion.

He caught impressions piecemeal, as their triumphal entry was interrupted by hugs, kisses, and bone-jarring slaps on the back, combined with questions piled on questions. "No, no trouble—except that Roy got mad and busted his leg . . . yeah, sure, we found what we went after; wait till you *see* . . . no . . . yes . . . Jackie! . . . Hi, Bob!—it's good to see you, too, boy! Where's Carmen . . . Hi, Grant!"

Cowper was grinning widely, white teeth splitting his beard. Rod noticed with great surprise that the man looked *old*—why, shucks, Grant wasn't more than twenty-two, twenty-three at the most. Where did he pick up those lines?

"Rod, old boy! I don't know whether to have you two thrown in the hoosegow or decorate your brows with laurel."

"We got held up."

"So it seems. Well, there is more rejoicing for the strayed lamb than for the ninety and nine. Come on up to the city hall."

"The what?"

Cowper looked sheepish. "They call it that, so I do. Better than 'Number Ten, Downing Street' which it started off with. It's just the hut where I sleep—it doesn't belong to me," he added. "When they elect somebody else, I'll sleep in bachelor hall." Grant led them toward a little building apart from the others and facing the cooking area.

The wall was gone.

Rod suddenly realized what looked strange about the upstream end of the settlement; the wall was gone completely and in its place was a thornbush barricade. He opened his mouth to make a savage comment—then realized that it really did not matter. Why kick up a row when the colony would be moving to the canyon of the Dwellers? They would never need walls again; they would be up high at night, with their ladders pulled up after them. He picked another subject.

"Grant, how in the world did you guys get the inner partitions out of those bamboo pipes?"

"Eh? Nothing to it. You tie a knife with rawhide to a

thinner bamboo pole, then reach in and whittle. All it takes is patience. Waxie worked it out. But you haven't seen anything yet. We're going to have *iron*."

"Huh?"

"We've got ore; now we are experimenting. But I do wish we could locate a seam of coal. Say, you didn't spot any, did you?"

Dinner was a feast, a *luau,* a celebration to make the weddings look pale. Rod was given a real plate to eat on—unglazed, lopsided, ungraceful, but a plate. As he took out Colonel Bowie, Margery Chung Kinksi put a wooden spoon in his hand. "We don't have enough to go around, but the guests of honor rate them tonight." Rod looked at it curiously. It felt odd in his hand.

Dinner consisted of boiled greens, some root vegetables new to him, and a properly baked haunch served in thin slices. Roy and Rod were served little unleavened cakes like tortillas. No one else had them, but Rod decided that it was polite not to comment on that. Instead he made a fuss over eating bread again.

Margery dimpled. "We'll have plenty of bread some day. Maybe next year."

There were tart little fruits for dessert, plus a bland, tasteless sort which resembled a dwarf banana with seeds. Rod ate too much.

Grant called them to order and announced that he was going to ask the travelers to tell what they had experienced. "Let them get it all told—then they won't have to tell it seventy times over. Come on, Rod. Let's see your ugly face."

"Ah, let Roy. He talks better than I do."

"Take turns. When your voice wears out, Roy can take over."

Between them they told it all, interrupting and supplementing each other. The colonists were awed by the beach of a billion bones, still more interested in the ruins of the Dwellers. "Rod and I are still arguing," Roy told them. "I say that it was a civilization. He says that it could be just instinct. He's crazy with the heat; the Dwellers were *people*. Not humans, of course, but people."

"Then where are they now?"

Roy shrugged. "Where are the Selenites, Dora? What became of the Mithrans?"

"Roy is a romanticist," Rod objected. "But you'll be able to form your own opinions when we get there."

"That's right, Rod," Roy agreed.

"That covers everything," Rod went on. "The rest was just waiting while Roy's leg healed. But it brings up the main subject. How quickly can we move? Grant, is there any reason not to start at once? Shouldn't we break camp tomorrow and start trekking? I've been studying it—how to make the move, I mean—and I would say to send out an advance party at daybreak. Roy or I can lead it. We go downstream an easy day's journey, pick a spot, make a kill, and have fire and food ready when the rest arrive. We do it again the next day. I think we can be safe and snug in the caves in five days."

"Dibs on the advance party!"

"Me, too!"

There were other shouts but Rod could not help but realize that the response was not what he had expected. Jimmy did not volunteer and Caroline merely looked thoughtful. The Baxters he could not see; they were in shadow.

He turned to Cowper. "Well, Grant? Do you have a better idea?"

"Rod," Grant said slowly, "your plan is okay ... but you've missed a point."

"Yes?"

"Why do you assume that we are going to move?"

"*Huh?* Why, that's what we were sent for! To find a better place to live. We found it—you could hold those caves against an army. What's the hitch? Of *course* we move!"

Cowper examined his nails. "Rod, don't get sore. I don't see it and I doubt if other people do. I'm not saying the spot you and Roy found is not good. It may be better than here—the way this place used to be. But we are doing all right here—and we've got a lot of time and effort invested. Why move?"

"Why, I told you. The caves are safe, completely safe. This spot is exposed ... it's *dangerous*."

"Maybe. Rod, in the whole time we've been here,

nobody has been hurt inside camp. We'll put it to a vote, but you can't expect us to abandon our houses and everything we have worked for to avoid a danger that may be imaginary."

"Imaginary? Do you think that a stobor couldn't jump that crummy barricade?" Rod demanded, pointing.

"I think a stobor would get a chest full of pointed stakes if he tried it," Grant answered soberly. "That 'crummy barricade' is a highly efficient defense. Take a better look in the morning."

"Where we were you wouldn't need it. You wouldn't need a night watch. Shucks, you wouldn't need houses. Those caves are better than the best house here!"

"Probably. But, Rod, you haven't seen all we've done, how much we would have to abandon. Let's look it over in the daylight, fellow, and then talk."

"Well . . . no, Grant, there is only one issue: the caves are safe; this place isn't. I call for a vote."

"Easy now. This isn't a town meeting. It's a party in your honor. Let's not spoil it."

"Well . . . I'm sorry. But we're all here; let's vote."

"No." Cowper stood up. "There will be a town meeting on Friday as usual. Goodnight, Rod. Goodnight, Roy. We're awfully glad you're back. Goodnight all."

The party gradually fell apart. Only a few of the younger boys seemed to want to discuss the proposed move. Bob Baxter came over, put a hand on Rod and said, "See you in the morning, Rod. Bless you." He left before Rod could get away from a boy who was talking to him.

Jimmy Throxton stayed, as did Caroline. When he got the chance Rod said, "Jimmy? Where do you stand?"

"Me? You know me, pal. Look, I sent Jackie to bed; she wasn't feeling well. But she told me to tell you that we were back of you a hundred per cent, always."

"Thanks. I feel better."

"See you in the morning? I want to check on Jackie."

"Sure. Sleep tight."

He was finally left with Caroline. "Roddie? Want to inspect the guard with me? You'll do it after tonight, but we figured you could use a night with no worries."

155

"Wait a minute. Carol . . . you've been acting funny."

"Me? Why, Roddie!"

"Well, maybe not. What do you think of the move? I didn't hear you pitching in."

She looked away. "Roddie," she said, "if it was just me, I'd say start tomorrow. I'd be on the advance party."

"Good! What's got into these people? Grant has them buffaloed but I can't see why." He scratched his head. "I'm tempted to make up my own party—you, me, Jimmy and Jack, the Baxters, Roy, the few who were rarin' to go tonight, and anybody else with sense enough to pound sand."

She sighed. "It won't work, Roddie."

"Huh? Why not?"

"I'll go. Some of the youngsters would go for the fun of it. Jimmy and Jack would go if you insisted . . . but they would beg off if you made it easy for them. The Baxters should not and I doubt if Bob would consent. Carmen isn't really up to such a trip."

13

Unkillable

THE MATTER NEVER CAME TO A VOTE. LONG BEFORE Friday Rod knew how a vote would go—about fifty against him, less than half that for him, with his friends voting with him through loyalty rather than conviction . . . or possibly against him in a showdown.

He made an appeal in private to Cowper. "Grant, you've got me licked. Even Roy is sticking with you now. But you could swing them around."

"I doubt it. What you don't see, Rod, is that we have

taken root. You may have found a better place . . . but it's too late to change. After all, you picked this spot."

"Not exactly, it . . . well, it just sort of happened."

"Lots of things in life just sort of happen. You make the best of them."

"That's what I'm *trying* to do! Grant, admitted that the move is hard; we could manage it. Set up way stations with easy jumps, send our biggest huskies back for what we don't want to abandon. Shucks, we could move a person on a litter if we had to—using enough guards."

"If the town votes it, I'll be for it. But I won't try to argue them into it. Look, Rod, you've got this fixed idea that this spot is dangerously exposed. The facts don't support you. On the other hand see what we have. Running water from upstream, waste disposal downstream, quarters comfortable and adequate for the climate. Salt—do you have salt there?"

"We didn't look for it—but it would be easy to bring it from the seashore."

"We've got it closer here. We've got prospects of metal. You haven't seen that ore outcropping yet, have you? We're better equipped every day; our standard of living is going up. We have a colony nobody need be ashamed of and we did it with bare hands; we were never meant to be a colony. Why throw up what we have gained to squat in caves like savages?"

Rod sighed. "Grant, this bank may be flooded in the rainy season—aside from its poor protection now."

"It doesn't look it to me, but if so, we'll see it in time. Right now we are going into the dry season. So let's talk it over a few months from now."

Rod gave up. He refused to resume as "City Manager" nor would Caroline keep it when Rod turned it down. Bill Kennedy was appointed and Rod went to work under Cliff as a hunter, slept in the big shed upstream with the bachelors, and took his turn at night watch. The watch had been reduced to one man, whose duty was simply to tend fires. There was talk of cutting out the night fires, as fuel was no longer easy to find nearby and many seemed satisfied that the thorn barrier was enough.

Rod kept his mouth shut and stayed alert at night.

Game continued to be plentiful but became skittish.

157

Buck did not come out of cover the way they had in rainy weather; it was necessary to search and drive them out. Carnivores seemed to have became scarcer. But the first real indication of peculiar seasonal habits of native fauna came from a very minor carnivore. Mick Mahmud returned to camp with a badly chewed foot; Bob Baxter patched him up and asked about it.

"You wouldn't believe it."

"Try me."

"Well, it was just a dopy joe. I paid no attention to it, of course. Next thing I knew I was flat on my back and trying to shake it loose. He did all that to me before I got a knife into him. Then I had to cut his jaws loose."

"Lucky you didn't bleed to death."

When Rod heard Mick's story, he told Roy. Having had one experience with a dopy joe turned aggressive, Roy took it seriously and had Cliff warn all hands to watch out; they seemed to have turned nasty.

Three days later the migration of animals started.

At first it was just a drifting which appeared aimless except that it was always downstream. Animals had long since ceased to use the watering place above the settlement and buck rarely appeared in the little valley; now they began drifting into it, would find themselves baffled by the thorn fence, and would scramble out. Nor was it confined to antelope types; wingless birds with great "false faces," rodents, rooters, types nameless to humans, all joined the migration. One of the monstrous leonine predators they called stobor approached the barricade in broad daylight, looked at it, lashed his tail, then clawed his way up the bluff and headed downstream again.

Cliff called off his hunting parties; there was no need to hunt when game walked into camp.

Rod found himself more edgy than usual that night as it grew dark. He left his seat near the barbecue pit and went over to Jimmy and Jacqueline. "What's the matter with this place? It's spooky."

Jimmy twitched his shoulders. "I feel it. Maybe it's the funny way the animals are acting. Say, did you hear they killed a joe inside camp?"

"I know what it is," Jacqueline said suddenly. "No 'Grand Opera.'"

"Grand Opera" was Jimmy's name for the creatures with the awful noises, the ones which had turned Rod's first night into a siege of terror. They serenaded every evening for the first hour of darkness. Rod's mind had long since blanked them out, heeded them no more than chorusing cicadas. He had not consciously heard them for weeks.

Now they failed to wail on time; it upset him.

He grinned sheepishly. "That's it, Jack. Funny how you get used to a thing. Do you suppose they are on strike?"

"More likely a death in the family," Jimmy answered. "They'll be back in voice tomorrow."

Rod had trouble getting to sleep. When the night watch gave an alarm he was up and out of bachelors' barracks at once, Colonel Bowie in hand. "What's up?"

Arthur Nielsen had the watch. "It's all right now," he answered nervously. "A big buffalo buck crashed the fence. And this got through." He indicated the carcass of a dopy joe.

"You're bleeding."

"Just a nip."

Others gathered around. Cowper pushed through, sized the situation and said, "Waxie, get that cut attended to. Bill . . . where's Bill? Bill, put somebody else on watch. And let's get that gap fixed as soon as it's light."

It was greying in the east. Margery suggested, "We might as well stay up and have breakfast. I'll get the fire going." She left to borrow flame from a watch fire.

Rod peered through the damaged barricade. A big buck was down on the far side and seemed to have at least six dopy joes clinging to it. Cliff was there and said quietly, "See a way to get at them?"

"Only with a gun."

"We can't waste ammo on that."

"No." Rod thought about it, then went to a pile of bamboo poles, cut for building. He selected a stout one a head shorter than himself, sat down and began to bind Lady Macbeth to it with rawhide, forming a crude pike spear.

Caroline came over and squatted down. "What are you doing?"

"Making a joe-killer."

She watched him. "I'm going to make me one," she said suddenly and jumped up.

By daylight the animals were in full flight downstream as if chased by forest fire. As the creek had shrunk with the dry season a miniature beach, from a meter to a couple of meters wide, had been exposed below the bank on which the town had grown. The thorn kraal had been extended to cover the gap, but the excited animals crushed through this weak point and now streamed along the water past the camp.

After a futile effort no attempt was made to turn them back. They were pouring into the valley; they had to go somewhere, and the route between water and bank made a safety valve. It kept them from shoving the barricade aside by sheer mass. The smallest animals came through it anyhow, kept going, paid no attention to humans.

Rod stayed at the barricade, ate breakfast standing up. He had killed six joes since dawn while Caroline's score was still higher. Others were making knives into spears and joining them. The dopy joes were not coming through in great numbers; most of them continued to chase buck along the lower route past camp. Those who did seep through were speared; meeting them with a knife gave away too much advantage.

Cowper and Kennedy, inspecting defenses, stopped by Rod; they looked worried. "Rod," said Grant, "how long is this going to last?"

"How should I know? When we run out of animals. It looks like—get him, Shorty! It looks as if the joes were driving the others, but I don't think they are. I think they've *all* gone crazy."

"But what would cause that?" demanded Kennedy.

"Don't ask me. But I think I know where all those bones on that beach came from. But don't ask why. Why does a chicken cross the road? Why do lemmings do what they do? What makes a plague of locusts? Behind you! *Jump!*"

Kennedy jumped, Rod finished off a joe, and they went on talking. "Better detail somebody to chuck these into the water, Bill, before they stink. Look, Grant, we're okay now, but I know what I would do."

"What? Move to your caves? Rod, you were right—but it's too late."

"No, no! That's spilt milk; forget it. The thing that scares me are these mean little devils. They are no longer dopy; they are fast as can be and nasty . . . and they can slide through the fence. We can handle them now—but how about when it gets dark? We've got to have a solid line of fire inside the fence and along the bank. Fire is one thing they can't go through . . . I hope."

"That'll take a lot of wood." Grant looked through the barricade and frowned.

"You bet it will. But it will get us through the night. See here, give me the ax and six men with spears. I'll lead the party."

Kennedy shook his head. "It's my job."

"No, Bill," Cowper said firmly. "I'll lead it. You stay here and take care of the town."

Before the day was over Cowper took two parties out and Bill and Rod led one each. They tried to pick lulls in the spate of animals but Bill's party was caught on the bluff above, where it had been cutting wood and throwing it down past the cave. They were treed for two hours. The little valley had been cleaned out of dead wood months since; it was necessary to go into the forest above to find wood that would burn.

Cliff Pawley, hunter-in-chief, led a fifth party in the late afternoon, immediately broke the handle of the little ax. They returned with what they could gather with knives. While they were away one of the giant buck they called buffalo stampeded off the bluff, fell into camp, broke its neck. Four dopy joes were clinging to it. They were easy to kill as they would not let go.

Jimmy and Rod were on pike duty at the barricade. Jimmy glanced back at where a couple of girls were disposing of the carcasses. "Rod," he said thoughtfully, "we got it wrong. *Those* are stobor . . . the *real* stobor."

"Huh?"

"The big babies we've been calling that aren't 'stobor.' *These* things are what the Deacon warned us against."

"Well . . . I don't care what you call them as long as they're dead. On your toes, boy; here they come again."

Cowper ordered fires laid just before dark and was studying how to arrange one stretch so as not to endanger the flume when the matter was settled; the structure quivered and water ceased to flow. Upstream something had crashed into it and broken the flimsy pipe line.

The town had long since abandoned waterskins. Now they were caught with only a few litres in a pot used by the cooks, but it was a hardship rather than a danger; the urgent need was to get a ring of fire around them. There had already been half a dozen casualties—no deaths but bites and slashings, almost all from the little carnivores contemptuously known as dopy joes. The community's pool of antiseptics, depleted by months of use and utterly irreplaceable, had sunk so low that Rob Baxter used it only on major wounds.

When fuel had been stretched ready to burn in a long arc inside the barricade and down the bank to where it curved back under the cave, the results of a hard day's work looked small; the stockpile was not much greater than the amount already spread out. Bill Kennedy looked at it. "It won't last the night, Grant."

"It's *got* to, Bill. Light it."

"If we pulled back from the fence and the bank, then cut over to the bluff— What do you think?"

Cowper tried to figure what might be saved by the change. "It's not much shorter. Uh, don't light the downstream end unless they start curving back in on us. But let's move; it's getting dark." He hurried to the cooking fire, got a brand and started setting the chain of fire. Kennedy helped and soon the townsite was surrounded on the exposed sides by blaze. Cowper chucked his torch into the fire and said, "Bill, better split the men into two watches and get the women up into the cave—they can crowd in somehow."

"You'll have trouble getting thirty-odd women in there, Grant."

"They can sit up all night. But send them up. Yes, and the wounded men, too."

"Can do." Kennedy started passing the word. Caroline came storming up, spear in hand.

"Grant, what's this nonsense about the girls having to go up to the cave? If you think you're going to cut me out of the fun you had better think again!"

Cowper looked at her wearily. "Carol, I haven't time to monkey. Shut your face and do as you are told."

Caroline opened her mouth, closed it, and did as she was told. Bob Baxter claimed Cowper's attention; Rod noticed that he looked very upset. "Grant? You ordered all the women up to the cave?"

"Yes."

"I'm sorry but Carmen can't."

"You'll have to carry her. She is the one I had most on my mind when I decided on the move."

"But—" Baxter stopped and urged Grant away from the others. He spoke insistently but quietly. Grant shook his head.

"It's not safe, Grant," Baxter went on, raising his voice. "I don't dare risk it. The interval is nineteen minutes now."

"Well . . . all right. Leave a couple of women with her. Use Caroline, will you? That'll keep her out of my hair."

"Okay." Baxter hurried away.

Kennedy took the first watch with a dozen men spread out along the fire line; Rod was on the second watch commanded by Cliff Pawley. He went to the Baxter house to find out how Carmen was doing, was told to beat it by Agnes. He then went to the bachelors' shed and tried to sleep.

He was awakened by yells, in time to see one of the leonine monsters at least five meters long go bounding through the camp and disappear downstream. It had jumped the barrier, the stakes behind it, and the fire behind that, all in one leap.

Rod called out, "Anybody hurt?"

Shorty Dumont answered. "No. It didn't even stop to wave." Shorty was bleeding from a slash in his left calf; he seemed unaware of it. Rod crawled back inside, tried again to sleep.

He was awakened again by the building shaking. He hurried out. "What's up?"

"That you, Rod? I didn't know anybody was inside. Give me a hand; we're going to burn it." The voice was

163

Baxter's; he was prying at a corner post and cutting rawhide strips that held it.

Rod put his spear where it would not be stepped on, resheathed Colonel Bowie, and started to help. The building was bamboo and leaves, with a mud-and-thatch roof; most of it would burn. "How's Carmen?"

"Okay. Normal progress. I can do more good here. Besides they don't *want* me." Baxter brought the corner of the shed down with a crash, gathered a double armful of wreckage and hurried away. Rod picked up a load and followed him.

The reserve wood pile was gone; somebody was tearing the roof off the "city hall" and banging pieces on the ground to shake clay loose. The walls were sunbaked bricks, but the roof would burn. Rod came closer, saw that it was Cowper who was destroying this symbol of the sovereign community. He worked with the fury of anger. "Let me do that, Grant. Have you had any rest?"

"Huh? No."

"Better get some. It's going to be a long night. What time is it?"

"I don't know. Midnight, maybe." Fire blazed up and Cowper faced it, wiping his face with his hand. "Rod, take charge of the second watch and relieve Bill. Cliff got clawed and I sent him up."

"Okay. Burn everything that will burn—right?"

"Everything but the roof of the Baxter house. But don't use it up too fast; it's got to last till morning."

"Got it." Rod hurried to the fire line, found Kennedy. "Okay, Bill, I'll take over—Grant's orders. Get some sleep. Anything getting through?"

"Not much. And not far." Kennedy's spear was dark with blood in the firelight. "I'm not going to sleep, Rod. Find yourself a spot and help out."

Rod shook his head. "You're groggy. Beat it. Grant's orders."

"No!"

"Well . . . look, take your gang and tear down the old maids' shack. That'll give you a change, at least."

"Uh—all right." Kennedy left, almost staggering. There was a lull in the onrush of animals; Rod could see none beyond the barricade. It gave him time to sort out his crew, send away those who had been on duty since sunset, send for stragglers. He delegated Doug Sanders and Mick Mahmud as firetenders, passed the word that no one else was to put fuel on the fires.

He returned from his inspection to find Bob Baxter, spear in hand, holding his place at the center of the line. Rod put a hand on his shoulder. "The medical officer doesn't need to fight. We aren't that bad off."

Baxter shrugged. "I've got my kit, what there is left of it. This is where I use it."

"Haven't you enough worries?"

Baxter grinned wanly. "Better than walking the floor. Rod, they're stirring again. Hadn't we better build up the fires?"

"Mmm . . . not if we're going to make it last. I don't think they can come through that."

Baxter did not answer, as a joe came through at that instant. It ploughed through the smouldering fire and Baxter speared it. Rod cupped his hands and shouted, "Build up the fires! But go *easy.*"

"Behind you, Rod!"

Rod jumped and whirled, got the little devil. "Where did that one come from? I didn't see it."

Before Bob could answer Caroline came running out of darkness. "Bob! Bob Baxter! I've got to find Bob Baxter!"

"Over here!" Rod called.

Baxter was hardly able to speak. "Is she—is she?" His face screwed up in anguish.

"No, no!" yelled Caroine. "She's all right, she's fine. *It's a girl!*"

Baxter quietly fainted, his spear falling to the ground. Caroline grabbed him and kept him from falling into the fire. He opened his eyes and said, "Sorry. You scared me. You're sure Carmen is all right?"

"Right as rain. The baby, too. About three kilos. Here, give me that sticker—Carmen wants you."

Baxter stumbled away and Caroline took his place. She grinned at Rod. "I feel *swell!* How's business, Roddie? Brisk? I feel like getting me eight or nine of these vermin."

Cowper came up a few minutes later. Caroline called out, "Grant, did you hear the good news?"

"Yes. I just came from there." He ignored Caroline's presence at the guard line but said to Rod, "We're making a stretcher out of pieces of the flume and they're going to haul Carmen up. Then they'll throw the stretcher down and you can burn it."

"Good."

"Agnes is taking the baby up. Rod, what's the very most we can crowd into the cave?"

"Gee!" Rod glanced up at the shelf. "They must be spilling off the edge now."

"I'm afraid so. But we've just *got* to pack them in. I want to send up all married men and the youngest boys. The bachelors will hold on here."

"I'm a bachelor!" Caroline interrupted.

Cowper ignored her. "As soon as Carmen is safe we'll do it—we can't keep fires going much longer." He turned away, headed up to the cave.

Caroline whistled softly. "Roddie, we're going to have fun."

"Not my idea of fun. Hold the fort, Carol. I've got to line things up." He moved down the line, telling each one to go or to stay.

Jimmy scowled at him. "I won't go, not as long as anybody stays. I couldn't look Jackie in the face."

"You'll button your lip and do as Grant says—or I'll give you a mouthful of teeth. Hear me?"

"I hear you. I don't like it."

"You don't have to like it, just do it. Seen Jackie? How is she?"

"I snuck up a while ago. She's all right, just queasy. But the news about Carmen makes her feel so good she doesn't care."

Rod used no age limit to determine who was expendable. With the elimination of married men, wounded, and all women he had little choice; he simply told those whom he considered too young or not too skilled that they were to leave when word was passed. It left him with half a dozen, plus himself, Cowper, and—possibly —Caroline. Trying to persuade Caroline was a task he had postponed.

He returned and found Cowper. "Carmen's gone up," Cowper told him. "You can send the others up now."

"Then we can burn the roof of the Baxter house."

"I tore it down while they were hoisting her." Cowper looked around. "Carol! Get on up."

She set her feet. "I won't!"

Rod said softly, "Carol, you heard him. Go up—*right now!*"

She scowled, stuck out her lip, then said, "All right for *you*, Roddie Walker!"—turned and fled up the path.

Rod cupped his hands and shouted, "All right, everybody! All hands up but those I told to stay. Hurry!"

About half of those leaving had started up when Agnes called down, "Hey! Take it slow! Somebody will get pushed over the edge if you don't quit shoving."

The queue stopped. Jimmy called out, "Everybody exhale. That'll do it."

Somebody called back, "Throw Jimmy off . . . *that* will do it." The line moved again, slowly. In ten minutes they accomplished the sardine-packing problem of fitting nearly seventy people into a space comfortable for not more than a dozen. It could not even be standing room since a man could stand erect only on the outer shelf. The girls were shoved inside, sitting or squatting, jammed so that they hardly had air to breathe. The men farthest out could stand but were in danger of stepping off the edge in the dark, or of being elbowed off.

Grant said, "Watch things, Rod, while I have a look." He disappeared up the path, came back in a few minutes. "Crowded as the bottom of a sack," he said. "Here's the plan. They can scrunch back farther if they have to. It will be uncomfortable for the wounded and Carmen may have to sit up—she's lying down—but it can be done. When the fires die out, we'll shoehorn the rest in. With spears poking out under the overhang at the top of the path we ought to be able to hold out until daylight. Check me?"

"Sounds as good as can be managed."

"All right. When the time comes, you go up next to last, I go up last."

"Unh . . . I'll match you."

Cowper answered with surprising vulgarity and added, "I'm boss; I go last. We'll make the rounds and pile anything left on the fires, then gather them all here. You take the bank, I take the fence."

It did not take long to put the remnants on the fires,

then they gathered around the path and waited—Roy, Kenny, Doug, Dick, Charlie, Howard, and Rod and Grant. Another wave of senseless migration was rolling but the fires held it, bypassed it around by the water.

Rod grew stiff and shifted his spear to his left hand. The dying fires were only glowing coals in spots. He looked for signs of daylight in the east. Howard Goldstein said, "One broke through at the far end."

"Hold it, Goldie," Cowper said. "We won't bother it unless it comes here." Rod shifted his spear back to his right hand.

The wall of fire was now broken in many places. Not only could joes get through, but worse, it was hard to see them, so little light did the embers give off. Cowper turned to Rod and said, "All right, everybody up. You tally them." Then he shouted, "Bill! Agnes! Make room, I'm sending them up."

Rod threw a glance at the fence, then turned. "Okay, Kenny first. Doug next, don't crowd. Goldie and then Dick. Who's left? Roy—" He turned, uneasily aware that something had changed.

Grant was no longer behind him. Rod spotted him bending over a dying fire. "Hey, Grant!"

"Be right with you." Cowper selected a stick from the embers, waved it into flame. He hopped over the coals, picked his way through sharpened stakes, reached the thornbush barrier, shoved his torch into it. The dry branches flared up. He moved slowly away, picking his way through the stake trap.

"I'll help you!" Rod shouted. "I'll fire the other end."

Cowper turned and light from the burning thorn showed his stern, bearded face. "Stay back. Get the others up. That's an order!"

The movement upward had stopped. Rod snarled, "Get on up, you lunkheads! Move!" He jabbed with the butt of his spear, then turned around.

Cowper had set the fire in a new place. He straightened up, about to move farther down, suddenly turned and jumped over the dying line of fire. He stopped and jabbed at something in the darkness . . . then screamed.

"Grant!" Rod jumped down, ran toward him. But Grant was down before he reached him, down with a joe worrying each leg and more coming. Rod thrust at one, jerked his spear out, and jabbed at the other, trying not to stab Grant. He felt one grab his leg and wondered that it did not hurt.

Then it did hurt, terribly, and he realized that he was down and his spear was not in his hand. But his hand found his knife without asking; Colonel Bowie finished off the beast clamped to his ankle.

Everything seemed geared to nightmare slowness. Other figures were thrusting leisurely at shapes that hardly crawled. The thornbush, flaming high, gave him light to see and stab a dopy joe creeping toward him. He got it, rolled over and tried to get up.

He woke with daylight in his eyes, tried to move and discovered that his left leg hurt. He looked down and saw a compress of leaves wrapped with a neat hide bandage. He was in the cave and there were others lying parallel to him. He got to one elbow. "Say, what—"

"Sssh!" Sue Kennedy crawled over and knelt by him. "The baby is asleep."

"Oh . . ."

"I'm on nurse duty. Want anything?"

"I guess not. Uh, what did they name her?"

"Hope. Hope Roberta Baxter. A pretty name. I'll tell Caroline you are awake." She turned away.

Caroline came in, squatted and looked scornfully at his ankle. "That'll teach you to have a party and not invite *me*."

"I guess so. Carol, what's the situation?"

"Six on the sick list. About twice that many walking wounded. Those not hurt are gathering wood and cutting thorn. We fixed the ax."

"Yes, but . . . we're not having to fight them off?"

"Didn't Sue tell you? A few buck walking around as if they were dazed. That's all."

"They may start again."

"If they do, we'll be ready."

"Good." He tried to raise up. "Where's Grant? How bad was he hurt?"

She shook her head. "Grant didn't make it, Roddie."

"Huh?"

"Bob took off both legs at the knee and would have

taken off one arm, but he died while he was operating." She made a very final gesture. "In the creek."

Rod started to speak, turned his head and buried his face. Caroline put a hand on him. "Don't take it hard, Roddie. Bob shouldn't have tried to save him. Grant is better off."

Rod decided that Carol was right—no frozen limb banks on *this* planet. But it did not make him feel better. "We didn't appreciate him," he muttered.

"Stow it!" Caroline whispered fiercely. "He was a fool."

"Huh? Carol, I'm ashamed of you."

He was surprised to see tears rolling down her cheeks. "You *know* he was a fool, Roddie Walker. Most of us knew . . . but we loved him anyhow. I would 'uv *married* him, but he never asked me." She wiped at tears. "Have you seen the baby?"

"No."

Her face lit up. "I'll fetch her. She's beautiful."

"Sue said she was asleep."

"Well . . . all right. But what I came up for is this: what do you want us to do?"

"Huh?" He tried to think. Grant was dead. "Bill was his deputy. Is Bill laid up?"

"Didn't Sue tell you?"

"Tell me what?"

"You're the mayor. We elected you this morning. Bill and Roy and I are just trying to hold things together."

Rod felt dizzy. Caroline's face kept drawing back, then swooping in; he wondered if he were going to faint.

"—plenty of wood," she was saying, "and we'll have the kraal built by sundown. We don't need meat; Margery is butchering that big fellow that fell off the bluff and busted his neck. We can't trek out until you and Carmen and the others can walk, so we're trying to get the place back into shape temporarily. Is there anything you want us to do now?"

He considered it. "No. Not now."

"Okay. You're supposed to rest." She backed out, stood up. "I'll look in later." Rod eased his leg and turned over. After a while he quieted and went to sleep.

Sue brought broth in a bowl, held his head while he

drank, then fetched Hope Baxter and held her for him to see. Rod said the usual inanities, wondering if all new babies looked that way.

Then he thought for a long time.

Caroline showed up with Roy. "How's it going, Chief?" Roy said.

"Ready to bite a rattlesnake."

"That's a nasty foot, but it ought to heal. We boiled the leaves and Bob used sulfa."

"Feels all right. I don't seem feverish."

"Jimmy always said you were too mean to die," added Caroline. "Want anything, Roddie? Or to tell us anything?"

"Yes."

"What?"

"Get me out of here. Help me down the path."

Roy said hastily, "Hey, you can't do that. You're not in shape."

"Can't I? Either help, or get out of my way. And get everybody together. We're going to have a town meeting."

They looked at each other and walked out on him. He had made it to the squeeze at the top when Baxter showed up. "Now, Rod! Get back and lie down."

"Out of my way."

"Listen, boy, I don't like to get rough with a sick man. But I will if you make me."

"Bob . . . how bad is my ankle?"

"It's going to be all right . . . *if* you behave. If you don't—well, have you ever seen gangrene? When it turns black and has that sweetish odor?"

"Quit trying to scare me. Is there any reason not to put a line under my arms and lower me?"

"Well . . ."

They used two lines and a third to keep his injured leg free, with Baxter supervising. They caught him at the bottom and carried him to the cooking space, laid him down. "Thanks," he grunted. "Everybody here who can get here?"

"I think so, Roddie. Shall I count?"

"Never mind. I understand you folks elected me cap—I mean 'mayor'—this morning?"

"That's right," agreed Kennedy.

171

"Uh, who else was up? How many votes did I get?"

"Huh? It was unanimous."

Rod sighed. "Thanks. I'm not sure I would have held still for it if I'd been here. I gathered something else. Do I understand that you expect me to take you down to the caves Roy and I found? Caroline said something..."

Roy looked surprised. "We didn't vote it, Rod, but that was the idea. After last night everybody knows we can't stay here."

Rod nodded. "I see. Are you all where I can see you? I've got something to say. I hear you adopted a constitution and things while Roy and I were away. I've never read them, so I don't know whether this is legal or not. But if I'm stuck with the job, I expect to run things. If somebody doesn't like what I do and we're both stubborn enough for a showdown, then you will vote. You back me up, or you turn me down and elect somebody else. Will that work? How about it, Goldie? You were on the law committee, weren't you?"

Howard Goldstein frowned. "You don't express it very well, Rod."

"Probably not. Well?"

"But what you have described is the parliamentary vote-of-confidence. That's the backbone of our constitution. We did it that way to keep it simple and still democratic. It was Grant's notion."

"I'm glad," Rod said soberly. "I'd hate to think that I had torn up Grant's laws after he worked so hard on them. I'll study them, I promise, first chance I get. But about moving to the caves—we'll have a vote of confidence right now."

Goldstein smiled. "I can tell you how it will come out. We're convinced."

Rod slapped the ground. "You don't understand! If you want to move, move ... but get somebody else to lead you. Roy can do it. Or Cliff, or Bill. But if you leave it to me, no dirty little beasts, all teeth and no brains, are going to drive us out. We're *men* ... and men don't *have* to be driven out, not by the likes of those. Grant paid for this land—and I say stay here and keep it for him!"

14

Civilization

THE HONORABLE RODERICK L. WALKER, MAYOR OF
Cowpertown, Chief of State of the sovereign planet
GO-73901-II (Lima Catalog), Commander-in-Chief of
the Armed Forces, Chief Justice, and Defender of Freedoms, was taking his ease in front of the Mayor's
Palace. He was also scratching and wondering if he
should ask somebody to cut his hair again—he suspected lice . . . only this planet did not have lice.

His Chief of Government, Miss Caroline Beatrice
Mshiyeni, squatted in front of him. "Roddie, I've told
them and told them and told them . . . and it does no
good. That family makes more filth than everybody else
put together. You should have seen it this morning.
Garbage in front of their door . . . flies!"

"I saw it."

"Well, what do I do? If you would let me rough him
up a little. But you're too soft."

"I guess I am." Rod looked thoughtfully at a slab of
slate erected in the village square. It read:

> ### To the Memory of
> ### ULYSSES GRANT COWPER,
> #### First Mayor
> #### —who died for his city

The carving was not good; Rod had done it.

"Grant told me once," he added, "that government
was the art of getting along with people you don't like."

"Well, I sure don't like Bruce and Theo!"

"Neither do I. But Grant would have figured out a
way to keep them in line without getting rough."

"You figure it out, I can't. Roddie, you should never have let Bruce come back. That was bad enough. But when he married that little . . . well!"

"They were made for each other," Rod answered. "Nobody else would have married either of them."

"It's no joke. It's almost—Hope! Quit teasing Grantie!" She bounced up.

Miss Hope Roberta Baxter, sixteen months, and Master Grant Roderick Throxton, thirteen months, stopped what they were doing, which was, respectively, slapping and crying. Both were naked and very dirty. It was "clean" dirt; each child had been bathed by Caroline an hour earlier, and both were fat and healthy.

Hope turned up a beaming face. " 'Ood babee!" she asserted.

"I *saw* you." Caroline upended her, gave her a spat that would not squash a fly, then picked up Grant Throxton.

"Give her to me," Rod said.

"You're welcome to her," Caroline said. She sat down with the boy in her lap and rocked him. "Poor baby! Show Auntie Carol where it hurts."

"You shouldn't talk like that. You'll make a sissy of him."

"Look who's talking! Wishy-Washy Walker."

Hope threw her arms around Rod, part way, and cooed, "Woddie!" adding a muddy kiss. He returned it. He considered her deplorably spoiled; nevertheless he contributed more than his share of spoiling.

"Sure," agreed Carol. "Everybody loves Uncle Roddie. He hands out the medals and Aunt Carol does the dirty work."

"Carol, I've been thinking."

"Warm day. Don't strain any delicate parts."

"About Bruce and Theo. I'll talk to them."

"Talk!"

"The only real punishment is one we never use— and I hope we never have to. Kicking people out, I mean. The McGowans do as they please because they don't think we would. But I would love to give them the old heave-ho . . . and if it comes to it, I'll make an issue of it before the town—either kick them out or I quit."

"They'd back you. Why, I bet he hasn't taken a bath this week!"

"I don't care whether they back me or not. I've ridden out seven confidence votes; someday I'll be lucky and retire. But the problem is to convince Bruce that I am willing to face the issue, for then I won't have to. Nobody is going to chance being turned out in the woods, not when they've got it soft here. But he's got to be convinced."

"Uh, maybe if he thought you were carrying a grudge about that slice in the ribs he gave you?"

"And maybe I am. But I can't let it be personal, Carol; I'm too stinkin' proud."

"Uh . . . Turn it around. Convince him that the town is chompin' at the bit—which isn't far wrong— and you are trying to restrain them."

"Um, that's closer. Yes, I think Grant would have gone for that. I'll think it over."

"Do that." She stood up. "I'm going to give these children another bath. I declare I don't know where they find so much dirt."

She swung away with a child on each hip, heading for the shower sheds. Rod watched her lazily. She was wearing a leather bandeau and a Maori grass skirt, long leaves scraped in a pattern, curled, and dried. It was a style much favored and Caroline wore it around town, although when she treated herself to a day's hunting she wore a leather breechclout such as the men wore.

The same leaf fibre could be retted and crushed, combed and spun, but the cloth as yet possessed by the colony was not even enough for baby clothes. Bill Kennedy had whittled a loom for Sue and it worked, but neither well nor fast and the width of cloth was under a half meter. Still, Rod mused, it was progress, it was civilization. They had come a long way.

The town was stobor-tight now. An adobe wall too high and sheer for any but the giant lions covered the upstream side and the bank, and any lion silly enough to jump it landed on a bed of stakes too wide now for even their mighty leaps—the awning under which Rod lolled was the hide of one that had made that mistake. The wall was pierced by stobor traps, narrow tunnels

175

just big enough for the vicious little beasts and which gave into deep pits, where they could chew on each other like Kilkenny cats—which they did.

It might have been easier to divert them around the town, but Rod wanted to kill them; he would not be content until their planet was rid of those vermin.

In the meantime the town was safe. Stobor continued to deserve the nickname "dopy joe" except during the dry season and then they did not become dangerous until the annual berserk migration—the last of which had passed without loss of blood; the colony's defenses worked, now that they understood what to defend against. Rod had required mothers and children to sit out the stampede in the cave; the rest sat up two nights and stayed on guard . . . but no blade was wet.

Rod thought sleepily that the next thing they needed was paper; Grant had been right . . . even a village was hard to run without writing paper. Besides, they must avoid losing the habit of writing. He wanted to follow up Grant's notion of recording every bit of knowledge the gang possessed. Take logarithms—logarithms might not be used for generations, but when it came time to log a couple of rhythms, then . . . he went to sleep.

"You busy, Chief?"

Rod looked up at Arthur Nielsen. "Just sleeping . . . a practice I heartily recommend on a warm Sabbath afternoon. What's up, Art? Are Shorty and Doug pushing the bellows alone?"

"No. Confounded plug came out and we lost our fire. The furnace is ruined." Nielsen sat down wearily. He was hot, very red in the face, and looked discouraged. He had a bad burn on a forearm but did not seem to know it. "Rod, what are we doing wrong? Riddle me that."

"Talk to one of the brains. If you didn't know more about it than I do, we'd swap jobs."

"I wasn't really asking. I know two things that are wrong. We can't build a big enough installation and we don't have coal. Rod, we've *got* to have coal; for cast iron or steel we need coal. Charcoal won't do for anything but spongy wrought iron."

"What do you expect to accomplish overnight, Art? Miracles? You are years ahead of what anybody could ask. You've turned out metal, whether it's wrought iron or uranium. Since you made that spit for the barbecue pit, Margery thinks you are a genius."

"Yes, yes, we've made iron—but it ought to be lots better and more of it. This ore is wonderful . . . the real Lake Superior hematite. Nobody's seen such ore in commercial quantity on Terra in centuries. You ought to be able to breathe on it and make steel. And I could, too, if I had coal. We've got clay, we've got limestone, we've got this lovely ore—but I *can't* get a hot enough fire."

Rod was not fretted; the colony was getting metal as fast as needed. But Waxie was upset. "Want to knock off and search for coal?"

"Uh . . . no, I don't. I want to rebuild that furnace." Nielsen gave a bitter description of the furnace's origin, habits, and destination.

"Who knows most about geology?"

"Uh, I suppose I do."

"Who knows next most?"

"Why, Doug I guess."

"Let's send him out with a couple of boys to find coal. You can have Mick in his place on the bellows— no, wait a minute. How about Bruce?"

"Bruce? *He* won't work."

"Work him. If you work him so hard he runs away and forgets to come back, we won't miss him. Take him, Art, as a favor to me."

"Well . . . okay, if you say so."

"Good. You get one bonus out of losing your batch. You won't miss the dance tonight. Art, you shouldn't start a melt so late in the week; you need your day of rest . . . and so do Shorty and Doug."

"I know. But when it's ready to go I want to fire it off. Working the way we do is discouraging; before you can make anything you have to make the thing that makes it—and usually you have to make something else to make that. Futile!"

"You don't know what 'futile' means. Ask our 'Department of Agriculture.' Did you take a look at the farm before you came over the wall?"

"Well, we walked through it."

177

"Better not let Cliff catch you, or he'll scalp you. I might hold you for him."

"Humph! A lot of silly grass! Thousands of hectares around just like it."

"That's right. Some grass and a few rows of weeds. The pity is that Cliff will never live to see it anything else. Nor little Cliff. Nevertheless our great grandchildren will eat white bread, Art. But you yourself will live to build precision machinery—you know it can be done, which, as Bob Baxter says, is two-thirds of the battle. Cliff *can't* live long enough to eat a slice of light, tasty bread. It doesn't stop him."

"You should have been a preacher, Rod." Art stood up and sniffed himself. "I'd better get a bath, or the girls won't dance with me."

"I was just quoting. You've heard it before. Save me some soap."

Caroline hit two bars of *Arkansas Traveler*, Jimmy slapped his drum, and Roy called, "Square 'em up, folks!" He waited, then started in high, nasal tones:

"Honor y'r *part*ners!

"Honor y'r *cor*ners!

"Now *all* jump *up* and *when* y' come *down*—"

Rod was not dancing; the alternate set would be his turn. The colony formed eight squares, too many for a caller, a mouth organ, and a primitive drum all unassisted by amplifying equipment. So half of them baby-sat and gossiped while the other half danced. The caller and the orchestra were relieved at each intermission to dance the other sets.

Most of them had not known how to square-dance. Agnes Pulvermacher had put it over almost single-handed, in the face of kidding and resistance—training callers, training dancers, humming tunes to Caroline, cajoling Jimmy to carve and shrink a jungle drum. Now she had nine out of ten dancing.

Rod had not appreciated it at first (he was not familiar with the history of the Mormon pioneers) and had regarded it as a nuisance which interfered with work. Then he saw the colony, which had experienced a bad letdown after the loss in one night of all they had built,

178

an apathy he had not been able to lift—he saw this same colony begin to smile and joke and work hard simply from being exposed to music and dancing.

He decided to encourage it. He had trouble keeping time and could not carry a tune, but the bug caught him, too; he danced not well but with great enthusiasm.

The village eventually limited dances to Sabbath nights, weddings, and holidays—and made them "formal" . . . which meant that women wore grass skirts. Leather shorts, breechclouts, and slacks (those not long since cut up for rags) were not acceptable. Sue talked about making a real square dance dress as soon as she got far enough ahead in her weaving, and a cowboy shirt for her husband . . . but the needs of the colony made this a distant dream.

Music stopped, principals changed, Caroline tossed her mouth organ to Shorty, and came over. "Come on, Roddie, let's kick some dust."

"I asked Sue," he said hastily and truthfully. He was careful not to ask the same girl twice, never to pay marked attention to any female; he had promised himself long ago that the day he decided to marry should be the day he resigned and he was not finding it hard to stay married to his job. He liked to dance with Caroline; she was a popular partner—except for a tendency to swing her partner instead of letting him swing her—but he was careful not to spend much social time with her because she was his right hand, his alter ego.

Rod went over and offered his arm to Sue. He did not think about it; the stylized amenities of civilization were returning and the formal politenesses of the dance made them seem natural. He led her out and assisted in making a botch of *Texas Star*.

Later, tired, happy, and convinced that the others in his square had made the mistakes and he had straightened them out, Rod returned Sue to Bill, bowed and thanked him, and went back to the place that was always left for him. Margery and her assistants were passing out little brown somethings on wooden skewers. He accepted one. "Smells good, Marge. What are they?"

"Mock Nile birds. Smoked baby-buck bacon wrapped around hamburger. Salt and native sage, pan broiled. You'd better like it; it took us *hours*."

"Mmmm! I do! How about another?"

"Wait and see. Greedy."

"But I need more. I work hardest. I have to keep up my strength."

"That was *work* I saw you doing this afternoon?" She handed him another.

"I was planning. The old brain was buzzing away."

"I heard the buzzing. Pretty loud, when you lie on your back."

He snagged a third as she turned away, looked up to catch Jacqueline smiling; he winked and grinned.

"Happy, Rod?"

"Yes indeedy. How about you, Jackie?"

"I've never been happier," she said seriously.

Her husband put an arm around her. "See what the love of a good man can do, Rod?" Jimmy said. "When I found this poor child she was beaten, bedraggled, doing your cooking and afraid to admit her name. Now look at her!—fat and sassy."

"I'm not *that* fat!"

"Pleasingly plump."

Rod glanced up at the cave. "Jackie, remember the night I showed up?"

"I'm not likely to forget."

"And the silly notion I had that this was Africa? Tell me—if you had it to do over, would you rather I had been right?"

"I never thought about it. I knew it was not."

"Yes, but 'if'? You would have been home long ago."

Her hand took her husband's. "I would not have met James."

"Oh, yes, you would. You had already met me. You could not have avoided it—my best friend."

"Possibly. But I would not change it. I have no yearning to go 'home,' Rod. *This* is home."

"Me neither," asserted Jimmy. "You know what? This colony gets a little bigger—and it's getting bigger fast—Goldie and I are going to open a law office. We won't have any competition and can pick our clients. He'll handle the criminal end, I'll specialize in divorce, and we'll collaborate on corporate skulduggery. We'll make *millions*. I'll drive a big limousine drawn by eight

180

spanking buck, smoking a big cigar and sneering at the peasants." He called out, "Right, Goldie?"

"Precisely, colleague. I'm making us a shingle: 'Goldstein & Throxton—Get bailed, not jailed!' "

"Keerect. But make that: 'Throxton & Goldstein.' "

"I'm senior. I've got two more years of law."

"A quibble. Rod, are you going to let this Teller U. character insult an old Patrick Henry man?"

"Probably. Jimmy, I don't see how you are going to work this. I don't think we have a divorce law. Let's ask Caroline."

"A trifle. You perform the marriages, Rod; I'll take care of the divorces."

"Ask Caroline what?" asked Caroline.

"Do we have a divorce law?"

"Huh? We don't even have a getting-married law."

"Unnecessary," explained Goldstein. "Indigenous in the culture. Besides, we ran out of paper."

"Correct, Counselor," agreed Jimmy.

"Why ask?" Caroline demanded. "Nobody is thinking about divorce or I would know before they would."

"We weren't talking about that," Rod explained. "Jackie said that she had no wish to go back to Terra and Jimmy was elaborating. Uselessly, as usual."

Caroline stared. "Why would anybody want to go back?"

"Sure," agreed Jimmy. "This is the place. No income tax. No traffic, no crowds, no commercials, no telephones. Seriously, Rod, every one here was aiming for the Outlands or we wouldn't have been taking a survival test. So what difference does it make? Except that we've got everything sooner." He squeezed his wife's hand. "I was fooling about that big cigar; I'm rich now, boy, rich!"

Agnes and Curt had drawn into the circle, listening. Agnes nodded and said, "For once you aren't joking, Jimmy. The first months we were here I cried myself to sleep every night, wondering if they would ever find us. Now I know they never will—and I don't care! I wouldn't go back if I could; the only thing I miss is lipstick."

Her husband's laugh boomed out. "There you have the truth, Rod. The fleshpots of Egypt . . . put a cos-

181

metics counter across this creek and every woman here will walk on water."

"That's not fair, Curt! Anyhow, you promised to make lipstick."

"Give me time."

Bob Baxter came up and sat down by Rod. "Missed you at the meeting this morning, Rod."

"Tied up. I'll make it next week."

"Good." Bob, being of a sect which did not require ordination, had made himself chaplain as well as medical officer simply by starting to hold meetings. His undogmatic ways were such that Christian, Jew, Monist, or Moslem felt at ease; his meetings were well attended.

"Bob, would *you* go back?"

"Go where, Caroline?"

"Back to Terra."

"Yes."

Jimmy looked horrified. "Boil me for breakfast! *Why?*"

"Oh, I'd want to come back! But I need to graduate from medical school." He smiled shyly. "I may be the best surgeon in the neighborhood, but that isn't saying much."

"Well . . ." admitted Jimmy, "I see your point. But you already suit us. Eh, Jackie?"

"Yes, Jimmy."

"It's my only regret," Bob went on. "I've lost ones I should have saved. But it's a hypothetical question. 'Here we rest.' "

The question spread. Jimmy's attitude was overwhelmingly popular, even though Bob's motives were respected. Rod said goodnight; he heard them still batting it around after he had gone to bed; it caused him to discuss it with himself.

He had decided long ago that they would never be in touch with Earth; he had not thought of it for—how long?—over a year. At first it had been mental hygiene, protection of his morale. Later it was logic: a delay in recall of a week might be a power failure, a few weeks could be a technical difficulty—but months on months was cosmic disaster; each day added a cipher to the infinitesimal probability that they would ever be in touch again.

He was now able to ask himself: was this what he wanted?

Jackie was right; this was home. Then he admitted that he *liked* being big frog in a small puddle, he loved his job. He was not meant to be a scientist, nor a scholar, he had never wanted to be a businessman—but what he was doing suited him . . . and he seemed to do it well enough to get by.

" "Here we rest!' "

He went to sleep in a warm glow.

Cliff wanted help with the experimental crops. Rod did not take it too seriously; Cliff always wanted something; given his head he would have everybody working dawn to dark on his farm. But it was well to find out what he wanted—Rod did not underrate the importance of domesticating plants; that was basic for all colonies and triply so for them. It was simply that he did not know much about it.

Cliff stuck his head into the mayor's hut. "Ready?"

"Sure." Rod got his spear. It was no longer improvised but bore a point patiently sharpened from steel salvaged from Braun's Thunderbolt. Rod had tried wrought iron but could not get it to hold an edge. "Let's pick up a couple of boys and get a few stobor."

"Okay."

Rod looked around. Jimmy was at his potter's wheel, kicking the treadle and shaping clay with his thumb. "Jim! Quit that and grab your pike. We're going to have some fun."

Throxton wiped at sweat. "You've talked me into it."

They added Kenny and Mick, then Cliff led them upstream. "I want you to look at the animals."

"All right," agreed Rod. "Cliff, I had been meaning to speak to you. If you are going to raise those brutes inside the wall, you'll have to be careful about their droppings. Carol has been muttering."

"Rod, I can't do everything! And you can't put them outside, not if you expect them to live."

"Sure, sure! Well, we'll get you more help, that's the only— Just a second!"

They were about to pass the last hut; Bruce McGowan was stretched in front of it, apparently asleep.

Rod did not speak at once; he was fighting down rage. He wrestled with himself, aware that the next moment could change his future, damage the entire colony. But his rational self was struggling in a torrent of anger, bitter and self-righteous. He wanted to do away with this parasite, destroy it. He took a deep breath and tried to keep his mouth from trembling.

"Bruce!" he called softly.

McGowan opened his eyes. "Huh?"

"Isn't Art working his plant today?"

"Could be," Bruce admitted.

"Well?"

" 'Well' what? I've had a week and it's not my dish. Get somebody else."

Bruce wore his knife, as did each of them; a colonist was more likely to be caught naked than without his knife. It was the all-purpose tool, for cutting leather, preparing food, eating, whittling, building, basketmaking, and as make-do for a thousand other tools; their wealth came from knives, arrows were now used to hunt —but knives shaped the bows and arrows.

But a knife had not been used by one colonist against another since that disastrous day when Bruce's brother had defied Rod. Over the same issue, Rod recalled; the wheel had turned full circle. But today he would have immediate backing if Bruce reached for his knife.

But he knew that this must not be settled by five against one; he alone must make this dog come to heel, or his days as leader were numbered.

It did not occur to Rod to challenge Bruce to settle it with bare hands. Rod had read many a historical romance in which the hero invited someone to settle it "man to man," in a stylized imitation fighting called "boxing." Rod had enjoyed such stories but did not apply them to himself any more than he considered personally the sword play of *The Three Musketeers;* nevertheless, he knew what "boxing" meant—they folded their hands and struck certain restricted blows with fists. Usually no one was hurt.

The fighting that Rod was trained in was not simply strenuous athletics. It did not matter whether they were armed; if he and Bruce fought bare hands or otherwise, someone would be killed or badly hurt. The *only* dangerous weapon was man himself.

Bruce stared sullenly. "Bruce," Rod said, striving to keep his voice steady, "a long time ago I told you that people worked around here or got out. You and your brother didn't believe me so we had to chuck you out. Then you crawled back with a tale about how Jock had been killed and could you please join up? You were a sorry sight. Remember?"

McGowan scowled. "You promised to be a little angel," Rod went on. "People thought I was foolish—and I was. But I thought you might behave."

Bruce pulled a blade of grass, bit it. "Bub, you remind me of Jock. He was always throwing his weight around, too."

"Bruce, get up and get out of town! I don't care where, but if you are smart, you will shag over and tell Art you've made a mistake—then start pumping that bellows. I'll stop by later. If sweat isn't pouring off you when I arrive . . . then you'll never come back. You'll be banished for life."

McGowan looked uncertain. He glanced past Rod, and Rod wondered what expressions the others wore. But Rod kept his eyes on Bruce. "Get moving. Get to work, or don't come back."

Bruce got a sly look. "You can't order me kicked out. It takes a majority vote."

Jimmy spoke up. "Aw, quit taking his guff, Rod. Kick him out now."

Rod shook his head. "No. Bruce, if that is your answer, I'll call them together and we'll put you in exile before lunch—and I'll bet my best knife that you won't get three votes to let you stay. Want to bet?"

Bruce sat up and looked at the others, sizing his chances. He looked back at Rod. "Runt," he said slowly, "you aren't worth a hoot without stooges . . . or a couple of girls to do your fighting."

Jimmy whispered, "Watch it, Rod!" Rod licked dry lips, knowing that it was too late for reason, too late for talk. He would have to try to take him . . . he was not sure he could.

"I'll fight you," he said hoarsely. "Right now!"

Cliff said urgently, "Don't, Rod. We'll manage him."

185

"No. Come on, McGowan." Rod added one unforgivable word.

McGowan did not move. "Get rid of that joe sticker."

Rod said, "Hold my spear, Cliff."

Cliff snapped, "Now wait! I'm not going to stand by and watch this. He might get lucky and kill you, Rod."

"Get out of the way, Cliff."

"No." Cliff hesitated, then added, "Bruce, throw your knife away. Go ahead—or so help me I'll poke a joe-sticker in your belly myself. Give me your knife, Rod."

Rod looked at Bruce, then drew Colonel Bowie and handed it to Cliff. Bruce straightened up and flipped his knife at Cliff's feet. Cliff rasped, "I still say not to, Rod. Say the word and we'll take him apart."

"Back off. Give us room."

"Well—no bone breakers. You hear me, Bruce? Make a mistake and you'll never make another."

" 'No bone breakers,' " Rod repeated, and knew dismally that the rule would work against him; Bruce had him on height and reach and weight.

"Okay," McGowan agreed. "Just cat clawing. I am going to show this rube that one McGowan is worth two of him."

Cliff sighed. "Back off, everybody. Okay—get going!"

Crouched, they sashayed around, not touching. Only the preliminaries could use up much time; the textbook used in most high schools and colleges listed twenty-seven ways to destroy or disable a man hand to hand; none of the methods took as long as three seconds once contact was made. They chopped at each other, feinting with their hands, too wary to close.

Rod was confused by the injunction not to let the fight go to conclusion. Bruce grinned at him. "What's the matter? Scared? I've been waiting for this, you loud-mouthed pimple—now you're going to get it!" He rushed him.

Rod gave back, ready to turn Bruce's rush into his undoing. But Bruce did not carry it through; it had been a feint and Rod had reacted too strongly. Bruce laughed. "Scared silly, huh? You had better be."

Rod realized that he *was* scared, more scared than he had ever been. The conviction flooded over him that Bruce intended to kill him . . . the agreement about

186

bonebreakers meant nothing; this ape meant to finish him.

He backed away, more confused than ever . . . knowing that he must forget rules if he was to live through it . . . but knowing, too, that he *had* to abide by the silly restriction even if it meant the end of him. Panic shook him; he wanted to run.

He did not quite do so. From despair itself he got a cold feeling of nothing to lose and decided to finish it. He exposed his groin to a *savate* attack.

He saw Bruce's foot come up in the expected kick; with fierce joy he reached in the proper *shinobi* counter. He showed the merest of hesitation, knowing that a full twist would break Bruce's ankle.

Then he was flying through air; his hands had never touched Bruce. He had time for sick realization that Bruce had seen the gambit, countered with another— when he struck ground and Bruce was on him.

"Can you move your arm, Rod?"

He tried to focus his eyes, and saw Bob Baxter's face floating over him. "I licked him?"

Baxter did not answer. An angry voice answered, "Cripes, no! He almost chewed you to pieces."

Rod stirred and said thickly, "Where is he? I've got to whip him."

Baxter said sharply, "Lie still!" Cliff added, "Don't worry, Rod. We fixed him." Baxter insisted, "Shut up. See if you can move your left arm."

Rod moved the arm, felt pain shoot through it, jerked and felt pain everywhere. "It's not broken," Baxter decided. "Maybe a green-stick break. We'll put it in sling. Can you sit up? I'll help."

"I want to stand." He made it with help, stood swaying. Most of the villagers seemed to be there; they moved jerkily. It made him dizzy and he blinked.

"Take it easy, boy," he heard Jimmy say. "Bruce pretty near ruined you. You were crazy to give him the chance."

"I'm all right," Rod answered and winced. "Where is he?"

"Behind you. Don't worry, we fixed him."

"Yes," agreed Cliff. "We worked him over. Who does

187

he think he is? Trying to shove the Mayor around!" He spat angrily.

Bruce was face down, features hidden in one arm; he was sobbing. "How bad is he hurt?" Rod asked.

"Him?" Jimmy said scornfully. "He's not hurt. I mean, he hurts all right—but he's not hurt. Carol wouldn't let us."

Caroline squatted beside Bruce, guarding him. She got up. "I should have let 'em," she said angrily. "But I knew you would be mad at me if I did." She put hands on hips. "Roddie Walker, when are you going to get sense enough to yell for me when you're in trouble? These four dopes stood around and let it happen."

"Wait a minute, Carol," Cliff protested. "I tried to stop it. We all tried, but—"

"But I wouldn't listen," Rod interrupted. "Never mind, Carol, I flubbed it."

"If you would listen to me—"

"Never mind!" Rod went to McGowan, prodded him. "Turn over."

Bruce slowly rolled over. Rod wondered if he himself looked as bad. Bruce's body was dirt and blood and bruises; his face looked as if someone had tried to file the features off. "Stand up."

Bruce started to speak, then got painfully to his feet. Rod said, "I tod you to report to Art, Bruce. Get over the wall and get moving."

McGowan looked startled. "Huh?"

"You heard me. I can't waste time playing games. Check in with Art and get to work. Or keep moving and don't come back. Now *move!*"

Bruce stared, then hobbled toward the wall. Rod turned and said, "Get back to work, folks. The fun is over. Cliff, you were going to show me the animals."

"Huh? Look Rod, it'll keep."

"Yes, Rod," Baxter agreed. "I want to put a sling on that arm. Then you should rest."

Rod moved his arm gingerly. "I'll try to get along without it. Come on, Cliff. Just you and me—we'll skip the stobor hunt."

He had trouble concentrating on what Cliff talked about . . . something about gelding a pair of fawns and getting them used to harness. What use was harness

188

when they had no wagons? His head ached, his arm hurt and his brain felt fuzzy. What would Grant have done? He had failed . . . but what should he have said, or not said? Some days it wasn't worth it.

"—so we've got to. You see, Rod?"

"Huh? Sure, Cliff." He made a great effort to recall what Cliff had been saying. "Maybe wooden axles would do. I'll see if Bill thinks he can build a cart."

"But besides a cart, we need—"

Rod stopped him. "Cliff, if you say so, we'll try it. I think I'll take a shower. Uh, we'll look at the field tomorrow."

A shower made him feel better and much cleaner, although the water spilling milk-warm from the flume seemed too hot, then icy cold. He stumbled back to his hut and lay down. When he woke he found Shorty guarding his door to keep him from being disturbed.

It was three days before he felt up to inspecting the farm. Nielsen reported that McGowan was working, although sullenly. Caroline reported that Theo was obeying sanitary regulations and wearing a black eye. Rod was self-conscious about appearing in public, had even considered one restless night the advisability of resigning and letting someone who had not lost face take over the responsibility. But to his surprise his position seemed firmer than ever. A minority from Teller University, which he had thought of wryly as "loyal opposition," now no longer seemed disposed to be critical. Curt Pulvermacher, their unofficial leader, looked Rod up and offered help. "Bruce is a bad apple, Rod. Don't let him get down wind again. Let me know instead."

"Thanks, Curt."

"I mean it. It's hard enough to get anywhere around here if we all pull together. We can't have him riding roughshod over us. But don't stick your chin out. We'll teach him."

Rod slept well that night. Perhaps he had not handled it as Grant would have, but it had worked out. Cowpertown was safe. Oh, there would be more troubles but the colony would sweat through them. Someday there would be a city here and this would be Cowper Square. Upstream would be the Nielsen Steel Works. There might even be a Walker Avenue . . .

He felt up to looking over the farm the next day. He told Cliff so and gathered the same party, Jimmy, Kent, and Mick. Spears in hand they climbed the stile at the wall and descended the ladder on the far side. Cliff gathered up a handful of dirt, tasted it. "The soil is all right. A little acid, maybe. We won't know until we can run soil chemistry tests. But the structure is good. If you tell that dumb Swede that the next thing he has to make is a plough . . ."

"Waxie isn't dumb. Give him time. He'll make you ploughs and tractors, too."

"I'll settle for a hand plough, drawn by a team of buck. Rod, my notion is this. We weed and it's an invitation to the buck to eat the crops. If we built another wall, all around and just as high—"

"A wall! Any idea how many man-hours that would take, Cliff?"

"That's not the point."

Rod looked around the alluvial flat, several times as large as the land enclosed in the city walls. A thorn fence, possibly, but not a wall, not yet . . . Cliff's ambitions were too big. "Look, let's comb the field for stobor, then send the others back. You and I can figure out afterwards what can be done."

"All right. But tell them to watch where they put their big feet."

Rod spread them in skirmish line with himself in the center. "Keep dressed up," he warned, "and don't let any get past you. Remember, every one we kill now means six less on S-Day."

They moved forward. Kenny made a kill, Jimmy immediately made two more. The stobor hardly tried to escape, being in the "dopy joe" phase of their cycle.

Rod paused to spear one and looked up to speak to the man on his right. But there was no one there. "Hold it! Where's Mick?"

"Huh? Why, he was right here a second ago."

Rod looked back. Aside from a shimmer over the hot field, there was nothing where Mick should have been. Something must have sneaked up in the grass, pulled him down— "Watch it, everybody! Something's wrong. Close in . . . and keep your eyes peeled." He turned back, moved diagonally toward where Mick had disappeared.

Suddenly two figures appeared in front of his eyes—Mick and a stranger.

A stranger in coveralls and shoes . . . The man looked around, called over his shoulder, "Okay, Jake! Put her on automatic and clamp it." He glanced toward Rod but did not seem to see him, walked toward him, and disappeared.

With heart pounding Rod began to run. He turned and found himself facing into an open gate . . . and down a long, closed corridor.

The man in the coveralls stepped into the frame. "Everybody back off," he ordered. "We're going to match in with the Gap. There may be local disturbance."

15

In Achilles' Tent

IT HAD BEEN A HALF HOUR SINCE MICK HAD STUMBLED through the gate as it had focused, fallen flat in the low gravity of Luna. Rod was trying to bring order out of confusion, trying to piece together his own wits. Most of the villagers were out on the field, or sitting on top of the wall, watching technicians set up apparatus to turn the locus into a permanent gate, with controls and communications on both sides. Rod tried to tell one that they were exposed, that they should not run around unarmed; without looking up the man had said, "Speak to Mr. Johnson."

He found Mr. Johnson, tried again, was interrupted. "Will you kids *please* let us work? We're glad to see you

—but we've got to get a power fence around this area. No telling what might be in that tall grass."

"Oh," Rod answered. "Look, I'll set guards. We know what to expect. I'm in ch—"

"Beat it, will you? You kids mustn't be impatient."

So Rod went back inside his city, hurt and angry. Several strangers came in, poked around as if they owned the place, spoke to the excited villagers, went out again. One stopped to look at Jimmy's drum, rapped it and laughed. Rod wanted to strangle him.

"Rod?"

"Uh?" He whirled around. "Yes, Margery?"

"Do I cook lunch, or don't I? All my girls have left and Mel says it's silly because we'll all be gone by lunch time—and I don't know *what* to do."

"Huh? Nobody's leaving . . . that I know of."

"Well, maybe not but that's the talk."

He was not given time to consider this as one of the ubiquitous strangers came up and said briskly, "Can you tell me where to find a lad named Roderick Welker?"

"Walker," Rod corrected. "I'm Rod Walker. What do you want?"

"My name is Sansom, Clyde B. Sansom—Administrative Officer in the Emigration Control Service. Now, Welker, I understand you are group leader for these students. You can—"

"I am Mayor of Cowpertown," Rod said stonily. "What do you want?"

"Yes, yes, that's what the youngster called you. 'Mayor.'" Sansom smiled briefly and went on. "Now, Walker, we want to keep things orderly. I know you are anxious to get out of your predicament as quickly as possible—but we must do things systematically. We are going to make it easy—just delousing and physical examination, followed by psychological tests and a relocation interview. Then you will all be free to return to your homes—after signing a waiver-of-liability form, but the legal officer will take care of that. If you will have your little band line up alphabetically—uh, here in this open space, I think, then I will—" He fumbled with his briefcase.

"Who the deuce are you to give orders around here?"

Sansom looked surprised. "Eh? I told you. If you

192

want to be technical, I embody the authority of the Terran Corporation. I put it as a request—but under field conditions I can compel co-operation, you know."

Rod felt himself turn red. "I don't know anything of the sort! You may be a squad of angels back on Terra . . . but you are in Cowpertown."

Mr. Sansom looked interested but not impressed. "And what, may I ask, is Cowpertown?"

"Huh? *This* is Cowpertown, a sovereign nation, with its own constitution, its own laws—and its own territory." Rod took a breath. "If the Terran Corporation wants anything, they can send somebody and arrange it. But don't tell us to line up alphabetically!"

"Atta boy, Roddie!"

Rod said, "Stick around, Carol," then added to Sansom, "Understand me?"

"Do I understand," Sansom said slowly, "that you are suggesting that the Corporation should appoint an *ambassador* to your group?"

"Well . . . that's the general idea."

"Mmmm . . . an interesting theory, Welker."

" 'Walker.' And until you do, you can darn well clear the sightseers out—and get out yourself. We aren't a zoo."

Sansom looked at Rod's ribs, glanced at his dirty, calloused feet and smiled. Rod said, "Show him out, Carol. Put him out, if you have to."

"Yes, *sir!*" She advanced on Sansom, grinning.

"Oh, I'm leaving," Sansom said quickly. "Better a delay than a mistake in protocol. An ingenious theory, young man. Good-by. We shall see each other later. Uh . . . a word of advice? May I?"

"Huh? All right."

"Don't take yourself too seriously. Ready, young lady?"

Rod stayed in his hut. He wanted badly to see what was going on beyond the wall, but he did not want to run into Sansom. So he sat and gnawed his thumb and thought. Apparently some weak sisters were going back —wave a dish of ice cream under their noses and off they would trot, abandoning their land, throwing away all they had built up. Well, *he* wouldn't! This was home, his place, he had earned it; he wasn't going back and

193

maybe wait half a lifetime for a chance to move to some other planet probably not as good.

Let them go! Cowpertown would be better and stronger without them.

Maybe some just wanted to make a visit, show off grandchildren to grandparents, then come back. Probably . . . in which case they had better make sure that Sansom or somebody gave them written clearance to come back. Maybe he ought to warn them.

But *he* didn't have anyone to visit. Except Sis—and Sis might be anywhere—unlikely that she was on Terra.

Bob and Carmen, carrying Hope, came in to say good-by. Rod shook hands solemnly. "You're coming back, Bob, when you get your degree . . . aren't you?"

"Well, we hope so, if possible. If we are permitted to."

"Who's going to stop you? It's your *right*. And when you do, you'll find us here. In the meantime we'll try not to break legs."

Baxter hesitated. "Have you been to the gate lately, Rod?"

"No. Why?"

"Uh, don't plan too far ahead. I believe some have already gone back."

"How many?"

"Quite a number." Bob would not commit himself further. He gave Rod the addresses of his parents and Carmen's, soberly wished him a blessing, and left.

Margery did not come back and the fire pit remained cold. Rod did not care, he was not hungry. Jimmy came in at what should have been shortly after lunch, nodded and sat down. Presently he said, "I've been out at the gate."

"So?"

"Yup. You know, Rod, a lot of people wondered why you weren't there to say good-by."

"They could come *here* to say good-by!"

"Yes, so they could. But the word got around that you didn't approve. Maybe they were embarrassed."

"Me?" Rod laughed without mirth. "I don't care how many city boys run home to mama. It's a free country." He glanced at Jim. "How many are sticking?"

"Uh, I don't know."

194

"I've been thinking. If the group gets small, we might move back to the cave—just to sleep, I mean. Until we get more colonists."

"Maybe."

"Don't be so glum! Even if it got down to just you and me and Jackie and Carol, we'd be no worse off than we once were. And it would just be temporary. There'd be the baby, of course—I almost forgot to mention my godson."

"There's the baby," Jimmy agreed.

"What are you pulling a long face about? Jim . . . *you're* not thinking of leaving?"

Jimmy stood up. "Jackie said to tell you that we would stick by whatever you thought was best."

Rod thought over what Jimmy had not said. "You mean she wants to go back? Both of you do."

"Now, Rod, we're partners. But I've got the kid to think about. You see that?"

"Yes. I see."

"Well—"

Rod stuck out his hand. "Good luck, Jim. Tell Jackie good-by for me."

"Oh, she's waiting to say good-by herself. With the kid."

"Uh, tell her not to. Somebody once told me that saying good-by was a mistake. Be seeing you."

"Well—so long, Rod. Take care of yourself."

"You, too. If you see Caroline, tell her to come in."

Caroline was slow appearing; he guessed that she had been at the gate. He said bluntly, "How many are left?"

"Not many," she admitted.

"*How* many?"

"You and me—and a bunch of gawkers."

"*Nobody* else?"

"I checked them off the list. Roddie, what do we do now?"

"Huh? It doesn't matter. Do *you* want to go back?"

"You're boss, Roddie. You're the Mayor."

"Mayor of what? Carol, do you *want* to go back?"

"Roddie, I never thought about it. I was happy here. But—"

"But what?"

"The town is gone, the kids are gone—and I've got

only a year if I'm ever going to be a cadet Amazon." She blurted out the last, then added, "But I'll stick if you do."

"No."

"I will so!"

"No. But I want you to do something when you go back."

"What?"

"Get in touch with my sister Helen. Find out where she is stationed. Assault Captain Helen Walker—got it? Tell her I'm okay . . . and tell her I said to help you get into the Corps."

"Uh . . . Roddie, I don't *want* to go!"

"Beat it. They might relax the gate and leave you behind."

"You come, too."

"No. I've got things to do. But you hurry. Don't say good-by. Just go."

"You're mad at me, Roddie?"

"Of course not. But go, *please,* or you'll have me bawling, too."

She gave a choked cry, grabbed his head and smacked his cheek, then galloped away, her sturdy legs pounding. Rod went into his shack and lay face down. After a while he got up and began to tidy Cowpertown. It was littered, dirtier than it had been since the morning of Grant's death.

It was late afternoon before anyone else came into the village. Rod heard and saw them long before they saw him—two men and a woman. The men were dressed in city garb; she was wearing shorts, shirt, and smart sandals. Rod stepped out and said, "What do you want?" He was carrying his spear.

The woman squealed, then looked and added, "Wonderful!"

One man was carrying a pack and tripod which Rod recognized as multi-recorder of the all-purpose sight-smell-sound-touch sort used by news services and expeditions. He said nothing, set his tripod down, plugged in cables and started fiddling with dials. The other man, smaller, ginger haired, and with a terrier mustache, said, "You're Walker? The one the others call 'the Mayor'?"

"Yes."

"Kosmic hasn't been in here?"

"Cosmic what?"

"Kosmic Keynotes, of course. Or anybody? LIFE-TIME-SPACE? Galaxy Features?"

"I don't know what you mean. There hasn't been anybody here since morning."

The stranger twitched his mustache and sighed. "That's all I want to know. Go into your trance, Ellie. Start your box, Mac."

"Wait a minute," Rod demanded. "Who are you and what do you want?"

"Eh? I'm Evans of Empire . . . Empire Enterprises."

"Pulitzer Prize," the other man said and went on working.

"With Mac's help," Evans added quickly. "The lady is Ellie Ellens herself."

Rod looked puzzled. Evans said, "You don't *know?* Son, where have you—never mind. She's the highest paid emotional writer in the system. She'll interpret you so that every woman reader from the *Outlands Overseer* to the *London Times* will cry over you and want to comfort you. She's a *great* artist."

Miss Ellens did not seem to hear the tribute. She wandered around with a blank face, stopping occasionally to look or touch.

She turned and said to Rod, "Is this where you held your primitive dances?"

"What? We held square dances here, once a week."

" 'Square dances' . . . Well, we can change that." She went back into her private world.

"The point is, brother," Evans went on, "we don't want just an interview. Plenty of that as they came through. That's how we found out you were here—and dropped everything to see you. I'm not going to dicker; name your own price—but it's got to be exclusive, news, features, commercial rights, everything. Uh . . ." Evans looked around. "Advisory service, too, when the actors arrive."

"Actors?!"

"Of course. If the Control Service had the sense to

197

sneeze, they would have held you all here until a record was shot. But we can do it better with actors. I want you at my elbow every minute—we'll have somebody play your part. Besides that—"

"Wait a minute!" Rod butted in. "Either I'm crazy or you are. In the first place I don't want your money."

"Huh? You signed with somebody? That guard let another outfit in ahead of us?"

"What guard? I haven't seen anybody."

Evans looked relieved. "We'll work it out. The guard they've got to keep anybody from crossing your wall— I thought he might have both hands out. But don't say you don't need money; that's immoral."

"Well, I don't. We don't use money here."

"Sure, sure . . . but you've got a family, haven't you? Families always need money. Look, let's not fuss. We'll treat you right and you can let it pile up in the bank. I just want you to get signed up."

"I don't see why I should."

"Binder," said Mac.

"Mmm . . . yes, Mac. See here, brother, think it over. Just let us have a binder that you won't sign with anybody else. You can still stick us for anything your conscience will let you. Just a binder, with a thousand plutons on the side."

"I'm not going to sign with anybody else."

"Got that, Mac?"

"Canned."

Evans turned to Rod. "You don't object to answering questions in the meantime, do you? And maybe a few pictures?"

"Uh, I don't care." Rod was finding them puzzling and a little annoying, but they were company and he was bitterly lonely.

"Fine!" Evans drew him out with speed and great skill. Rod found himself telling more than he realized he knew. At one point Evans asked about dangerous animals. "I understand they are pretty rough here. Much trouble?"

"Why, no," Rod answered with sincerity. "We never had real trouble with animals. What trouble we had was with people . . . and not much of that."

"You figure this will be a premium colony?"

"Of course. The others were fools to leave. This place is like Terra, only safer and richer and plenty of land. In a few years—say!"

"Say what?"

"How did it happen that they left us here? We were only supposed to be here ten days."

"Didn't they tell you?"

"Well . . . maybe the others were told. I never heard."

"It was the supernova, of course. Delta, uh—"

"Delta Gamma one thirteen," supplied Mac.

"That's it. Space-time distortion, but I'm no mathematician."

"Fluxion," said Mac.

"Whatever that is. They've been fishing for you ever since. As I understand it, the wave front messed up their figures for this whole region. Incidentally, brother, when you go back—"

"I'm not going back."

"Well, even on a visit. Don't sign a waiver. The Board is trying to call it an 'Act of God' and duck responsibility. So let me put a bug in your ear: don't sign away your rights. A friendly hint, huh?"

"Thanks. I won't—well, thanks anyhow."

"Now how about action pix for the lead stories?"

"Well . . . okay."

"Spear," said Mac.

"Yeah, I believe you had some sort of spear. Mind holding it?"

Rod got it as the great Ellie joined them. "Wonderful!" she breathed. "I can feel it. It shows how thin the line is between man and beast. A hundred cultured boys and girls slipping back to illiteracy, back to the stone age, the veneer sloughing away . . . reverting to savagery. Glorious!"

"Look here!" Rod said angrily. "Cowpertown wasn't that way at all! We had laws, we had a constitution, we kept clean. We—" He stopped; Miss Ellens wasn't listening.

"Savage ceremonies," she said dreamily. "A village witch doctor pitting ignorance and superstition against nature. Primitive fertility rites—" She stopped and said to Mac in a businesslike voice, "We'll shoot the dances three times. Cover 'em a little for 'A' list; cover 'em up a lot for the family list—and peel them down for the 'B' list. Got it?"

"Got it," agreed Mac.

"I'll do three commentaries," she added. "It will be worth the trouble." She reverted to her trance.

"Wait a minute!" Rod protested. "If she means what I think she means, there won't be any pictures, with or without actors."

"Take it easy," Evans advised. "I said you would be technical supervisor, didn't I? Or would you rather we did it without you? Ellie is all right, brother. What you don't know—and *she* does—is that you have to shade the truth to get at the real truth, the underlying truth. You'll see."

"But—"

Mac stepped up to him. "Hold still."

Rod did so, as Mac raised his hand. Rod felt the cool touch of an air brush.

"Hey! What are you doing?"

"Make up." Mac returned to his gear.

"Just a little war paint," Evans explained. "The pic needs color. It will wash off."

Rod opened his mouth and eyes in utter indignation; without knowing it he raised his spear. "Get it, Mac!" Evans ordered.

"Got it," Mac answered calmly.

Rod fought to bring his anger down to where he could talk. "Take that tape out," he said softly. "Throw it on the ground. Then get out."

"Slow down," Evans advised. "You'll like that pic. We'll send you one."

"Take it out. Or I'll bust the box and anybody who gets in my way!" He aimed his spear at the multiple lens.

Mac slipped in front, protected it with his body. Evans called out, "Better look at *this*."

Evans had him covered with a small but businesslike gun. "We go a lot of funny places, brother, but we go prepared. You damage that recorder, or hurt one of us, and you'll be sued from here to breakfast. It's a serious matter to interfere with a news service, brother. The public has rights, you know." He raised his voice. "Ellie! We're leaving."

"Not yet," she answered dreamily. "I must steep myself in—"

"Right now! It's an 'eight-six' with the Reuben Steuben!"

"Okay!" she snapped in her other voice.

Rod let them go. Once they were over the wall he went back to the city hall, sat down, held his knees and shook.

Later he climbed the stile and looked around. A guard was on duty below him; the guard looked up but said nothing. The gate was relaxed to a mere control hole but a loading platform had been set up and a power fence surrounded it and joined the wall. Someone was working at a control board set up on a flatbed truck; Rod decided that they must be getting ready for major immigration. He went back and prepared a solitary meal, the poorest he had eaten in more than a year. Then he went to bed and listened to the jungle "Grand Opera" until he went to sleep.

"Anybody home?"

Rod came awake instantly, realized that it was morning—and that not all nightmares were dreams. "Who's there?"

"Friend of yours." B. P. Matson stuck his head in the door. "Put that whittler away. I'm harmless."

Rod bounced up. "Deacon! I mean 'Doctor.'"

"'Deacon,'" Matson corrected. "I've got a visitor for you." He stepped aside and Rod saw his sister.

Some moments later Matson said mildly, "If you two can unwind and blow your noses, we might get this on a coherent basis."

Rod backed off and looked at his sister. "My, you look *wonderful*, Helen." She was in mufti, dressed in a gay tabard and briefs. "You've lost weight."

"Not much. Better distributed, maybe. You've gained, Rod. My baby brother is a man."

"How did you—" Rod stopped, struck by suspicion. "You didn't come here to talk me into going back? If you did, you can save your breath."

Matson answered hastily. "No, no, no! Farthest

201

thought from our minds. But we heard about your decision and we wanted to see you—so I did a little politicking and got us a pass." He added, "Nominally I'm a temporary field agent for the service."

"Oh. Well, I'm certainly glad to see you . . . as long as that is understood."

"Sure, sure!" Matson took out a pipe, stoked and fired it. "I admire your choice, Rod. First time I've been on Tangaroa."

"On what?"

"Huh? Oh. Tangaroa. Polynesian goddess, I believe. Did you folks give it another name?"

Rod considered it. "To tell the truth, we never got around to it. It . . . well, it just *was*."

Matson nodded. "Takes two of anything before you need names. But it's lovely, Rod. I can see you made a lot of progress."

"We would have done all right," Rod said bitterly, "if they hadn't jerked the rug out." He shrugged. "Like to look around?"

"I surely would."

"All right. Come on, Sis. Wait a minute—I haven't had breakfast; how about you?"

"Well, when we left the Gap it was pushing lunch time. I could do with a bite. Helen?"

"Yes, indeed."

Rod scrounged in Margery's supplies. The haunch on which he had supped was not at its best. He passed it to Matson. "Too high?"

Matson sniffed it. "Pretty gamy. I can eat it if you can."

"We should have hunted yesterday, but . . . things happened." He frowned. "Sit tight. I'll get cured meat." He ran up to the cave, found a smoked side and some salted strips. When he got back Matson had a fire going. There was nothing else to serve; no fruit had been gathered the day before. Rod was uneasily aware that their breakfasts must have been very different.

But he got over it in showing off how much they had done—potter's wheel, Sue's loom with a piece half finished, the flume with the village fountain and the showers that ran continuously, iron artifacts that Art and Doug had hammered out. "I'd like to take you up

202

to Art's iron works but there is no telling what we might run into."

"Come now, Rod, I'm not a city boy. Nor is your sister helpless."

Rod shook his head. "I know this country; you don't. I can go up there at a trot. But the only way for you would be a slow sneak, because I can't cover you both."

Matson nodded. "You're right. It seems odd to have one of my students solicitous over my health. But you are right. We don't know this set up."

Rod showed them the stobor traps and described the annual berserk migration. "Stobor pour through those holes and fall in the pits. The other animals swarm past, as solid as city traffic for hours."

"Catastrophic adjustment," Matson remarked.

"Huh? Oh, yes, we figured that out. Cyclic catastrophic balance, just like human beings. If we had facilities, we could ship thousands of carcasses back to Earth every dry season." He considered it. "Maybe we will, now."

"Probably."

"But up to now it has been just a troublesome nuisance. These stobor especially—I'll show you one out in the field when—say!" Rod looked thoughtful. "These *are* stobor, aren't they? Little carnivores heavy in front, about the size of a tom cat and eight times as nasty?"

"Why ask me?"

"Well, you warned us against stobor. All the classes were warned."

"I suppose these must be stobor," Matson admitted, "but I did not know what they looked like."

"Huh?"

"Rod, every planet has its 'stobor' . . . all different. Sometimes more than one sort." He stopped to tap his pipe. "You remember me telling the class that every planet has unique dangers, different from every other planet in the Galaxy?"

"Yes . . ."

"Sure, and it meant nothing, a mere intellectual concept. But you have to be afraid of the thing behind the concept, if you are to stay alive. So we personify it . . . but we don't tell you what it is. We do it differently each year. It is to warn you that the unknown and

203

deadly can lurk anywhere . . . and to plant it deep in your guts instead of in your head."

"Well, I'll be a— Then there *weren't* any stobor! There never were!"

"Sure there were. You built these traps for them, didn't you?"

When they returned, Matson sat on the ground and said, "We can't stay long, you know."

"I realize that. Wait a moment." Rod went into his hut, dug out Lady Macbeth, rejoined them. "Here's your knife, Sis. It saved my skin more than once. Thanks."

She took the knife and caressed it, then cradled it and looked past Rod's head. It flashed by him, went tuck-*spong!* in a corner post. She recovered it, came back and handed it to Rod. "Keep it, dear, wear it always in safety and health."

"Gee, Sis, I shouldn't. I've had it too long now."

"Please. I'd like to know that Lady Macbeth is watching over you wherever you are. And I don't need a knife much now."

"Huh? Why not?"

"Because I married her," Matson answered.

Rod was caught speechless. His sister looked at him and said, "What's the matter, Buddy? Don't you approve?"

"Huh? Oh, sure! It's . . ." He dug into his memory, fell back on quoted ritual: " 'May the Principle make you one. May your union be fruitful.' "

"Then come here and kiss me."

Rod did so, remembered to shake hands with the Deacon. It was all right, he guessed, but—well, how old were they? Sis must be thirtyish and the Deacon . . . why the Deacon was *old*—probably past forty.

It did not seem quite decent.

But he did his best to make them feel that he approved. After he thought it over he decided that if two people, with their lives behind them, wanted company in their old age, why, it was probably a good thing.

"So you see," Matson went on, "I had a double reason to look you up. In the first place, though I am no longer teaching, it is vexing to mislay an entire class. In the second place, when one of them is your brother-in-law it is downright embarrassing."

"You've quit teaching?"

"Yes. The Board and I don't see eye to eye on policy. Secondly, I'm leading a party out . . . and this time your sister and I are going to settle down and prove a farm." Matson looked at him. "Wouldn't be interested, would you? I need a salted lieutenant."

"Huh? Thanks, but as I told you, this is my place. Uh, where are you going?"

"Territa, out toward the Hyades. Nice place—they are charging a stiff premium."

Rod shrugged. "Then I couldn't afford it."

"As my lieutenant, you'd be exempt. But I wasn't twisting your arm; I just thought you ought to have a chance to turn it down. I have to get along with your sister, you know."

Rod glanced at Helen. "Sorry, Sis."

"It's all right, Buddy. We're not trying to live your life."

"Mmm . . . no." Matson puffed hard, then went on. "However, as your putative brother and former teacher I feel obligated to mention a couple of things. I'm not trying to sell you anything, but I'll appreciate it if you'll listen. Okay?"

"Well . . . go ahead."

"This is a good spot. But you might go back to school, you know. Acquire recognized professional status. If you refuse recall, here you stay . . . forever. You won't see the rest of the Outlands. They won't give you free passage back later. But a professional gets around, he sees the world. Your sister and I have been on some fifty planets. School does not look attractive now—you're a man and it will be hard to wear boy's shoes. But—" Matson swept an arm, encompassed all of Cowpertown, "—this counts. You can skip courses, get field credit. I have some drag with the Chancellor of Central Tech. Hmmm?"

Rod sat with stony face, then shook his head. "Okay," said Matson briskly. "No harm done."

"Wait. Let me tell you." Rod tried to think how to explain how he felt . . . "Nothing, I guess," he said gruffly.

Matson smoked in silence. "You were leader here," he said at last.

"Mayor," Rod corrected. "Mayor of Cowpertown. I *was* the Mayor, I mean."

"You *are* the Mayor. Population one, but you are still boss. And even those bureaucrats in the control service wouldn't dispute that you've proved the land. Technically you are an autonomous colony—I hear you told Sansom that." Matson grinned. "You're alone, however. You can't live alone, Rod . . . not and stay human."

"Well, yes—but aren't they going to settle this planet?"

"Sure. Probably fifty thousand this year, four times that many in two years. But, Rod, you would be part of the mob. They'll bring their own leaders."

"*I* don't have to be boss! I just—well, I don't want to give up Cowpertown."

"Rod, Cowpertown is safe in history, along with Plymouth Rock, Botany Bay, and Dakin's Colony. The citizens of Tangaroa will undoubtedly preserve it as a historical shrine. Whether you stay is another matter. Nor am I trying to persuade you. I was simply pointing out alternatives." He stood up. "About time we started, Helen."

"Yes, dear." She accepted his hand and stood up.

"Wait a minute!" insisted Rod. "Deacon . . . Sis! I know I sound like a fool. I know this is gone . . . the town, and the kids, and everything. But I *can't* go back." He added, "It's not that I don't want to."

Matson nodded. "I understand you."

"I don't see how. *I* don't."

"Maybe I've been there. Rod, everyone of us is beset by two things: a need to go home, and the impossibility of doing it. You are at the age when these hurt worst. You've been thrown into a situation that makes the crisis doubly acute. You—don't interrupt me—you've been a man here, the old man of the tribe, the bull of the herd. That is why the others could go back but you can't. Wait, please! I suggested that you might find it well to go back and be an adolescent for a while . . . and it seems unbearable. I'm not surprised. It would be easier to be a small child. Children are another race

206

and adults deal with them as such. But adolescents are neither adult nor child. They have the impossible, unsolvable, tragic problems of all fringe cultures. They don't belong, they are second-class citizens, economically and socially insecure. It is a difficult period and I don't blame you for not wanting to return to it. I simply think it might pay. But you have been king of a whole world; I imagine that term papers and being told to wipe your feet and such are out of the question. So good luck. Coming, dear?"

"Deacon," his wife said, "Aren't you going to *tell* him?"

"It has no bearing. It would be an unfair way to influence his judgment."

"You *men!* I'm glad I'm not male!"

"So am I," Matson agreed pleasantly.

"I didn't mean that. Men behave as if logic were stepping on a crack in a sidewalk. I'm going to tell him."

"On your head be it."

"Tell me *what?*" demanded Rod.

"She means," said Matson, "that your parents are back."

"What?"

"Yes, Buddy. They left stasis a week ago and Daddy came out of the hospital today. He's well. But we haven't told him all about you—we haven't known *what* to say."

The facts were simple, although Rod found them hard to soak up. Medical techniques had developed in two years, not a pessimistic twenty; it had been possible to relax the stasis, operate, and restore Mr. Walker to the world. Helen had known for months that such outcome was likely but their father's physician had not approved until he was sure. It had been mere coincidence that Tangaroa had been located at almost the same time. To Rod one event was as startling as the other; his parents had been dead to him for a long time.

"My dear," Matson said sternly, "now that you have thrown him into a whingding, shall we go?"

"Yes. But I had to tell him." Helen kissed Rod quickly, turned to her husband. They started to walk away.

Rod watched them, his face contorted in an agony of indecision.

Suddenly he called out, "Wait! I'm coming with you."

"All right," Matson answered. He turned his good eye toward his wife and drooped the lid in a look of satisfaction that was not quite a wink. "If you are sure that is what you want to do, I'll help you get your gear together."

"Oh, I haven't any baggage. Let's go."

Rod stopped only long enough to free the penned animals.

16

The Endless Road

MATSON CHAPERONED HIM THROUGH EMIGRANTS' GAP, saved from possible injury a functionary who wanted to give Rod psychological tests, and saw to it that he signed no waivers. He had him bathed, shaved, and barbered, then fetched him clothes, before he let him be exposed to the Terran world. Matson accompanied them only to Kaibab Gate. "I'm supposed to have a lodge dinner, or something, so that you four can be alone as a family. About nine, dear. See you, Rod." He kissed his wife and left.

"Sis? Dad doesn't know I'm coming?"

Helen hesitated. "He knows. I screened him while Deacon was primping you." She added, "Remember, Rod, Dad has been ill . . . and the time has been only a couple of weeks to him."

"Oh, that's so, isn't it?" Used all his life to Ramsbotham anomalies, Rod nevertheless found those concerned with time confusing—planet-hopping via the gates did not seem odd. Besides, he was extremely edgy without knowing why, the truth being that he was having an attack of fear of crowds. The Matsons had anticipated it but had not warned him lest they make him worse.

The walk through tall trees just before reaching home calmed him. The necessity for checking all cover for dangerous animals and keeping a tree near him always in mind gave his subconscious something familiar to chew on. He arrived home almost cheerful without being aware either that he had been frightened by crowds or soothed by non-existent dangers of an urban forest.

His father looked browned and healthy—but shorter and smaller. He embraced his son and his mother kissed him and wept. "It's good to have you home, son. I understand you had quite a trip."

"It's good to be home, Dad."

"I think these tests are much too strenuous, I really do."

Rod started to explain that it really had not been a test, that it had not been strenuous, and that Cowpertown—Tangaroa, rather—had been a soft touch. But he got mixed up and was disturbed by the presence of "Aunt" Nora Peascoat—no relation but a childhood friend of his mother. Besides, his father was not listening.

But Mrs. Peascoat was listening, and looking—peering with little eyes through folds of flesh. "Why, Roderick Walter, I *knew* that couldn't have been a picture of you."

"Eh?" asked his father. "What picture?"

"Why, that wild-man picture that had Roddie's name on it. You must have seen it; it was on facsimile and Empire Hour both. I knew it wasn't him. I said to Joseph, 'Joseph,' I said, 'that's not a picture of Rod Walker—it's a fake.'"

"I must have missed it. As you know, I—"

"I'll send it to you; I clipped it. I knew it was a fake. It's a horrible thing, a great naked savage with pointed teeth and a fiendish grin and a long spear and war paint all over its ugly face. I said to Joseph—"

"As you know, I returned from hospital just this morning, Nora. Rod, there was no picture of you on the news services, surely?"

"Uh, yes and no. Maybe."

"I don't follow you. Why should there be a picture of you?"

"There wasn't any reason. This bloke just took it."

"Then there *was* a picture?"

"Yes." Rod saw that "Aunt" Nora was eyeing him avidly. "But it was a fake—sort of."

"I still don't follow you."

"Please, Pater," Helen intervened. "Rod had a tiring trip. This can wait."

"Oh, surely. I don't see how a picture can be 'a sort of a fake.'"

"Well, Dad, this man painted my face when I wasn't looking. I—" Rod stopped, realizing that it sounded ridiculous.

"Then it *was* your picture?" "Aunt" Nora insisted.

"I'm not going to say any more."

Mr. Walker blinked. "Perhaps that is best."

"Aunt" Nora looked ruffled. "Well, I suppose *anything* can happen 'way off in those odd places. From the teaser on Empire Hour I understand some *very* strange things did happen . . . not all of them *nice.*"

She looked as if daring Rod to deny it. Rod said nothing. She went on, "I don't know what you were thinking of, letting a boy do such things. My father always said that if the Almighty had intended us to use those gate things instead of rocket ships He would have provided His own holes in the sky."

Helen said sharply, "Mrs. Peascoat, in what way is a rocket ship more natural than a gate?"

"Why, Helen Walker! I've been 'Aunt Nora' all your life. 'Mrs. Peascoat' indeed!"

Helen shrugged. "And *my* name is Matson, not Walker—as you know."

Mrs. Walker, distressed and quite innocent, broke in to ask Mrs. Peascoat to stay for dinner. Mr. Walker added, "Yes, Nora, join us Under the Lamp."

Rod counted to ten. But Mrs. Peascoat said she was *sure* they wanted to be *alone*, they had so *much* to talk about . . . and his father did not insist.

Rod quieted during ritual, although he stumbled in responses and once left an awkward silence. Dinner was wonderfully good, but he was astonished by the small

210

portions; Terra must be under severe rationing. But everyone seemed happy and so he was.

"I'm sorry about this mix-up," his father told him. "I suppose it means that you will have to repeat a semester at Patrick Henry."

"On the contrary, Pater," Helen answered, "Deacon is sure that Rod can enter Central Tech with advanced standing."

"Really? They were more strict in my day."

"All of that group will get special credit. What they learned cannot be learned in classrooms."

Seeing that his father was inclined to argue Rod changed the subject. "Sis, that reminds me. I gave one of the girls your name, thinking you were still in the Corps—she wants to be appointed cadet, you see. You can still help her, can't you?"

"I can advise her and perhaps coach her for the exams. Is this important to you, Buddy?"

"Well, yes. And she is number-one officer material. She's a big girl, even bigger than you are—and she looks a bit like you. She is smart like you, too, around genius, and always good-natured and willing—but strong and fast and incredibly violent when you need it . . . sudden death in all directions."

"Roderick." His father glanced at the lamp.

"Uh, sorry, Dad. I was just describing her."

"Very well. Son . . . when did you start picking up your meat with your fingers?"

Rod dropped the tidbit and blushed. "Excuse me. We didn't have forks."

Helen chuckled. "Never mind, Rod. Pater, it's perfectly natural. Whenever we paid off any of our girls we always put them through reorientation to prepare them for the perils of civil life. And fingers were made before forks."

"Mmm . . no doubt. Speaking of reorientation there is something we must do, daughter, before this family will be organized again."

"So?"

"Yes. I mean the transfer of guardianship. Now that I am well, by a miracle, I must reassume my responsibilities."

Rod's mind slipped several cogs before it penetrated

211

that Dad was talking about *him*. Guardian? Oh . . . Sis was his guardian, wasn't she? But it didn't mean anything.

Helen hesitated. "I suppose so, Pater," she said, her eyes on Rod, "if Buddy wants to."

"Eh? That is not a factor, daughter. Your husband won't want the responsibility of supervising a young boy—and it is my obligation . . . and privilege."

Helen looked annoyed. Rod said, "I can't see that it matters, Dad. I'll be away at college—and after all I am nearly old enough to vote."

His mother looked startled. "Why, Roddie dear!"

"Yes," agreed his father. "I'm afraid I can't regard a gap of three years as negligible."

"What do you mean, Dad? I'll be of age in January."

Mrs. Walker clasped a hand to her mouth. "Jerome . . . we've forgotten the time lag again. Oh, my baby boy!"

Mr. Walker looked astonished, muttered something about "—very difficult" and gave attention to his plate. Presently he looked up. "You'll pardon me, Rod. Nevertheless, until you are of age I must do what I can; I hardly think I want you to live away from home while at college."

"Sir? Why not?"

"Well—I feel that we have drifted apart, and not all for the best. Take this girl you spoke of in such surprising terms. Am I correct in implying that she was, eh . . . a close chum?"

Rod felt himself getting warm. "She was my city manager," he said flatly.

"Your *what?*"

"My executive officer. She was captain of the guard, chief of police, anything you want to call her. She did everything. She hunted, too, but that was just because she liked to. Carol is, uh—well, Carol is *swell.*"

"Roderick, are you *involved* with this girl?"

"Me? Gosh, no! She was more like a big sister. Oh, Carol was sweet on half a dozen fellows, one time or another, but it never lasted."

"I am very glad to hear that you are not seriously interested in her. She does not sound like desirable companionship for a young boy."

212

"Dad—you don't know what you are saying!"

"Perhaps. I intend to find out. But what is this other matter? 'City Manager!' What were *you?*"

"I," Rod said proudly, "was Mayor of Cowpertown."

His father looked at him, then shook his head. "We'll speak of this later. Possibly you need, eh—medical help." He looked at Helen. "We'll attend to the change in guardianship tomorrow. I can see that there is much I must take care of."

Helen met his eyes. "Not unless Buddy consents."

"Daughter!"

"The transfer was irrevocable. He will have to agree —or I won't do it!"

Mr. Walker looked shocked, Mrs. Walker looked stricken. Rod got up and left the room . . . the first time anyone had ever done so while the Lamp of Peace was burning. He heard his father call after him but he did not turn back.

He found Matson in his room, smoking and reading. "I grabbed a bite and let myself in quietly," Matson explained. He inspected Rod's face. "I told you," he said slowly, "that it would be rough. Well, sweat it out, son, sweat it out."

"I can't *stand* it!"

"Yes, you can."

In Emigrants' Gap the sturdy cross-country wagons were drawn up in echelon, as they had been so often before and would be so many times again. The gate was not ready; drivers gathered at the booth under Liberty's skirts, drinking coffee and joking through the nervous wait. Their professional captain was with them, a lean, homely young man with deep lines in his face, from sun and laughing and perhaps some from worry. But he did not seem to be worrying now; he was grinning and drinking coffee and sharing a doughnut with a boy child. He was dressed in fringed buckskin, in imitation of a very old style; he wore a Bill Cody beard and rather long hair. His mount was a little pinto, standing patiently by with reins hanging. There was a boot scabbard holding a hunting rifle on the nigh side of the saddle, but the captain carried no guns on his person; instead he wore two knives, one on each side.

213

A siren sounded and a speaker above the Salvation Army booth uttered: "Captain Walker, ready with gate four."

Rod waved at the control booth and shouted, "Call off!" then turned back to Jim and Jacqueline. "Tell Carol I'm sorry she couldn't get leave. I'll be seeing you."

"Might be sooner than you think," asserted Jim. "My firm is going to bid this contract."

"Your firm? Where do you get that noise? Have they made him a partner, Jackie?"

"No," she answered serenely, "but I'm sure they will as soon as he is admitted to the Outlands bar. Kiss Uncle Rod good-by, Grant."

"No," the youngster answered firmly.

"Just like his father," Jimmy said proudly. "Kisses women only."

The count was running back down; Rod heard it and swung into saddle. "Take it easy, kids." The count passed him, finished with a shouted, *"ONE!"*

"Reins up! Reeeiins *UP!"* He waited with arm raised and glanced through the fully-dilated gate past rolling prairie at snow-touched peaks beyond. His nostrils widened.

The control light turned green. He brought his arm down hard and shouted, "Roll 'em! *Ho!"* as he squeezed and released the little horse with his knees. The pinto sprang forward, cut in front of the lead wagon, and Captain Walker headed out on his long road.

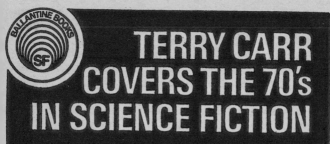

RAVE REVIEWS FOR THEA DEVINE:

For DESIRE ME ONLY:

"DESIRE ME ONLY takes the reader on a lush and sensual journey . . . Once again Thea Devine redefines women's erotica with her highly sensual love scenes and titillating story line."

—Romantic Times

"DESIRE ME ONLY is a page burner that will keep you enthralled and on the edge of your seat!"

—Romance Forever

For SINFUL SECRETS:

"A divinely sinful erotic read with a wildly unexpected twist!"

—Bertrice Small, author of DECEIVED

"This time, the Queen of American Erotic Romance blends the heated sensuality of the finest Victorian erotic novels with the suspense and chilling aura of an Ann Rice tale . . . A one night read!"

—Romantic Times

"Thea Devine has the right combination to keep readers riveted . . . SINFUL SECRETS is as hot as it gets. Don't miss it!"

—Romance Forever

For SECRET PLEASURES:

"Thea Devine continues to reign supreme as the divine queen of sensually spicy love stories . . . Ms. Devine's heavenly talent is growing by leaps and bounds."

—Affaire de Coeur

For DESIRED:

"I'm surprised the pages didn't burn to a crisp this story is so hot."

—Rendezvous

By Desire Bound

Thea Devine

Zebra Books
Kensington Publishing Corp.
http://www.zebrabooks.com

ZEBRA BOOKS are published by

Kensington Publishing Corp.
850 Third Avenue
New York, NY 10022

Zebra and the Z logo Reg. U.S. Pat. & TM Off.

First Printing: September, 1998
10 9 8 7 6 5 4 3 2 1

Printed in the United States of America

Prologue

Goole Abbey, Croxfordshire, England—1895

She had fallen in love with the face in the portrait the moment she walked into Goole Abbey as a new bride.

"That's the good brother," Roger had said mockingly. "The dead brother."

The brother who had been the heir of the house of Pengellis, jewelers to the Crown.

The brother whose face was rugged and ascetic both, with piercing dark eyes and a firm carved mouth, who carried himself like a king.

The brother who had died in quest of a legendary diamond nine years before, his exploits documented in a hundred sepia photographs that were kept enshrined at the London town house and at Goole.

The brother who was mourned and revered and almost canonized.

The brother who was still alive.

Not only that, but Roger and his mother had known that Connack Pengellis was alive all those years they were publicly mourning his death.

And now she knew, dangerous knowledge for which she was locked in the tower at Goole Abbey like Rapunzel.

And at the door, Gorgon, in the form of her malicious malevolent mother-in-law, Lavinia, just waiting for the moment to pounce.

And the only thing that was keeping her alive was the thing Lavinia coveted most: she was carrying Roger Pengellis's child.

One

He lay sprawled on the thickly tufted sofa, grizzled, touseled and naked, just another anonymous male body in a brothel full of them.

"He's new," the madam said. "Just brought in last night. He's . . . asleep—but very willing, as my lady can see."

Oh yes, she saw: he was long and lean and strong and beautifully made. His body was canted at an angle so that one of his legs was supporting his torso, and the other was crooked up on the sofa in a seemingly unconscious pose that put him deliciously on display.

He looked utterly knocked out; he could have been unconscious or drugged, or maybe he was just playing coy.

She couldn't tell.

But she knew who he was. Instantly and shockingly she knew, the way she tended to know odd things, and she believed it was he, and she immediately understood that she had to keep them both safe at any cost.

Any cost.

How much did she have? Her hands shook. A wad of banknotes she had stolen from Lavinia, and in her bag, an armload of unmarked silverware she had taken from Goole Abbey.

Enough to keep the dogs at bay for how long—an hour? A day?

She had to tread very carefully because she knew the madam had recognized her from a half-dozen forays she had made to the brothel when she was newly wed and skirting the thin edge of ostracism with the fastest social set in London.

She had been good at pretending. She had always been good at pretending. Roger hadn't cared what she was doing; he had only cared about the gold her father had dowered to his quirky only child to buy a baronetcy, which was as close to a title as Leonard Boulton would ever come.

Not that she had cared. She had been his willing partner in complicity, eagerly reaching with both hands for the title, the money, the freedom. They had done it before, she and her father, only this time, he had required she make a lifetime commitment to an indissoluble marriage and unending privilege.

What obedient daughter could refuse such a request? Especially one who had been as avaricious as she?

"My lady?"

The madam knew not to show her impatience, but it was there, a thin thread in her sharp question.

Her heart was pounding wildly but she didn't hesitate; you didn't, with these people, and she needed to get out of Madame's sight as quickly as possible. Too much had happened too quickly. She needed to act quickly, *now*. She could think about it later. "I'll take him."

"As my lady wishes. For how many nights?"

Oh lord— She drew herself up. "We'll see how he works out. And since he's new, I will of course expect a more favorable fee, since I will be the one breaking him in."

Such daring . . . but she had always lived on the edge of disaster . . . it was the only way she knew.

The madam eyed her skeptically for a long moment. This one had never bargained for anything a day in her life, she thought. And never in a brothel. She knew this one: this one had never ever chosen from the menu in all the times she had ventured into the house.

It was amusing, really. "Very well," Madame said. "And payment will be arranged how?"

She calculated quickly, but she already knew she could not give up her banknotes. "I have silver."

"Indeed?"

"Which you can convert easier than I."

"You think so."

Awful woman—but still, the safest place she could think of with Lavinia in pursuit—she had no choice; she had to convince her.

"Unmarked, Madame. Who is to know?"

Now the madam was curious; it showed plainly in her eyes.

"My lady surely has money."

She gritted her teeth; she had to gamble, and her bluff was cloud thin. "I will buy this gentleman for the night with silver. Let me say that I know you are probably aware of its origin. Therefore this will be my only offer, Madame. Take it or leave it."

"Let me see."

She opened her bag and removed a silver sugar bowl and handed it to the madam who held it to the light and examined it thoroughly.

"If you have the entire set, my lady, you may have him for two nights."

"I have the teapot and cream jug, and I must be assured I am buying your discretion."

"If you add in the tray and trivet, I believe we may have a bargain."

Any cost . . .

It was all she had of the silver, and she thought how sharp it was of the madam to understand exactly what the whole comprised and to bargain accordingly.

Madame knew she had no choice. But Madame *was* willing to bargain; she had picked up on that right away.

She handed them over reluctantly, with the madam examining and nodding over each exquisite piece.

"We have a bargain. Two nights. And of course you may be assured *I* know that such a one as my lady would never venture forth to such a place. I have never seen you. I don't even know who you are. Is that satisfactory? Good. Then I will have him transported to a more private room."

Madame clapped her hands and two burly men appeared with a pallet onto which they lifted the inert body of her would-be lover, and then they proceeded to a more private room on an upper floor of the brothel.

It was a very utilitarian room—with a bed, a washstand, an upholstered chair, an armoire for clothes, and carpeted floor. A fireplace for warmth, which was crackling with a banked fire, and nothing in the way of decoration except for fabric-draped walls in a neutral color.

Good enough for her purposes. And isolated in the back of the house.

Any cost . . . did it matter now?

She watched as the porters unceremoniously rolled their burden onto the bed, and exited the room.

Alone at last . . .

She locked the door with shaking hands, marveling at her bravado and her reserves of sheer nerve.

Or was it the familiar rush of triumph at having outwitted an adversary yet again . . . ?

But then—it was *him* . . . his face, thinner, longer, gray with fatigue and something else, and buried under a bushy growth of beard and hair—but *his face* none-theless.

And that body, that unimagined body that she had looked at every day, three and four times a day, in his portrait at Goole Abbey.

That painted body, clothed as plain as a priest, with no clue to the sinew and power that lay beneath.

It was a body made to be touched. Even in repose, even with him unconscious, she felt the awful urge to feel the texture, the heat, the muscularity of him.

. . . the him of her dreams . . .

Really him? Or just a demon of her imagination?

She stretched out her hand and laid it on his shoul-der—and jumped back. His skin was hot, burning hot.

Like a demon . . .

. . . oh, God—this wasn't real . . . it couldn't be—she wasn't in a brothel with the man who had been canonized by his family who had known all along he hadn't died . . .

—and she hadn't just buried her husband of five years and escaped from her tower prison . . .

. . . dear Lord . . .

The stuff of gothic romance . . .

Even she didn't believe it.

But there he was, on the bed, naked as a baby and burning with fever, and she was his sole lifeline, even if only she knew it.

She took a deep breath to slow her drumming heart and calm her jangling nerves.

What to do now, with a complication she could never have envisioned in her life?

Except she hadn't planned anything, not the how, the where, the what, not even Roger's unexpected death; all she had was the amorphous dream of killing Lavinia—yes, destroying Lavinia—somehow, and escaping.

But then Roger had died instead, suddenly and inexplicably, and as his grieving widow, she had had to put on a public show, which had given her time, precious precious time, to act on her impulses.

And to this moment, she didn't know how she had done it, how she had had the rational thought to overpower Lavinia, steal the money and the silver, and to escape with her life and her lies.

And escape to this . . . the unforeseen, inconceivable, unbelievable coincidence of finding Connack Pengellis in the very last place anyone would expect or look.

And naked and for sale.

How likely was that?

And yet, the brothel had been the first thought that came into her mind as she fled the grounds of Goole.

She reached out to touch him again just as he shifted and rolled onto his side.

She had been meant to find him.

No!

Unthinkable.

Her hand shook as she laid it against his bearded cheek. He was hot, hot as the devil, consumed in hell.

She had known somehow he was here.

Irrational . . .

Inconceivable.

Maybe.

Not.

But she didn't want to consider the incomprehensible and the implausible. She liked reasons, explanations, and possibilities grounded in reality.

But there was no explanation for this.

For him.

Who had been thought dead.

Or somewhere in South Africa.

At the very least.

And who was where he wasn't supposed to be, with her who was somewhere she wasn't supposed to be—

And both at the mercy of Lavinia who wouldn't scruple to kill them both.

She lifted the edge of the bedspread and draped it over his naked body.

She wanted to climb into bed with him—

Dear God— That was insanity.

She sank wearily into the chair, and rested her head in her hands.

There wasn't a sound except the crackle of the fire in the hearth.

She couldn't hear the wind, or a guest, or a mouse.

There was nothing—just her own injudicious thoughts as she rummaged through the events of the last twenty-four hours.

She was safe—for the moment.

And so was he.

She had known Roger was going to die. She knew the way she always knew things—a moment before and a step ahead.

She had watched him from the slit of the window in the tower where they had imprisoned her; everyday she had watched him careering over the fields of Goole Abbey until the fatal day he had tried to jump a downed tree trunk and his horse didn't make it.

And neither did he.

The funeral was lavish and overcrowded.

Lavinia chained her to her side, and everyone commented on how devoted they were and how fortunate it was that there would be an heir to carry on the family business and Roger's name.

Only there was no baby. There would be no heir.

And it would not have been too long before Lavinia found out and her life would have had no value.

Lavinia would have killed her without blinking an eye.

And so, in that infinitesimal moment when Lavinia was distracted by the intricacies of unlocking her manacles before incarcerating her again for the last time, she attacked her, disabled her, and managed to elude the servants, steal the silver and money, and escape.

And all on a tide of driving fear and sheer gut instinct.

She had no reserves left.

She couldn't think beyond the next minute.

She had no idea where next to go or what to do.

She had two nights.

And the limp naked body of Con Pengellis to burden her down.

And she wasn't going to leave Croxfordshire without him.

Everyone knew the story of Connack Pengellis, Bart., head of Pengellis-Becarre Company. He was the man who had mined a fortune in diamonds and then left the company at the height of its production and expansion to devote his life to pursuing a legend.

No one knew if he had ever found the mythic diamond they called *The Eye of God*.

Everyone thought he had died seeking the fabled Valley of the Diamonds.

Only Roger and Lavinia knew he had survived.

And then her—long after Roger had inherited his brother's wealth, his mines, his title, and his properties.

They couldn't take the chance she wouldn't tell; they knew she hated Roger and, since she had her own money in a trust set up by her father, that she felt no loyalty to him either.

She knew they would have no compunction about killing her—but she saved herself by giving Lavinia the one thing she wanted above all else—a child of Roger's blood.

And with that quick-witted, brilliant and inventive lie, she bought herself some time.

Two months and two nights.

She felt as if the whole of her life were compressed into that time. One more month and Lavinia would have wondered why she did not show. One more night and she would have been condemned forever.

And she couldn't begin to think what might have happened to *him* if she had not escaped.

She was meant to find him.

She shuddered at the thought, but she felt it to the very marrow of her bones.

That, and the loss of everything. Just everything.

First her father, and now this. And she could count her money gone as well.

Dear God—all that money . . .

Her share of her father's initial profit from his partnership with Roger: he had banked it in Funds before his death, and now she couldn't risk trying to get hold of it.

All she had was the silver and a fistful of banknotes. And an unconscious naked man who didn't know that she was his savior.

She didn't even have a plan.

No . . . she had the barest sketch of a plan: she had bought two nights, so they would stay there the two nights.

Beyond that, she couldn't think.

She couldn't move, she wanted to stay immobile for-

ever and never have to make another decision. Her
body felt heavy, constricted. Tight, as if something were
squeezing her very vitals.

She jerked awake in panic, unable to move, unable
to breathe—choking, choking, choking on her words,
her breath, her life.

He was behind her, on his knees, his muscular arm
around her neck, pulling back on her throat to almost
the point of no return.

He had tied her up in the thin bedspread with which
she had covered him, and she felt the murderous anger
emanating from him in waves.

He was going to kill her. A wild naked man on his
knees was going to finish what his family had started.

He increased the pressure on her throat. She felt her
helplessness in the face of his strength, his fury, his heat.

She couldn't see: there was only darkness and his
panting breath and her futile gasps for air.

She felt the life going out of her. Another minute . . .
and then darkness and gone—she would be with her
father, soon, to eternity—

She welcomed it, she did . . .

"Who the hell are you?"

The pressure against her throat eased—just enough
so that she could gulp some air.

"Where are we?"

His voice was savage with an explosive frustration.

She heaved against him in an impotent attempt to
loosen his hold.

He clamped her against the back of the chair more
tightly, the tension in his body palpable.

"Jesus God, who am I . . . ?"

Two

Red . . . bright, burning, liquid . . .

In her eyes, her mouth, clotting in her throat, constricting in her veins . . . no help, no hope . . . he was too powerful, and fueled by pure animal rage . . . she was losing, losing to his strength, his heat, and his savage instinct to defend himself.

All the answers—she had all the answers . . . if he would just—she couldn't breathe . . . agonizing—smelled his fear, felt the beast roar, felt her body giving up, going limp, words gagging in her mouth . . . last gasp—last ounce of strength . . .

She twisted her body wildly against the encroaching darkness . . . such a puny defense against a lion . . .

. . . and yet—

. . . she gasped for breath as his arm eased away from her throat . . . coughing, rasping, inhaling weakly, her body shaking, gulping air now as she felt him release the pressure just enough . . . just—

Not an animal then; *something* had broken through the fury, the fear.

He wanted those answers. Maybe.

She swallowed convulsively. *He might kill her anyway.*
He would, if he didn't like the answers.
She didn't like the answers.

The silence took on a heavy sentient quality. He waited

with the patience of a predator, his muscular arm around her throat, tense, taut and hot.

She swallowed again, just to feel the movement in her throat.

And he waited, his body alert, poised as if he were marking the passing moments by a dozen other senses.

The silence became elastic, stretching just to the breaking point of his patience and her fear.

And when he finally spoke, his voice was deep, rich, and rough with the hard edge of a man who was on the knife edge of sanity.

"Who are you?"

And she thought, she didn't have the answers, not even that one. What could she say to vanquish a lion?

"My name is Darcie Boulton," she said finally, her voice raspy from the tightness in her throat.

He ingested the information. There was no other word for it. It was as if he took every word and turned it over and examined it to see if it had any meaning.

She could feel it, the long slow parsing of that one sentence.

"My name is . . ."

Liar. Cheat. Thief. Relation by marriage . . .

He locked his arm against her throat again in a sudden sharp move.

"Who are you?"

She choked. "I—"

"Goddamn it . . . !" He pulled tighter.

"Darcie . . .

Tighter still.

"Truth . . ." she gasped.

He moved his arm—just a fraction. "Why should I believe you?"

"Tell you . . ." she panted, between deep gulping breaths, ". . . everything . . ."

"I live to hear it—Darcie. Boulton."

"Stop . . . please . . ." she whispered, and he eased the weight on her throat, but his arm remained like an iron bar across her shoulders.

"Talk."

She felt the aftershock immediately. Her body quaked like she was in a firestorm. Her throat cramped up. She couldn't think of one coherent word that would make sense or that he would believe.

Her throat was so raw, she sounded like a croaking frog.

"I know who *you* are," she whispered.

Tension: immediate and palpable. She felt as if she had a knife at her throat; his arm inched threateningly closer.

"Tell me."

"I—"

"Tell me—"

Pressure just at her collarbone; she coughed violently, then she caught her breath and choked out: "Pengellis—your name—" Another spasm of coughing and then: "Connack Pengellis . . ."

Again she had that sense of him absorbing the sound, the texture of the words. His hold loosened slightly and his body shifted.

"Tell me more," he commanded, his voice guttural and hard.

She heard just the faintest wariness in his tone. He didn't know. He had meant it: he really didn't know. And so how could he believe *her?*

She drew in a long shuddery breath. "Please . . . don't— I'll tell you everything—just don't . . ."

"Don't what? Strangle you? Attack you? I'm to believe a stranger—Darcie? I can't tell the truth from a fairy tale. I wonder what lies you'll spin to gain your freedom."

"I'll tell you the truth," she said desperately.

"Whose truth? Your truth? How can I know it when I don't even know that name."

"Let me tell you what I know." She wasn't pleading; God, she hoped she didn't sound like she was begging. But even so, what she would tell him was the stuff of a penny novel. He wouldn't believe her anyway.

She felt a swamping hopelessness. His situation was fantastic, incredible, improbable, and she had been rash and imprudent. He could kill her as easily as believe her.

But he *needed* her. And she had to make him understand.

"Let me tell you," she whispered, "and maybe something will strike you."

"Tell me who you are."

She thought about it—one beat, two, how much, how little, the details, the omissions.

He is real; he is here. He must have found the diamond. The biggest, most legendary diamond on earth . . . he knows where it is. And if I could get a piece of it, I could be free forever—

"I told you—my name is Darcie Boulton. I was married to your brother. I'm your sister-in-law."

His arm tightened. "My . . . *brother* . . . ?"

She closed her eyes against the inevitable. "You have . . . had—a brother. He inherited your wealth, your companies, your title. He died in an accident not a week ago."

"And his wife wound up—*where*?" His voice now was dangerous, silky with a kind of repressed anger.

"In a . . . whorehouse," she whispered. "A *male* brothel."

That silence again. Long and rubbery, thick with all the conflict within him. His arm moved closer to her throat.

"And what exactly am I doing here?"

"I don't know."

"And you—"

"Hiding . . ."

"Hiding," he echoed. "Hiding. You buried your husband and you're hiding."

"From your mother."

His arm tightened again. "Jesus God—my *what?*"

"Mother—" she choked out. "Dead. They said—dead . . . you. Died. Years ago. No one knew. *No one.* I found out. Dangerous. They wanted to kill me."

"No—no . . . I don't believe you—God, are you a liar—"

And she was. She knew it. Just not about this, which sounded, even to her, like the biggest lie of all.

She swallowed raggedly. "Roger—your brother—he took over everything. He ran the companies, the mining operation, the store. He . . ."

"Liar."

"They made you a saint."

"Really?" he sneered. "And on what altar was I sacrificed?"

"You gave yourself up to *The Eye of God.*"

He went still. A tight eerie stillness as if he were obliterating himself. As if he recognized *that* in some deep recess of his forgetfulness.

"Go on," he hissed.

"Nine years ago—*they* said. You disappeared. *They* said you'd died. Somewhere in India. It was in the newspapers—everything. You gave up the company, the day-to-day operation of the diamond mines. You wanted *The Eye of God.* You went after it. And you never came back. *Aghhhh . . .*"

He jerked his arm against her throat again.

"Jesus God . . . what hell is this? What kind of shit is this? Who the hell are you?"

She gulped a precious mouthful of air. ". . . married your brother five years ago . . . I—father . . . money, gold—Roger wanted . . . to fund company—"

"What company?" he growled.

". . . Pengellis-Becarre . . . mining . . . jewels—diamonds . . ." she gasped out.

He went dead still again.

She had a moment, the merest moment, to persuade him that her story wasn't a fairy tale, that it was real, *he* was real, and *she* could save him.

"My father—looking for investment and a title. Roger needed the money. Knew you were still alive. Knew it, and he and your mother, kept the secret for years. I found out. Couldn't risk my telling. Imprisoned me. Everyone thought you were dead. *Everyone.* Roger took everything—years before I came. And then they thought—they knew—I would tell everything. They locked me up. They would have killed me."

"They didn't," he said flatly, coming out of the silence and filling in the one detail that could puncture her story.

And now, and now—the biggest lie of all. She sagged against the chair, rolling the phrasing around in her mind to find the way to say it that wasn't a lie and didn't bend the truth.

"I told them I'm pregnant," she whispered.

He listened to the words and the tone of her voice closely, too closely, as if he were weighing every nuance.

"Are you?"

She chose not to answer that. "Lavinia—your mother—wanted the baby. I was to stay locked in the tower at the Abbey until it was born."

He heard that too. He *heard* it.

She took advantage of his hesitation as he absorbed the information.

"You need me." Brash of her when he could choke her to death in one abrupt motion. But he had eased the pressure, and considered her words even as he dismissed them.

"Hardly," he said sardonically.

"No—somewhere inside you know it's true, and you need me."

"I know *nothing*, Darcie Boulton, except you are a consummate liar."

"I know," she said with a hint of desperation. "It sounds impossible. But I paid the madam with the silver from Goole Abbey to have you for two nights."

Another hard pull against her collarbone.

"What a sweet detail, Darcie," he growled close to her ear. "You just can't stop yourself, can you? What kind of woman are you?"

"It's true. All of it."

And she thought maybe he felt it, viscerally, because he hadn't killed her—*yet*.

"So let me summarize what we already know," he murmured, his voice icy now with danger and distrust. *"My* name is Connack Pengellis, and I am believed to have died nine years ago in quest of something called *The Eye of God*. But my family has known and kept secret that I am alive, and meantime, my brother took over my business properties, but conveniently died last week, and his pregnant wife, who had discovered I was still alive, escaped from a tower where she was kept prisoner in order not to reveal to the world the mesmerizing secret that I had survived, and somehow wound up in a brothel in order to hide from my nasty—I guess my mother *now*— who allegedly wants to kill her . . . have I got it right, Darcie? Is that what I'm to believe?"

It sounded awful. It sounded spur of the moment, out of her mind, ridiculous, crazy, absurd, impossible.

Insane.

"Yes," she whispered. *"Yes."*

"Bravo, Darcie. Bravo. You're good. It's a fabulous tale. *Fabulous.* A tale out of *A Thousand and One Nights.* You made it all up. Am I right?" His arm tightened. "I have to be right, Darcie, because nothing else makes sense."

"It's the truth," she muttered. "It is. I swear it. I'll take you to Goole. You'll see. It's all there. The scrapbooks, your portrait. Yes—the portrait. That's how I knew. There's a painting of you in the entrance hall at Goole . . ."

He pulled against her throat and choked off her words.

"You're good, Darcie. You're very good. Take me to Goole—it sounds so authentic—what the hell is Goole? No!—don't answer. Someplace you'll make sound impossibly plausible that has a portrait that looks amazingly like me . . . how clever of you, Darcie . . . how damnably clever of you . . ."

His hold loosened. She felt his hands on her shoulders as he rose to his feet and came around the chair so that his hips and his blatant nakedness were level with her gaze.

He was a big man, bigger than was evident when the porters had lifted his unconscious form to carry him to this room.

He scared her. She could never have imagined the reality of him from her pristine daydreams about his powerful figure in the portrait. Nothing she knew about him had prepared her for the sight of him, and the scent of him, as he knelt beside her so that now his face was devastatingly close to hers.

That face—she had studied that face forever, in pictures and in his portrait. She thought she knew that face, she thought she loved that face, but he looked older than in the portrait, and his face was pale from lack of sun and carved with lines from years in the field. His brows were thick and well defined, and his mouth, sensual in the portrait, was thin with impatience and frustration both.

"Take a good look, Scheherazade."

His eyes bored into hers; they saw into her every lie, her every deceit, and straight into her soul.

And then he lifted his hands and touched her face. Moved his fingers to feel the shape of her eyes, her nose, her lips, the curve of her jaw, the line of her neck.

Cupped her cheeks and moved his head still closer, as if he were about to kiss her—

—but he didn't.

Instead, he settled his hands lightly around her neck, exerting that slight threatening pressure that told her clearly and firmly who was in control.

And then she understood: those eyes that looked so clearly and frighteningly into the deepest recesses of her mind saw nothing.

He had not only lost his memory, he was also blind.

And now she had the power.

And she didn't need to state the obvious. He needed her, and he had known it all along. He wasn't going to fight her: he would use her, just as she would use him. And nothing more needed to be said.

The silence lengthened.

"You're a real terror," she said finally. "You ought to untie me."

"I ought to kill you."

"I can help you."

"I don't think so."

"I'll be your eyes."

"For the five minutes it takes to get out of here."

"Why did I save you?"

He looked down at himself, his naked body, his turgid member. "For just the reason you said, Scheherazade. For two nights, no questions asked."

"Damn you. Don't you understand—if she finds you, she'll kill you."

"I thought that was your story," he said nastily.

"She wants Roger's baby."

"Roger . . . my brother, do I have it right? Roger's dead. They should welcome *Con* back with open arms."

"They heard you'd escaped, that you were on your way to England. I overheard them . . . they were going to find you first—contain you, kill you if they had to—"

"And Roger died first," he interpolated. "Or maybe *Con* killed him?"

"Don't do this . . . Lavinia will kill you. She inherits everything. She wouldn't stand for anyone getting in her way."

"Or maybe they're trying to smoke *Con* out?" he suggested with a note of irony.

She froze. *Oh, my God . . . he thought it was a joke. He didn't know, he didn't remember—anything was possible, anything, with Lavinia, even such a bizarre scheme to find Con before he found them. It was so likely, so like Lavinia.*

And Roger.

But she had seen Roger fall, seen him in the coffin, attended the lavish funeral . . .

Insane that she was even considering the ridiculous theories of a blind amnesiac . . . they were both insane because she could almost believe it.

She would believe anything to stay safe and keep him alive long enough to lead her to The Eye of God.

And maybe Lavinia wanted that too. She was evil enough, and devious, and cold-blooded.

Anything was possible.

Anything.

"You—*you*—are Con Pengellis, and if they want to get to you, they will get to you. You need me. You're as helpless as a baby."

"I got here," he pointed out.

"And you don't remember how or from where. You have no clothes, no money, no papers, no eyesight. Exactly how do you expect to proceed?"

"I'll figure it out."

"You need me."

"What's in it for you?"

"You won't kill me," she answered imprudently.

He smiled nastily and cupped her neck again with his large callused hand.

"So you'll kill *me* instead. Or turn me over to the dreaded Lavinia. I don't think so. Maybe *you're* the trojan horse. Maybe you'd better make up a better story than this poppycock about a baby and a wicked stepmother because I'm going nowhere with *you*, Darcie Boulton."

He leaned into her menacingly, and for one moment she could have sworn he saw everything. And then she thought, he would be a millstone, a drag, he would load her down, and pull her back. She was crazy to consider going on the run with him.

But without him, she would have nothing. And with him, with his memory, with the most legendary diamond in the universe, she could own the world.

She considered the ramifications of being totally honest. Always, always, it was a delicate balance of how little to say, how much to withhold to accomplish her purpose.

She was skilled at it; she and her father had dealt with the incongruities of fate for all the years they had sifted for gold. But Con Pengellis blind and naked was a proposition she could never have conceived of.

How much truth, how much lie? What would convince him to go with her, to let her be his eyes, his memory, his motive power?

Honesty. And on a point he couldn't remember. Maybe that was a plus. Maybe.

She had another moment to decide.

He smiled knowingly, almost as if he sensed her struggle. "Give up, Darcie. It was a good try."

She made up her mind.

"I want a piece of the diamond," she said abruptly.

"—the diamond—?"

"The Eye of God."

"The thing that Con Pengellis supposedly died for—?"

"I think you found it," she interrupted relentlessly. "I think you know where it is, and I think Lavinia thinks you know where it is, and they want it, and that's why they want you."

He started clapping. "Scheherazade is back in form again. Excellent story, Darcie."

"Roger said you thought it was real, and that you knew where to look. And that's why you gave up the company, the mines, everything."

"Just like that? Some businessman I was."

"Or a romantic," she said, and the words dropped like falling stones between them and settled into the sudden, startling silence.

She met his steady gaze, and it was so eerie to be looking into his eyes that could see nothing—

Or was it nothing?

Was he that clever? Was she? She still had the sense that he could see everything. Or was he learning to use his power in other, more disconcerting ways? God, he was formidable, but without his sight, he was defenseless, and that was the endgame.

He needed her. And he knew it.

"An eye for an eye," she said softly, "My eyes for a piece of the diamond."

"And she barters too; what a splendid trade, Darcie, and all on the strength of your belief I'm this Con Pengellis. Who are *you*, I wonder."

"I'm a gambler," she said bluntly. "I always have been."

"Or maybe you're a bigger fool," he said roughly, "and much more of a romantic than I."

His words hung between them, truths she didn't want to admit.

A romantic? No . . . a pragmatist, maybe, doing whatever was expedient to get what she wanted. She wasn't accustomed to viewing herself through someone else's eyes; she sounded like a madwoman. Worse, her scheme sounded like a hoax.

His hands tightened gently on her neck. She felt as if her skin were singed by his touch. His dark eyes bored into hers. His skepticism was palpable. "Why should I believe you, Darcie Boulton?"

But he had no choice. She might be a lunatic, but she had a plan, whereas he had no memory of anything prior to waking up in this room. *Not anything.*

A crazy woman. But she meant it about the jewel. That was real, and he felt her intensity, and the underlying greed to possess it, in her words.

"You have to trust me," Darcie whispered, watching as he considered every angle. This was the throw of the dice, and he had no idea what was at stake. "You can't leave without me. And I can't go without you."

He rolled it over and over in his mind. But she *could* go without him. She would be stronger, move faster, go further without a blind man hanging onto her skirts. If he let her go, she could disappear in a minute, leaving him at the mercy of any stranger.

His gut knotted. This wasn't a duel of wits. He either put himself in the hands of a madwoman, or he fended for himself. That was his only choice because he didn't know how to reclaim his life.

Yet.

He moved closer to her, sensing a desperation in her. There was something more here, but she wasn't ready

to tell him. For the moment, he could trust her. She
needed him.

"*I'll* be your memory," she whispered. "I'll be your
eyes."

"What else will you be?" he murmured, leaning into
her so that again, his face was inches away from hers.
This was the way. Maybe the only way he could tell anything about her motives and her desires. He needed her
irrevocably bound to him and he would do what he had
to do to insure it.

He knew women; he felt it viscerally. And she didn't
fight him, she didn't plead for her virtue. She stayed still
as stone as he felt for the soft lush lips he had touched
with his fingers.

And then his mouth settled on hers with a surety and
possessiveness that jolted him. She opened to him with a
keening little sigh of surrender that sparked a spiralling need
deep in his belly. The taste of her was electrifying, and almost
catapulted him out of control. He wanted to live in her
mouth, surround himself with that hot wet heat forever.

It told him everything he needed to know, and more.
Miss Darcie Boulton had feelings for this Con Pengellis.
And that suited him just fine. He was perfectly willing to
be Con Pengellis until he got back his memory.

He pulled away from her slowly, softly before he
drowned in her honey. "We have a bargain, Darcie Boulton. An eye for an Eye."

A kiss for a kiss. He felt her relief, her surge of energy,
and suddenly everything became clear. Darcie had more
than feelings for Con Pengellis.

She was in love with him.

She had thought she had another whole day to plan
out their escape. "But the first thing we have to do is get
you some clothes."

He had untied her, and she was massaging her wrists as she talked. "There has to be a laundry in this place. Those men didn't arrive here buck naked. And we have to get some food. I'm starving. Being nearly choked to death gives you an appetite." She stopped abruptly. "Con?"

He didn't respond.

"Con?" she said more insistently.

He turned then, with the sheet wrapped around his lower torso. "I have to get used to your calling me that."

"It's your name," she said briskly. "Listen. I'm going to find the laundry, we're going to eat, rest and in the morning, we're going to get out of here."

"It's a plan," he agreed, eyeing her warily as he eased down onto the bed. *She loves Con Pengellis; she won't abandon me now.*

She slipped out into the hallway and down the back stairs. She heard laughter, voices, moans; inhaled the scent of whiskey and musky sex. Found the door under the stairs that led to the basement.

Heard the pounding at Madame's front door, and froze.

"Open up! Open! Now, Madame!"

"Yes?" Madame's smooth continental tones. "What can I do for you?"

"We are looking for this woman."

A silence. Darcie edged toward the basement door and opened it a crack.

"I do not know this woman," Madame said.

The door banged against the wall, as if her questioner had thrown it open and entered without Madame's invitation. And what could she do? She could not call the police.

"And what's this?" a burly voice demanded.

"Payment," Madame said, but her voice was less certain now. "Silver."

"You know whose silver," the voice said.

Darcie fled down the stairs, as Madame told them, "A young woman like the one you described, came and left in one night. She did not give me her name, I did not ask. Indeed, my clientele trusts me to be discreet. She paid for the evening with the silver."

Madame's lies might buy them an hour, Darcie thought in a panic, but if she had to give back the silver, she wouldn't scruple to give them up altogether.

Suddenly, she had no time at all and she had no idea where to find him clothing. She whirled, racing from one end of the belowstairs hallway to the other, and almost knocking down a maid who had emerged from one of the doors.

"Where's the laundry?"

She must have sounded crazed; the woman opened her mouth, closed it, and pointed to one of the doors.

No time, no time. Lavinia's henchmen were already climbing the stairs. They wouldn't find *her*, but they might recognize Con.

Oh God. She burst into the laundry and scanned the room. A fat old woman lounged by the washtub. In the corner, a maid was fitfully ironing a shirt.

"I need . . . I need—" She raced around the room, piling clothes into her arms. And shoes. Where did Madame store the shoes?

"Where are the shoes?" The younger maid looked up from the shirt, her eyes wide as saucers.

"In the cupboard, my lady," she whispered, pointing to a built-in cabinet along one wall. Darcie threw open the doors to find shelf upon shelf of shoes and boots of all shapes and sizes.

She grabbed the largest pair of boots and ran.

Down the hall. Up the steps. Easing into the parlor hallway and around to the back staircase. Not thinking.

Acting on pure instinct. Frantic that Lavinia's men had already found Con and had dragged him from the room.

She raced up the stairs, flattening herself against the first floor landing wall as she heard a loud thumping on a nearby door.

"Open up!"

The same authoritarian voice. Protests from within the room at the untimely interruption.

Darcie jumped and took the steps two by two. There was still time. Just a little time. She almost fell into the room, weak with relief that Con was still there, and that his expression mirrored her own.

She had come back for him, she had kept to the bargain.

"We have to hurry," she whispered, tossing the clothes at him. "Lavinia's men are after me. I brought you some clothes."

He rummaged through them quickly, picking out a shirt, trousers and a coat, and began dressing hurriedly.

A kiss for a kiss. An eye for an eye.

She had meant what she said: they were in this together, for better or for worse, and the journey had already started.

Three

Goole Abbey loomed up in the darkness like a monster, a hulk of a building set on a dreary crag, surrounded by winter-weary trees with branches reaching to the sky like skeletal fingers. Her prison. Her nightmare.

She shivered at the sight of the tower outlined menacingly against the light of the moon, the dead stillness, the frigid cold, the soulless windows, dark and shuttered.

Lavinia was not at home.

Danger lurked, she felt it in her bones. The price of saving Con Pengellis was already too steep. She wasn't sure at the moment she wanted to pay it.

And yet, she had planned to bring him to Goole before he had shocked her with the fact of his blindness.

It could still work, she thought. They could hide in the tower—no one would think to look for her there. Not now.

She could retrench, take stock. Try to jog his memory with the smells, the sounds, the familiarity of Goole. She could steal food and clothes and more things to sell, and then, in a few days, they could be on their way.

It didn't matter where. Anywhere. Until he got his memory back.

India, perhaps, where he was alleged to have died . . .

An owl screeched above them, and she jumped. He

felt the movement and grasped her arm tightly. "Where are we?"

"We are at Goole," she whispered. "Can't you tell?"

He breathed deeply and all he inhaled was the cold night air and the sense of eerie dislocation. This was the devil's own quest, and he was still wondering how he had let her talk him into it.

Diamonds. Death. Dust.

The stuff of a thousand and one nights, just as he'd said.

And yet—*yet* . . .

He was disturbed by it, an indefinable something that felt familiar and just skimmed the edge of his consciousness. It was within reach, and he cursed his sight, his memory, his clumsiness, his stupidity that he couldn't quite . . . *quite* . . . grasp it.

In the dark, there was an obliterating nothingness, and he *hated* it; he would die before he gave in to it. He was certain he had been a man of action once; now he was a creature of the senses, as weakened as Samson without his hair. And he had no idea how it had happened— how he had *let* it happen.

The woman was insane. But he was in no position to disclaim a savior. Even a lunatic.

And then there was that simmering sense of familiarity.

She slipped her arm around his waist. "There doesn't seem to be anyone around. We can go to the tower now. It's tricky here, in the dark."

He cursed the fates that had killed his sight as he slipped and tripped down the path beside her. Her body was almost too fragile to support him; and he could feel how elegant her bones were. Touch was a marvelous thing. He had imprinted her face, her shoulders, her throat, in the very tips of his fingers.

And yet he knew the tensile strength in her too, in the way she bore the burden of him, and in the way she had fearlessly stood up to him and gotten, in the end, what she wanted.

What had he to lose, after all? He couldn't remember a thing, and she offered a momentary safe harbor.

An eye for an Eye . . .

The owl screeched again, and this time both of them reacted; she slipped and he pulled her back against him tightly.

"Not much further to go," she breathed, almost as if she were afraid to disrupt the night with even a hint of noise.

But it seemed to him that this night had been a succession of torturous time-warped passages to nowhere. He was feeling edgy, as if unseen entities were all around him. He wanted sanctuary, out of the endless night, away from the cold dank air.

"Shhh . . ."

He sensed they were in the shadow of the building now. But he felt the blow of the wind and an eerie openness beyond. He heard the scrape of a key. The squeal of a hinge, and then there was a deep enfolding feeling of darkness.

He reached out a hand. Cold stone walls. A straw-strewn floor. A sudden lighting, as if she had lit a torch or a lamp.

"Come . . ."

Into a narrow confining space then, a stairwell. Up the stone steps, their footsteps echoing unnaturally as they climbed to the tower room.

Another door, opened this time without a key, and then they were safe inside.

Safe—? No one was safe anywhere . . .

And this place—it felt hollow, it smelled musty, and he felt a palpable aura of danger.

"Here . . ."

She guided him downward; he sank onto a mattress, and he sensed her beside him.

"This is the tower room," she murmured. "I extinguished the light. Soon, I'll forage for food and—" she broke off, and he sensed, in his darkness, what she did not say: clothes. Items to barter. Money.

She was, after all, a thief, and it was how—if she were to be believed—she had paid for him.

"—water," she finished. "You can't move away from this place."

"How could I?"

"You have to believe me," she added urgently.

"I'm here," he said mordantly. God, he hated the darkness.

"I'll be back soon."

A rustle of clothing. A step, two, three toward the door. The subtle latching of the door.

Alone again.

Alone . . .

The thought struck a chord somewhere.

Alone. He had known aloneness. An absolute crushing loneliness. A bottomless emptiness. His skin prickled, and he rolled onto his knees in a defensive movement.

This place reminded him of something.

*Not some*one. *Some* thing.

He reached out his hands. Stone floor. Stone wall. Mattress on a platform. Thin cotton coverlet. A pillow.

He moved forward on his hands and knees. And fell off the bed.

Dammit, dammit, dammit . . . goddamn dammit—

He had scraped the palms of his hands, but he pushed

forward, crawling past the bed, and all around the perimeter of the room.

It was larger than the empty place in his consciousness. It was furnished with a clothes press, a table and chair, a washstand. A palace in comparison to . . . *what?*

Where he had been—

What? Mist. A moment of clarity, and then that goddamned everlasting mist. And he couldn't see through it. Just the musky edge of something— Dark. Dirt. Dank. His memory playing tricks.

He stood up, and inched his way back to the bed again.

Nothing familiar.

And yet—yet . . .

Maybe it was the feeling of helplessness; and the sense that he'd fallen headlong into a pit . . .

. . . a pit—

Something about that . . .

He sank onto the bed.

Deep—

Something about that . . .

To hell and gone—

Hell—life without sight was hell on earth . . .

It was a puzzle with pieces that didn't fit, and a flirty sense of familiarity that beckoned him like a lover. Goddammit, *why* couldn't he remember? He pounded the mattress. No memory even of the moment before he woke up in the brothel. Just a thick fog, and a mind-numbing sense of desolation.

He shrank back against the wall as if something were threatening him. *Fool. He was falling headlong, suddenly, into an abyss—helpless, hapless, furious, in his mind, with his body, dizzying, endless—*

REAL . . .

"NO-O-O-O-O-O!!!!"

Dead . . .

He jerked awake violently and opened his eyes to the isolating darkness. Sweat poured down his face and he gripped the edge of the mattress, trying to shake off the bone-jarring sense of tumbling into nothingness. He felt as if he were weightless, mindless, and he was the only soul in a sea of oblivion.

It scared him all to hell. He couldn't conceive of it. Someplace in the blankness of his mind, he knew—he *knew*—he had had a life before the nothingness. It was like a blank canvas with shadings here and there that might form into recognizable shapes. But his brain refused to fill in the shadows or the colors. There was just the dark, the indefinable, shapeless, hopeless *dead* dark . . .

"I'm back."

Reality . . . he swam up up up toward the voice, Darcie's voice, an anchor in the void.

"Here." Her touch. He wasn't dead, not yet. He grasped her hand and felt something cold spill onto his leg. "Water."

He sipped, the elixir of life. *He lived.* He drank greedily.

"Lavinia isn't in residence." She spoke in a whisper. "The servants . . . we have to get by the servants so I can take you around the house. I think our best chance is to do it tonight. We're risking a lot just by being here. We have to get out by tomorrow. I brought you something to eat." She pushed something into his hands.

Bread. *Staff of life.* He tore off a piece and stuffed it into his mouth. His stomach growled. *He wasn't dead yet.*

"And what exactly are we trying to accomplish on this midnight foray?" *We* . . . he thought of them as *we.*

"I'm not sure. I thought something might jar your memory." *It has to, she thought; she was counting on it, depending on it, on him, and his strength and his ferocious will to remember. He would remember.*

She would make *him remember. And then she could forget
that devastating kiss.*

"And we need things . . ." she went on.

". . . *we* . . ."

"Things we can wear. Things we can sell. We're going
to need money. Papers, if we travel . . ."

. . . *we* . . .

She had thought of everything. *We.*

"When?"

"Soon." It had to be tonight. Lavinia could return
at any time. A servant could be keeping watch. She
would have to be very clever with him. Take him to the
areas of the abbey that Con Pengellis would have lived
in. The entry hall with the portrait. The great long parlor with its beamed ceiling and massive fireplace. The
dining room. The library. She was sure that he, of all
of them, had used the library . . .

She shivered. This was the biggest gamble she had
ever made: staking both of their lives on his regaining
some of his memory.

"I want us out of here soon. I spent too much time
here after . . ." After she had found out the truth. After
Roger had caught her listening, and hauled her into
the dining room for a thorough cross-examination.

She hadn't understood what she was dealing with,
that *they* had been holding him prisoner for nine years
while they tried to coerce out of him the location of
the diamond.

And now it was only Lavinia. Unless . . . unless they
had plotted and planned the unthinkable ruse that *he*
had suggested.

It was too complicated to even think about. Roger
wasn't that devious. He had just wanted his brother's
wealth, his title, his life.

But Lavinia was . . .

She shivered. Lavinia was evil, and she had felt the force of it all around her as she prowled the house tonight. How did you escape the evil? What if Lavinia already knew she was there?

"After . . . ?" he prompted.

"This is where they put me after I found out you were still alive."

"Con Pengellis was still alive," he amended.

She didn't argue. Time was going slowly enough without engaging him in a war of semantics. And so much tonight depended on time. Where she could take him, what she could appropriate that she could turn into money, if she could swipe some of Roger's clothes for him. Whether they could stay safe and undetected in the tower for just this one precious night.

She couldn't let herself think of the alternatives. It would work. It *had* to work. Something about Goole would rewaken a memory in him. And then they could go on from there.

A clock somewhere in the distance struck midnight.

He reacted, an involuntary movement in response to sound of the sonorous gong.

"What? . . . What?" she whispered urgently.

"I don't know. I don't *know.*"

She heard the frustration in his voice, felt the tension in his body. "You've heard this clock."

"I don't know. I don't remember." He sounded angry, confused. There *was* something—and once again, it curled around the edges of his body, and then just drifted away.

"We have to go."

He wanted to go, he wanted to *do* something tangible and concrete to help him grasp the wisps and turn them into something real.

"I have a candle. We don't need much light."

No, a blind man didn't need light to *see*, he thought angrily, as she led him slowly down the tower stairs.

"There's a way to the house from the tower. Down some steps and underground."

It was noticeable instantly. He stepped down into the dank cold air, five steps down, ten. And then there was grit and water beneath his feet, wet, icy cold, and their footsteps echoing faintly against the moist walls of the tunnel. And the sound of hinges squeaking, his foot hitting a stone step, and her hand carefully guiding him up and into warmth and sanity.

A long long moment while she listened for other voices. There was only a dead stark silence and then the scrape of a match as she lit the candle.

"Come." He heard her unlatch another door and then she took his hand and pulled him forward.

And then she stopped.

"Where are we?"

"In the reception hall," she whispered barely above a breath. "I'm looking at the portrait. It's *you.*"

He stood as tight and still as if he were paralyzed. Something about this place was familiar. He had a sense of soaring space, and a scent that pricked his consciousness—but he had felt that about the tower too.

He couldn't trust his senses. Darcie wanted him to be Con Pengellis too badly and it would be so easy to fall into that trap.

Bong . . . the clock struck the half hour and he shuddered.

He knew that sound.

No . . . !

She propelled him forward, into the parlor.

Here . . . here—soft deep carpets, he knew them. The edge of a sofa, deeply carved and curved. He knew it. The stones of the massive fireplace. Familiar.

And always, always, the scent in the air, lurking in some hidden place, waiting for him to identity what it was, what he remembered.

The dining room was next, and it was the same, just that spiralling feeling of something familiar but unidentifiable, something pushing the edges of his consciousness, waiting for one particular connection. Like turning up the flame on a gas fixture, and illuminating everything that had been in the dark.

But no matter if he remembered, he would still be in the dark . . .

A door slammed.

"Oh my God," she breathed. "Lavinia's home." She doused the candle, and pushed him behind the thick dining room draperies. "Stay here."

And she was gone. He grasped the thick damask curtains just to have something to hang onto. He knew these curtains; and the scent that was so familiar seemed to be caught in the folds.

As he was caught in Darcie's fantasy. There wasn't a sane man alive, blind or sighted, who would have fallen for her story the way he had.

Or had he just fallen for her?

He gripped the curtains as he heard footsteps. And then the voice:

"Salit!"

Her voice.

Whose voice?

"Mem?" The liquid tones of her butler at the door of the dining room.

"I trust all is quiet."

"Just as you would wish."

"She has not returned?"

A flash in his mind: obsidian eyes . . . glittering, greedy,

*her hands holding a large unprepossessing stone—she says it's
not that one, not the one she wants . . . and he doesn't care—*

"We watch and wait, mem."

. . . he is dressed in white and always wears a turban . . .

"See that you do."

. . . she slaps a quirt against her thigh . . . always impatient, always filled with dark dreams . . . no, that one is not
her . . .

"She has not come." The voice of Salit, gently emphasizing her well placed trust.

Salit—

That was why . . .

*He understood now . . . he almost had it . . . and then,
and then—everything went dark and slipped out of his grasp.*

"Shhh . . ."

He was on the floor; somehow he had slipped down
on the floor and Darcie was beside him, behind the
curtain which was suffocating him with its scent.

He almost had it, the scent, the voices, everything . . .
and all he remembered was Darcie and her leaving him
behind the curtain, and it was as if that curtain had
closed off his mind entirely.

"Come. We have to go."

He crawled to his feet, and let her lead him.

"We have to chance it—one more room. I don't think
they'll come back again yet. She went up to her room."

*She. Yes. The voice. And something else he had remembered
that now had slipped away.*

He followed, edging after her as best he could in a
fog of disorienting feelings.

"In here." She opened another door and guided him
into another room.

He knew this room.

A different scent this time. Leather. Parchment. Something else.

He didn't resist when she took his hand and brushed it over the thick tufted chairs; the leather desktop; the glass inkwell; the leather-bound books, the ladder that ran on a brass track around the room.

He knew it—and he didn't.

And maybe she wasn't hoping for any epiphanies tonight. It was too dangerous to linger with that woman in the house.

"We have to go."

A nightmare passage back to the tower, as they edged their way back to the tunnel in the dark, desperately trying not to make a sound.

We watch and wait, mem.

Where? Where were they waiting? Who?

He had a bad feeling about her going back to the house again.

. . . Salit . . . bowing his turbaned head—he could see it, and then the picture was gone.

"Stay here. I'm not done. We need food and clothes, and whatever I can find that we can sell."

"We'll find some other way to do it."

. . . we . . . he had said it without thinking.

"There is no other way. How else can I get food and money? I'll do that now, while they sleep. But you—you *have* to remember. I think you did, a little."

"I don't know . . . I think I recognize something, and then the thing just slides away from me. The whole thing is too crazy, Darcie. It's too chancey for you to go back to the house."

"I'll be back soon. Just . . . just don't do anything but think about what you felt, what was familiar. You *are* Con Pengellis. You just have to find the thing that will trigger your memory."

She slipped away from him again. Holding onto her

was like trying to grasp the wind. She was so determined, and it worried him that the whole of her plan depended so heavily on *his* memory.

No, Con Pengellis's memory.

But . . . but—something flashed in his mind and spiralled away. The scent. *The scent* . . . he felt himself reaching for the idea of the scent. That was something real and tangible, something that connected somewhere inside him.

And all those pinpricks of recognition. Suggestion because Darcie wanted it so much?

. . . The clock . . .

Faintly, in the distance, the sonorous gong—once, twice . . .

. . . leather-topped desk, his hands pressing down, facing the back of the leather chair . . . I'm going—you're crazy, but I won't stop you; we want it, if you find it, you'll bring it back—you won't have it . . . obligation to the company—our money—my money, I made it—I made the company . . . bong, bong, bong—late late late so mother wouldn't hear . . . between him and his conscience and—and . . . and . . . turn the chair around—speaking to who who— Who? Scent of . . . what, permeating the room? Inhale, think—I know that smell . . . I can just just just—taste it . . .

Taste it . . . bong bong bong bong argument endless . . . he's eating—that's what . . . white turban—arguing . . . company the company all the time the company . . . And the smell . . . What is that smell?

He shifted, rolling this way and that on the narrow bed, enclosed by the silence and the dark. It was all around him now, the scent, immersed in a dream.

It *was* a dream, he thought from somewhere in the depths of it, but it was someone else's dream. And somehow he had to find a way to make it his own.

Four

Bong . . .

"Hurry . . ." Someone shaking him, whispering in his ear. "Shhh . . ."

Dark, dark, dark . . . he emerged from the dark suddenly, violently, utterly disoriented, groping for the location of the voice. *The voice . . . but it was a woman's voice . . . a different voice—the clock . . . the voice, the smells, he was eating. He remembered that much—in the dream, someone had been eating.*

"Con—" *her* voice, not the other one, barely above a breath.

. . . watching and waiting . . .

"We have to go." She grasped his arm and he shook her off. Not that voice, the one in the dream. Another voice, a different dream. . . . *the company, always the company . . .*

"Con . . ."

"What?" he answered ferociously, full voice.

She winced. Dear God, if he failed them now . . . *but he had answered to his name . . . !* "We have to get out of here—then we'll talk."

"Who are you?"

"I'm Darcie, remember?" Her patience was running out. This was a bad idea. He'd obviously had a dream, and he had no idea who he was or the danger of the situation. "Please come."

"Is *she* coming?"

She managed to maneuver him to his feet. He sounded, he acted almost as if he were inebriated.

"No. But she will. We have to get away from here."

"Good idea," he muttered, and swayed against her containing arm around his waist.

"Quick now; don't think. Be quiet. They're watching and waiting . . ."

 . . . *watching and waiting . . . the turban had said that to the voice . . . yes, this voice was right—they had to get away from her . . . even he knew that—*

The scent followed them, and the incessant *bong* of the clock.

Bong, bong, bong, bong, bong . . .

"It's almost dawn," she whispered as they stumbled down the tower steps.

The scent was everywhere, in his consciousness, in his pores. *He was eating . . . no, the other one was eating. And the company, he had made the company—yes—*

The image faded; the scent remained.

"Quick . . ." She thrust open the door and shoved him into the cold night air.

He hated the dark, God, he hated it. Like he was swimming, drowning, pushing up up up for air, and there was no air, only the numbing reality of the dark, and death.

She pushed him forward and he collided with a wheel.

"I stole a cart and a horse. Hurry."

He fumbled for the step, feeling her hands guiding him, cursing his inadequacies. The horse was restive, dancing, moving, he couldn't get purchase to hoist himself up and into it.

And he was so confused, so bewildered. Everything

was fuzzy, indistinct; he didn't understand about the cart, the horse, *her.*

But the scent was gone, and the ominous *bong* of the clock . . .

She pushed him and heaved him up, face first, into the cart, and clambered up and over him. He heard the snap of the reins and the cart lurched forward, and he pitched backward onto a pile of *things.* And then he lay very still.

She glanced back at him quickly, but she didn't have time to tend to him. She didn't have time for anything but getting as far into the woods and out of sight of the Abbey as possible. And she had chosen the oldest, the calmest of horses, the one who wouldn't get spooked, unruly, or disturbed by a blind man fumbling all around it. One that would stand still, and respond to her unfamiliar commands.

But it was the slowest animal on God's earth, and it plodded at a sedate pace that was as nerve-racking as watching a child's first steps as the first light of dawn rimmed the horizon.

Her heart pounded like a sledgehammer. *Dear God, what had she done? Made things worse was what. And now he was in a stupor, and so disoriented, her every plan was shot to hell.*

It took too much time to reach the shadow of the trees, and she grit her teeth as she pulled hard on the reins and brought the cart to a stop. There was no shelter here. She twisted around to check on Con; he was sprawled across the bag of clothes and food that she had appropriated, and he looked either unconscious or asleep.

Maybe this was better. He could only be a hindrance in his present condition, and she had a half-dozen decisions she needed to make right now. For both of them.

He was hers now for real, she thought, though her dream of acquiring *The Eye of God* was beginning to seem like the fairy tale he thought it was.

What if she had damaged him with her precipitate return to Goole? What if he never remembered anything more than he knew now? She'd have to come to terms with it. She'd lost the gamble. She let the words sink in slowly. *She'd lost.* Only she didn't feel as if it were over. Something told her it wasn't over.

But if Lavinia or Salit had seen them . . . it *would* be over.

Fear shot through her. She jumped down from her perch and edged out toward the open field, trying to quell her panic. Thank God, *he* was still as limp as the morning laundry; that was a blessing right now. She needed to concentrate, to think logically and to see if she could sense anything.

She took a deep cleansing breath. Reasonably, it was too early for anyone at the Abbey to have found the horse and cart missing. But she had to get moving. Daylight was creeping over the horizon, and the stablehands would be about soon. And when the thefts were discovered, Lavinia would know she was the culprit.

Lavinia wouldn't give up looking for her. Lavinia wanted the child.

She flattened her hands against her belly. The danger wasn't over yet. She felt that as clearly as if it were a spoken thought.

But at this point, it didn't matter where they went, but maybe it made sense to go as far from London as possible. Maybe toward Portsmouth, she thought, where there would be places to sell the items she'd stolen and obtain papers if they should need them.

Yes, Portsmouth. It felt right in her bones, and she always listened to those feelings. The threat she sensed was still beyond—and far away. She would not be able to outrun it. All she could do was find a place of safety and security and consider what next to do.

He slept. Through the whole horrible excruciating journey, he slept and she worried, about the stamina of the horse, about Lavinia following them, about his memory, the course she'd chosen, and she berated herself for her folly, her gambler's nature, her feckless soul.

She sat in a slipper rocker beside his bed in a small inn at Savernake, and rocked gently back and forth, feeling for the moment safe. And guilty for telling the innkeeper a storehouse of lies.

Con was her brother, she told him. They had driven out to the country for a picnic. He'd fallen. He was conscious, but he had fallen asleep, and she couldn't travel with him in this condition.

They needed a doctor, and a doctor was duly summoned to lend credence to the lie, even though it cost her a precious couple of pounds. It was worth it, to maintain the fiction.

And Con had slept, through the bouncing and jouncing of the cart all those long miles, through the awkward lifting of him into the inn, through the doctor's perfunctory examination, and now, as her demons receded into the darkness, he slept through the night.

An owl screeched outside the window and she jerked awake. She'd slept. What a fine thing, to find a moment in the midst of her turmoil to sleep. She'd thought she would never sleep again.

She leaned over and checked on Con. He looked so peaceful, as if nothing had disturbed him in the past twenty-four hours. She wished she could penetrate his mind and unlock his memories. All it would take was one connection, one detail recognized, and she would have the key to a fortune.

All she could do was keep trying, she thought. But that was her nature. She had learned long ago how to keep moving and chase the dream.

They had to keep moving, she amended her thought, even with a lumberous horse and a rickety cart, and she had to believe his memory would return.

I'm funding this myself, he told them. This has nothing to do with the company. You'll have no claim on it. You won't get a piece of it—

If it exists. Roger, skeptical, petulant.

It's my risk. And it will be my gain.

Roger hadn't liked that. Roger was too eager to take over the Company and everything else. But even having control of Pengellis-Becarre in South Africa was not enough for him.

It would have to be enough. He had decided that long ago, when he had first decided to undertake the quest. It would be all his, something apart from Lavinia and Roger and all the Pengellises before them.

Bong, bong, bong. The clock tolled the hours of their secret meeting.

A knock on the door—Lavinia, barging in, followed by Salit carrying a tray. Always there, Lavinia, never leaving a soul in peace. Playing the mother when she really wanted to play God.

And food was the excuse.

Salit set the tray down on the leather-covered desk and uncovered the plates. The scent of cumin wafted up from the tray—

. . . the scent . . . the scent—

He bolted upright, his heart pounding. *The scent,* Spices. *Spices.* He swallowed, almost as if he could taste

them. Spices, always a part of the meal. The cooks Lavinia had imported on the advice of Salit to recreate
the food of her childhood.

Spices. Oh my God.

But he remembered nothing else about the dream
except the spices.

Maybe it was enough. One tenuous thread linking
him to the fantastic tales of Scheherazade.

He groped his way around the bed. The scent was
different, the sense of his surroundings. The bed and
its coverings. The wall—smooth and plastered. This was
a new and different place, and he couldn't remember
how he'd gotten there.

Where is she?

He slipped to the edge of the bed, and reached out
a hand, blind, blind, blind. She was there, in a chair
beside the bed, her skin warm to his touch.

Reassured, he eased back against the pillow and
closed his eyes.

Spices. The thought flowed away from him like a
stream.

The last he remembered, they were in the tower.

And the clock. *Bong, bong, bong, bong . . .*

*. . . The longest journey of his life . . . plotting, planning,
digging . . . disappointments. Thieves. Lies. Loss. Pursuit.
Scenes speeding past him like a train gone out of control. And
then into a tunnel, a dark dank dungeon, crashing into the
wall. Dead and gone, as if he never existed.*

Bong, bong, bong, bong . . .

*Another clock, a lighter more musical sound now, and some-
where below. But there was no below; he was below, deep deep
deep in a hole that only God could find . . .*

*No! He wasn't going to think about the hole . . . and the
putrid food they threw at him as if he were a dog . . .*

Animal; he'd become an animal. Everything he remembered,

everything he was, he subjugated to the rage to survive and escape.

Bong, bong, bong, bong, bong . . .

He jerked awake again, his arms flailing.

"Con?" Her voice was soft as rain.

"Where are we?" It seemed like he was always asking that question.

"Far away from Goole."

He swung his long legs over the bed, and rubbed his face. He felt as scruffy as a chimney sweep, and his mouth was thick with an unholy thirst.

He looked focused, Darcie thought, he looked . . . *there,* and she felt a huge swing of hope. *It wasn't over.*

"There's food," she said. "It's cold, but it's edible. There's some wine. There's water to drink and in the basin. It's cold, but it'll do for a quick wash. What do you want to do first?"

"Damned if I know."

She poured him some water. He drank it greedily and gestured for more. Then she helped him wash up, and set what was left of dinner in front of him.

He tackled it with a gusty appetite that was heartening to see. She studied him carefully as he ate, trying to discern what was different. He was alert and fully awake now, and she thought there was an attentiveness about him that there hadn't been before.

"Con?"

He looked up sharply, and her heart leaped. *He had answered to his name again. It wasn't over . . .*

She cleared her throat. "We're going to Portsmouth."

"Why is that, Miss Darcie?"

"It makes sense. It's away from London, and we can get anything we need there. And I don't think Lavinia will think of looking for us there. She'd more likely try Dover."

"It sounds like we're going someplace," he murmured. "Where would that be?"

"Wherever the diamond is," Darcie said sharply, "whenever you remember."

"Ah, the diamond . . ." *The diamond* . . . the minute the word struck his consciousness, he felt himself falling. *The diamond—not meant for man to find . . . he'd held it in his hands, the weight of it almost insupportable . . . he saw himself lifting it, marveling at it . . . the myth, the story, the tale of a thousand years—and then somewhere outside of it, alone, on the ground as if he had been blasted from its very presence . . . He'd dreamt it. He knew he'd dreamt it. And then they put him down the hole . . .*

He shook himself, pulling himself out of the blackness, and away from the splendor. He sensed her watching him.

"An eye for an eye," she said softly.

"I remember." His voice was rough with frustration.

"What else do you remember, Con? I know you're starting to remember."

He didn't answer. He didn't want to remember. Who was this Darcie Boulton who was forcing him to remember? Roger's wife. The perfidious Roger's wife. The *dead* Roger's wife, who was carrying his child. How could he trust *her*? All he could trust was his sense that she was in love with him. No, with Con Pengellis, the man in the portrait.

And that wasn't him. He was a shell of the man he'd been. A husk, hollowed out by forces out of his control. Blinded by greed, youth, fame, and the need to always be in the spotlight. Arrogant Con Pengellis, setting off on a quest that was worthy of the *Arabian Nights*.

A legend in his own time. The story read well, though it didn't quite go the way he had planned. What did that matter? Con Pengellis had died for a madman's dream. It was only fitting that he should be brought back to life by a madwoman in love with that dream.

How much of what she told him was real? Even he couldn't define the line because he didn't know what was real and what was the dream. All he could see was the darkness. And now, imprinted in his memory, in his touch, the weight of the jewel he'd died for; the taste of the greed that had saved him.

A fairy tale, without the ending; her kiss would not turn him into a prince.

"Some of it," be said finally. "Some of it's coming back."

"Then you know you *are* Con Pengellis."

"I'm someone named Con Pengellis," he corrected. "I'm not the man in the portrait."

But he was, she thought. He was. Only older and more dangerous, especially as be honed his senses against his frustration with his blindness. She had to bring him back on course, make him understand that the threat from Lavinia was real, and that he could not renege on the bargain. Nothing could get in the way of that. *Nothing.*

"You're the man who knows where to find a legendary diamond," she said pointedly. "And that's close enough for me."

"We're going to sell the horse and cart, and hire a coach to take us to Whitechapel," she announced after he had finished eating and she'd called for a pot of tea. "It would take us a week to get there otherwise."

"That's rather profligate," he commented.

She shrugged. "It's Lavinia's money. And I don't think you are taking her threat seriously. You understand, if you turn up alive, you are a hero. You can claim everything Roger took from you, and you'll still know where to find the diamond. Do you think for one moment that Lavinia will stand for that, if she and Roger kept you incarcerated all those years because you wouldn't reveal its location? Do you think she'll let you live now that she's running the company? Or that you'll die this time without telling her?"

Lavinia. The other voice locked in his memory. He shook his head as if he were trying to grasp something. *Something about the voice . . .*

"Lavinia wants the baby," she whispered. "We have to protect the baby."

. . . the baby . . . yes, she'd said something about a baby— and it was all jumbled up with the voice, and his flooding memories . . .

"I saved your life. I want my share of the diamond."

Always the diamond, always the greed and the desire for power . . . he hadn't been immune himself, he thought, but Darcie Boulton was something else again. And what was the diamond? He knew that now: it was something to balance out the fates, exactly as nature intended.

All the pieces tumbling around in his mind like dice. Luck and the throw of the dice—he'd played Hazard and gone down the hole, just like Alice, into a dark upside down world where nothing made sense. And now, the Queen of Hearts was after him, and he was years too late. And anyway, the thing probably wasn't even there . . .

There—where? That was the question . . . and the price that had bought his life. And now he was fully aware that Darcie was waiting to collect.

"I have no memory of that," he said into the darkness. God, he cursed the darkness. He needed to see her eyes, her face. He couldn't sense a thing except her stillness.

"But you will," she said finally. "And we'll go there,

and you'll think about it, and you'll remember. We'll wait in Portsmouth until then.''

It would take a day to get to Portsmouth by coach and by train; he stared unseeingly into the darkness as their carriage careened down the connecting roads from Savernake to Whitechurch, and a tide of memories careened through his mind.

Think . . . he'd had enough of that for a lifetime. How many years in a dungeon, with the rats and his ferocious determination not to lose his mind and keep his secret? All they wanted was the location of the diamond. The biggest, most valuable uncut octahedron ever discovered. A legend no one believed existed except him, and from the moment he believed, others did too.

He'd known he was being followed as he made preparations for his journey. Roger, certainly, because Roger had been enraged that his quest was not all for the company. Roger had been a company man, and insanely jealous of him. He had known Roger would usurp everything when he was gone.

But Roger wouldn't appropriate the diamond. The diamond was his, if he could find it, if he could claim it. If, if, if . . .

He closed his eyes against the crushing memories that were as real as if they were happening right before his eyes.

They'd caught him in Delhi, on one of his sojourns into the city for supplies. And they had no mercy. They wanted The Eye of God, and nothing less would appease them. And he refused to tell.

They thought isolation and imprisonment would loosen his tongue. They thought the beatings, the torture, the moldy food would debilitate him, and instead he became more determined more indomitable, able to withstand the most heinous cruelties, ready to die rather than divulge the location of the diamond.

They wanted to kill him.

Some powerful hand stayed his execution. The barbarians

could not gnaw on his bones, and until his captor possessed his knowledge, he knew he would live. But how he escaped, he couldn't remember. And how he got from where he'd been to a bordello in London was a complete blank in his mind.

No matter. The important things were still there: the sharpness of mind, the decisiveness, the hunger, the memories. He ought to have been grateful he'd only lost one of his senses.

But if he were planning to go after the diamond, he thought, he might have lost them all . . .

They had an hour layover before they changed for the train to Portsmouth. They arrived at dusk and Darcie stepped out first into the crisp night air and stopped so abruptly that he walked right into her.

She felt it there, on the platform, that sense of lingering evil, suffocating and aware.

"Oh my God," she whispered, clutching his arm. "Oh my God. We can't stay here, Con. I can't explain it, but it's not safe—*I swear . . .*"

Five

It was the worst of hotels, but the best she could do
with the furies following them. When she finally closed
the door of the room, she still felt the pull of amorphous lurking evil, and that somehow he might be a
part of it.

But how so? She had found him; no one else knew
he was alive. And she'd left no clue to their whereabouts
at Goole—and yet all around her, she sensed a foulness
that didn't bode well. Lavinia could not have known
they were coming here, but she couldn't take the
chance.

"We have a lot to do in the morning," she told him
briskly. "We're going to France before Lavinia finds us."

That shocked him. It was too soon. Too fast. And he
was deeply suspicious of her desire to move quickly.
"You've assured me time and again, Lavinia knows
nothing about us."

"I'm not so sure now."

He felt a chill. They were on the edge of nowhere
because of her certainty about Lavinia. He didn't like
this new permutation at all. "The story suddenly
changes? How convenient, Darcie."

"It would be more convenient if you remembered
the location of the diamond," she snapped. "That's all

I care about; that's all the payment I want for saving your miserable life."

"And if you hadn't, you'd probably be exactly where you are now. Roger's widow and on the run from Lavinia, if your story about the baby is even true. What difference is a chip of a legendary diamond going to make?" he asked venomously.

"All the difference in *my* life. And maybe yours."

"I'm better off dead," he said brutally, "and the diamond left buried."

"Unless someone else finds it," she retorted. "Someone else could find it. Roger caught *you*, so they must have some idea where to look."

He went completely still, every nerve in his body on alert, cursing his blindness, and his inability to *see* what should have been obvious before.

She was either his savior—or his assassin, and she could be his whore. But there was more than one side to this equation, and it was time to dig out more.

He smiled mirthlessly. "That's right. Roger's men caught me. I remember now."

He was slipping away suddenly, and she didn't know what to do to contain him. She couldn't tell him about her feelings; he wouldn't understand them, or believe them. She had no leverage at all except his waning gratitude for her saving him. And right now it sounded as if he wished she hadn't tried.

"Stop it! You couldn't recall a thing until I took you to Goole. You need me and I need you."

"I was probably better off," he muttered.

"That diamond is worth a bloody fortune. And you found it. You have to claim it before someone else does."

"So you can exact your tithe for saving me."

No use lying. "Exactly," she said. "What's wrong with

that? What would have happened to you otherwise? I might still have come to Portsmouth—but you might be dead. And if you survived all those years in captivity, you don't want to die. Or to have your secrets to die with you."

She was so so clever. Everything she said was designed to galvanize him toward the goal of retrieving the diamond. She didn't know what she was asking for. He was staring to remember, piece by piece, bit by bit, all dredged up from that dark place in his soul.

The darkness was the key to everything. Even a diamond could be buried in darkness.

"If we go to France, there's less of a chance we'll be followed," she said.

"If anyone is after us at all."

"Don't do that, Con. The danger is very real. You don't know Lavinia."

"I'm staying here for the moment," he said obdurately. "You can go on without me."

"What will you use for money? How will you get around? Are you insane?"

"Hell, I probably got from Portsmouth to London by myself. I'll just do it again."

"You'll be killed before you leave Hants. Why are you doing this?"

He was amused he ever thought she would abandon him. "Just trying to get a fix on who you are, Darcie Boulton. And how much I can trust you."

"You can trust me," she whispered, her voice breaking.

It was an excellent touch, so sincere. A man could melt under the throbbing emotion in that voice. He hardened himself against it, against her. She was a gambler, playing the odds and taking the risk that he was only testing her. And she was good, very very good to have gotten him with her this far.

And she was smart enough to know when to stop pushing.

Who was Darcie Boulton, really? He had only one card to play, and he decided right then and there that they weren't going to France until he found out.

How did everything get so out of control? She didn't like it that suddenly everything seemed out of her grasp. But she knew why: he was remembering more and more, he thought she was a liar, and she had to make him trust her again.

How stupid of her to say anything when they got off the train. That had only aroused his suspicions about her motives. She shuddered to think what this layover would cost them. But she would work around that. She always did when she was confronted by an obstacle.

"All right," she said finally, "we'll stay in Portsmouth for a while. We have a lot to do anyway."

That roused him. "Really? Do let me hear."

"I have to sell the—" she broke off.

"Sell what, Darcie—the jewelry you stole from Lavinia?"

"How did you know?"

"Deduction—what else is small, portable and valuable enough to pawn? And why isn't a diamond necklace enough for you, Darcie Boulton? You could have taken a fortune in jewels from Lavinia any time in the last five years. Why does it have to be *The Eye of God?*"

How could he understand? She had been born seeking castles in the air, weaned on the sacred quest for El Dorado. She didn't know anything else. And this one was for her father as well.

"It's the next big strike," she whispered fiercely, "and I want it."

He wasn't shocked; she saw it in his all-seeing eyes. He comprehended it perfectly, because he had wanted it too. And he had almost died for it.

He sifted through the impact of her words. They were too alike, he thought mordantly. She had thrown him completely off-balance by giving him something he completely understood and making it sound real. She'd found the one thing he might respond to, the craving and the greed.

"And you're starting to remember more and more," she added, "and you don't want anyone else to have that diamond but you."

He didn't respond to that; what he remembered, what he wanted were his only leverage right now. "What did you take from Lavinia?"

She recognized a distraction when she heard it. She had made her point, and now she had to convince him to continue on. "Nothing too obvious. A couple of diamond rings, a diamond bracelet, three necklaces, a choker. I'm sure you know what's in her jewel box better than she does. She'd buried these at the bottom. If I had to guess, I'd say she hadn't seen them in years."

"Likely not," he agreed, but he wished he could see them. He could tell her their worth, their price. He felt the frustration rise again, and then shift. *He could tell her . . . if he could goddamn see, he could—he could—remember . . .* "Give them to me. Let me see if I can figure out what you took."

He heard rummaging sounds, and then he felt her take his hand and place something cool into it. A bracelet, by the feel, all edges, sixteen stones, flat-planed and faceted, with gold-pronged settings and clasp.

He could just picture it, and then, in a wash of memory, his mother at dinner, and his father handing the narrow velvet box across the table. Mother's long clever fingers opening it, her mouth rounding into an "oh," as she saw what was within. Father coming around the table and fastening it to her wrist. That bracelet. That warm wonderful time before he was old enough to become greedy and saturated with the day-to-day running of the Company and the lack of adventure in his life.

That bracelet in the hands of a charlatan . . . he crushed it in his hand, feeling the prongs prick his palm. "Don't take less than fifty pounds for it," he said, keeping his voice neutral. "Those diamonds are perfectly matched, and set in a custom design. A gift from my father. Probably everything you took was one of my father's many gifts to her."'

"*Lavinia?*"

"Lavinia," he said flatly.

His reaction bothered her. He couldn't understand about Lavinia. She wasn't soft or lovable. She was as avaricious as the rest of them. More so, because she had been the driving force to keep the secret that Con was still alive. But obviously, from the expression on his face, the bracelet had aroused some deep cozy memory, and if he had a choice, she thought warily, he wouldn't let it go.

But he had no choice; Lavinia would kill him if she could find him, and they had to get out of England as soon as possible.

"Not less than fifty pounds," she echoed. "And the necklaces proportionately more, I would guess. Do you want to . . . ?"

"No," he said abruptly. "I don't want to know."

"But you remember," she persisted. "And you know we have to go."

He hesitated before he answered. How much, how

little to tell her. She didn't know it, but she had, with her words, aroused in him again the instinct of the hunter. And she had said it more than once: he didn't want anyone else to claim *The Eye of God*. He had found it, and it was his, and while it remained hidden, he still owned it.

But now, without a doubt, Lavinia was searching for him, just as Darcie said. And Lavinia wanted both of them, to claim different treasures.

No one will have The Eye of God *but me* . . .

Darcie had called it. He was every bit as much the mercenary as she.

"Sell the bracelet," he said, his tone firm and devoid of emotion. "We'll go to France."

Dark, dark, dark . . . time meant nothing to him. It could have been morning or midnight when Darcie left him, and he railed against the darkness that held him captive. He was helpless as a baby in the darkness, much more so than he had been in any prison when he'd had his sight.

To depend entirely on Darcie . . . a liar, a cheat, a thief. A woman married to one man for privilege and power, and hopelessly, impossibly in love with another—

Darcie, who'd given him back his life . . . and he, like a genie, could grant her fondest wish . . .

"Con . . ." Darcie, at the door.

"How much did you get?"

"More than your estimate," she whispered. "Shhh . . . the walls are thin as paper." He felt her weight depress the mattress where he lay. "Listen, everything is arranged. In two days, we can sail for Le Havre. I have the papers, I bought suitcases, and some things we'll need, and I figured out a disguise. We're going to be a nurse and her elderly patient. No one will think to question it. I don't suppose you speak French?" she added hopefully.

Her efficiency was stunning. "As it happens, I do," he said dryly.

"I should have known," she murmured. "Well then, I've got a wheelchair down at the front desk. You'll pretend to be old and ill, and we'll just wheel you on board, keep to our cabin, and any time we go on deck, I'll take you in the chair and no one will think we're anything but nurse and patient."

He was shaking his head, and she felt her heart plummet. "Don't you think it's a good idea?"

"I forgot: we're not safe in Portsmouth, whatever that means. What does it mean, by the way? And I think you're crazy if you imagine anyone's going to think I'm elderly."

"But you haven't seen yourself. Your hair and your beard are longer than St. Nicholas's. All we have to do is powder it and you'll hunch over, so you don't look so tall, and you'll wear this hat—" She put a slouchy felt hat in his hands, "—and no one will know the difference."

He pulled the hat over his ears, and slouched down. "Like that?"

"Absolutely. That's very good, Con. Have you done this before?"

"In another life," he muttered, removing the hat. "God, I *hate* the darkness."

"Con—" she touched his arm. "I don't think Lavinia knows we're here, but I felt something ominous when I stepped off the train."

"That's too nebulous for me," he said, a bad feeling settling in his gut. *Something ominous* . . . he had a feeling he was about to *hear* something ominous.

"They're trying to get a step ahead of you. They're

after *The Eye of God*, and if they can find you, they think you'll lead them to it."

And who had him so obviously in tow? Who conceivably could be working for Lavinia? Whose every word could be a lie? Who was in love with Con Pengellis? And how badly did she want a piece of the prize?

"So why exactly am I going to do that, Darcie?"

"Because," she said emphatically, "you want it for yourself."

She lay beside him on the rickety bed, her body stiff as a board so that she wouldn't inadvertently touch him. God, if she touched him . . . if he even knew, even had a hint about what she felt about him—

It was all she could do to keep the goal in sight. *The diamond. Her father. What he lived for. What she could die for.*

She could do it. She was strong enough for both of them. She had taken care of her father all those years before, now she would take care of Con. She saw it as a simple extension of what she had done all her life.

Only now, so much more was at stake.

What would she have done if none of this had happened? If Con had really died? How long could she have evaded Lavinia?

Her heart pounded painfully. *An easier task than eluding her with a blind man keeping pace behind her.*

It didn't matter. She could do it. And no matter what happened, it was still easier to travel with him than to go on by herself.

She hadn't forgotten that kiss. She had a feeling he hadn't either. But it had been a kiss to exert domination. She had understood that and reacted accordingly.

She hoped.

What could a man tell from a kiss?

What kind of dreams had she woven around the feelings from that kiss? Impossible dreams. Dreams she had tamped into nothingness because she had no right to have them.

But *she* was the one lying next to him in a seedy hotel on the edge of oblivion. *Fate . . . ?* She had thought that when she'd found him. She didn't trust in fate; fate was capricious. Anything could tip the balance.

If she moved one inch, it would tip the balance. One inch and she would fall fast and hard into the darkness, and welcome it with open arms.

Thank God, she had kept them moving so she could defy the darkness. But moments like these scared her. She felt his heat, his skepticism, his need, and she didn't know what she feared most.

She feared herself.

She shifted slightly, unable to maintain the rigid tension of her body.

And he knew it.

This wasn't supposed to happen.

What could happen? Another kiss? What was a kiss in the scheme of things? A moment two people were moved to connect with each other, nothing more, nothing less. What could he tell from a kiss? Even she, who had flirted with lovers in the course of her marriage, knew a kiss meant nothing. She had learned to be as hardhearted as the rest of her set during her marriage to Roger. She could handle Con Pengellis.

She shifted again toward the edge of the bed. Easy. She could put all feelings aside in pursuit of the dream.

Con Pengellis had been a dream, she reminded herself.

. . . A nightmare, given his blindness—but if she hadn't found him, she might be settling down in some small village

in Ireland or France, using Lavinia's jewelry to maintain a modest and circumspect lifestyle.

This was infinitely better. It was like her days on the trail with her father through Colorado and Nevada. Over the hill to the next big one. Around the pass to the place where no one else had ever thought to look.

Familiar territory even though she was a thousand miles away from it, and her father had realized his dream of becoming a respectable gentleman.

All that gold . . . they found it—one big strike, one huge profit from the takeover by a mining company in Colorado. And then her father's last dream: marry a title. Marry money. His itinerant daughter set for the rest of her life; himself aligned with an honorable, giving luster to his otherwise vagrant family tree.

And somewhere the future, he expected her to appropriate a piece of The Eye of God, *whenever it would come into Roger's possession. It had been all he wanted before his death; she could do nothing less than oblige him as she'd always done. And then fate handed her Con Pengellis . . .*

She woke with a start . . . oh God—she was backed up tight against his chest, the last place she wanted to be. And she had slept, when she'd had no intention of doing so. Why on earth hadn't she stayed in the bedside chair, as she had last night? You couldn't get into trouble if you slept upright and as far from temptation as possible.

Or had she unconsciously wanted to provoke something? Oh, nonsense. They were conspirators, he waxed hot and cold about her motives anyway, and she was making more of this than it was.

He was sleeping; he needed his sleep after their strenuous trip and his grappling with his returning memory: his breathing seemed regular, she thought, there was no reason not to be at ease with the situation. This was not a scene for seduction.

She couldn't relax. Her body tensed up. Her muscles contracted as she tried so hard not to make an untoward movement. *He mustn't ever think* . . . She'd make sure he didn't think . . .

The hours stretched on, punctuated by the sound of a foghorn, the squawk of a seagull, her pounding heart, the feeling of his arm around her waist, the touch of his mouth against her hair.

What did he *see*? She could be anything to him, *anyone*. She could look exactly like his deepest fantasy. He could be hers. He had been hers in her dreams, but it had been the Con Pengellis in the portrait, who could be anything *she* wanted.

But in the portrait he hadn't had this world-weary face, or that mouth with its harsh words and ingrained cynicism. His lips had been, in her dreams, soft, coaxing, obedient, teasing her, tempting her, letting her lead him to the places where dreams were made.

His arm had not been hard, veined and muscular. His hands, in her dreams, were not rough, callused, hot. His body didn't pulse with that raw heat that was so disturbingly male.

In dreams, he was cool, elegant, aloof, and he pursued her with an ardor that placed all the power squarely in her hands. And yes, she did show him mercy, she did. She allowed him to touch, to kiss, to command.

The man beside her would allow no such thing. The reality of him was different, dangerous, *hell*.

How far into the darkness did she want to leap?

. . . *as far down as I have to go to* . . .

No! She made a restive movement, and regretted it instantly. He shifted closer, and now against her buttocks she could feel the thrust of his erection, thick and hard as wood.

. . . that far down . . . and he could take her and break her and she wouldn't care . . .

A slight lift of her head, a wiggle of her derrière, a twist of her body . . . she could have him. He was awake, aware, his hand tensing as he grasped her hip.

This wasn't part of the bargain.

Maybe it was . . .

She was an adventuress, after all—and her father had taught her by words and by example that no sacrifice was too great for the bigger picture. And how many times had he used charm and guile to get them food and lodgings and transportation. She wasn't stupid—and she had known exactly what the whole entailed, even when she agreed to marry Roger.

And she'd kept her side of the arrangement, submitting all those bloodless, passionless nights that Roger had taken her, doing his duty, a lackluster lover, and earning the gold her father had stuffed into his coffers.

But Con—oh, but Con . . . all she had ever longed for, in his hands, within her sight. Maybe she was a creature of the senses after all.

But—she felt it instinctively: a bargain with Con, would be something else again.

She had to decide if she was willing to pay the price.

"Con?" Her voice was barely above a breath, pulling her back to him magnetically. She wanted no words; words would disturb it, disperse the fog of heat and need.

"Yes or no, Darcie?" She liked that; a man who knew what he wanted, would take what he wanted if it were offered.

"Yes," she whispered, and the word floated in the air, as firm and fragile as a bubble. She twisted her body toward him. She felt his hand skim from her hip to her shoulder, to her neck and her chin, and she shuddered.

The touch of a sightless man, feeling his way in the dark. Unfamiliar territory but for her traitorous mouth. That he knew, and he hadn't forgotten. She *had* given too much, and it was too late to backtrack now.

He cupped her chin firmly to position her mouth for the devastating press of his lips, faintly moist, against hers. The sensation spiraled all the way to her toes, and she parted her lips and invited him in.

The dark enfolded her. She felt as if she were an island, alone with him, a part of him, and that nothing existed outside of him. Hot, wet, hungry: she couldn't get enough of him; she was neither mistress nor slave to him. She just *was,* drowning in his heat, her need, the taste, the feel and the sensation of him living in her kisses.

He had all the time in the world; he explored her mouth as if it were a new world, as if the taste of her nourished his soul. She took him greedily, feeding on her dreams, her unacknowledged desires.

She had thought she could hide in the dark, that nothing would be visible that she didn't want to show. But he knew everything, just from the taste, the touch, the ache in her. And then, it was too much, and too late to refuse him anything.

She stretched against him like a cat, her body swelling with a shimmery longing that settled definitively between her legs.

His had nestled between her breasts, feeling the contour, the shape, caressing one stiffened nipple beneath the soft worn bodice of her dress.

Heaven . . . luscious heaven, as if that hard peak were the only pure pleasure point of her body. His kisses drove her; the nebulous feelings in her took shape into something more potent and powerful as his fingers shaped her nipple in concert with her moans.

But the contact was not real, not strong; in a frenzy, she ripped her dress, her underclothes away from her breast to bare her nipple to his stroking fingers.

And she almost convulsed when he touched it, circling it gently and enclosing it in his long callused fingers. And she wanted it; she never knew how badly she wanted it. Her body sunk into a morass of voluptuous sensation. He knew just how to touch it, how to play with it and stroke and squeeze it. Never too hard, never too little. Always just the right amount of pressure and delicate massage.

She arched herself against him, lost in his kisses and the keening excitement of his manipulating her naked nipple. She never wanted him to stop.

His hot mouth, her feverish kisses, his knowing fingers, her frantic body writhing beneath his expert caress of her hot hard nipple—she wanted more and more and more. Both nipples at the mercy of those fingers, both at once. Her mouth, her body, her soul, he could have everything if only he never stopped the movement of his stroking thumb.

The pleasure was too sharp, too necessary for her very being. And it was building, steeply, deliberately, deliciously to a hot hard peak that she willingly ascended if only to ask for more.

He gave her more. He deepened his kisses, and the pressure of his fingers against her nipple. Just that much more feeling, just that much more sensation. It crashed over her like a wave as he squeezed her naked nipple deliberately hard.

Her body convulsed, she pushed against his invasive fingers, seeking the last hot spasm of pleasure, and he gave it to her. He wrenched his mouth from hers and squeezed her nipple hard between his lips that were wet with her honey, and she bucked against him like a gun as her body fired off one exquisite sensation after another deep between her legs.

On and on, he wouldn't give up her nipple. He wanted it, and she pushed him to squeeze her, to suck it, until she was hot and dry.

But she was wet, sopping wet, with her tumultuous climax and sobbing now it had ended, because that he had gently let her go.

More . . . more than she'd ever dreamed—how could there be more? She was insensate with the pleasure of it, and the way he pulled her against his chest in the dark.

She made a motion toward him, and he pushed her hand away.

"Next time," he murmured.

Next time. She savored the words and curled up against him, awash in the lingering scent of her sex, and the heat of him.

Next time. He smiled faintly in the darkness. Next time. A world of promise in his consideration and his skill.

He had done what he had planned: tonight he had made her his.

Six

Next time.

Everything had changed. The next morning she felt satiated and raw. And she didn't know quite how she was going to face him.

But of course, she thought ruefully as she tugged at her torn bodice, it wasn't a case of him *looking* at her. It was her shame, her need. If she hadn't crept into the bed, if she hadn't rolled against him, hadn't turned . . . if she hadn't let her fantasies override the reality of the situation . . .

She needed a needle and thread, instead of recriminations. It was all of a piece. They would find the diamond, Con would reclaim his life, his position, and his mercenary sister-in-law would probably have to find another place. Why not take her pleasure where she found it?

Oh my God—next time . . .

He was still asleep, doomed to the darkness forever. *Poor Con.* She leaned over and stroked his face. *The pleasures of the night would always take place in the darkness,* she decided. *If there were a* next time. *If she really were that weak. That needy. That bold.*

She threw a cape over her shoulders and went out into the brisk morning air.

There was nothing like a seacoast town. The smell of fish, the fishmongers already hawking the first catch of the day, the caw of the gulls, the stiff wind off the water, the sun burning hot by contrast.

She sensed no threat today. She felt awake and alive, and everything she saw touched her awareness as sensitively as he had touched her last night.

She really had to stop dwelling on that. It had been a moment, cut out of many more moments to come where things like that would never happen. She wouldn't think about it. She wouldn't hold him to a promise he might never keep.

Next time . . . she could make it happen, she thought, as she hunted up a seamstress from whom she could purchase a sewing kit, and then bought some bread and cheese for their breakfast. Did she want to make it happen?

The innkeeper had already provided morning tea and a pitcher of lukewarm water for washing, but little else, and he had brought both items to the room, which saved her the exertion of fitting her purchases around the pot and cups, and going back downstairs again for the wash water.

She set the tray on a table. "Are you awake?"

"Very," he said dryly, and she understood exactly what he meant. *Next time. He wasn't going to conveniently forget last night.*

"There's tea, and I have bread and cheese."

He swung his legs over the bed. "That will do. Can I wash?"

"Yes. On the other side of the bed, there's a stand with a pitcher of water."

She watched him as he groped his way across the room. He was no less powerful and desirable for his blindness. Perhaps he was more so, because he was vulnerable.

But a man like Con Pengellis would hate that. He would trade on his strength and his intelligence. He was a man who had conquered a universe and made a legend real. And he had possessed *her* last night. He had taken her need and her lust and made it his own. He had given her pleasure and worshipped her like a queen.

Who wouldn't dream of a next time with one such as he? Her heart constricted just thinking about it, and she wheeled away from him to pour the tea. Useless thinking like this. He had probably come to his senses, and she was still out of hers.

"There's tea."

He inhaled deeply and moved toward the scent, letting her guide him to a chair beside the table.

"Do you take sugar?"

He shook his head and she placed the cup in his hands. *His hands. That hand, an instrument of pleasure.* He sipped, and she watched his lips jealously. *Those lips, savoring her sex or liquid heat with equal pleasure. Either. Both. Next time.*

Her breath caught, and she poured herself a cup and went to sit on the bed. She couldn't think of a thing to say.

"The ship sails tomorrow?" he said finally.

She swallowed hard, and wrenched her mind away from the image of his hands caressing her. "At the tide. The booking is made. The papers are in order. The bracelet bought us time and money."

He listened to the nuances of her voice. For the first time since they'd begun this journey, she wasn't thinking about Lavinia, Roger or the diamond.

Just what he'd wanted. Just what he'd hoped. She was

thinking about him, and the explosive demands of her body.

Even he wasn't immune to them. He'd been isolated and removed for so long. He had thought he was dead, dry, dust; he had suppressed every urge and all emotions, pushed every thought of a man's desire as deep into the pit as he was.

But a man never forgot. A man never lost the capacity to rise to the occasion. His ferocious lust to possess her shocked him. And this morning: he wanted her. He hadn't nearly had enough of her. He wanted to explore that passion and that driving need with which he sent her plummeting over the edge. He wanted her to erupt like that always and ever only for him.

And he was staggered by how deep and hard the feeling went.

This was something he hadn't planned. Something he needed to think about. He folded his hands around the hot cup and lifted it to his lips to sip.

One didn't sip a woman's body . . .

Jesus . . . he slammed the cup down on the table. "There's bread and cheese?"

She bit her lip. *That was a violent reaction. What was he thinking? What was he sorry he had done?* "Right by your elbow."

He ripped off a piece of bread like it was the neck of his worst enemy and bit into it aggressively.

"All right," he said finally, after he'd demolished the bread and several chunks of cheese, "so—we sail tomorrow. And what did you plan in the meantime?"

"I didn't." *Uh-oh. Better clarify that.* "I thought it would take longer to arrange things," she amplified.

"I see." Did he? *He saw her naked body writhing in his hands. Next time. Now? Never? He had to decide. But he had promised—those very words—next time.* "So all we have to do is . . . ?"

"Pack," she said, distracted by the movement of his lips. "Remember."

The air thickened. "Remember what, Darcie?"

"You . . ." she started and couldn't quite get out the rest of the sentence. Not when he was looking at her as if he could see her, and as if he wanted her again.

"*I* remember," he said softly, and the decision was made, had been made since the moment he discovered she loved the demon adventurer whose portrait launched a thousand dreams.

He shook himself. One dream. Darcie's dream.

The distance between her sex and a legendary diamond didn't seem so remote now. He could almost taste the secret yearning in her, so excellent to use to his own advantage.

And what about all his secret appetites, dredged up from the grave?

"It was a mistake," she whispered, her heart pounding. *He remembered. This could be—next time. And more . . . And an even bigger mistake.*

She didn't care. She wanted him to counter her hesitation, to give her a reason to willingly give herself to him.

What about your swollen lips, your aching breast, your own dreams and desires? She could subordinate them, she could.

No, she couldn't.

She felt the sweet ache between her legs that had nothing to do with reason or respect.

"Let's see if it was," he said softly, and her whole body twinged at the note in his voice. "Take off your clothes, Darcie."

Her breath caught. He wouldn't see a thing. He would go crazy imagining it, and she wanted that. She wanted him hot and melting at her feet, where there was no mercy for a man who could make her feel like that.

"Darcie . . . ?" There was a catch in his voice.

Next time . . . "Come and get me," she breathed, and backed against the bed.

He came toward her as surely as if he could see her, and she didn't know how. How he knew, how he reached out and unerringly found the torn flap of her dress, and then just ripped it from her trembling body.

"Now, Darcie."

She wished it were dark. Even knowing he could see nothing, she wished it were dark and that she were more perfect, that it was a love more perfect—but in absence of all of that, she would willingly take this much from him, and maybe even more.

She peeled off her underclothes, unhooked the unwieldy corset, tossed off her shoes, wriggled out of her underslip and stockings, and finally her drawers. God, how long it took to get ready to sin. A man could lose all his heat in the time it took a woman to divest herself of the props of civilization.

But once they were gone, she felt as primitive as Eve. "Con . . . ?" she murmured, and she knew he heard the excitement in her voice.

"Come."

She walked into his arms and lifted her mouth to his and surrendered to the darkness.

And in the darkness, there was light: he nestled himself against her hips, so she could feel his length, his pride, his power. He lifted her against him, and she wrapped her legs around him and ground her hips against his driving erection.

Oh God—she wanted him. All of him buried to the hilt deep within her. All that heat and power contained in her . . .

She pulled her mouth from his mesmerizing kiss. "Do

it now," she whispered, wriggling her derrière against his questing hands and his thrusting member.

"Soon." A breath against her swollen lips, and then he claimed them again, while his hands stroked her and probed her from behind.

Her body jolted against him as his fingers slipped into her slick wet folds and deep into her very core.

"How many fingers?" he murmured against her lips.

It didn't matter; they felt hard and thick and full sheathed in the heat and velvet of her, and she didn't want him to move, ever.

"Three? Four?" She licked his lips, seeking his tongue. "I love what you're doing. I love what you did yesterday."

"I know." He moved to the bed and sat, still holding her wrapped around him. "Don't move. I want to feel you just like this."

"I want you inside me."

"Not yet. Do you feel my fingers?"

She drew in a deep breath as he stroked her. "Yessss." She made a sound as he probed deeper. "Oh God— Con . . ."

"I know you like that. I'm going to find out everything you like and I'm going to give it to you, Darcie."

She squirmed against his fingers. "I want you to." A groan. A wave of sensation as he pumped his fingers between her legs.

"You love a man there."

"He's not there yet," she whispered pointedly, grinding down on his fingers.

"Oh, he's there. Give me your tongue, Darcie. We're not nearly done yet."

She arched against him and gave him her tongue. Gave over her naked body to his expert fingers as they stroked and felt between her legs, prodding her, priming her, teasing her. He never touched her nipples. His free hand explored her buttocks, and found the hidden place at the small of her back that turned her into a wild woman.

"Oh God, Con—I'm so wet—"

"Good. I want you wet and hot, Darcie, and only for me."

"Ohhh . . ." she sighed from deep in a haze of swamping pleasure. Those incredible fingers . . . she rode them like a stallion, whipped into a frenzy by his words, his caresses, his desire.

She felt every spurt of his penis. It was like an untamed animal waiting to break free. She wanted to mount it high and hard and deep inside her and keep it there forever.

But she was losing it, to him. His fingers worked inside her, pulling her inexorably toward the edge.

"Con . . . !" she cried in anger.

"Come to me, Darcie, come . . ."

"I can't . . ."

"You don't have to . . . come—"

"Con . . ." She was trying to hold it back.

"I want you. I want you to come—" His voice was so soft, his fingers were so hard, so coaxing; they wanted her fire. They wanted *her* draining her juices into his hand.

And she came, climaxing on a long soft sigh into the light. Into glitter and gold. Into a spiking pleasure that attacked her very vitals and drained slowly slowly slowly from between her legs. Just like that. Just there.

Into silence as he held her tightly against him.

He had seen everything.

"Shhhh . . ." he laid her reverently down on the bed and curved his body around her. "Shhhh . . ."

And then she slept.

* * *

And now he knew her. He knew her luscious mouth, and her responsive nipples, the special place at the small of her back. And in the heat of her woman's flesh, her gorgeous wanton sweet spot.

He lay with his fingers gently inserted, just there. She spread her legs slightly to ease his way, and from time to time in her rest, she wriggled erotically against him to let him know she was awake and aware.

There was something so voluptuous about lying with her like this. He had forgotten those small delectable pleasures. His every nerve ending pulsated with the need to possess her. His penis was as stiff and heavy as stone; he wanted to penetrate her, embed himself in her, and drive them both to completion.

But the waiting . . . the waiting heightened the intensity of his need, he liked that. He was accustomed to waiting; there was something very potent about it, when the imagination conjured up pleasures and delights for the taking. And he liked having her waiting, naked, and yearning, naked, just for him.

He felt her restive movements beside him.

"Con . . ." There was a slight thread of supplication in her tone.

"Tell me what you want, Darcie."

"Where do I start?" she murmured, wriggling urgently against his fingers.

He pushed deeper. "I need to hear one thing you want."

"Don't make me beg."

"Tell me, Darcie."

She shimmied desperately on his fingers. "Con . . . you know—"

He pushed again, to give her a taste of the pleasure to come.

"Say it, Darcie. How else can I know?"

She grit her teeth. "I want you—you *know* I want you between my legs . . . oh! Don't . . . don't take away your fingers . . . you beast—that's what you wanted to hear . . ."

He loomed over her. "I needed to know you crave *my* penis."

She stretched out her hands and grasped him. Oh dear God—he had forgotten this too—what it was like to have a woman take him purposefully with both hands, surrounding him, feeling him, pumping him, lavishing him with caresses and murmurs until he was out of his mind with rocketing need.

"Oh God, Darcie . . ."

"No, *no*—I have you now, and I'm not giving you up. You're mine now, do you hear me? And you'd better not move."

He couldn't move; he was braced on his hands and knees over her slender body, poised to penetrate and sink himself into hot velvet. And instead, instead, she had brought him to worship before her, with her pure erotic possession of his throbbing member.

She caressed it, she felt its length and thickness; she played with it, sliding her fingers all over it, tapping the lush slick underside of it, and then finger walking back down to the base of it to entangle her fingers in the crisp hair, and finally to cup the taut scrotum below.

And then the attention she gave his scrotum—sliding her palm under it, stroking it, stroking him deep between his legs and almost to his crease . . . his knees went weak. His arms trembled. He tried to kiss her and she wouldn't let him. She wanted to watch his face as she caressed and pumped every long inch of him until he was ready to explode.

And then she began feeling around the very tip and sensitive crown.

"Darcie . . ."

"I'm going to bring you down, Con . . ."

"Darcie . . ." he managed before she began the steady rhythm just at the crown, on and on and on, her relentless hand taking him as no woman had ever taken him before.

She licked her lips as he began thrusting in concert with the movement of her hand. She held his scrotum with her one hand as she pumped and pulled with the other. She brought him close to her mouth and licked and sucked at the turgid tip of him, and when he reared back for that one last roaring thrust into her circling fingers, she caught some of the cream of his desire on her breasts and tongue.

And he was gone—spewing himself all over her body in concert with her ecstatic moans.

And when it was over, he collapsed on top of her and she held him lightly, tightly, possessively as if they had always been lovers, and she would never let him go.

"Con?" It was dark now; they had slept, but he wouldn't know the dark from the daylight.

"Ummm."

The dark was better, she thought, sliding her hand down to cup his quiescent penis. It immediately leaped to attention. She liked that, she liked how things were more explosive in the dark and how she was hungry for him all over again.

"Are you awake?"

He grunted.

She rubbed him with both hands, moving them lightly in opposite directions.

"Ah, Darcie . . ."

"Are you hungry?"

"I am now."

Her body twinged. *Next time. As many next times as she could desire. Anything she wanted, borne of his celibacy and need. As many times as she wanted, as many ways as they could invent.*

"Do you want me?"

"Don't be coy, Darcie."

"I'm naked for you, Con. What are you waiting for?"

"I like the waiting. It makes everything deeper, more powerful."

She loved this game. She loved him talking rough in counterpoint to her caressing his potent manhood, and she reveled the power of her touch when he couldn't suppress a groan.

"I think you want me," she murmured, her fingers squeezing and working up and down his quivering length.

"Spread your legs then."

"Do you want me?" She twisted the palm of her hand around his shaft.

"You know what I want, Darcie. You want it too, so spread your legs."

"How much do you want it?" she asked coquettishly, her hands still working her erotic magic on him.

"I've had all I can take of your silly game. I don't want to talk, I want to cram myself into you . . ." he wrenched himself out of her grasping hands . . . *"now . . ."* and he pushed her legs apart and rammed himself into her, deep, oh so hot and deep and just when she thought he was totally embedded within her, he drove himself deeper still.

"Oh God . . ." Who said it . . . one or both . . . the raw nakedness of him penetrating her so deeply, so immeasurably, so darkly; he almost rocketed out of control.

"Darcie . . ."

She whispered against his mouth, "Take me *now* . . ."

"I don't want to move."

"Do it—"

He'd never had a woman like this, who shimmied and writhed and spread her legs and pushed down demandingly on him and commanded him to give her everything he had.

"I'm never going to let you get dressed again," he growled in her ear. "I want you naked so I can take you whenever I want."

"Do it, Con . . ."

He shoved himself deeper. "I can't wait for it now . . ." and he pulled himself back, so long and strong and thick that his withdrawal made her feel bereft. And then he rocked back into her with deep, hot thrusts, one, two, three, withdraw, thrust, a rhythm that made her whimper with need. He was too far away too far; she reached for him desperately when he removed himself. She needed him deep inside her. She needed to feel him, to squeeze him, to know he was hers.

Short, stiff thrusts, suddenly, hard against the flaring center of her heat. No kisses. No caresses. Just his potent power lunging and plunging and driving her home.

He felt her body seize up and her resistance to it. "Come for me *now*, Darcie—"

"No. I want you to work for it."

"Do you?" He could go on forever, a machine, pumping and thrusting into the encompassing heat of her. He was hot for her, out of his mind for her. *She* was the light in the darkness and he drove into her wildly to appease her, to pleasure her, to bind them even tighter so that she would stay.

"*Now*, Darcie . . ."

She made a sound at the back of her throat, almost a whimper. She didn't want it to end, but they both wanted it too badly; five thrusts later, she careened out of control, sliding down the shaft of his power, and riding him to oblivion, triumphant at last when he followed her into the darkness and satiety.

Seven

They lay side by side, exhausted. She thought at one point she slept because there was a short spate of time in which she was not thinking about him, and his sex, and their explosive coupling. And then she was awake suddenly, stretching her body luxuriously to just touch his, to experience what feeling his bare skin did to her.

There was something so illicit and delicious about knowing he was there, naked and hard, and waiting for her.

"Are you awake?"

"I'm here."

Did she dare . . . ? "How *here*?" she whispered, her voice trembling just a little.

"As *here* as you want me to be," and there was no doubt what he meant. She reached out her hand to grasp him and he groaned and rolled toward her.

His heat enveloped her as she welcomed his weight and parted her thighs. His mouth settled on hers, feeding off the intensity of the desire that had aroused them both quick as a flame. He slipped inside her, thick as a cloud, and they moved in unison to her rhythm.

He was the man in the desert who had found an oasis, and he didn't want to find out if it were an illusion. All he knew, all he could feel was *her*—soft and slick and enfolding a starving man as deeply as his aching soul. Slowly and softly, she moved with him, coaxed him, adored him. His sweet discharge, when it came, spiralled them endlessly outward toward oblivion, and then she held him tightly while they slept.

When she awakened again, it was still dark. She reached out to touch him and he wasn't there. She panicked, scrambling over the side of the bed and reaching for the lamp on the night table.

"Con . . . ?"

"I'm here." His voice, strangely disembodied, from the other side of the room.

"What are you doing?"

"Thinking about you."

She liked that. She sat back on the bed and considered his words. "Tell me what you're thinking."

He wanted her again. He was rigid and rampant with it and he didn't understand a need so consuming it kept him awake and hot and throbbing for almost a day and a night. If he took her now, he would want her again in an hour. He didn't like feeling that out of control after so many years of denial. But—her craving for his sex was every bit as strong as his desire for her.

He had accomplished what he had set out to do—he had enslaved her, only he had ensnared himself in the process. But at the moment, it didn't seem to matter. There was something about the dark and her untamed response, and the sense that he could say what he wanted, he could do what he wanted—in the dark—and somehow it would all be absolved.

"I can't get enough of you," he growled.

She loved that. "Tell me how much."

"I want you now."

She swallowed. His words made her breathless, made her body quicken with desire. She loved the idea of coming to him in the dark; in the dark, they were equals. In the dark, they were the same.

This was time out of reality. It didn't count when it was in the dark and filled with such devouring pleasure. They didn't have to acknowledge the things that they did in the dark. And she could hold those memories in her heart forever.

She felt her way across the room to where he was sprawled in the chair, and she knelt between his legs and placed her hands on his knees. She loved this, feeling for him in the dark, where every sense was heightened by the scent of their sex, the knowledge of everything they had done before, and the drive of their mutual desire.

She rubbed her face against his penis, loving its texture, its length, its rigidity, its power. And then she buried her lips at its base, in his hair, her mouth taking him at the root in a ferocious love bite.

"Get up here."

"I like it better down here." She nipped him again, a little further up his shaft. And then another and another, until she encircled him at the ridge and pulled on him in a long wet sucking kiss.

His body jolted against her rapacious mouth. "Je-esus . . ." he groaned. He felt himself spinning, pushing himself into her mouth, and he didn't want to let go, not now, not there. Not yet. *"Darcie . . . !"* he reached forward and grasped her arms.

"I'm hungry," she protested.

"Me, too. Get up here." He pulled her onto his lap and she straddled his legs, spreading her thighs and settling herself precisely on his rigid length with appreciative little murmurs of delight. "I like this; I like sitting on you like this."

He cupped her breasts. "I like it too."

She arched her back inviting a caress.

"You're very hot, Darcie."

"It's because I'm pressed down on you. Make me wet," she begged, bracing her hands against his shoulder and pushing her breasts closer to his mouth.

He pushed her breasts closer together, and then he brushed her nipples with his lips, first one, then the other, back and forth equally, one and the other, in a lush erotic rhythm that made her writhe and moan.

She ground her body down tightly against his hard length as he started kissing her nipples, one and the other with deep wet sucking kisses, over and over, licking, pulling, sucking until she almost couldn't stand it. And then, without breaking the rhythm, he began concentrating on each hard pointed tip, swirling his tongue, cushioning, pulling, squeezing with his lips, pulling, pulling, pulling, one and the other.

She arched up against his mouth in an erotic haze, begging for more, bracing herself against his knees, and feeling for his length, so she could stroke him there in concert with his relentless sucking.

The minute she touched him, he was ready to blow. Her nipple was tight and taut in his mouth, wet and hard from his sucking; he felt her fingers rubbing him, caressing him, feeling him. He pulled harder just at the sex-engorged tip in a dark ferocious sucking kiss.

"Ahhhhhhhhh . . ." She threw her head back and bore down on his manhood as her climax broke and streamed all through her body, a river of hot silver skeining down down down and exploding between her legs.

And then she melted against him, pressing her aching breasts against his chest.

He took her mouth in a soft soft kiss, waiting, waiting, until she was ready, waiting even though he was stoked to the bursting point. Waiting, with every one of his senses screaming for release.

"Let me come inside you."

"Please . . ." she whispered, rubbing her lips against his mouth.

She shifted to her feet, and then she slowly climbed back onto him; he held her hips, guiding her as she grasped his penis and positioned it at the point of penetration, and then she just sank onto his jutting length with a muffled groan.

His hands moved upward as she bore down; he covered her breasts, he cupped them, he caressed her nipples as she set the primitive rhythm, her whole body centered on her two most pleasure points: her tight taut nipples and the precious flesh between her legs.

There was just nowhere else for a woman. He fingered her nipples and let her move, and she thought she would just explode. But he came first, erupting into her with one volcanic thrust that lifted her from her erotic seat as spasms racked his body and finally made him complete.

His dreams were suffused with visions of sex and surrender, but the thing that held him captive were the memories surfacing from someplace down below, from beyond all conscious remembrance.

He couldn't quite grasp what he wanted to know. It was all tangled up with tunnels and pits and diamonds and trains and the Con Pengellis he used to be. The darkness mattered. Sometimes he thought he could see more clearly in the darkness. And sometimes he felt like he had to fight it like a demon, and blast his way up and out.

He remembered the diamond, remembered touching, lifting it, feeling the weight of it in his hands.

. . . leaving it . . .

Where?

No—it was the slender weight of Darcie he lifted in his hands . . . and then he was falling, top over tail, through the tunnel, down the pit, into the darkness, his eyes focused on the brilliant light beyond . . .

. . . wait . . .

He had waited. Patiently he had waited. Wait. A train. A tunnel. He was running. Wait. He knew what Con Pengellis knew. And The Eye of God was following him . . . The Eye of God saw everything and cast out a sinner . . . wait—

. . . the single largest octahedron ever found . . .

. . . balancing fate—

Darcie was fate.

And he would remember because he felt the hunger of the hunt all over again. The hunt for sex. The hunt for riches. And he would find his way to the tunnel before somebody else did.

And now he had Darcie to help him.

She never wanted morning to come. She wanted to curl up in that seductive fog and warm herself against his heated skin forever.

Instead, she was up and about before him, packing what few clothes they had, and seeing to breakfast.

It felt strange, this morning, to be folding away the memories of this room, where no one and nothing could touch them, but dreams couldn't last forever. They would never be as safe again, she thought. And she would never be as free.

Risks—they both had taken risks, and now it was time to go beyond the walls. And they couldn't turn back, he wouldn't turn back now, and let someone else claim it all.

She had gotten him a shabby old suit to wear, in the guise of her elderly patient. But she wondered, as she laid it out at the foot of the bed, how she thought she could contain his intense masculinity with any kind of disguise.

Well, he would find it, and know what to do with it. She needed to take the pitcher downstairs to bring back some hot water.

"I trust my wheelchair is safe," she said to the innkeeper.

"Yes, mum. We was hoping the mister would recover some, as you said."

"He can sit up, and he seems well enough to travel. I'll pay the bill now and then I'll need some help bringing him downstairs." She hadn't told Con that part, but her senses were so disordered, she felt she needed to take every precaution. The charade had to begin, now.

"Ring the bell, mum, and I'll come."

She entered the room to find him half dressed, and groping toward the table. "That's right, you're almost there. There's tea and pastries, and I've just brought up some hot water."

He sat down heavily in the chair. "You sound disgustingly chipper this morning."

She pushed every other consideration aside, like his warm bare chest, and her rising desire. That was over now. It *was*. "We *have* to go."

"I'd rather stay here." Even he was feeling it, the reluctance and the need.

"We're going. There's a suit at the foot of the bed. And after you've eaten and washed, I'm going to powder your hair."

"Jesus." She really meant it, he thought; she was going to make him into an invalid. But he was already feeling like one now that the magic of darkness was gone.

"Everything else is packed and I've paid the bill," she said briskly. "I've asked the innkeeper to come help me take you downstairs, by the way."

He put down his cup hard. "Why is that, Miss Darcie?" he asked, his tone just a little dangerous.

"The play starts here, Con. I can't take the chance no one is watching us. I haven't been out and about in two days. I don't know what's going on out there. So we have to start play-acting now."

She knew he wasn't going to like that. She felt his skepticism clear across the room. But it didn't matter. She'd put the whole thing together in her mind the first day and she wasn't going to deviate from it.

"The story is, you've been recuperating for the past couple days from an attack of some kind, and now you're better and ready to travel. We have . . . oh, maybe two hours, and we'll need at least an hour to get you dressed and down those steps. And don't glower. It has nothing to do with anything else."

"It has to do with a fool's quest, and your stupid determination to find this damned diamond, that I still goddamned can't remember where or if I even found it."

"But you will," she said confidently, ignoring his frustration and his outburst. "You know what's at stake, and I know you will."

It was over, so abruptly he couldn't quite comprehend it. But it was nothing he hadn't expected, he thought. Darcie was eminently practical. She had spent the money for tickets to France, they were going to France, no matter what magic they had created in that room.

He couldn't afford to fall for her. Above all else, she wanted her share of the diamond. In one corner of that sensible mind, she had never forgotten the endgame. Nor would she ever let him forget he owed her his life.

And now he had made sure he had bound her to him like a wife. And he couldn't ever forget that had been his plan.

She eyed him like an artist surveying a masterpiece. "You wouldn't want to see yourself, Con. You look— fifty." She jammed the slouchy hat down on his head. "Perfect."

"I feel fifty," he grumbled.

"It's time to go." She jerked the bellpull. "I think I have everything. We have two suitcases, one each, and I tried to estimate what size clothes for you. I think I did all right. I didn't want to take too much, in case we had to move fast."

"Darcie—no one is after the diamond."

"You can't know that."

"And Lavinia has probably given up looking for you."

"I doubt it," she said, and she felt a rush of heat. Oh dear God, in all that happened, she had forgotten about the baby; how could she have forgotten about the baby. "I told you, she wants Roger's baby."

He felt like he'd been kicked in the gut. *The baby. The baby had utterly slipped his mind. She was carrying a child in that beautiful flat belly. How far along was she?*

There was a knock at the door so he couldn't pursue that thought; she opened it to admit the innkeeper.

"If you'd just let him lean against you, and I'll take our bags—I think we'll be fine."

He felt himself being heaved up roughly against a tall

male body. He felt Darcie lifting his arm on the other side, and he let it drape around her neck.

"That's good," she said brightly, wrapping her left arm around his waist and pinching his side. "That'll be fine. Just down a flight of steps, darling, and you won't have to walk again."

"Mmmph," he grunted, as they shuffled into the hallway.

"He's deeply appreciative," Darcie said, as they carefully descended the stairs.

"Grrmph," he growled when they reached bottom.

"And he couldn't have done it without you," she added, as they settled him in the rickety wicker wheelchair she'd bought on the cheap, and she dumped the suitcases in his lap.

She flashed a smile at the innkeeper as she slipped him a couple of pence. "Thank you so much."

"Good luck, mum."

"We'll need it," Con muttered.

"You never can tell," she whispered hotly. "Come on now, hunch your shoulders. Look *old.*"

She wheeled him into the sunshine, swerving around objects with the skill of a lorry driver. He felt the sun in a burst of light against his eyes. He heard the raucous noise of an afternoon in a coastal town: mongers and drays, and gulls and dogs, and voices and horns, all meshing together in one indelible picture in his mind.

And Darcie, determinedly wheeling him toward the dock.

"How many days to Le Havre?" he asked, his voice muffled because he had crushed his chin against his chest.

"Two days," she said, jerking the chair around sharply to avoid a cat, before her step faltered. She hadn't thought about that.

Two days. Even out in the bright fresh air, the words sat between them, a bridge between pleasure and promise. *Two days.*

But no—she wouldn't let it happen; that part was over. They had things to do now, and memories to resurrect. By the time they stepped foot in Le Havre, she had to know where their course would take them.

She wheeled the chair around purposefully, and bumped it up onto the gangplank, and pulled it up the slanted walkway from behind.

"Jesus, Darcie."

"Shhhh," she whispered fiercely. "Be quiet. You don't *know.*"

What didn't he know? he thought, and he almost fell out of the chair as with another clump and bump, she pulled the wheelchair onto the solid foredeck of the steamer *Rossignol.*

"We're here."

"I can tell." The sea-scent was more pungent here, the cry of gulls, the sound of voices as the crew shouted orders back and forth in preparation to sail.

"We just have to go through checks and ticketing. Act *old.*" There was an odd note in her voice.

"There's something wrong."

"No. Everything is fine," she said. But she wasn't sure. She didn't feel any aura of evil. There was no palpable sense of danger. But something wasn't right, and she couldn't quite put her finger on what.

Better to say nothing. Better to just get him to the cabin so they could settle in.

She felt all of her senses start to tingle. She would allow nothing to distract her now: the real journey had just begun.

* * *

The cabin was small, dishearteningly small, with two berths one over the other, and the top one folding up against the wall so the lower could be used for seating.

Darcie was appalled at the cramped space. Admittedly, she had bought a single cabin, but still—a pullman car on a train was roomier than this. Well, it was too late now, and there were at least a hundred other passengers, which meant there probably would not be any other space available.

They would make do. She was good at making do.

She asked one of the mates to help them down the narrow stairs to the lower deck over Con's furious protest.

"Shhh . . . you're infirm, remember?"

Oh, he was infirm all right, but it had nothing to do with age. He felt like throttling her. He didn't like this plan. He didn't like the mate settling him into the bunk like a baby while Darcie cooed instructions on the side.

He was amazed he had the patience to wait until they were alone in the cabin before he exploded. "What the hell was that all about?"

"That was about appearances," she said loftily, pulling a blanket over him against his struggles to sit up. "I'm going to leave you for a while. All you have to do is remember you're an invalid, and stay put. I have to arrange to have food delivered to the cabin. And you need to stop fighting me and—*think.*"

"Damn it to hell, Darcie—I . . ."

"Con, there isn't anything else you can do right now."

"I can think of one thing."

She patted the blanket. "We don't have time for that now."

Just as he'd thought. Practical, sensible Darcie. Put it all in a compartment and store it neatly away.

He heard the door close softly, and he kicked off the

blanket. *Goddamn darkness. Goddamn everything a stupid black blank . . . God, he hated it, he* hated *it . . . there weren't words for what he felt, how helpless he felt, how crazy he felt depending on a mercenary adventuress who turned her desires on and off like a faucet.*

He swung his legs over the edge of the bunk. A man needed to scout things out his surroundings. He'd been pinioned between Darcie and one of the deck hands, so he'd gotten no sense of where he was, and he knew how dangerous that was. He'd been careless once and—

What . . . ?

. . . careless—once . . . ?

—And what? What? What couldn't he remember?

He got up and began groping around the cabin. The berths were on the wall opposite the door. There were built-in drawers on either side and two doors, one of them leading to a minuscule water closet. There was a fold-down table, and two chairs tucked under the lower bunk. Neat for sleep and very little else, he thought, feeling his way back to the bunk. A tribute to Darcie's thrift. Nothing more or less than they needed for the short trip across the Channel.

. . . short trip . . .

That struck a chord somewhere.

He eased himself back against the wall. *Where had he been when they'd gotten to him?* His eyes narrowed. *Not with the diamond.* He closed his eyes. *He remembered that. Not with the diamond. So they'd been after him then. Roger would not have left it alone, just as he recalled. His memory had not failed him: Roger would have wanted it too, a coup for the company. An expansion into other realms. All of that was clear to him now. All the arguments, the anger, the recriminations. What he didn't remember definitively was what came after. That was just a grab bag of odd jagged pieces, a jigsaw puzzle in his mind.*

Think . . . As if he could wave a magic wand and conjure it all up. But the lulling movement of the ship reminded him of something.

A short trip. Precautions not taken.

. . . *careless once* . . .

He had known there was danger. He would work backward—or forward—from that.

She stood topside at the deck railing, watching the commotion on the dock, and being jostled by late boarding passengers and deckhands wheeling their luggage alongside.

They were a half hour away from sailing into calm waters against a cloudless blue sky. Overhead, gulls screeched and dove for food. She watched as one wheeled and swooped down low over the dock and toward the boat, toward her, she thought in shock as she moved to dodge it. But then at the last minute it veered nose-down into the water.

She could have sworn the thing was coming after her. But that was ridiculous, she chided herself. It was all of a piece with her feeling of disquiet. Everything would seem threatening underscored by that.

She did trust her feelings. She and her father hadn't gotten where they were by following the rules. There were no rules. The last two days had proven that.

But even though she'd given in to her feelings, she had learned long ago never to have regrets. Never to be afraid to be wrong. There was always another love. Always another strike.

Always someplace else to go.

Well, Le Havre was the first place they would go. And from there she would study how to get them to India.

And somewhere between those two points, Con would remember all about the location of the diamond.

It was too late to back out, she thought. The die had been cast with Roger's death.

But the thing was to remember the details. Lavinia. The baby. The legends. The lore.

The game.

The game—the undefinable game against an opponent who wasn't there. And rules that didn't exist.

She stayed at the rail until the lines were cast and the ship moved out of the harbor and she could see the gulls no more.

Eight

She had arranged for tea, and breakfast and dinner, to be brought to the cabin. So she was expecting the knock at the door shortly after she returned to the cabin, and she opened it without cautioning Con to pull up the blanket.

The deckhand who had helped them when they boarded was at the door, the tea tray in his hands. She took it from him, mesmerized for a moment by the burning look in his eyes. But he wasn't looking at her; he looked beyond her, at Con sitting on the bunk with every evidence of physical vigor.

She grabbed the tray and slammed the door in his face, and she turned to face Con, her eyes wide. "He was looking at you."

"So what? He was just one of the sailors—didn't I recognize his voice?"

"He was the one who brought us down here." She folded down the table and set the tray on it, and then pulled out the chairs and set them up. "Come." She held out her hand. "I didn't like the way he was looking at you."

He fumbled his way across the room. "What could he have seen? I was sitting on the bed."

"You don't look old." She guided him to one of the

chairs, and took the other opposite. "You don't look *slouchy.*" She poured him a cup and put it into his hands.

"I hate this."

"Well, we all know that, but we're committed now."

"You know, I don't feel quite the same urgency you do."

"And I'm feeling it more."

"You don't think, if Lavinia were after you, that you would have seen some evidence of it by now?"

She shook her head. "She's very subtle. She and Roger managed to get to you, right?"

"I can't remember that."

"What do you remember? You remember the diamond." She was as certain of that as her life.

He nodded. "And all the arguments before I even set out on the expedition to find it. They wanted it for the company. They wanted this great big huge diamond that they didn't even know if it existed, and they wanted to cut into it and turn it into a fortune in crown silver. I left the company because of it, probably the only noble thing I've ever done, and all in service of this *grand guignol* gesture which was pure selfishness. *I* was going to find the thing, and be the mythic hero."

"And you found it."

"I found it. But I don't know where, and I don't know how, and all I next remember is being in a deep dark pit for an endless amount of time. And nothing after that until I woke up in the brothel."

She sipped her tea thoughtfully. All that was encouraging, she thought. "You touched it."

"Yes."

Very encouraging. "You held it."

"Yes."

"You didn't remove it."

"No."

"Why?"

Why? Maybe he hadn't been asking himself the right questions. Why?

He gave it a long moment's consideration. "I don't know."

"Think—maybe you knew they were after you."

Maybe . . . had he known? He must have known . . .

She saw his confusion. "Roger and Lavinia told everyone you'd died in India in search of the diamond. Long before I married Roger. It had been announced in the papers. They had a memorial service for you at St. James. They even put up a tombstone on the grounds of Goole."

"Was my funeral well attended?" he asked sarcastically.

"I wasn't there—more's the pity. I thought you were dead. This was the deepest buried secret, Con. No one knew."

"They knew," he said darkly, "—and you found out. I remember what you said. You found out. But you never said how."

"You escaped."

He slammed down the cup. "Jesus, Darcie—that's the most important point. I *escaped . . . ?*"

"You don't remember?"

"I keep goddamned telling you . . ."

"All right, I believe you. This is what happened: A messenger had come during dinner—something urgent. Roger was absolutely panicked. I heard them say they would talk later, in the library, after I'd gone upstairs, and I was desperate to know what had happened. I hid behind the curtains . . .

. . . the curtains that were redolent with the scent of spices . . .

". . . and I heard the whole thing, that they thought

they'd had you contained, they thought that the latest torture had weakened you to the point that you might be ready to tell. They wanted the diamond, they wanted it over, and they wanted you dead. And somehow you got away. Does any of this sound familiar?"

He shook his head. "You're chasing after ghosts."

"Lavinia knew I was there. How did she know? I understood what was at stake. I didn't move a muscle. I didn't breathe. I didn't make a sound. And still she knew I was there."

He tried to envision it. Lavinia, stalking around the library, in a rage because he had somehow escaped. Roger, placating, shaken, agitated. The two of them, plotting and scheming all to naught: they didn't know how he'd gotten away or where he was.

And then what? Darcie in the curtains. Lavinia dragging her out from behind, and pushing her in front of Roger.

Can't you control your wife?

Darcie said the words out loud even as they formed in his mind.

"And of course, I was so righteous about it. Roger looked about ready to kill me."

We can't let her run around loose, Lavinia would have said.

What are we going to do with her? Roger had asked. *How can we contain her? You know she'll tell the world.*

We'll—we'll lock her up, Lavinia decided. *In the tower. She always thought she was a fairy-tale princess, now we'll make her one. And then we've got to find Con. Do you understand, Roger? We* must *find Con.*

"And then what?" Con asked.

"They couldn't find you. She was living in dread fear you'd walk in the front door and accuse her of attempted murder, and she couldn't see any reason why they shouldn't kill me—that would be one more threat out of the way. But there was the baby. And then Roger died and I got away."

Yes, he remembered her telling him that. And now he remembered Roger. Greedy lustful Roger grasping for something to placate Lavinia that would draw him out in the open.

If I have to, I'll die for the company.

He remembered Darcie's stillness when he'd suggested it. He could just see Lavinia considering the possibilities.

That's an interesting idea, my boy. That's a very interesting idea. He might fall for that. He might come and reclaim everything, and then we'll have him.

They'd safely put Darcie away so they could concentrate on finding him. What better way than to lure him with everything he'd renounced.

"I think Roger's death was a ruse."

She didn't answer for a long few minutes. "You shocked me when you said that before. And I thought maybe you were right, that Lavinia and he could have pulled it off. But I was at the funeral. I saw him in the coffin . . ." her voice trailed off.

"Anybody could play a corpse in a coffin," he pointed out, defining the thing she didn't want to say.

"They buried him," she whispered.

"The coffin was closed . . ." He knew it even without her confirming it.

"Yes." She could still see it in her mind's eye: the gray day, the naked branches bending in the wind. The crowd. The coffin. The gaping hole. The prelate sonorously extolling Roger's life.

Herself, chained to Lavinia, playing the bereaved widow to the hilt. Lavinia who hadn't cried, who'd been as tight and controlled as an automaton, who must have been desperate to preserve the lie and still come away with the prize.

She shook her head. "I don't know now. Anything's possible."

He sent her a speculative look that was so direct, she was shaken by it. He saw too much, she thought. And he saw too clearly.

"It all sounds ridiculous, doesn't it?" she whispered.

. . . And then Roger died and I got away . . .

He rolled that detail over in his mind.

She got away.

It sounds ridiculous.

Anything's possible.

How much was real, how much was illusion?

Clever Darcie. She was Scheherazade, who could spin a thousand tales over a thousand nights and one night.

She was Helen who launched a journey of a thousand miles on the strength of his quest for a legend.

She had the audaciousness of an adventuress, the guile of a gambler, and the confidence of a queen.

Who was Darcie Boulton, really?

And when did he stop playing the game?

"It sounds insane," he said bluntly.

"But if Roger's alive—?"

He didn't answer, and she got up and began pacing agitatedly. He heard her impatient footfall, the swirl of her skirt, her abrasive breathing.

"This is crazy," she said finally, explosively. "We don't know that Roger's still alive. We don't know anything except that you found the diamond and that somehow you were caught and imprisoned so that they could torture the location out of you. And we know that Lavinia said you'd died in India. We have to assume that's where they kept you isolated, and maybe even where the diamond is."

"I don't know that, Darcie. I still don't know that."

She ignored him. "That's why we're going there. It will help your memory, just like my taking you to Goole. You started to remember."

He didn't deny it. He had a lot of the pieces of the puzzle now: he'd been a strutting cock who'd tried to pull off the exploit of the ages. It hadn't been enough to own diamond mines in South Africa worth a million pounds. It hadn't been enough to be the head of Pengellis-Becarre, jewelers to kings, queens, and the wealthy of the world.

No, he'd wanted the intangibles—adventure, glory, notoriety. Risks and rewards. Slicing close to the edge, and sliding through. All of that. And more. The admiration. The envy. The women. The wealth.

It hadn't been some mystical quest. It had been greed, pure selfish greed, and an arrogant desire to annoy Roger and provoke his mother.

He'd been blind to how much was at stake. He never thought it was critical. And he'd been wrong. Dead wrong.

    . . . careless once—
Words to live by.
    . . . careless twice—
A man could die.

He had to exercise caution on every level. He knew nothing about Darcie Boulton other than what she told him, and for all he knew every word was a lie.

And now he was thinking like Darcie, he thought mordantly as he lay wide awake in his berth that night, and maybe it was better than being distracted by her.

It was too easy to slip into her body; she was so hot and too willing, a Circe at his beck and call, and if she climbed on top of him now, he would sink himself into her without a second thought.

"Con?" her voice was a whisper above him, shaping the wish into reality. "Are you awake?"

He hesitated a moment. "Yes." He heard the soft sound of her feet hitting the floor, and then he felt her hand on his arm as she knelt next to the bunk.

"I can't sleep." But she couldn't tell him why. It was the excitement of the hunt coupled with her heightened sense of him in this tiny cabin. He filled it. He heated it. He heated *her*. She wanted him, simply as that. "Con?"

"I don't think so, Darcie." The willpower it took to say that, when his body leaped to contradict him. She was a siren, tempting him in the dark.

"Then—just let *me* . . ." she whispered, fumbling with his clothes.

She had him at the point where he couldn't say no. He closed his eyes as her hand closed around him, enveloping him in pure pleasure in the dark.

She held him like a lover, her lips nuzzling him as she covered him with hot little kisses. Cloaked in kisses. Drowning in kisses and the heat of her mouth. Feeling both of her hands containing him, and her tongue slick and knowledgeable defining his length. Feeding off of her excitement as she pulled him into her mouth and begin rhythmically sucking on him.

There, there, there—his whole world was centered at the point of light surrounding her avid mouth. Right there. He could see it; he thrust into it, feeling its heat, its wet, its need. She pulled him toward the light, slowly, lusciously, inexorably, until it exploded behind his eyes and he soared into the incandescent light.

He fell back slowly, luxuriously, soft as a cloud, into the dark, into her hands, into the tight wet mystery of her femininity. And he was the core, the hot center, and she worshipped him. She adored him. And she erupted all around him in a shimmering spasm of radiant light.

And still it was dark. But he needed no other illumination to see her body. He took her with his hands, with his mouth, with every sense tuned to her lust and her longing.

The way he had defined her face, he delineated her body—the fragility, the strength, the long legs, the curve of her buttocks that fit so neatly in his hands. The texture of her skin. The contour of her breasts. The sweep of her belly that nurtured another life.

He lay his head against it, listening, trying to sense the quickening and the flutter of new life. He moved down her taut belly, swiping her navel with his tongue before he settled his relentless mouth between her legs.

The essence of her, the embodiment of Eve; he could take her with his mouth and create the chaos of fulfillment. On the tip of his tongue, he positioned her, poised for him to possess her.

She hovered above him, her hips grinding and writhing against him, seeking to envelop him in the perfume of her need. And suddenly she was sitting on the tip of a star, its center shining and golden, and without warning, she slipped and she plummeted into a backwash of sensation that furrowed through her body and down down down to break sumptuously at the precious point between her legs.

And then it was dark again, it always ended in the dark. It was better that way, he thought. Promises didn't exist in the dark. Time stood still, and threats receded, and the only thing that counted was the one forbidden moment of pure uncomplicated pleasure.

And the danger was, he thought warily, as he folded her against his chest, a man could get very very used to that. And it could be the very thing that Darcie was counting on.

They debarked at Le Havre the next day. It was late in the afternoon under an angry gray sky. The deck mate with the burning eyes came to help him maneuver the narrow interior stairs.

Darcie watched him with a vigilant eye as she followed behind with their suitcases. There was something about the man, even though he had been nothing but courteous and prompt during the trip. Still, the way he looked at Con worried her. He was too solicitous to a stranger, and he had the wheelchair, which had been stored above deck because it was too wide to go below, waiting as they emerged onto the foredeck.

"I'll wheel 'im off for you, mum," he offered, in that same respectful voice he had addressed her the last two days. "He is a heavy man, I can manage better and make sure all is right and tight. That is, if you want."

She took a surreptitious look around her. Passengers were streaming down the gangplank, deckhands with their luggage in tow. It seemed reasonable enough, she thought. It would cost a ha'penny, maybe two.

"I'd appreciate it," she said, bending down to Con who was once again hunched over his chest. "The deckhand is going to wheel you down. Do you think you could hold one of the suitcases?"

"I'm not dead yet, girl," he snapped in a crackly voice that made her smile. She placed his case on his lap and nodded to the deckhand, and he wheeled the chair into a queue of passengers advancing toward the gangplank.

"Have you got transportation, mum? Or a place to stay?"

She looked up at him sharply. He was staring straight ahead, minding the steps of the people in front of him, and keeping the footrest of the chair at a precise foot from the person in front of him.

It was an idle question, in aid of procuring another few pence for a recommendation. Nothing more. Nothing less.

"Thank you, yes."

"That's good," he said.

They shuffled forward another foot, surrounded by the hum of conversation, and the cry of screaming gulls swooping overhead.

The gray sky enfolded them as an unexpected wind blew up, whipping the waves.

They waited at the head of the gangplank for the next knot of passengers to pass below. The mate lifted the chair onto the walkway ahead of her and stopped. She wasn't watching, and she bumped into him, and that jarring movement seemed to make him relinquish his grip on the chair.

She watched in horror as the wheelchair pitched down the gangplank like a drunken sailor, gaining momentum and speed.

She screamed his name as it hit the dock and hurtled a hundred feet beyond.

He heard her in the throes of the nightmare where everything was pitch black, and nothing was real except the fearsome sensation of falling down down down into a pit.

He had to get out of there, even if he died. He wrenched sideways, felt himself suddenly flying through the air. He couldn't hang onto the suitcase—he couldn't hold onto his life. He was falling like wind-driven rain, his past spinning and spiralling before his sightless eyes.

He hit the dock with a sickening thud, his head glancing off a piling. For one fulminating moment, his vision cleared, and the light flooded in. He saw angels all around him. He saw Darcie and *him*.

Far above him on the deck, rooted there as if he were made of stone, the mate with the burning eyes, watching, watching, watching as Darcie flew down the gangplank to kneel by his side.

"Con . . ." she cried, and he looked into her beautiful tear-filled eyes.

The danger was real; the danger was *there*.

"I can see," he whispered, pulling his gaze from her to look toward the top of the gangplank.

He saw what he expected: the deckhand was gone.

And then his eyes clouded over and he could see no more.

Nine

He swam slowly up from the bottom of the pit, feeling as if he had been fighting wind and ice and fire and all the reigning evils in the world.

He opened his eyes to the darkness. "Darcie!"

"I'm here."

He felt the panic in spite of the calm tone of her voice, and he fought to come to the surface. "Where?"

"Shhh . . . this is the hospital of Dr. Rivard. He's been taking care of you."

"What happened?"

She hesitated. Even she didn't know, and what she felt and what she had seen were two vastly different things. "The deckhand . . . he let go of the chair. It fell. You fell. The doctor tells me there are no broken bones, and that the blow to your head caused minimal damage. He expects you will have a vicious headache at the worst. But he foresees no permanent damage."

"I saw you," he said suddenly, unable to comprehend anything she was saying because of the sharp pain behind his eyes. He waited, to see if it would materialize into a vision, the vision of Darcie.

But there was only the dark, the awful, deadly, god-forsaken dark.

Her eyes swelled with tears. He couldn't have seen

anything, but she wasn't about to point that out. "What did you see?"

"Black hair. Blue eyes. Tears. A gray sky. Heaven."

No—careless twice . . . he licked his dry lips. *That close to death he had come . . . down another pit, across another lifetime.*

The danger was real. The danger was there.

Darcie grasped his hand and he held it fast. "This is the doctor's infirmary. We'll be safe here."

"Will we?" he asked, his voice raspy.

"As anywhere. The mate—"

"I saw him."

"You dreamt it, Con. The doctor says you couldn't have."

"I saw him—I saw you."

"You need to rest."

"Will you stay?"

"There's nowhere else to go," she said gently. "The wheelchair went into the water. The one suitcase is wrecked. I salvaged what I could. Everything else is safe. And we'll be safe here for the moment."

"That sailor . . ."

"I don't know, Con. I don't know if he just let go or if it was an accident. How can anyone tell?"

"He was watching you, just the way you said he was looking at me when he came to the cabin."

"You could *not* have seen that."

"I saw it," he said adamantly, and she started to protest, and then decided it would be better not to agitate him.

"I just remember screaming and running down the gangplank," she said finally, reliving that horrific moment in her mind. "God, I couldn't believe it. But you're all right. We can go on."

"And everything's safe."

"I made sure of it. I tied pouches all over my underthings. And there are places I can convert what we have to francs."

He closed his eyes. No difference in the darkness. It felt heavy, weighting him down. He would pull her down if she had to carry him across two continents. "You know how long a trip it is."

"I know. And we'll go. As soon as you're able."

"Tomorrow," he murmured, rousing out of his lethargy one more time before allowing himself to float.

"Tomorrow," she agreed, squeezing his hand.

It took a week, time in which he battled the demons in his dreams. The sailor led them all, dancing tantalizingly just out of reach of his memory, and goading him to the edge of sanity.

The danger was there; the danger was real. All he had to do was get one step closer, and all the answers would be clear.

He lay in a fever those first couple of days, and Darcie feared for his life. But she felt safe in their sanctuary as she tended him through the night.

The infirmary was quiet as a church. The doctor moved among his patients like the most holy father, stopping to lay his hand across Con's hectic brow, and nodding reassuringly as if his touch could heal.

"He progresses," the doctor said.

He was a sweet little man, with the most serene of faces, who spoke fluent English and she felt the utmost confidence in him and she didn't know why.

"He is delirious," she contradicted. "He thought he could see."

The doctor smiled. "So many things we cannot know between earth and heaven, my dear. Maybe he did."

Maybe he did. He knew her eyes were blue. He thought he'd gone to heaven . . .

The doctor touched her shoulder. "Stay with him again tonight, my dear. Tomorrow he will be fine."

She sat by his side in the dark in the silence. She felt surrounded by the darkness, as she saw through his eyes. Imagining hurtling blindly, plummeting through space. Praying for your life and calling on every one of your senses to save your soul.

She didn't know how he had survived with so little bodily harm.

I can see . . .

Or maybe he was delusional. Maybe this one accident was a portent of the end.

Oh dear God—all for nothing? All to end in some blind alley?

There was a part of her that couldn't stand the thought. The gambler in her that would take every risk, walk every line. And without him, there was nothing. She needed his memories; he needed her eyes. The bargain was the bargain, and she couldn't let anything stop them now.

She'd carry him on her shoulders if she had to, she thought fiercely. She'd carry him to hell and beyond for a piece of that diamond.

And what about a life with him?

Which is more important to you, Darcie?

She bit her lip. *Conscience couldn't enter into it at this point. Did it have to be both or neither, with no middle ground?*

That wasn't even a question for consideration right now. She didn't know why she was thinking about it. Maybe it was because she was nestled beside him, enveloped by the dark. The dark did funny things to you; erotic things, forbidden things, and it made you think about things that were buried deep in your soul.

All those things in the dark . . . *his* dark.

And now she had made it hers.

She stayed by his side for the succeeding three days. Dr. Rivard moved a bed into the cubicle for her, and every day, he came by to check, to murmur, to approve.

"He progresses," was the only prognosis he would give her. "He will be fine."

How did he know? What did *he* see? She saw no appreciable difference in Con's appearance. He was still pale, still feverish, delusional with visions of monsters and madness.

"Another day," Dr. Rivard murmured. "It will all come clear."

She fed him soup, water, crackers, barely eating herself.

"He needs a different kind of nourishment," the doctor told her. "You keep doing as you are doing. He will be fine."

She slept. They slept. The next two days drifted by.

Dr. Rivard came to see him. "He is well," he murmured, laying his hands on Con's head. "He is fine. Another day and you can go."

Five days' delay, she thought. And all they had was faith to propel them on. Well, she had enough for both of them. And today they were free to go.

She left the nurses to dress him while she got their things together and then went to find Dr. Rivard.

But the head nurse didn't understand English. She kept shaking her head and spewing words that Darcie did not understand. Finally in frustration, she went to get Con.

He hobbled into the lobby of the infirmary between the two nurses who had tended him, and cocked his head questioningly at Darcie.

"Ask them about Dr. Rivard," she said. "I want to see Dr. Rivard before we go."

He relayed her request in a spate of fluent French that really impressed her, and the head nurse answered in kind. They went back and forth for a moment, and then Con turned to her.

"She says there is no Dr. Rivard. This is not his hospital. Or his infirmary. She says she's never heard of him, that there is no such a one."

They took the afternoon train to Paris. Con slept. Darcie ruminated on the mystery of Dr. Rivard.

. . . no such a one . . .

And yet she could picture him so clearly moving among the patients, touching, soothing, listening.

Healing?

She sat bolt upright at the thought, and then sank back again.

Always in the dead of night he had come, she thought suddenly. *Always after the witching hour—always in the dark.*

And she had better stop making more of these incidents than they warranted. Both were merely a case of a careless deckhand and a kindly doctor who perhaps was doing a good deed in secret. Nothing more.

Nothing more.

They were going to Paris because Con remembered going there after sailing from Dover. Paris was a start, a good start. They had money, he spoke French, and he was slowly slowly remembering the details.

She was content with that. She put out a calming hand as he moved restively in his sleep. He felt her touch, he heard the clickety-clack of wheels, the wail of the whistle. He had come to Paris by boat and by rail, he felt the memories in his bones.

The swaying train. The vitality of the city. All of its extremes. A good glass of wine. A view of the street and the baudets gawking at whatever was the exhibition of the moment. The wealthy flitting back and forth between the hunt and the Opera; coutouriers and concerts; Biarritz and the Bois de Boulogne.

They used to send for him in the summer to come to Chatelguyon to display the latest in diamond jewelry . . . Roger would go sometimes, and sometimes he, because there was so much in the way of entertainment in France. And their hosts would foot the bill, no small amount of francs in order for them to have the exclusive right to purchase the latest creation from Pengellis-Becarre.

"We'll find a pensione near the Bois," he said. "A few days there . . ."

A few days here—five days gone—she felt itchy with the urge to keep moving. She had to give him time to heal, and curb her awful impatience to keep ahead of their enemies.

They didn't even know who their enemies were.

She felt them out there, closing in, coming closer and closer. *That deckhand had been their enemy. He had deliberately let go of the wheelchair. It had not been an accident . . .*

She shook herself sharply. Every suspicion had the substance of fog and air. And then it dawned on her what he had said. *Near the Bois. As if he were that familiar with Paris. Details. He was starting to remember the details.*

"We'll do that," she said. "We'll stay a few days and figure things out."

"We'll take Lavinia's things to Poiteau's. We'll get a fair price there, at least. I used to know everyone there—but that was years ago. We came over often in the eighties."

Details. One after the other, spilling from him as if he were reliving them in a dream.

"Did you?" she murmured.

"Pengellis had a designer of jewelry, a man named Valery, whose pieces were coveted all over the world. Every year, they would summon us to Chatelguyon or Biarritz or Nice for the newest display. And they would buy, lavishly and open-handedly, cost no object as long as the thing was one of a kind. We made our reputation on those pieces. And they *were* exquisite."

She got the connection. "Are the pieces I took the work of Valery?"

"I think so. I don't want to know. We'll just sell them."

"We still have some money," she told him.

"We're going to need a lot of it," he said, turning his blank gaze toward the window.

That sounded as if he were committed, she thought. And as if he were planning ahead. "We're coming into the station," she said.

"I know. I feel the train slowing down." All the telltale signs by which he was learning to negotiate his way without sight. Did a man ever get used to it? Could he, after that one heaven-struck moment of seeing his attacker and his savior?

He felt like he was reining himself in, that if he let himself, he would explode all over everything and everyone around him.

One step at a time, he told himself. *Methodical and well-planned, step by step as he started to remember. And just put the two incidents out of your mind. The whole thing with the wheelchair was an accident. And Darcie must have misunderstood the doctor's name. Simple and reasonable explanations. He hadn't been seriously injured, and now they were finally on their way.*

On a damned long trip.

The thought popped up from nowhere.

To where?

He tried to recall the previous time he'd come through Paris. From Dover. He knew exactly where to go because he'd been here before. He'd conserved money by staying at an inexpensive pensione. He had been at the beginning of his journey. *That* journey. But what he'd done next utterly escaped him. And he couldn't remember for his life where he had been going.

And that was crux. *Where.*

"We're here." Superfluous to say it, when the train had heaved into the station with a huge burst of steam and come to a lurching halt.

She guided him off of the train and onto the platform where dozens of hansom cabs vied for passengers.

"Where to now, Con?"

He shook his head, and then: "Rue Mirbeau, I think."

She signalled and one of the drivers pulled over. *"S'il vous plaît—"* she began, and then she looked up into the driver's face, and into the dark burning eyes of the deckhand of the *Rossignol;* into the evil smile and dark malevolence of their enemy, just as the horse reared up and the carriage shot toward Con.

And he could see! In that mind-flashing moment, as Darcie shrieked and tackled him and he fell heavily to the ground, he saw everything clearly and concisely: the horror of the faces in the crowd rushing forward, the deckhand working masterfully to get his horse under control, and then the fiendish rictus of his triumphant grin.

And then in a split second the man vanished, and the dark came on again.

* * *

He kept insisting he was all right, and he didn't tell her what he had *seen.*

"Well I'm *not,*" Darcie said tartly. "I didn't imagine that. Everyone saw it. It was the same man . . . the deckhand of the *Rossignol.* I'd know those eyes anywhere."

"He won't find us again."

"How do you know? How do we know anything?"

"It's a coincidence," he said, but he knew it was a half-hearted excuse. "No one will find us here."

"We're not there yet," Darcie grumbled. "Rue Mirbeau—suppose he heard you tell me that."

"He didn't hear." He didn't know how he could sound so confident. The incident had shaken him badly, far more so than the accident at the dock.

Two occurrences since they'd arrived. And in short order too. But he wasn't going to think about that. It had to be a coincidence, just as he'd said; it was easier to believe that.

Meantime, they could only go one step at a time. First, the boardinghouse he remembered on the Rue Mirbeau. Then a good night's sleep and Poiteau's tomorrow.

They had walked a good number of streets beyond the train station.

"I think it's safe to call a cab here," she murmured, lifting her hand to signal. Immediately, one came rolling over, handled this time by an older cabman who was courteous and kind.

"*S'il vous plaît—*" she began, and Con interrupted, "*A la Rue de la Croix, et vite.*"

He pushed her into and climbed in beside her.

"What was that about?" she whispered.

"I decided not to take the chance. We'll be close enough where he's taking us."

Close enough. Details. Memories. Little by little. Piece by piece.

The cabdriver set them down on a broad avenue that skirted the Bois, and Darcie paid him.

"Now what? It's getting dark."

"Across the boulevard on the far side, and down that street. Rue Mirbeau is down that way. Hurry."

They hurried as much as they could with her having to guide his every step.

Details. As if he'd had a map in his mind.

"Left down Mirbeau," he said, when she hesitated. "You'll see, there'll be discreet signs advertising rooms."

Details.

Ten more minutes before they made their way slowly down Rue Mirbeau in the oncoming twilight and she tried to find the signs.

"Ah! Here . . ."

"No. Keep going."

Details. What did he sense? What could he hear?

They continued on.

"Here's one."

"What does it say?"

"The sign says *restez ici.*"

He thought about it a moment. "Yes."

She would have questioned it, but it was getting too dark too fast, and she felt as if they were alone in a vast unknown. She stepped down to the basement entrance and rang the bell.

A pretty maid answered, and Con spoke for them, quickly, concisely, and several minutes later, she led them up into the hallway while she summoned the concierge. He made the rest of the arrangements with equal brevity, told her how much money the room would require, and to sign the register as husband and wife and in her maiden name.

She didn't question it. He had his reasons, obviously. The place seemed well kept, the gas-lit corridors were narrow, with two rooms to the side and one each front and rear as they came up the steps.

They were allocated a front room on the third floor. Darcie took the key and closed the door after them gratefully.

It was a small, small room, with a large bed tucked under the eaves, and a dresser, a washstand, a table and chair, and a closet.

"Do you think we're safe here?" she asked as she swung their suitcase onto the table and began to unpack.

He sank onto the bed. "I think we have a place to stay for the moment."

"And you remembered it." *Details.*

He considered that and nodded. "I think I did. And I saw the driver of the cab."

She stopped what she was doing instantly. "You didn't."

"I swear to you."

"Con—this is getting crazy."

"I had my sight, Darcie; I'm as certain of it as when I found the diamond. I saw him."

"Do you know him?"

He hesitated. "No."

"But you're remembering other details. Like Poiteau and the trips to Paris. So you're bound to recall things as we get deeper into the journey."

"Maybe." *But who needed him to do that more—their nebulous enemy as embodied by the deckhand—or Darcie?*

The answer was obvious, and it disturbed him even more that he was leaping from the mysterious deckhand to *her* as the source of his disquiet.

She felt the change in him instantly, sharply, like the connection between them had broken off somehow, and she had to reestablish it quickly or she'd lose him forever.

"Con . . . you don't think . . ."

"What, Darcie? What don't I think?"

He'd gotten up and he was moving toward her as unsteadily as if he were walking on quicksand.

". . . he has some other way to track us—to follow us?" *Uh oh—wrong question.* She saw it in his eyes.

"Maybe he does, Darcie."

"What are you thinking?" she asked, suddenly scared. He was too intense, too wary. And she couldn't back away and let him fall on his face.

"I just keep thinking there's one person who has a greater stake in this than anyone else. Someone who very easily could be helping my so-called enemies track me. Us. One person, Darcie."

"No . . ."

"You."

"No." She put up her hands protectively against the hot wall of his chest.

"How do I know?"

"You *have* to know, Con."

"I don't know. Tell me again, Darcie."

"I've told you—every way I know how," she whispered.

"A woman's way," he said scornfully.

"It's the only way I know." *She just couldn't believe what he was saying.* She felt brittle, like fine china that could fracture into a hundred pieces.

"You do it well, too. Who put you up to it? Lavinia? Roger? Who, Darcie? Your father?"

She broke. "My father's dead, Con. He died before he got to be an esquire. He gave over my dowry, he saw me married to Roger, and then he was gone. It's just me. My dream. My quest. And yours, if you still want to go."

"I don't goddamned know what I want to do," he snarled. She'd got him off-balance again. Her father was dead. To whom could she have allegiance then? Was she that good an actress that she could pretend to hate Lavinia so?

"Your secrets, Con."

"Till I die, Darcie."

"Then we'll make sure you don't die."

"Darcie—" It was so dark, and he was so alone.

"I'm here."

"Goddamn you," he growled, and he swept her into his arms and into the roaring tide of his heat, his rampant sex, and his punishing kiss.

She melted against him. His anger was potent and swift. He tore off her clothes and she helped him. He pushed against her and pushed against her until she backed up against the door.

Secrets. Hard driving secrets. Against her back. Against all reason.

She wrapped herself around him, her arms, her legs, her naked body pressing against the hard edgy core of his desire. He was like lightning, bolting into her without priming or preparation, and pinning her against the door.

It was absolutely what she needed from him: a storm of emotion binding him to her, and obscuring everything she didn't want him to see.

She clung to him as he pounded her toward the precipice; she climbed—slowly then, slowly, drawing him out, pulling with her.

And then she fell into the breakwater as he emptied himself into her, and she opened herself to him and, in that bone crackling moment of surcease, she gave him her soul.

Ten

They lay together on the bed, silent, quiescent, spent.

She felt liquid, satiated, golden, loving his hands playing on her bare skin and the feel of her naked body against his clothes.

He trailed his fingers down her shoulder, her arm, her hip; and then he slipped his hand to her belly and spanned its width.

She recoiled instantly.

The baby . . . she kept forgetting the baby. But that was the thing—it hadn't even been that long. Not nearly enough for her to think in terms of it being real.

Her body tensed as she waited for his question, but it wasn't the one she expected.

"When did your father die?"

She took a deep breath to calm herself. *He'll get to the baby, I know he will.* And it seemed to her that all that lust and sex evaporated in the face of his question.

"About six months after Roger and I married."

He sensed the reluctance in her and she cursed herself for letting that emotion show. She brushed his hand away and reached to pull the blanket up over her naked body, a movement she knew he would read correctly.

But it didn't matter; her father's death was still a sore point. And she didn't want to tell him why, even though she knew exactly what his next question would be.

"How?"

She tried to keep her tone neutral, but she couldn't keep out the slight tremor. "The doctor said it was a heart attack."

"So soon," he murmured, his response instinctive and quick. He wondered about it immediately. "He made the next big strike, he came to England, he sold you to Roger, and then he died."

"That's just how it happened."

"And Roger did what with the money?"

"Paid operatives to search for you," she said tartly, "because *The Eye of God* is more valuable than gold, jewels, diamonds, life—if it's real."

"It's real," he said succinctly, but that was all he wanted her to know. "And once Roger had the money, your father was expendable, and probably you were too."

"And you," she said bluntly.

"And yet, we're both still here," he pointed out.

"How can you believe I could betray you?"

"One wonders," he said, levering himself up and away from her and swinging his legs over the bed. Only he didn't know where he could go in the dark. Always always, he had to consider the dark. He wanted to pace, he wanted to *see*.

What did he see? Everything she didn't say. The breadth of his family's duplicity, and the lengths to which they would go to possess The Eye of God. *Their greed. Their gluttony. Their viciousness and immorality.*

Inherited traits, all. He had them. He'd had no compunction about using them.

Darcie's father had been sacrificed on the altar of the Pengellis greed.

The quest had killed him.

The Pengellis curse.

He had to decide now: did he continue to take the risk or did he walk away?

Balance. It was always a question of balance.

And trusting what he couldn't see.

A woman. A baby. His desire. Her motives. His memories.

Tenuous things, with all the substance of the dark in which he was immured. He had to come to terms with it: the dark was a place from which he couldn't walk away.

"We'll go to Poiteau's in the morning," he said, and the decision was made. "We're going to need all the money we can get."

Details.

She'd pulled away from the cliff—this time. She could see him weighing the details, determining their lives.

One misstep. One wrong move . . .

Forget it. She'd dealt with things like that before. The only tricky part was the death of her father. It was the only thing about which she thought there was something more.

They were past it now, she thought, as she dressed. She shouldn't have to defend her deceased father. She needed to focus on the baby. It was still early enough, and the baby would be fine. She just had to remember to consider the baby.

She was down to one dress, one skirt and one shirt-waist now. Two sets of underclothes, excluding the corset which he had ruined last night, and the little bags of jewelry, no bigger than sachets, that she pinned to her camisole and her waistband.

She buttoned the high collar of her dress and she was ready to go.

"We won't come back here tonight," he said, and she packed what was left of their belongings in the suitcase, they signed out with the concierge, and then they made their way back to the Rue de la Croix.

"Let's walk," he said suddenly.

"You're being awfully cautious," she murmured, but she was not immune to the feeling that someone could have followed them.

But there wasn't anything remotely suspicious along the sun-bright avenue.

"Which way shall we go?"

"The opposite direction where the cab left us last night."

They walked; he held onto her, which he hated, and he listened to the burgeoning morning sounds. It was early. There was only the intermittent rumble of a dray or cab along the avenue. A certain sense that there were no crowds and that they were alone. The heat of the sun beating on his face. Her sure step as she guided him along.

Her impatience grew with every step. They were wasting time, she thought, and she had no idea where she was going.

"I wish I had a map," she said fretfully.

"We'll get one." That was a problem he could solve. "The store is on the Boulevard des Anges. I think it's safe to find a cab."

Still, her hand trembled as she signalled one and another of the few hansoms canvassing for passengers along the avenue, and she didn't like that. She couldn't let herself be intimidated by anything. They were both counting on her strength, and she lifted her chin haughtily as the driver looked askance as Con gave directions.

They looked like paupers, she thought. They didn't look like anyone who would patronize the elegant stores along the Boulevard des Anges. People who shopped there were blessed by the angels, and dripping with diamonds.

Nevertheless, the wealthy knew, as Con did, that Poiteau's was one of the few stores where they could discreetly dispose of those assets, and no matter what they looked like, no matter who they were, they would not be turned away.

As the cab slowed before the tall golden double doors of the entrance to Poiteau's, Darcie was gripped by a sudden fear. "What if they recognize the settings, Con? What if they know it's you?"

"It's been ten years or more. Who could still be there who would care?"

"I don't know." It was stupid; she was being an alarmist. Evil could exist on the beautiful Boulevard des Anges.

She pushed open the golden door and they entered. A gentleman in formal clothes immediately came to greet them.

"Con?" she whispered. "There is a gentleman here who probably would like to know what we're doing here."

Con nodded and made their needs known. "He says to wait in one of the salons at the rear of the store."

She took his arm and followed the man as he led them past counters of glittering jewels set enticingly on gold-corded creamy satin pillows in locked display cases.

Their gentleman indicated the first door along a hallway of doors the same creamy color with moldings picked out in gold. Darcie opened the door to a room that was papered in cream and gold stripes and furnished with an upholstered bench, an elegant escritoire and two chairs.

"Someone will come," Con told her, "and will ask to examine the stones. You'll give him one piece—a ring, if you have one—and he will determine the cut and grade of the stone, the value, and what Poiteau might be willing to pay."

"Sounds like a lengthy process," Darcie said. She was getting very nervous. She reached under her waistband and fished in one of the pouches for a ring. She'd taken two. Or maybe three. Or maybe she'd forgotten already in the heat of all that had happened during the journey.

She slipped it on her finger and stretched out her hand. The ring had a filigreed band and a round stone that flashed rainbow colors in the artificial light.

The kind of ring she would have liked: simple, elegant and visible. But it was Lavinia's ring, from a time when someone had loved her.

She felt Con's hand touch her and then slide down her arm to feel the ring. She saw by his face he knew which one it was, and that there were memories. Always memories.

"Monsieur, madame—" Their gentleman at the door.

"He says to follow him," Con murmured. "The appraiser will see us now."

She took his arm and guided him back into the hallway. The gentleman was moving toward the sales floor, and she turned in that direction.

"At the rear of the store," Con directed.

She turned to the right and maneuvered them past the sparkling display cases where customers were already on the sales floor. She could just see where to follow; Con slowed her up just ten steps behind.

"Where is he going?"

"There's an area back there they can evaluate gems. At least that's what he told me.

"Did you tell him what we have?"

"No."

That was quick and to the point. She only had time to wonder why when they reached the end of the aisle. There was only one place to go: she pushed him to her left where there was a smoky glass door through which their gentleman had gone.

"I guess this is it." She grasped the brass knob and opened the door.

Another man stood with his back to them across the room and their gentleman was nowhere in sight.

Darcie tapped on the door. *"Monsieur . . ."*

The man turned.

The deckhand . . . ! Trussed up in formal clothes, brandishing a loupe, his smile as malicious as a shark. Dear God, what was he doing here? How could he be here?

He took a step toward her and she screamed, "Con . . . !" And she grabbed his hand and she ran.

Down the aisles, through the store, knocking over tables, chairs, customers, pushing aside salespeople, oblivious to the shouts and screams that followed them. Con, lumbering blindly behind her, his one arm outstretched, crashing against everything in his path.

Oh God, oh God, oh God . . .

She smashed through the doors and into the sunlight, hauling him with her. *They're coming, coming, coming . . .* Her fear was monumental. They had to escape, she didn't care how. She bolted across the avenue, oblivious of vehicles, horses, pedestrians, curses following them as she ran interference for him.

She heard them shouting behind her, but she was oblivious to everything but getting them out of sight of the store.

"Con!" She was panting so hard she could barely get out his name.

"Jesus God." He was right with her. "What the hell . . . !"

"Can't . . . talk—" She didn't slow down, wasn't aware of the stares of pedestrians who saw a frenzied young woman and a blind man racing like furies down the street. "Can't . . . stop—"

Another block and another. She would never get far enough away. But she was running out of breath. She had a stitch in her side, and she was suddenly aware that she'd left their suitcase in the little salon in the store, and that all she had with her now was the money and jewelry pinned under the clothes she wore.

Oh my God . . . She slowed her pace to a walk, and waited as he fell in step beside her.

"God almighty, Darcie, what the hell was that all about?"

"Are you all right?"

"I don't know." He felt dizzy, disoriented, and dependent on her. And he hated it. Hated, hated, hated it. And more than that, he despised her eyes. And he was so intent on that, he almost didn't hear what she said.

"He was there."

He shook himself and tried to concentrate. *"Who?"*

"The deckhand. In the store, in the appraisal room." *"What?"*

"We have to get out of here. He's everywhere. He was even in the store, and for all I know, he's somewhere out here." Now she was panicked; she sounded close to hysteria. "We have to get away from here. Right now. Before he comes after us."

He felt himself going calm in the face of her agitation. Something he could *do*, he thought. He could focus and direct her and get her back in control. They had nothing, if Darcie couldn't maintain control.

"All right," he said with more composure than he felt. "We'll get out of here now; we'll take the first train, no matter where it goes."

* * *

Details. A train rocketing through the night. Arrangements made by telegraph for him to be met in Switzerland. In the dead of the night. Money exchanged. Confidentiality assured.

Another long night in transit. Munich next. Change trains. Board for Vienna. Another two days beyond that to Budapest. He's busy, mapping and plotting where he has to go.

No interruptions here. He's alone in the railroad car. Money buys that, and luxury. He's too used to it. His mother had told him. Money doesn't buy everything. It buys him the wherewithal to travel in luxury. To purchase silence. To buy loyalty. To possess a legend.

His mother's voice, always in his ear . . .

They were going to Munich, economy class, surrounded by passengers who knew to travel with picnics and pillows.

"We can buy food; it doesn't matter," he said, and he knew he was speaking with the voice of a man accustomed to having all the money he ever needed at his command.

"What if he's on the train?"

"He's not on the train."

"Next you'll say he wasn't in the store."

"No. I believe he was in the store. Just like I saw him, on the dock and in the street. Maybe he's a figment of both our imaginations."

She shook her head. "You're remembering more now, aren't you?"

"I think so. I goddamned hope so. I hate being blind."

Balance. Always a question of balance. He had to maintain the balance, to stay calm and clear, and focused on the result. He couldn't allow himself to think about whether his blindness was permanent.

"Do you speak German?" she asked idly.

"A little. I learned just enough of everything to get me whatever I needed."

She could envision that. Con Pengellis was definitely a man who would always know exactly how to get what he wanted.

He got me.

She shook away the thought and turned her attention to the screaming children of the family across the aisle. A tidy middle-class family with two young ones, two older ones, a weary mother and autocratic father who portrayed a semblance of normalcy, direction, home.

Things she'd never known.

She felt a crushing sense of loneliness. *Father . . . I want my father—Her need slicing as keenly as a knife through her heart. Daddy—*

How awful—in the midst of bedlam . . . tears streaming down her cheeks; she wiped them away impatiently, thankful that he couldn't see them.

They came to Munich in the dark, and she refused to take a cab, go to a hotel, be stranded in the dark; nothing except stay in the station until the next connecting train arrived in the morning.

In the station, there was light. They could see everything, everyone—and they could blend into the crowd.

They bought food from vendors who came to the station, and she slept with his shoulder cushioning her head.

Late in the morning after most of the crowd was gone, they bought a ticket for a private car, and they boarded the train for Vienna.

As the train rolled through the countryside, she counted the money. Too little money. Not many more pounds and francs, and they had so much more to travel, and supplies to fund.

"We have to get some money."

"I know. We'll just have to take what we can get."

She closed her eyes wearily. It sounded more and more hopeless. There were too many factors operating against them. They were running out of money. They needed gear. His blindness was an obstacle almost impossible to overcome.

Crazy, crazy, crazy . . .

Finally, she slept.

They came into the Western Railway Terminal in Vienna early in the morning, and emerged from their car rumpled, tired, and cautious in the extreme, something they'd discussed the whole of the trip.

"We've taken the obvious route all along," Darcie kept saying irritably. "I want to know now—are we on a wild-goose chase?"

He wondered that himself. Things were going too slowly; he remembered moving fast when he had been alone, by steamer, by train, by horse and wagon when necessary, with all the Pengellis money paving the way.

Now they had near nothing, no gear, no clothes, no money, and an outside chance of selling Lavinia's diamonds for anywhere near what they were worth.

And all for *The Eye of God*.

He closed his eyes and he saw the grotto, the altar of ancient stone, the light pouring down as if from heaven . . . oh yes it was real, it was a dream, it was his, and he was going to claim it.

"For all you know, Lavinia has sent her operatives back to India just to wait for your return."

"Probably," he agreed, a little shocked that it didn't worry him.

"They're probably on this train."

"Don't get delusional, Darcie. We have work to do."

They found the Ringstrasse, which was like the center of the world. Here, on one side or the other of the cobbled boulevard, were the parliament and city hall. The university, the museum; the opera house, all built in grand gothic scale, and overlooking a seemingly endless stretch of malls and esplanades.

There were clubs and theaters, the woods and wine gardens. There was life in this place, teeming, rollicking, vigorous, and they walked right into it and lost themselves in the crowd.

The quest for a mythical diamond seemed like a fairy tale here, in a country that had lost its fairy tale prince to an operatic tragedy.

But Vienna was not only the Ringstrasse. It was also the Ottakring district, where they headed on a horse-drawn streetcar an hour later. Here the working class labored and their wives ran the anonymous boarding-houses that they sought. Here they could find a way to dispose of a diamond ring without approaching the better known dealers or stores.

He felt insanely hampered by his sightlessness. He felt like a ventriloquist's dummy, speaking only when Darcie needed a direction, an answer, a translation in his raw German.

But it was enough: enough to procure a room, enough to buy food, and to find a tailor who had some ready-made clothes in his store.

And nobody asked questions. It was the part of the city in which you could disappear like air. They bought food and maps and melted into the fabric of the poorer quarter as if they'd lived there all their lives.

"We can stay here for a day or two," Con said.

"I hate wasting time."

"Time is all we have. No one else knows where to look for *The Eye of God*."

She eyed him across the narrow table where they had spread their dinner.

"Do you?"

Do you? Studying all the myths and legends. Separating the wheat from the chaff; pinpointing the reality in the fairy tales; the concrete from the dream. Poring over maps and directions. Did he know where to look? Did he remember?

Did he?

"Yes."

One word and he gave her everything she wanted to know. He felt the tension ease out of her, heard her pour some wine, felt her press his glass in his hand, heard her move things from the table and then the rustle of paper as she unfolded a map and spread it out.

"How do we go?"

Now he had to give more. "Just the way I originally went: by express through Budapest to Bucharest, and then a connecting train to Varna. We take a steamer across the Black Sea to Istanbul, and then it's by horse and camel across to Baghdad . . . and then over the Zagros Mountains to Isfahan and on to Lahore."

Her throat went dry. So many days. So many miles. So much time. And he needed his eyes. She had had no idea how much he needed his eyes. Hers were just not enough for the rough trip ahead.

She was silent for a long time, studying the route on the map. It wasn't enough, she thought, not his dream, not her desire, not their sex, not their greed. Nothing was enough to compel her to go on from here. It was too much, and they had too little. And even his confession that he remembered the location of the diamond was too little too late.

He couldn't do it without his sight. And she couldn't do it leading him blind. And she didn't know how they could do it altogether.

He sensed her withdrawal. "Darcie?"

"What?" She knew she sounded terse, unsure.

"You need a bath and a good night's sleep. It might be the most you get for the next three or four weeks."

"That's not funny, Con."

"It's truth. We're halfway there, you know."

"I don't know. I feel like we're halfway from anywhere."

"Like you felt travelling from—say Colorado to New York?"

She felt an instant flash of recognition. *Narrow gauge railroads and five car trains. Wagons. Dust. Dirt. Mountains. Rain. Flash floods. Dangerous crossings. Mules, sometimes, or horses. And other times, on foot.*

Nothing had ever stopped her or her father. Not weather, not impenetrable wilderness, or lack of money. Or thieves, outlaws, or dead dry claims.

They just stepped right over the bones of their losses, and kept on looking.

What was different then? And what did the obstacles matter when the next big strike was just over the hill? Or over a mountain. Or across the Black Sea.

"Halfway there," she echoed softly, moving her finger across the map and following the route he had outlined. Halfway to India, she thought, and riches beyond her wildest dreams.

There was a knock at the door, and she started.

"Probably the bathwater," Con said coolly. "Don't panic."

It was a little luxury she had paid extra for, and they both were going to use it. She opened the door to admit the landlady caring two pitchers of steaming water, and her husband and son carrying a narrow copper tub.

"Just in the middle," she said, and then she pointed. The landlady said something, which Con translated. "She'll be back in a moment with soap, towels and some more water."

But it took three trips to fill the tub. Darcie locked the door behind the landlady and stared at it doubtfully. "I guess I'll go first. You don't have to turn your eyes."

"I guess not," he murmured, settling back on the bed.

She watched him for a moment, and then she began stripping off her clothes. It was easier without corsets and hooks; she unpinned the little pouches of jewelry and set them on the dresser.

How long ago was that when she had stolen through Goole Abbey to search out those pieces? It seemed like forever ago.

She pushed away the thought and slid out of her camisole, petticoat and drawers. And then she was naked, and she trailed her finger in the steaming water to test the heat.

The water looked so inviting, but he looked even more enticing sprawled out on the bed, attuned to something that she would never be able to share.

She wanted to know suddenly if he wanted her still, or if he still thought she could be his enemy.

If he knew she were naked, would he come to her?

She needed to know. She wanted to explore her power and test his potency. She walked slowly to the side of the bed, watching his body, watching his face.

His body reacted first, spurting indelibly to life before her eyes.

This was power. She loved it. She reached out her hand and touched him. Hot. Thick. Hard. Yes.

She climbed onto the bed and straddled his legs, and

she was absolutely certain by the look in his eyes that he could see everything.

She wrenched apart his trousers decisively, mercilessly ripping the cloth that impeded her way. And then his penis was free, springing into her hands as if it were home.

"Is that what you want?"

"Bathe me," she whispered, sliding her hands all up and down his erection.

"I'll drown you in it."

"Do it," she breathed.

Her hand worked harder, faster, slower, lightly, tightly; his eyes closed, his body undulated beneath her, his breathing came fast, his hands reached for her nipples as she bent forward into his pleasure.

It was coming. Slowly it was coming, building volcanically underneath pumping of her hands.

Her excitement escalated. She wanted him now, all over her, every last drop of his desire, she wanted.

"Come to me," she goaded him. "Come."

She rose onto her knees and bore down on him. He was just ready, so ready. She held it all in her hands: his strength, his vigor, his power.

She grasped him tightly, pushing him, pulling him, bringing him on. She felt all his muscles contracting, she felt him gathering, and he jacked himself up and thrust against her encircled fingers, and erupted in one mighty blow.

He spewed all over her, on her breasts, her face, her belly, her hands. And still he came, his ejaculate spurting with each convulsive spasm. She held him until his last shuddering climax, and even then, she didn't let him go.

"I'm covered with your essence," she whispered. ". . . do you see me?"

"I see you," he said hoarsely. "I feel you." He reached up and grasped her at the waist. "I want you." He pulled her down to him and rolled her over onto her back.

This he was sure of—in the dark. Her body was a landscape he could negotiate, in the dark.

"The water will get cold," she murmured, as she welcomed his weight and parted her legs.

He positioned himself to breach her heat, slanting his mouth down within a breath of hers.

"It can't quench my thirst," he whispered against her lips.

And he drove into her like a drowning man who had finally reached the shore.

Eleven

In the Ottakring, it was simple to find shops catering to every need, and brokers anxious to buy or sell, or to lend you money. What they liked best of all was collateral, and they examined the ring that Darcie wanted to sell, one broker after the other, and made their unacceptable offers.

"And then they'll resell to whatever jeweler with which they have a connection and make a profit of a hundredfold," Darcie said disgustedly, as they entered a pawnshop on the Schloss Alee.

"We don't have a choice now," he told her in an undertone. "We're too conspicuous. What do you think they see? Two vagrants hawking a diamond ring—we don't have the option of going to one of the bigger stores. They'd have the authorities after us before we could count to three."

She looked at the shopkeeper, who was old, with papery skin, and dressed in a long black frock coat, and she could have sworn he understood every word. And his eyes . . . his knowing eyes as he took the ring and examined it under a magnifying glass and with his loupe.

He made her nervous as he turned the ring over and over and tested it every way possible, and then he looked up at Con and made his offer.

"It's a little more money than the others."

"It's not nearly enough," she said, knowing how she sounded.

He handed her a stack of gulden. "Come on now. It's just a little setback." He said some words to the shopkeeper, and motioned Darcie toward the door.

She took his arm and turned back to look at the man.

He was old and stooped and losing hair, and he looked as if he were gloating over the bargain he had made. And then he looked up at her, and his eyes . . . his burning, knowing eyes—

She slammed the door behind them as they stepped into the street.

"That man . . ."

"Darcie . . ." he said warningly. "I didn't sense anything."

"You didn't see him. His eyes—"

"Forget his eyes. I have a plan. We're going to use the money to dress ourselves like gentry who might be stranded and in need of cashing in some valuables. You said it yourself: we have to *pretend*. This is just the first step."

Her senses began to tingle. "All right. You're right. We had to accept less so we didn't have to explain things. I understand. But that man's eyes . . ."

"Let's go shopping," Con interrupted her. "Find a cab."

She was even leery of doing that. She could still see those eyes that had followed them from Paris to Vienna. Those eyes could be anywhere, even in a pawnshop. Or driving the next cab.

"The driver says we want the Kohlmarkt," Con said, climbing into the carriage after her. "And Rosteck's for gold and gifts. I think we'll do very well with our stake."

And that was what it was: a stake, and she didn't think

they'd do well at all, but by late afternoon, they had accomplished a lot. They found in the Kohlmarkt stores that sold clothing ready to wear. She purchased an elegant dove gray suit over an underdress of lavender satin, and they fitted him out in a severe black suit which emphasized his height and gave him an elegance that belied his blindness.

They were able to buy one outfit each, with underclothing, and toiletries, and a suitcase that didn't look as if it had weathered a war, and they had left a handful of kreuzer.

"That might buy us a pastry for lunch," Darcie grumbled as she guided him along the boulevard.

"Then it's time to find Rosteck's and proceed to the next step."

Rosteck's was the equivalent of Poiteau's in Paris. An elegant shop that sold gift items and jewelry. A place where nothing was advertised and everything was understood.

"We need to sell a necklace this time," Con said. "We're going to need a lot of money."

They were taken once again to the rear of the shop, straight to the appraiser's office. Darcie removed a pouch and handed it across the desk. Con did the talking, and she could tell he was playing on the gentleman's sympathy.

They had concocted the story before they even reached the store, and it was paper thin to begin with. They were on their honeymoon. They ran out of money. They had no family to turn to. The necklace was a wedding present, an heirloom, but they were willing to sacrifice to continue on their journey. They were young and gay and so much in love.

Darcie rolled her eyes. The appraiser took the necklace and began his examination.

He spent a nerve-racking half hour, going over each of the stones, calling for consultations, and excusing himself at least twice to confer with another appraiser on the premises.

"They are calling the authorities is what," Darcie fretted. "They think we're thieves. We don't look like people who would own such a piece."

"They will pay the price," Con said, but even he was a little unnerved by the amount of discussion that was going on about the necklace, and he resolutely pushed the picture of Lavinia wearing the necklace out of his mind.

He had been—what?—five or six . . . ? He couldn't quite remember. But there was his father, with an oblong velvet box which he had not placed under the Christmas tree.

My dear . . .

Oh my darling—as his father lifted the necklace from its satin nest and held it up in the light.

It might well have been that he had fallen in love with diamonds that night. He remembered how they glittered and shot rainbow light down to the floor; how they sparkled like ice as his father's long fingers slipped the necklace around Lavinia's neck.

She stroked the center stone. It looked smooth as water, deep as the ocean, and bright as a star . . . her voice soft, murmuring her appreciation at the thoughtfulness of his father.

That Lavinia . . .

"Mein herr . . ." The appraiser, an hour later, the necklace spread across his hands like a waterfall.

He jerked out of his reverie. The amount the appraiser was offering was beyond even what he had estimated. He nodded his head in agreement.

"We have to sign a paper that says we are free to sell the item, and that it wasn't stolen or obtained by illegal means. They want all kinds of assurances about it."

"I suppose technically you *are* free to sell it."

"Technically." He wished he could see her face as he told her the sum. "It's a lot of money."

"Is it enough?"

Even he didn't know. "It's enough . . . for now."

They bought the tickets on the Direct Express that afternoon. "I think we need to leave here as soon as possible" Con said. "Even if this is the most obvious route, once we reach Istanbul we can make modifications. And at least we'll travel in comfort."

They would leave the next morning from the Southern Terminal, which meant another night in the Ottakring. She wasn't happy about that, but she agreed that their money was better spent purchasing more clothes, sturdy shoes, personal items, a small stash of dried food, and another suitcase, for him.

It was like starting off on the next adventure, Darcie thought, as they bought packages of roast pork and vegetables from a vendor to bring back for their dinner.

She felt the growing excitement that always preceded the thrill of the hunt. And the fact they now had money eased some of her fears.

There was always a way to get money if one had something to sell. And the further away from Europe they travelled, the fewer questions they would be asked and the less trouble they would have.

She felt reassured by the thought. And she decided she'd imagined the man with eyes, and she had better stop feeling so overwrought.

No one was following them. Lavinia could not have known where she had gone from the brothel. And if she were still after Con, she probably had operatives searching all over India for him. And she had a business to run on top of that. She couldn't be everywhere. She couldn't be in Vienna at any rate.

And Con's blindness hadn't hampered them all that much, she thought, as she laid out their dinner on the small table in their room. They'd bought some beer and wine as well, and she poured the beer into a glass for him and handed it across the table to him.

"Let's toast the fact we've done well," he proposed.

"Certainly," she said before she could stop herself. "We'll congratulate ourselves on the fact you were almost killed—twice—and that we sold a flawless diamond ring for no money at all, and we were that close to having the authorities arrest us at Rosteck's."

"Pessimist." He sipped his beer and made a face. "I hope the food is better."

"This is the Ottakring. What do you expect?"

"You adapt well," he murmured, feeling for the food and lifting a piece of pork to his mouth. "That's not bad."

"Con—we should be moving faster . . ."

He shook his head. "Do you know it's almost seventy hours by train to Istanbul from Paris? And that includes the ferry from Varna. If you were travelling alone, you still wouldn't get anywhere any faster, Darcie, so just shelve the idea of going on without me. You'd wind up dead, and you couldn't tell them where to bury you."

"I didn't mean that."

"Sure you did," he said, setting aside his beer and pushing away the pork. He lost his appetite suddenly. Sometimes . . . sometimes, he forgot about the blindness and it almost seemed a condition he'd lived with all his life. And he didn't want to get used to it. He wanted to remember when it happened, because he hadn't always been blind. And that meant there was a chance he could regain sight at some point in his life.

There was always the hope. Always the next dream. Darcie had lived her life that way, and to some extent, so had he. Only he had always had the advantage of money, and all she had had was faith and guile.

Sometimes he forgot they were only partners in a game to outwit an unknown enemy. Unholy partners, he thought; both of them rapacious, hungry, and bound by desire.

A perfect trinity. A blind man. A greedy woman. And *The Eye of God.*

Their compartment was in the fifth of seven sleeping cars on the Direct Express, and one of the smaller ones at that. But it did have its own lavatory, and a small closet beside the door to the room.

On either side of the car there were berths that folded up against the wall during the day; and there were seating benches beneath, and a clever table that pulled up from under the window.

Darcie guided Con to the tufted bench on the left hand side, and sank into the seat opposite by the window. She would unpack later, she thought, as she watched the porters hauling piles of expensive luggage toward the rear car. Their two small suitcases suddenly seemed awfully meager when she measured them against what other people were bringing on this trip.

Or maybe she was feeling the weight of the gloomy weather. They were leaving in the rain, and rain was always a bad omen, although they had arrived before it had begun. Others were just now scurrying down the platform, ill prepared for the weather, and covering themselves with whatever came to hand.

The train would leave in an hour, the next stop Budapest. And meantime, they would dine royally in the dining car, have the luxury of a porter making up their beds at night, and the diversion of new acquaintances in the bar car.

Con sat very erect, staring straight ahead. The darkness today seemed overwhelming, especially on top of the chaos of the departure he sensed beyond the compartment door.

Things he used to be able to *see*—

Things he couldn't remember. When he'd escaped; how he'd gotten to England; what happened to his eyes . . . blank spaces in his mind, as black as the vista in front of him.

And Darcie . . . what did he see? The softest of hair, long and flowing down her shoulders; smooth silky skin, magical hands—but not a face or figure came to mind when he pictured her. She was a presence, ephemeral by night, and solid practicality by day. The sum of the parts of her body that he now knew as intimately as his own.

Even the thought of her aroused him.

He didn't need to see her to want her. It was a continual ache in his groin. He was suspicious of it. He hated his dependence on it. And worst of all, he never stopped wanting it. But he couldn't live a life obliterating himself in a sexual void.

It was too easy.

She was too easy.

It was the thing he couldn't quite get around, at night, in the dark, when he couldn't sleep.

A man with no eyes could see more clearly in the dark.

But a man with no eyes, he thought warily, was also a very easy mark.

She saw the man with the eyes as the train pulled out of the Southern Terminal station. On the platform, beside an empty luggage cart, staring up at her, smiling, smiling smiling, that evil knowing smile. The face of the deckhand, the cabdriver, the money lender. He was all of them—and none.

And then he vanished as quickly as a ghost.

But when she turned her head and looked behind, she thought she saw him again, swinging up onto the steps of the last car as the train left the station.

Oh my God . . . oh my God— She rose from her seat and then slumped down again. She'd imagined it. She had. The train had been going too fast. Even if he had been on the platform, he wasn't strong enough to jump on a train moving at full speed.

Her imagination was playing tricks. How was she going to tell Con?

She wouldn't . . . It was a threat he couldn't see, and there was no purpose at all in telling him.

She would have to take all the precautions.

If she had seen what she thought she had seen.

I'm going crazy now. Just when I think things have calmed down, that there is no threat. That everything's behind us . . .

She was trembling. She was shaking like a belly dancer.

. . . and the baby—she mustn't forget the baby, it was too easy to forget the baby . . .

She stared out the window as the train rolled through the outskirts of the city. She would have to bring their food to the compartment, and she would have to scrutinize every stranger.

And every stranger would look like the man with the burning eyes . . .

She jumped at the knock on the compartment door.

"Who is it?" The first words Con had spoken since they entered the car.

"A porter." She could see his face through the window, benign, respectful, smiling. Nothing to be afraid of. "I'll get it." But her legs were shaky as she got up and went to the door.

And then impossibly, before her very eyes, he changed, his face metamorphosing from the elderly porter to the man with burning eyes, evil personified, bent on getting through the door.

She threw herself against it, shrieking, "Con!" and he bounded up, and, with his arms stretched out, fumbled his way toward her, and the thumping sound of something trying to enter their room.

"Con!" She wasn't strong enough, and he wasn't fast enough. "Hurry!"

The man with the eyes had superhuman strength, and he was beating her; slowly, inexorably he was forcing the door, and she just didn't have the power to stop him.

And then Con heaved himself against her and his weight in combination with hers enabled her to slam shut the door. She fumbled with the lock. Click. Click. The most welcome sound she'd ever heard. She ripped the curtain across the window, effectively closing out their nemesis.

But for how long? She was absolutely certain that if she pulled the curtain he would still be there.

She swallowed hard as he started pounding on the door, and Con looked questioningly at her.

"Don't open it, Con."

"Darcie, what the hell's going on?"

"You won't believe it."

"You sounded scared to hell."

"It was the man. And I don't know that this isn't him." The pounding grew louder.

"Ma'am . . . Ma'am—is anything wrong? Can I help you? Let me make sure you're all right. Ma'am? Ma'am? If you'd be so kind—open the door."

"That's crazy," he said under the pounding.

"I know." She cursed the fates that Con couldn't see him, and that he couldn't see how scared she was to open the door, "What should I do?"

He was so logical. "See who's there."

"But he looked—" she started to say, but what the man looked like made little difference to him. He'd seen him twice—if he had seen him at all, and he wouldn't be able to see the evil beyond the window.

No one could, except her. If it existed. If she could believe her eyes.

She drew the curtain slowly, slowly, her hand shaking, her breath shallow with fear.

The elderly porter outside the door looked at her quizzically, and mouthed, "Are you all right, ma'am?"

"Stay close to me," she whispered to Con as she unlocked the door and opened it a fraction of an inch. "I'm fine, thank you," she said to the porter.

"Could I bring you some tea, ma'am?"

He was a kindly man, she could see it in his eyes, and she would have loved some tea. But she couldn't trust anything, not even him.

"That's fine, thank you. I'll see to it myself. Later."

"As you wish, ma'am."

She eased the door closed and locked it again. And looked up once again to see the man with the burning eyes, laughing at her gullibility from beyond the window of the double-locked door.

"We're not going to eat. We're going to spend two days on this train and we're just not going to eat."

She knew she sounded delirious, but she didn't care. She was shaken beyond anything she cared to admit.

He, however, was practical. "We paid for the food, we're going to eat it."

"And how, pray tell, if we can't go to the dining car and we can't trust a porter to deliver it?"

"Darcie, you can't fall apart now."

"You didn't see that man."

"I saw him twice."

And that was the thing. Had he or had he imagined he could even see at all?

She decided not to comment on that. "I'll make arrangements to get some food," she said finally.

"And I'll lock the door."

Con alone and in the dark in their compartment? No, no, no. She couldn't leave him. If the man could transform himself from a porter into a portent of evil, Con would have no defense against him. None. And he'd already tried to kill him twice.

"That won't work either. We'll have to starve. I will not leave you at the mercy of that fiend."

"If you want to find a diamond, Darcie, you'd better feed me."

"I don't think you should even say that out loud."

He heard the note in her voice and cursed the darkness. "God, he's got you terrified."

"He's stalking us, Con."

He felt as helpless as a fly. He remembered looking up at the eyes, seeing the evil, and the lustful grin. Malevolence rising from the dust and dirt of a thousand years, provoking fate, disturbing the balance.

Sometimes death was the only solution.

"Then we have to destroy him," he said, as if he were pronouncing a sentence. "And you'll have to find the way."

They'd eaten some of the dried food they'd packed for the trip, fruit and beef, washed down with water, a makeshift dinner at best, and now she lay in her berth, staring into the dark, seeing what he saw every moment of every day.

Nothingness. Dark blank nothingness.

. . . I'll be your eyes . . .

And anything else you ask of me . . .

How could he live like that, staring endlessly into the dark, depending on someone else's eyes?

She turned restively in the narrow bed.

What if the man with the eyes was at the compartment door now? What if he watched them all night long? What if she couldn't get out tomorrow to get some food? What if, what if, what if?

She slipped down from the berth and folded up the bed. She wasn't going to get any sleep tonight. Instead, she was going to prowl the room and chew on the *what if's* until night turned into day.

She drew back the curtain on the door. A muted light filled the window from the sconces in the passageway. No shadows. No sense of a lurking presence.

She had no idea of the hour. She unlocked the door and opened it, and stepped out into the passageway. Not a sound but the rhythmic click of wheels on the rails. Not a breath intruding on the silence.

She inhaled deeply to calm her pounding heart. No one was about. There was nothing to fear. Maybe this was the time—her stomach was growling—she could just make her way to the dining car, and procure something for them to eat.

She heard Con stir in the bunk behind her. If she slipped out now, she could be back before he was ever aware.

And then she wouldn't feel utterly terrorized by that man.

The dining car was between the third and fourth

sleeping cars. She carefully locked the compartment door and slipped down the passageway, surrounded by silence and enfolded by the dim light.

Late as it was, there were still a couple of passengers sitting in the dining car, and one tired waiter waiting patiently at a table at the far end of the car for them to finish.

He got up wearily as she approached. Five minutes later, he returned with a tray; she took it from him, waving away his polite offer to carry it back to the compartment for her.

Another couple of moments, she would be safely there. She pushed her way through the first of the connecting doors into sleeping car number four.

He jolted awake suddenly as the train rounded a sharp curve.

Goddamned dark; can't see a goddamned thing. Shit. Hell. Bloody blast . . .

He toppled off of the bunk, his arms flailing, shouting her name.

No answer. He got up off the floor and groped his way around the room. No Darcie.

He felt his way to the door. Locked.

Damn and blast.

The key—taken. Where the hell had she gone?

He ripped open the locks and eased into the passageway.

No help there. No point in him going one foot further.

He had never felt more useless. He slammed the door furiously behind him.

And then he heard Darcie scream.

Twelve

He jumped her from behind between the cars, catching her totally unaware. She screamed as his arm wrenched her neck, and everything on the tray went crashing to the floor.

Careless. Her sole coherent thought before he pulled her backward into the darkness. She heard his animal panting in her ear, and she pulled and twisted, trying to get purchase to resist him, holding the tray in a death grip, her only weapon to defend herself.

But he was too strong. He dragged her toward the door, toward the steps, wrestling her as she fought him, as she hooked her feet in the doorframe, as she grabbed for the door.

He was choking her; she couldn't swallow. She could barely summon the energy to fight. He yanked her backward, and she relinquished the door and he forced her toward the steps. She heard the ominous clack of the wheels and felt the cold night air.

She was that close to death. He would kill her to get to Con—

Nooooo . . . !

She went limp against him, making him drag her full weight as he jerked her toward the steps.

Last chance—no room to turn, can't breathe . . . tray—

Both hands, no strength—
In the name of The Eye of God . . .

With both hands, with the last vestige of her feeble strength, she lifted the tray backward over her head and bashed it against him.

She didn't know what she hit—his arm, his shoulder, his head . . . but immediately his grip loosened; he fell, and she fell on top of him; she scrambled to her knees, and lashed out at him blindly, crashing the tray over his head, and breaking it in two.

He lay bleeding, his head propped against the second step from the bottom. Moaning. Limp. Vanquished.

. . . *we must destroy him . . . and you must find the way*—

She didn't think twice. She lifted his legs and pushed, tumbling him legs over shoulders down the steps and off the train.

She managed to salvage some of the food, as the porters came running, and one of them summoned the train manager to report the accident.

They'd paid for the food, she thought practically, as she gathered the basket of croissants and fruit. At least they would eat. Thank God she was still alive and she could eat.

A porter brought tea to the compartment, where Con was pacing like a caged tiger, and was just setting it on the table when she entered.

The train manager, she saw, was already there.

"Now madame . . ." he said, his voice calm and respectful, and Con translated.

She had determined her story as she made her way shakily back to the room, and she was going to stick to it. No one could prove it happened otherwise, and, she thought, she did not need to attribute a motive to the man with the eyes. He could have been any lecher seizing an opportunity to seduce an unchaperoned woman. And anyway, the fewer details the better.

"There isn't much to say. The man attacked me, and in the course of my defending myself, he slipped and fell from the train."

The manager made a tcching sound. "Did madame know the man?"

"I never saw him. He came at me from behind, his arm around my neck. I was coming from the dining car with a tray of food. I hit him with the tray. He fell backwards and slipped, and before I could do anything, he was gone."

"I see, madame." The train manager finished his notes and then bowed. "I think that will be all for now. I can see you are overcome."

She didn't know how she maintained her composure until they left. And then she just collapsed onto one of the benches and buried her head in her hands.

"Have some tea," Con said, groping for the bench opposite her.

"Is the door locked?"

"I locked it."

"I can't forgive myself for this. I couldn't sleep. I was so hungry . . . and no one was there." She looked up at him, even though he couldn't see her. "But this is the lesson I learned: he's everywhere. That man is *everywhere.*"

"He's gone now."

"I don't know that, Con. He fell off the train, but—I can't tell you he's gone." She felt tears on her cheeks and she wiped them away impatiently. He'd scared her again. He'd targeted her this time. She couldn't even think beyond that.

She could feel Con's frustration, that he could do

nothing while she had almost died. But his voice betrayed nothing of that as he said, "Pour yourself some tea, Darcie. Eat something. I've already thought about what to do."

She poured the tea and wrapped her cold hands around the cup. "All right, what can we do?"

"Well, you were right. We're on the most obvious course, and we have to get off of it. We're going to debark at Budapest, and change trains for Belgrade. The line goes straight through to Istanbul. From there, we can disappear, and they'll never find us."

"You're crazy. A blind man and a Western woman. Everyone will know who we are."

"So we'll playact," he said reassuringly. "Just like you said. You've been right about everything; you're much better at this than I am."

But she'd always had to be, she thought. Invariably she and her father had been one step ahead of someone they'd swindled or who had cheated them. She knew all about dodges and disguises. She'd just never had to cope with a sightless accomplice before.

She felt a spark of inspiration. "I think we have to hide. On the train. Do you know when we get into Budapest?"

"Early evening, I think. The timetable should be on the ticket folder. And where might we be hiding on the train?"

"The kitchen. Think, Con. It's perfect."

"We'll get fed, at least," he said dryly.

She ignored that. "We'll steal in after the midday meal, when they're cleaning up and we won't be too much in the way. We'll leave things just as they are here—locked door, curtained windows—pack everything up and maybe stash the suitcases before the lunch hour. That makes sense. Then we won't look as conspicuous when we go to the dining car for lunch, and we can sneak off from there the moment the train comes into the station."

She liked that plan. It felt good to be able to define some action and not to be at the mercy of forces she couldn't understand.

"Doesn't that make sense? We'll be right out in the open. No one can get to us in broad daylight. And by the time anyone tries, we'll be long gone."

It was as good a plan as any, he thought. He was just along for the ride. Helpless. Hopeless. Hapless. He felt like a doddering old man as she helped him along the passageway for the second sitting of the midday meal.

She'd reserved a table very close to the kitchen, and she had managed to get their bags into a storage cupboard in the pantry.

"You need not rush the meal, madame," the waiter told them as he guided Con into his chair. "We will not set another service until dinner since we arrive in Budapest at four o'clock."

"Perfect," Darcie mouthed as Con translated and then asked the waiter to recite the menu. They decided on cream soup to start, stuffed breast of turkey, a vegetable salad, with cheeses and tea to finish.

"We can take the cheese," Darcie said practically. "And whatever vegetables will keep. We ate a lot of that dried meat, and you never know when we might need it."

That, Con thought humorously, should be his line of reasoning. But Darcie had obviously been in that situation as well, in another country, another world away.

They ate in silence, with Darcie packing away the fresh bread and crackers that accompanied the soup.

She hated the fact he couldn't see the countryside as the train rolled on toward Budapest. It was one of the pleasures of the dining car, with its narrow tables, soft lighting, and superbly efficient service.

But at least, they would have one meal, and a moment's peace before the rest of the journey. Sometimes that was all you could expect.

The turkey was rolled and stuffed with a breaded dressing and walnuts, the most luxurious meal Darcie had had since before Roger died. The more so because she shared it with Con, because she could help him by covertly cutting his meat and arranging food, as he directed her, in a way he could manage them comfortably.

She loved his expression, as intent as a child's, as he dug his fork into the turkey—at three o'clock on the plate, and the dressing—at twelve, and the salad, at nine. A very efficient system which diminished his awkwardness and gave him some measure of control.

She picked at the salad, setting aside the lightly steamed and still-crisp julienned carrots to add to the food she had already squirreled away in a spare linen napkin.

They ordered dessert: fruit tart, and chocolate pots au crème. Darcie loved chocolate, he discovered, listening to her sensual moans as she slowly ate the creme.

She packed away the cheese, and poured their tea. "Still another hour until Budapest."

"All right. This train comes into the South station. We'll need to get over the river to the East station in the Elizabeth district. We may have less than a half hour before this train gets on its way again. They'll take on provisions and mail and they'll be gone."

"All right. In a half hour, we'll get into the kitchen. can you make a pot of tea stretch thirty minutes?"

"I can if you can."

More difficult done than said. There was nothing they could talk about in public, so she made light conversation about their fellow passengers until the waiter came to clear the table, after which he signalled that they could remain as long as they wished.

She watched the car clear out. A couple of passengers remained at the far end, reading a paper, or playing cards, or in deep conversation.

She thought the coast was clear. "I think we can do it now." She rose from the table and came around to take his arm. "This way." She didn't look back as she led him through the closer door and into the kitchen car.

It was the most clever arrangement. All the stoves and preparation counters lined one side of the car, with an icebox at the far end, and two chefs in constant attendance.

They wove their way around the assistant chefs and the boys who were washing up from the midday meal, and they pressed forward into the anteroom of the car which was lined with cupboards and closets full of provisions.

"I think they'll let us stay here until we come to the station," Darcie whispered. "Just press back against the wall, and I'll get the suitcases."

She was proud of how she'd managed that, so early in the morning, pretending to the boy on duty that she was taking them to a forward car. It worked perfectly; she'd had time to scout the cupboards, which were emptier now because the train would be reprovisioned in Budapest, and she had found an undercupboard with the requisite space.

And now they waited, as the washer-boys noisily rinsed the luncheon dishes, as the chefs shouted back and forth instructions for the preparation of the evening meal, as the sound of the clacking wheels slowed imperceptibly, and the wail of the train whistle announced they had reached the outskirts of the city.

In the frenzy to get things done before the train came to a halt, no one in the kitchen took notice of them. Or, Darcie thought, no one cared.

She edged her way to a small side window in the pantry. Almost there. Just a few minutes more, and they'd be off and gone.

She turned to Con to tell him—and she saw him out of the corner of her eye: the man with the burning eyes, coming at Con, a knife in his hand from across the kitchen car.

No. No. No. No!

"Con . . . !" she screamed as she hurled herself at him. "Get down . . . ! Damn it, get *down* . . . !"

She rammed him against the opposite wall just as their nemesis threw the knife. It hit a cabinet door, just above their heads.

She heard the babble of voices behind her and shouts and scuffling.

She pulled herself away from Con, and helped him to his feet, just as the train steamed to a jolting stop and everyone lurched off-balance again.

Where was the man? The chefs and assistants had him pinned to the floor, kicking and cursing, and struggling to get free.

She took all that in with one lightning glance, and the lethal dagger just above her head. She didn't even think. She grabbed it, and thrust it into the waistband of her skirt, and then she picked up the suitcases and grasped Con's hand.

"Darcie . . ." *Useless. Helpless. At the mercy of sound.* He held onto her hand like a lifeline.

"Shhh—It was the man . . . and we have to go—
now . . ."

She picked the first door in the pantry that looked
likely, and thanked the fates when it opened onto a
narrow passage that led to the loading dock.

She took one look behind her to see if anyone were
following, and then she kicked into a run and they were
off and gone.

From that point until they reached Istanbul, everything was a blur. They took a cab from the South station
to the East. They got second-class passage on a train
that left in the morning for Belgrade. There, they connected with the Venice Express which went through to
Istanbul.

Everywhere, she looked for the man with the burning
eyes, certain he followed them, and that they could
never escape him.

"He wants the diamond," Darcie said tiredly, as they
huddled against the leather banquette in their sleeping
car. She had laid the various foods she'd saved on the
table, and she was encouraging him to eat when neither
of them had an appetite.

"He wants me," Con said, "dead or alive."

That was worse. She refused to consider it. "Eat something."

"You eat. You need your strength."

"Hogwash."

"And what am I good for, Darcie? All I am is a re-
pository, a map to the location of a legend and a
dream."

"How long will it take to get there?" she asked, making a feeble joke.

"You have to fall down a rabbit hole, and hope that the queen doesn't take off your head."

"Lavinia," she murmured. "*She* can't be everywhere."

"No. Only her men."

The man with the burning eyes. The thought pursued them as tangibly as their nemesis, as the train steamed eastward.

Istanbul in the bright white hot light of the afternoon.

She had never felt such heat. It settled on her like a second skin and seeped into her pores. She felt as if she would melt under the relentless sun and that she would just be absorbed in the streets of the city.

It was a place where old and new existed side by side, domes and minarets interspersed with modern European architecture, and ringed by avenues lined with towering palms and enclosed by a wall that seemed to both contain and intensify its contradictions.

The Bosphorus glittered on the horizon, merging with the cloudless blue sky, and the sun beat down mercilessly on whitewashed houses crammed in narrow alleyways that led through the city's native bazaars.

It was here they were headed, after debarking from the train.

"There isn't a vendor in the *souk* who won't bargain and buy," Con said, "and we'll be able to sell some more jewelry. Although—we should register at the hotel first. The Pera Palace will do. It's a little further from the market, but the price is better."

And had she not known she was in heat-drenched Istanbul, she would have thought she was in a luxurious European hotel where they would be waited on hand

and foot and she could have soap and a bath and soft cotton sheets.

And she could have *him*.

They stored the suitcases in the room, and went back out into the sun-baked streets, as visible a target as the sky.

Con told her what they needed: the shrouding tunic and veil of the submissive woman, and the cloak and headdress of the dominating male. Heavy boots for protection and walking. Henna to dye their skin so they would blend into the crowd.

Even dressed like this, she didn't think the disguises would work. He was far too dependent, she was nowhere near enough subdued.

But he knew the language of the *souk*, and the ways of the moneylenders and the thieves. And he knew how to get around the vendors' obvious distaste of showing their wares to a woman, so by the end of the day, he had accomplished all he wished.

Shockingly, converting the jewelry to cash had been the easiest of the transactions once he had garbed himself in desert dress.

He told them he was a trader of white women, and he was taking her to Baghdad, with a dowry of diamonds for which he now needed cash.

Pretend. She had to force herself to act submissive, standing as the moneylenders examined her, with her hands tied behind her and her eyes downcast.

It was enough. "They said you were very beautiful for a Western woman," he told her as they returned to the hotel. "They deeply pitied me for my affliction. They paid me extra in sympathy, the bastards, because Allah would never grant me the blessing of seeing your unusual blue eyes. They envied the man who would buy you. They offered to top whatever his offer might be."

She didn't see the humor. She was sapped by then, utterly wretched in the heat, and the Pera Palace looked like heaven in the sweltering afternoon sun.

They ordered bathwater as they came into the hotel, and dinner, to be brought to the room.

"All I want to do is take off my clothes and lay naked in a pool of water," Darcie said, throwing herself down on the luxurious bed.

It was a very westernized room, designed to cater to travellers on the Orient Express. There was a proper bed, a commodious wooden dresser, two chairs and a table for in-room dining, a cool tile bath, luxurious carpeting, shuttered windows instead of the ubiquitous latticework that could be seen everywhere else; the only thing that differentiated it from a hotel in Mayfair was the godawful heat.

And she supposed, as she watched Con prowl the room still dressed in his *aba*, she might just as well get undressed; there was no question of modesty, there was just the everlasting heat and her feeling that this journey had not yet begun.

She divested herself of everything but her camisole and her drawers, and folded the clothes neatly on the bed.

"This is what we're going to do," Con said, pausing by the shuttered window, and staring out of it as if he could see the streets of the city below. "We're going to disguise you as a man."

"What?!"

"I'd wear women's clothes if I thought I could get away with it, but I'm too tall by Eastern standards, whereas you are approximately the right height for a man."

"And how will we diminish your height?"

"I'm feeling extremely diminished already, Darcie."

Ah! She felt the pinch and emotional sting of those words. Now was not the time to argue with him. And she didn't want to. She wanted something else from him altogether.

"That's a good plan," she agreed.

"It's reasonable, given the circumstances, and it'll allow us to disappear in the crowd. We shouldn't stay here more than just tonight. We'll outfit ourselves for the remainder of the trip tomorrow in the market. We have about another two weeks' journey to Lahore. And I think we'll take the train through to Baghdad."

"But the question is, did *he* get off the train in Budapest and follow us here?"

He sat down heavily in one of the chairs by the window. "Possibly. I keep forgetting Lavinia. Maybe she has operatives everywhere from here to the border. We'll just have to proceed as if she does."

Dinner arrived then, and a queue of servants bearing water carafes on their shoulders, which they poured into the shallow bath, while Darcie huddled under the blankets until they were gone.

And then she immediately darted into the bathroom and knelt by the tub. "Oh God, that looks good," she sighed, trailing a hand in the warm water and then flicking it in Con's face. He smiled, a little.

"Enjoy it. We won't see a bath for another month."

"I'm going to eat first."

"Feast away; you won't get a decent meal either."

She came back into the room and sat down at the table. There was wine and a samovar of tea; lamb in kebobs, rice and beans, a roasted chicken, cheese and fruits. She laid everything out for him, and then poured herself some tea, and some wine for him.

"We can toast the success of the journey," she said. "We're close to the end of the journey, aren't we?"

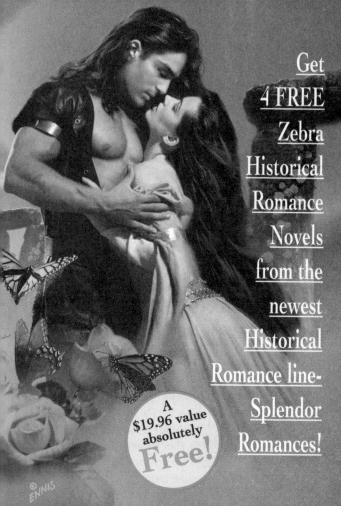

Take advantage of this offer to enjoy Zebra's newest line of historical romance novels....Splendor Romances (formerly Lovegrams Historical Romances)- Take ou introductory shipment of 4 romance novel -Absolutely Free! (a $19.96 value)

Now you'll be able to savor today's best romance novels without even leaving your home with o convenient and inexpensive home subscription service. Here's what you get for joining:

- 4 BRAND NEW bestselling Splendor Romances delivered to your doorstep every month
- 20% off every title (or almost $4.00 off) with you home subscription
- Shipping and handling is just $1.50.
- A FREE monthly newsletter, *Zebra/Pinnacle Romance News* filled with author interviews, member benefits, book previews and more!
- No risks or obligations...you're free to cancel whenever you wish...no questions asked

To get started with your own home subscription simply complete and return the card provided. You'll receive your FREE introductory shipment o 4 Splendor Romances and then you'll begin to receive monthly shipments of new Zebra Splendor titles. Each shipment will be yours to examine for days and then if you decide to keep the books, you pay the preferred home subscriber's price of just $4.00 per title. That's $16 for all 4 books with $1.50 added for shipping and handling. And if you want us to stop sending books, just say the word... that simple.

4 Free BOOKS are waiting for you!
Just mail in the certificate below!

If the certificate is missing below, write to: Splendor Romances, Zebra Home Subscription Service, Inc., P.O. Box 5214, Clifton, New Jersey 07015-5214

FREE BOOK CERTIFICATE

Yes! Please send me 4 Splendor Romances (formerly Zebra Lovegram Historical Romances), ABSOLUTELY FREE! After my introductory shipment, I will be able to preview 4 new Splendor Romances each month FREE for 10 days. Then if I decide to keep them, I will pay the money-saving preferred publisher's price of just $4.00 each... a total of $16.00. That's 20% off the regular publisher's price and I pay just $1.50 for shipping and handling. I may return any shipment within 10 days and owe nothing, and I may cancel my subscription at any time. The 4 FREE books will be mine to keep in any case.

Name _____

Address _____ Apt. _____

City _____ State _____ Zip _____

Telephone ( ) _____

Signature _____ SP0798
(If under 18, parent or guardian must sign.)

Terms and prices subject to change. Orders subject to acceptance by Zebra Home Subscription Service, Inc. .
Zebra Home Subscription Service, Inc. reserves the right to reject or cancel any subscription.

A $19.96 value.
FREE!
No obligation
to buy
anything,
ever.

He didn't answer. He lifted his goblet. "I'll toast to the journey, Darcie. I couldn't tell you where it's going to end."

She didn't like that, but she clinked her cup with his goblet and sipped the tea thoughtfully. There would be an end, she thought, the end *she* wanted, the one that wouldn't have the stamp of her father on it, or someone else's needs or desires. She'd saved him for one reason only, and her life—and his came to that—were worth nothing if they returned to England without *The Eye of God.*

The jewel of power. She knew all about that too— about the dreams that made men kill; the legends for which they died. The man with the burning eyes was counting on that; and Lavinia, so far in the background now as to seem negligible, was gambling on it too.

That didn't mean the threat she posed wasn't there. Lavinia wanted *The Eye of God,* and she wanted Con dead. And she yearned for the child of Roger's blood, and to have Darcie's head.

Two treasures for the House of Pengellis, to bejewel her crown. Time and distance meant nothing to her. However long it took, whatever she had to do, Lavinia would wait the course. Lavinia had patience. Seven years, she'd waited like Lot's wife for Con to give up the prize. What was a half year more to accomplish Con's demise?

But always, when she thought about Lavinia, she felt a sense of urgency, as if the mere conjuring of her name made her a tangible presence to be reckoned with.

A gull screamed outside the window and she felt a chill course all over her body. She pushed away her plate, her appetite gone, and she saw that Con had hardly eaten either.

"If we could leave tonight, I would," he said suddenly. "But it's dark now . . ."

"Yes."

"It's dark everywhere," he murmured. "God, I would give my soul for a moment of light."

"Don't say that."

"Perpetual darkness, Darcie. It's like being dead."

"Not if we bring back the diamond."

"You have no idea what lies ahead."

"I've climbed mountains, Con. I've gone without food. I've shivered in snowstorms. I've been thought buried for good. You were absolutely right. There's no difference."

She watched him wrestle with his anger, his frustration, his need.

"You should have left me at the bordello."

"I was meant to find you."

"Oh Jesus, Darcie."

"Explain why it was me then. Explain all of this."

"I listened to a lunatic."

"I saved you. I brought you back. And now we're both going to be wealthy as kings. What's wrong with that?"

"That simple."

"Absolutely." She knew; she remembered. There was nothing like the feeling of hitting the strike, finding the vein and bleeding the wealth into your pockets as fast as it would flow.

Nothing like it.

"All about the diamond."

"I never lied about that," she murmured. That was skirting it, she thought. That was paring it down to the extreme. She wondered if he'd have been as willing to come with her initially if he hadn't known about the child.

This was meant to be. With every gambler's instinct,

she believed it. She was as bad as Lavinia, she thought. However long it took, whatever she had to do . . . she was going to get him through.

"No. You never did."

"You want it, too."

"It will change nothing for me."

"It will get you back your life, Con."

"And what life was that, Darcie? The one where I spent seven years in a dungeon? Or the years I spent searching for *The Eye of God*? Whose life will be resurrected? Mine? Or yours? I think we know the answer."

"Don't." Oh God, she hated this. She didn't want to hear this.

"Oh, no, Darcie, why shouldn't you live with this too: you may walk away a wealthy woman. But I'll always be in the dark."

Always the dark. It was like the symbol of their quest. She lay beside him in the dark, damp from her bath, naked in the sultry heat, listening to the faint street sounds that echoed up through the open window.

Life in the dark. She heard him in the bath, the soft lapping of the water as he got out of the tub. His hesitant step as he made his way back toward the bed.

In the dark. Always in the dark.

Feeling for the edge of the bed. Feeling for his life. *In the dark.*

How had be survived?

No help wanted or needed. Forever.

No . . . !

She felt his weight depress the mattress, as he settled in beside her.

Wet. Naked. Delicious notions. Luscious words.

But the heat was so oppressive, even in the dead of

night, and the sheen of moisture from her bath had already evaporated.

She didn't want to move.

She wanted him to move, to want her, to take her, and to remove the sting of his ugly words.

In the dark.

Where nothing was seen, and everything could *be.*

Arousing, lying naked and hot next to him in the dark. All she had to do was reach out her hand. She could take him, and he would come.

She lay tense as a bowstring beside him, her muscles as taut as her swelling desire.

All he had to do was touch her, and she would come.

In the dark of the night, when all things were possible, he came to her, slipping sleekly and silently between her legs, embedding himself in her forgiveness and her heat.

It was just the way she wanted it: forceful, hot, focused, and *there.* She cradled him between her legs, wanting to keep him safe and sheltered inside her forever.

But in the dark, she had to learn, nothing was safe, not even her.

He took her with the fury of a sandstorm. He swirled all over her, his mouth, his hands insatiable, primal, raw; his penis centering within her, deep, throbbing, elemental as stone.

And she threw herself against it. She clung to it. She willingly gave herself up to it in a bone-crackling free fall to oblivion.

And that was all it took: a sultry night, a naked man, and the benediction of the dark to cover her, and absolve her of her sins.

Thirteen

They slipped away at the break of day, leaving everything behind that wasn't necessary.

They had arisen early, before dawn, to dress, to pack away their belongings, and by the light of a candle, to remove the stones of the remaining jewelry from their settings which now sat in just one of the pouches that Darcie pinned to the camisole she wore under her tunic.

Everything they were taking with them, they tied under their tunics in bundles made from their underclothing and sheets. It amounted to very little: a change of clothes, soap, the remaining cheeses and breads, the dagger.

She had to carry the dagger. "We will need the dagger," Con told her, even as she recoiled from the thought of touching it again. She had consigned it among her underclothes in the dresser, but in the dim secret light of the candle, as they finished packing, she finally took a good look at it.

It was a good six inches long with a short gold-tipped handle of black obsidian. And it was sharp; sharp as a wound, its tip honed to a fine icy point, as deadly as the man who had carried it.

Reluctantly, she added it to her bundle and tied it around her waist and then they were ready.

They were going one more time to the *souk*, where

they would trade the gold settings for the provisions they needed on this part of the trip.

She made a terrible-looking man, she thought as she caught a fleeting glance of herself in a hallway mirror. Especially when she felt so all-consumingly female. It seemed to her that everyone could tell just by a casual glance at her features, and that the dye she had applied to her skin was not enough to obscure her femininity or her eyes.

But Con was another matter altogether; in his headdress and cloak, he looked like a desert brigand, born to the saddle and the sand. At the very least, he blended in with the passersby with much more ease than she. It was the unfamiliar feel of the boots, the trousers, and the headdress, set low on her forehead as a precaution to shield her distinctive eyes. And the dagger, bound into its makeshift sheath. Maybe the dagger made her feel the most uncertain of all.

Nevertheless, as they made their way through the narrow streets toward the market, she felt more hopeful than she had in days. It was just a matter of hours now until they were on their way.

He took care of business quickly. Now that she was outfitted as a man, there were no questions asked. As they'd arranged, she communicated with him by signal, kept her eyes down, her senses keen, and counted the money with the skeptical eye of a moneylender.

They came away with hundreds of piastre notes, and food and drink, and he'd bought a revolver, a necessary precaution against desert raiders. After, they purchased third-class seats on the train to Basrah, a two-day journey from there.

From Basrah, they caught the steamer *Magid* for the three-day trip down the Tigris River to Baghdad. Here, there was some luxury, with *hamals* to serve breakfast, and a constant river view of endless muddy brown plains, mud huts and tent villages at intervals in the distance, and strings of camels and horses plodding along the horizon.

They passed a military post and countless marshes, and places with Biblical names, and faster, fleeter sailboats raced the steamer downstream while women and children waved from the shore.

And he could see none of this, Darcie thought, as she walked Con around the deck on the second morning after breakfast. To live a life not being able to see any of this.

She closed her eyes to try to imagine it; but all she could sense was the bright relentless sunlight reflecting off the river, and the presence of people she couldn't see.

Buried in darkness. Walking death. Take back your life. The part you can't see.

She felt someone knock against her shoulder, hard, and she opened her eyes. But whoever had jostled her had merged among the crowd at the rails watching the scenery, except for one lone anonymous figure on the hurricane deck who seemed to be watching *her.*

Baghdad in the morning, under the glow of an orange sun. A panoply of mosques and minarets, bridges and boats, golden domes and orange groves, and date gardens as the boat steamed slowly into the harbor.

A phalanx of officials and porters to greet them. Offers of transportation and guides for hire. A swirl of color and noise and crowds so close-packed, it was impossible to see anything.

"What do we do now?" Darcie whispered under the babble of voices.

"We go to one of the Mission Houses. We'll have a

room for the night, and they'll help with letters of transit and supplies."

They still had to get past the officials who routinely examined the passengers' baggage, that easily done by offering a bribe, and then they were ferried to shore.

They passed through the Custom House with no problem and engaged one of the eager young boys who were hawking their services to take them to the Mission House. There, they were provided with accommodations which were little more than dormitories set up in a basement beneath the mission, and the price of admission was a donation and their presence at the evening service.

In the morning, the mission doctor set about helping those who were travelling to the interior obtain the necessary papers, equipment and guides.

"All of which is very expediently done when you have money," Con said wryly as the number of piastre notes and krans diminished drastically.

"I would kill for a bath," Darcie muttered.

"I warned you."

Their guide, Karun, provided the mules they would need for their journey over the mountains to Isfahan. They scoured the market for trunks and tents, sheepskin coats and boots, *dhurries* to sleep on, cooking apparatus and food.

"But note, everything of value is brought from the market to the home of the prospective buyer," Con told her. "The upper castes do not come out to shop here."

And they travelled, making around fifteen miles a day, over rough roads, camping by the side of mud villages by night, passing caravans of voyagers like themselves, and bedouins seeking rest, walking into the endless expanse of desert toward the mirage of the mountains in the distance.

And Con saw none of it. He felt the heat of day and the cold of night, and he walked quickly and efficiently, for he held in his memory the places he'd travelled all those years before.

They began the ascent of the mountain two days later, and into the rain, and camping in the mud, and making do with little graces, like having water for tea. They huddled at night under their sheepskin coats on their muddied *dhurries,* and they hardly slept at all.

Karun tended mules and set up the tents, took his turn at watch, and was as taciturn as a rock.

They pressed on. Higher and higher, colder and colder, until nothing could be seen but sand and sky, and mud and brush. And onward, over rock and soil, ravines and hillocks, until they breasted the pass that would bring them to the other side and prepared to go over the bridge.

Karun took the mules across first, with their gear. The sun was just setting; he stood motionless at the end of the bridge, his body limned against the purpling light.

"It is safe," he called. "You can come."

Oh, but the fall on the one side was steep, and twilight was coming fast. It was the end of the world. Darcie felt it in her bones. She stepped onto the narrow edge of the footbridge, with Con right behind her, and slowly eased her way along the rocky ledge.

There was brush and scrub to hang onto, but it was even more difficult with Con gripping her hand and slowing her as he felt his way.

And then the wind whipped up with a drizzling rain.

On the other side, Karun waited as they shuffled cautiously across the bridge.

"Only a little, m'em. Just a little more."

She looked up as she heard his voice, and she saw him at the other edge, waiting for them, his eyes burning, his hands tensing for the confrontation to come.

She stopped abruptly. *"Oh my God*—Con . . . it's *him*— it's Karun . . ."

He heard the terror in her voice. "Darcie—the dagger . . ."

"Oh dear Lord, I *can't* . . ."

"You have to . . ."

"He's coming toward us."

"He'll kill us. Darcie—throw the dagger . . ."

His voice was so calm in her ear, as if he had no idea of the danger. As if a wrong step wouldn't hurtle them over into the ravine, and death.

Karun paced slowly toward her.

No words needed. No choices. They couldn't back up, they couldn't go forward. They couldn't escape, one way or the other. It was the dagger or nothing.

She slipped her hand under her tunic and pulled it from its sheath just as Karun lunged threateningly toward them.

She lifted the dagger.

He stopped abruptly, balancing himself against the rock wall with his right hand. There was no doubt he recognized it. "Ahh . . ." His voice was guttural, cruel, different from the tone of sailor and cabman. "But you know—you cannot kill me . . ."

She felt the horror right through to her bones, and she grasped the dagger in her shaking hand by the tip just the way he had on the train. He watched her, with that feral cunning, looking for that telling moment of hesitation, marking her weakness, sapping her fight.

"I can try . . ." she hissed but she couldn't steady her hand; she was never going to be able to use it. Not accurately.

And he knew it.

"Use it." Con's voice in her ear.

Oh God.

"Kill him." The desert bandit, merciless at the kill.

"I *can't.*" The dagger wobbled in her hand.

"Do it, Darcie—or we die."

He couldn't see the man; but he sensed death a foot-step away.

"You are doomed," Karun intoned. "You won't escape. Wherever you are, I will come for you." He started toward her again. "I come for you now . . ."

"Noooooo . . . !" she shrieked and hurled the dagger straight at his face, at the burning eyes that reflected the fires of hell.

He stopped short, shocked, and clamped his hand over his forehead, where the dagger protruded like another evil eye. He looked at her disbelievingly, his eyes two dark pools of malevolence and hatred, and he stepped threateningly toward her, blood spurting from between his fingers.

"No . . ." the word was a gurgle as blood spumed up from his mouth. "No . . ." as if he were invincible and it wasn't possible. "NOOOO . . . !" he shrieked, and then he dropped to his knees and with a keening wail, he pitched over the side of the bridge and into the void.

The rest, after that, was easy. They joined a caravan going through Isfahan to Kandahar, a border town in Afghanistan. They stayed but two days in Isfahan, taking time only to find a place to bathe, to rest their mules, and to buy new rugs, bedding, candles, and a fresh store of food, including tins of preserved meat, tea, flour and rice.

Now Darcie began feeling again that sense of urgency. She had been numb since she knifed the man with the burning eyes. She refused to believe he was dead, even after that fall off the cliff. Nothing was certain, not after everything they had seen.

But surely they were less vulnerable among the travellers in the *caravanserai*. Safety in numbers, and among men. The leader of the *caravanserai* thought her an ef-

feminate and managing young man and called her
mast—curdled milk—because she was always sour and
bossed around the tall *malek,* her chief.

It was saner to be in company as they crossed mountains and borders and fended off marauding thieves;
Con knew just enough of the language to have some
conversation, and they found one or two others who
were interested in going on to trade in Lahore.

They stayed three days in Kandahar, and went forward
finally, to Lahore, just inside the border of India.

There they left the traders of the *caravanserai,* and
there, before them, was the end of their journey, and
there, suddenly, they were on their own.

*God's tears. Somewhere it was written that diamonds con-
tained the essence of God, and that when God created man, his
tears of joy embedded themselves in the ground to solidify into
gemstones, superior to any other on earth.*

*Somewhere, in the vast reaches of all the research he had done,
the myths he'd studied, the clues he'd discarded, the theories he'd
evolved, he had determined the location of the fabled Valley of
Diamonds, from which Scheherazade spun the tale of the eagles
and the sheep and valley walls so steep that no man could climb
them.*

*There, on the fringes of the magic carpet of her thousand and
one nights, did she weave a story for the ages, a valley floor
adrift with diamonds and no man brave enough or clever
enough to come and take them away.*

*And then he had come, and he had seen, but he had not been
clever enough to remove them. And because it was a question of
balance, penance had to be paid.*

*The indomitable force and the unspeakable evil . . . perfect
in nature, and blessed in all things . . .*

* * *

They caught him in Srinagar, watching for him, waiting for the moment he must surface to buy supplies. He should have stayed in the mountains forever, Christ in the wilderness, knowing he was about to be betrayed.

But he had thought they were far away, and as a man alone, he was safe.

A man with a secret is never safe.

In the deep of the night, they came for him in the *dak* bungalow where he took his rest. They caught him sleeping, they caught him off guard, and they caught him as neatly as a spider catches a fly.

After that, the days and nights were a blur. They'd planned everything; the hell-hole of his prison pit had been prepared beforehand, and when, after inducements and torture, he refused to reveal the location of the valley, they incarcerated him without a blink.

And then time had no meaning at all.

Somewhere outside of Srinagar. They'd been so wrong.

Now he was here, everything came rushing back like a tidal wave. He needed to think, to eat, to sleep.

And so the tall impassive *malek* and his sour-faced secretary who never looked you in the eye took a *dak* bungalow along the trunk line to Srinagar, to spend a profitable two days in sleep.

Darcie was certain she'd never sleep again, even though the hardships of the journey had taken a toll. She was sunburned, she was aching and sore, and the burden of being Con's eyes had taken a lot out of her and she felt exhausted to the core.

If only she didn't see that man every time she closed her eyes.

Con had no compunction whatsoever about sleeping. He was dead tired, and not even thinking what awaited them. Two rupees was a small price to pay for a measure of security to obtain some rest. And with that, for a nominal sum, they were served dinner as well.

Roasted chicken, stuffed eggplant, baked custard—a feast after what they had endured on the trip.

"How long must I remain *Mast-sahib* then?" Darcie asked, as she devoured the chicken and custard.

"We'll continue on with it, I think. Along the border, there are enough traders going back and forth that we won't be conspicuous."

"And we're going—where?"

"Up into Kashmir, in the Dhambra Mountains."

Dear God—more mountains. More climbing. More hardships. She was tired of it, suddenly; she wanted desperately to go home.

Except there was no home, for either of them.

"When?"

"In a day or two."

She hated those words. She hated the waiting. The faster they travelled, the sooner they'd get there, and they'd been travelling for two months at least.

But time meant nothing here. Not to him, in the darkness. And not to her in a place where it was measured by how many miles you could make in a day.

At least they would be going up to Srinagar by train, travelling third class, wedged among fifty commuting locals, assorted livestock and bundles of all shapes and sizes, going first through Sialkot and along the Jhelum River up into the mountains to Srinagar in the Vale of Kashmir.

Srinagar was the land of hills and houseboats, where the *pukka-sahibs* came to escape the summer heat. But in the off-season, there were plenty of houseboats available to rent, and they found one on the Nagin Lake, a short distance from the town, that came with a house servant, a cook and a *wallah* to drive the *tonga*.

It was Darcie's idea of heaven: the lulling rock of the boat on the gentle tide of the lake. The views, the vista, the weather, the servants, the conveniences.

Con however seemed coiled and tense, ready to spring, primed to explode. "Two weeks," he said. "Two weeks at the most is all we'll be here." He was amazingly calm given how close they were to the objective. It was all swirling around him, the agony and the urgency. The time had come. The balance had shifted. He was meant to be there. She'd been right all along.

"Darcie . . . !" He turned from the window where he'd been staring into his own dark soul.

"I'm here."

"Tomorrow, you will go into town and you will seek out the *box-wallah* called Sidhu Hamil. And you will tell him this: the *Chowkidar* awaits him. He will know what to do."

He was an unprepossessing man, an itinerant peddler, and people in the town called him either a beggar or a saint. He was a man who had given his allegiance to Con Pengellis all those years ago. He knew how to appease the gods of the mountains, how to go, what to take, and Darcie was instructed to expend on him one of the small diamonds so he could purchase their stake.

They were on their way again two days later, up on the snow-covered track toward Gilgit, over the Burzil pass, by mule and by foot, over goat trails and icy rivers, and death defying ravines.

Up up up to the mystical juncture of four mountains, the Hindu Kush, the Himalaya, the Dhambras and the Nanga Parbat, camping under sheepskin-shrouded tents, warmed by two portable stoves, cradled in the howl of the wind.

"Jesus was said to have walked here," Sidhu said in his thin high voice as they drank tea after their meager dinner on the second night, "in the valley, in the grotto where *The Eye of God* rests, and it is said that this diamond is blessed."

"But there's no proof He ever passed here," Con said, his tone dry. "It's part of the legend that just seems to grow."

Sidhu shook his head. "You must believe, *sahib,* and with that belief will come success."

"There's a pass four miles ahead that they call the Top of the World, and from there, you can just see the Panput Valley. It looks inhospitable, impossible to negotiate. A steep fall into a thousand trees."

"The valley?" Darcie whispered.

"The valley. My Valhalla, Darcie. The palace of *The Eye of God.*"

He had marked the place on an outcropping of rock on the ridge at the Top of the World all those years ago. But seven years had effected many changes, the most discouraging of which was that the marking was almost completely effaced. They spent a frustrating half a day looking for it in the midst of the swirling snow. And then, the growth in the valley looked so thick and impenetrable, Sidhu didn't see how they would make it down.

They waited until the snow abated, and then they descended by ropes pulled tight around the rock-bound trees at the edge of the track. Sidhu went first, Con next, and Darcie after.

Slowly slowly down the face of the valley wall, certain no one could follow them, they levered themselves down thick rough hemp ropes, their legs bouncing against the scrub and boulders, sending little rock landslides down into the valley below them.

The sky darkened over, as if the gods were displeased.

Darcie felt her muscles cramp in her legs and arms, and the fear of death invaded her soul. She didn't dare look up, couldn't bear to look down, had no idea whether Sidhu or Con had reached the ground below.

And how would they return? she wondered frantically. *What if they could never get out? Dear God, she couldn't think this way. She would let go and she would die, and someone else would reap the rewards of finding The Eye.*

It was enough to keep her going in the face of her terror, the cold, the impossible descent, with her grip on the rope her sole lifeline. She had nothing else, only this. She *had* to come through.

"Darcie . . . !" Con, below her.

"I'm here . . . !" She wasn't there; she floated above them, lightheaded, surrounded by angels, heading toward the light.

"Come, *memsahib*, come." Sidhu's voice slicing through the icy air.

"I'm coming." She focused on it like a beacon. Just a little bit more. A few feet more. Ever more.

"Come—" Sidhu's thin musical voice pulling her on, "you are almost here . . ."

Almost here . . . she could let go, she had nothing to fear—

She relinquished her grip, her fingers stiff with the cold, and she fell heavily to the ground, she heard Con's voice above her: "Jesus God—the baby . . . !" and she gave up her soul.

Fourteen

Silence. An all-consuming heavenly silence.

She lay cradled in a bed of leaves and scrub at the base of the valley wall, and contemplated heaven. Sidhu knelt beside her, touching her gently in various places.

She opened her eyes in reaction to the pressure of his fingers at a point on her belly. Con stood, leaning against a tree, a couple of yards away, his expression stony.

"An—*memsahib* awakens." Sidhu removed his hand and pulled her coat over her. "All is well."

"Is it?" Con murmured. "Is all well, Darcie?"

Her answer stuck in her throat. She struggled to a sitting position, taking in the details around her: the soft needles on the valley floor; the stones, the trees, the sense of desolation which only mirrored how she felt.

And somewhere, in this witch's forest, riches and dreams. They were that close, and something like this was going to get in the way.

"You didn't jar anything, Darcie? There isn't any bleeding? Any evidence of *anything* wrong?"

She swallowed convulsively. Sidhu must have noticed; Sidhu must have said something. "I'm fine," she managed.

"And how is the baby?"

The loaded question. She could have killed the baby. She had fallen hard, on her back, and all she felt was an ache at the base of her spine. A jolt like that could have injured the baby.

She looked up at Sidhu, whose eyes were sharp and comprehending, and she knew he knew. And something in his expression told her not to dissemble.

"There is no baby," she whispered.

The silence fell like a stone. Sidhu rocked back on his heels and bowed his head. She couldn't even look at Con.

"No baby." He was looking into the darkness, and seeing the limits of her soul.

"There was never a baby," she said stoically. "Lavinia wanted a baby. And I wanted to save my life. The lie kept me alive long enough to escape. And long enough to find you."

He was still silent.

She wouldn't have believed the story either. The whole thing, every detail, true as it was, still sounded like a lie. And the only lie was really the truth.

"Scheherazade," he muttered. "Jesus God—more stories. Do you never end, Darcie? You really are something."

She bristled. "And you are damned fortunate I found you, and even more fortunate that I wanted this . . ."

"This is all you want, Scheherazade, but you've never lied about that."

She supposed he thought that admission gave her something. But it wasn't enough—when she was on the verge of losing everything. "They were going to kill me."

And they'd come all the way to Srinagar to kill him, he

thought. *What wouldn't a person do to stay alive? Who knew better than he?*

He didn't have to be so obdurate. They were rogues, the two of them, and they were not averse to using any weapon they had at hand. He understood that. He just didn't comprehend why the lie was so devastating to him.

But everything was strange. The scents, the sounds, the feeling in the air . . . and the lie. He had no more time to deal with the lie. They could sort all that out later.

"Lavinia could still kill you," he said brutally.

"And she would, after I had given birth to that baby."

That stopped him. There was something about that he knew he should consider, but he couldn't take the time. Time suddenly was more precious than diamonds. He couldn't see the light but he knew it was lowering faster than they had planned.

And they still had to cut through the brush to the excavation.

"We have work to do," he said abruptly. "Sidhu."

"Sahib?" He listened to a barrage of instructions and then turned to Darcie. "Come. I will lead, you will follow. It is but a short distance from here. And we must think about the time—now time is fleeting."

Of everything she had imagined, she could not have conceived of this: one nondescript stone of hundreds, backed up the valley wall.

She couldn't have told one from the other, but Sidhu could. It was the one stone with markings cut by wind and weather, visible only to the knowledgeable eye. Now Sidhu's eyes. And that stone blocked a tunnel cleverly cut into the valley wall.

Uncover the tomb and find resurrection . . .

Together, they rolled away the stone to reveal the gaping tunnel entrance.

Sidhu raised his hand in benediction. "It is good, *sahib*. And now it is time." He handed a lantern to Darcie. *"Memsahib*—please to go first."

"Me?" She was flabbergasted. And scared out of her wits. "But—"

"Sidhu remains on guard," Con said. "He cannot enter a place of the infidel. And we don't have that much time."

So . . . she was going to be first to crawl into a tunnel that no one had breached in seven or more years. She swallowed the clog in her throat. She'd wanted this. And she'd been in tighter places down in the mines in Colorado. What was here that could touch her?

She knelt beside the entrance to the tunnel and immediately a flat musty scent assaulted her nose. She held up the lantern that Sidhu had lit for her. It looked to be a fairly short tunnel. She saw a sharp drop about fifty feet in. And then—what?

Nothingness. Everything about this quest was connected to the dark and nothingness . . .

"I'll be right behind you," Con said. "There's a place about a dozen yards in where the tunnel breaks. You'll see it. I'll talk you through it."

That didn't reassure her.

Going into the dark. Endless dark. On her knees and slowly pushing the lantern forward, the light reflecting back into her eyes. She might as well be blind.

"I'm behind you," Con said as he grasped the hem of her tunic and followed her in.

An awkward eight-legged humping monster making its way through the tunnel . . . and the aura of evil washing over them a dozen feet within the tunnel entrance. Cold. Musky. Murderous.

"Con"

"Keep going—"

Evil wasn't tangible; it didn't whip you in the face. And there was nothing to grasp onto. She couldn't shine her light on it. She wanted to back out of the tunnel and never look back.

"Move, Darcie . . . !"

He felt it too. She heard it in his voice; the evil was immutable, spreading all over and around them like a cocoon.

"I can't . . ." she protested.

"Darcie—we're that close. *That* close."

It wasn't worth it, it wasn't. "But Con—there's something . . ."

"Defeat it."

He knew this thing.

He pushed her forward relentlessly, and she moved involuntarily, creeping creeping forward, with his hand on her derrière, pushing, goading, coaxing, inch by malignant inch.

And only the pulsating dark and the bright glaring light before her eyes.

And that terrorizing evil somewhere in the dark.

"We're almost there," he whispered.

"Almost where?"

"At the drop. Be ready for the drop. Just swing your legs over. It's about four feet, and we'll be able to stand up."

"What aren't you telling me, Con?"

"I'd give my soul to be able to see."

She heard the torment in his voice—and then suddenly, silently, the evil presence laughing at them, mocking them.

"Con . . ."

His voice turned to steel. *"Keep going . . ."*

Her knees turned to jelly. "I can't."

"You will. You *must.*"

She closed her eyes, to close out the presence, to close in his voice and the motivation, the goal. To see what he saw, to know what he knew. In moments, she would see before her eyes the diamond, the mythical, mystical *Eye of God.*

And nothing would prevent it.

But nothing like this lived in a Colorado mine. She had defeated claim jumpers, robbers, outlaws, cheats. Things she understood; things she could see.

She felt the taunting laughter of the presence, and she girded herself, and creeping slowly forward, she continued on. Lantern first, right hand, left knee; left hand, right knee, with Con creeping in tandem right behind her.

She almost fell over the drop. She didn't expect it. Or the presence had distracted her from it.

She put out the lantern and set it onto nothingness, and it fell to the ground.

The presence jeered.

"Quick—over the drop." Con's voice behind her, pushing her on. She swung her legs over and jumped; a moment later he followed her, and they stood crouched, and wary, and determined.

Slowly, she eased into an upright position. The sense of evil was palpable here. She picked up the lantern, relit it, and took Con's arm, and pulled him to his feet.

"Now what?" Her voice shook.

"Straight ahead."

She lifted the lantern. "There is no straight ahead. It's a sheer wall."

"Then we move the headstone of the tomb."

She saw it then, the subtle fit of the stone against stone into the wall.

"Help me then."

The presence was almost unbearable as they each took a side of the stone and pushed and shifted it until it moved.

"It doesn't want us in there," Darcie whispered.

"It has a lot to lose."

They stood at the entrance to the second tunnel, tempted and afraid.

"At the end of this tunnel," Con said, his voice barely above a breath, "is the realization of your dreams."

But even that was not enough to galvanize her. She held up the lantern and swung it around. There was nothing in front of her but darkness, and the heavy sense of evil waiting.

"It's blocking the way."

"We'll pass through it."

"What if it's *him*?"

"He can't stop us. He hasn't yet."

Con leaned against her, forcing her to step over the threshold. And then they were in, past the barrier, into the evil, and moving slowly and hesitantly forward into the dark.

The sense of evil followed, a weight on their shoulders.

"There are stone steps, about a hundred feet down. Watch it."

She held the lantern low to the ground. "All right." She thought she sounded calm, but her voice came out breathless. "Take my arm."

She closed her eyes for a moment, again to try to imagine what he was seeing, what he was thinking. *Darkness. The unending, unnerving silence stretching to infinity. And the air: close, dank, malignant.*

*And they were so close. But she hadn't counted on this on-
going unspeakable evil. She had thought they'd just walk into
a cavern somewhere and pluck the thing up and spirit it away.*

*Naïve. Foolish. Short-sighted. Dumb. Still hadn't learned
that the next big strike never never came easily. That it was
always over the hill and the obstacles were almost insurmount-
able.*

And it was always always always buried in the dark.

And for Con, it always would be.

She shivered, in spite of the close musty air.

"Darcie." Con's voice, steely again, set with purpose,
his fingers convulsive against her arm. "This is what you
wanted. This is why we're here."

"I know." But she'd never felt like this at the kill—
wary, reluctant, faltering at the very moment she should
pounce.

The evil thing knew it; she felt it all around them,
mocking them, provoking them, daring them to go forward and claim the treasure.

"Then *move* . . ."

She moved, holding the lantern in front of her like
a shield, one hesitant step at a time with Con draped
around her like a cloak. Moved like a snail, moved like
a crone who had nothing to live for.

What was wrong with her?

The air was stultifying, the closer they came to the
stone steps. She saw them finally just ahead. "We're almost there."

"Go down the steps, Darcie."

She inched toward them, feeling her way in the light
as if she were blind. There was something beyond, something below. The thing was waiting. The evil was there.

She paused at the top. The steps descended into darkness.

"Just go," Con whispered.

They fumbled down the steps together. Steep steps, sharply angled, easy to misstep and fall to eternity. She held onto the wall, she held onto him. And she held onto the thought of what awaited them.

"The tunnel veers to the right at the bottom," Con murmured.

She held up the lantern. To the right, into more ominous darkness, and the suppurating evil.

"You'll see columns of rock. Like guardians at the gate," he went on in an undertone as they shuffled on.

She grabbed his hand as they came into view, a horizontal line of thick, coruscated stalagmites, sentinels of the divine.

"The grotto is just beyond."

She felt a chill down her spine. *This close. Almost there. Steps away. She almost couldn't breathe. The strike of a thousand lifetimes . . . and nothing to stand in their way.*

And then she felt it, a violent swirl of malevolence enveloping them, and blocking their way.

She almost dropped the lantern; no—*it* almost made her drop the lantern.

"He's here," she hissed.

"He's dead," Con said, his voice like iron. "Keep walking."

She couldn't. She couldn't move; she felt the evil surrounding her, holding her immobile like the tentacles of an octopus.

"I *can't* . . ."

He lost patience. "Then I *will* . . ." He relinquished her arm, stretched out his arms and pushed forward in the dark.

Immediately he felt the wall of resistance.

"*Con*—!" she screamed as he merged with the fog. *Oh dear God*—! She felt the malevolence drain away from her; her body felt boneless, powerless. But she could move. She took an experimental step after him.

"*Con* . . . !" But he'd disappeared through the columned portal, and all she could see by the light of the lantern was a swirl of turbulence trailing after him, and the dark unknown beyond.

Her heart pounding crazily, she passed through the stone column, holding the lantern in front of her like a talisman.

There—just ahead of her—light . . .

She moved cautiously toward it, through a natural stone arch that framed the entrance to the grotto. The evil was all-pervasive here, its scent strong, awful, fecund, dead. She felt her throat gag, she wanted to turn and run away, and she resisted the impulse with all her might.

She forced herself to creep through the arch. "*Con* . . ." Her whisper reverberated in the stone. She was in what looked like an anteroom, and straight ahead of her, there was yet another arch, and beyond that, the glow.

She felt the evil trying to repulse her, and she pushed against it, her heart constricted with fear. It was so strong, so wicked, so all encompassing, she almost felt she couldn't defeat it.

And then suddenly, maliciously, it released her, and she tumbled into the grotto.

She was enfolded by the light. It seemed to her that the whole cavernous space was infused with light, emanating from *The Eye of God*. The holy grail of a diamond, placed on a ledge that looked like an altar, side by side with a stone of similar proportions and brilliance that was black like the night.

She stepped into the brilliance of the light, she was

enveloped by it, enthralled by it. She felt shocked that the stone was no bigger than a large jelly mould, and then it didn't matter at all. The stone glowed as if something holy were watching over her. She felt a sense of well-being and saneness, as if everything in the world had suddenly come right.

She moved toward it unerringly as if its power pulled her. And she walked willingly into its light.

Con knelt on the ground before it, and leaning over him, subjugating him was the man with the burning eyes. The sailor, the cabman, the guide they'd called Karun. The personification of the evil that saturated the air.

If she moved one step toward the black stone, it would attack her. It would imprison her as it had Con. It wanted to. It wanted to destroy her for what she had inflicted on it.

But she knew, she felt, all she had to do was stay in the light and she would have the power to do battle with the malevolence from there.

But it went even deeper than that entity called Karun. It felt as if it were thundering in the grotto, waiting to erupt from someplace deep in the ground.

The thing called Karun stood over Con menacingly, with some kind of implements in its hand.

And there was a silence like death as it awaited its command.

"Don't move," Con breathed. "Don't say anything and I will tell you the whole story. This is the altar of the dark and the light. The black diamond is called *The Stone of Samael* after the Judge of the Dead. It sits in balance with *The Eye of God,* and they are never to be touched or moved. They neutralize each other, and bring good and evil into harmony. It is said whoever lays eyes on them will be cursed forever."

"As were you," she whispered, stunned to the bone.

"And now," the entity Karun intoned, "you will be damned to eternity."

He lifted the implements and she was shocked to see he held a cleaving tool and a chisel. He whirled and in a heart-stopping moment, in the blink of an eye, he chiseled into the black diamond, set the angle, and struck it with one sharp, awful rap.

"Jesus God . . ." Con breathed in horror. "Oh my God—"

A dark dense foul-smelling fog spumed into the cavern and enveloped them, freezing them in place. And then it moved unerringly to the entity called Karun, and slowly and completely it devoured him.

It hovered, fetid, putrid, all enfolding, obscuring *The Eye of God* and contaminating the air.

It paralyzed them; it rendered them immobile. Almost imperceptibly it began to re-form, the fog gathering into itself in eddying swirls, solidifying, elongating, transmogrifying itself incrementally before their very eyes.

And suddenly something was there: tall, spare, ascetic, cloaked in black, emanating an aura of depravity and ungodliness from every pore.

It was a man—and it was an entity—possessed of sharp, black, piercing eyes that saw everything and missed nothing.

He lifted his bony hand and Darcie recoiled from the malodorous smell that issued from him.

He pointed at Con, and Con felt the power of his diabolic touch. He reacted violently, pushing up from the floor, and tumbling back down again as the entity lowered his hand.

"Who are you?" he demanded sharply. "Who's there?"

"I am called Lazarin," it said, its words measured, its voice raspy and hollow. "And the power of Samael is dispersed upon the land."

It raised his hand again and pointed to Con, and Con felt the repercussions of the heat and soul-sapping energy through to his bones.

"You have transgressed upon the holy place of Samael, and so you will be judged," it intoned, and then it lifted its leonine head for a moment, as if it were listening to some supernatural power.

And then it nodded and turned its burning gaze back to Con.

"I lay my hand upon you, in the name of Samael, and in his name and in the sight of *The Eye of God*, I offer you the gift of your vision. The judgment of the merciful Samael is as follows: that you may know there is good in evil and evil in good."

It walked toward Con, its decaying essence enveloping them, making them sick.

"The decision is yours, infidel," it whispered, making a sign over Con's head. "The hand of Samael is upon you."

"Don't do it . . ." Darcie whispered. "Con . . . don't— you can't see it, it's a walking corpse . . . a phantasm from the grave . . ."

He felt like he was dying, and like he was being reborn. He'd said it over and over—to see again, he would sell his soul. He felt fractured, the way he envisioned Karun had cleft the black stone. His own depravity cracked within him, splitting him down the middle, and he knew that he had made the decision months ago, and that now he was damned, just as the Karun had foretold.

"I will have my sight," he whispered.

"Con . . . !" Darcie shrieked as Lazarin laid his bony

hand on his forehead. "The will of Samael shall be done," he intoned, sketching the sign with his thumb.

Darcie watched, horrified, as Con slumped over at Lazarin's feet.

And then the fog rose up around them, thick, rank, malodorous, foul. It filled the cavern, penetrating every crevice, every pore. It settled on *The Eye of God,* negating its powers. It rendered her helpless in its wake.

She saw Lazarin's burning eyes, warning her, condemning her, damning her through the billowing vapor, and it was the last thing she saw before she crumpled to the ground.

Fifteen

"*Memsahib . . . memsahib—*" Someone was shaking her. "Please . . . please to wake, *memsahib . . .*"

She shook her head groggily. She had no idea where she was or who was calling to her. The hand was gentle, respectful, urgent.

"*Memsahib . . .*"

She brushed the insistent hand away.

"Please—we must go . . ."

She didn't want to go; it seemed to her she was always going and she was tired of it. She just wanted to lie on the soft ground and fall back into her peaceful dreams.

"*Memsahib—the sahib* still sleeps . . ."

She opened her eyes. Sidhu! And in this sanctuary. She shook her head again, and then struggled to sit up. Something about that was odd and she couldn't remember what.

And Con—oh God—*where was Con?* But no, he was right there, on the grotto floor beside her, in deep unconscious sleep.

And there was light—but that came from Sidhu's lantern.

She was oriented now, except she couldn't quite remember what had happened. And then she did. The horror. The evil. The scent.

Oh dear God—The diamonds—!

She jumped to her feet and whirled toward the ledge. *The Stone of Samael* was gone.

Everything came back to her then full force. The fog. The entity. The unholy bargain. Con, limp as a puppet, on the ground. And Sidhu beside him, frantically trying to rouse him.

"Sidhu! When did you come?"

"After a day and a night had passed, *memsahib*. And the sky turned black and the mountain gods became angry."

She was stunned. *A day and a night. They'd lost that much time. Always at the mercy of time.*

She rubbed her eyes. *Her* eyes. What about *his* eyes? Surely they had dreamed everything about the ungodly entity. And where was the black diamond? Or had she dreamt that too?

But no, *The Eye of God* was on its resting place, the light around it extinguished. And something had compelled Sidhu to come.

She got down beside him. "Con—" He was so unresponsive.

Sidhu held up his hand. "All will be well, *memsahib*."

"How?"

"We will make do. I will make a pallet. Come."

She didn't know what was more frightening: leaving Con or going with Sidhu. "I can't leave him. The thing might come back."

Sidhu considered her words. "This is true. I will find the branches. It is daylight, we have time." He picked up his lantern and with it, lit hers. "Take courage, *memsahib*. I will return, soon."

She wrapped her arms around Con as Sidhu disappeared into the darkness, his lantern a faint glow in the distance.

She huddled closer to Con, avoiding the shadows, staring at *The Eye of God.*

Balanced to neutralize evil. Never to be touched or moved. Cursed forever—

Samael loose upon the land . . .

She shuddered convulsively. Whatever had happened, the black stone was gone. She wondered if she had the nerve to remove *The Eye of God.*

It wasn't that big. It couldn't be that heavy. She could just tie it up in a piece of her underclothing and hide it under her tunic.

She got to her feet, took the lantern, and went over to the ledge.

There was a scorch mark at the place where *The Stone of Samael* had been. *The brand of the Judge of Death . . . ?* And there was nothing left of the sundered stone except several minute slivers of crystal.

She swept them up onto her fingers. All that remained of a horrible dream. She slipped them into the pouch in which she carried the remaining Pengellis diamonds.

And then she considered *The Eye of God.*

Remembered the enfolding light, the warmth, the sense of well-being . . .

She reached out a hand and touched it. *Cool. Smooth. The object of desire. Wealth and riches at her fingertips.*

Did she dare . . . ?

She took it in her hands and lifted it. Just picked it up in her hands as easily as if she were taking a piece of fruit.

She held it up to the lantern light. Nowhere in its depths could she see the light, the power, or the mystical properties of its legend. It looked like less than it was.

Only Con could tell her. She turned to look at him,

still unconscious on the ground. No help there. And a decision to be made before Sidhu returned.

She held it up to the light again, a stone the size of a pineapple in her hand. And then she set it back on the ledge, and removed her tunic, thankful that for this bone-cold journey, she wore several layers of clothing.

Con had insisted on the trousers, and the sheepskin outer clothes. But she'd also worn a shirt and she reached for her shirttail now, and ripped it into a long oblong piece.

That would do. She placed the stone in the center, and tied the ends of the material over it, around it, and finally around her neck and then tucked it into her bosom, where it hung like a third breast.

And not a moment too soon. She heard Sidhu along the passageway, saw his light before he appeared, and then he emerged from the shadows carrying two thick long branches.

He looked immediately at the altar ledge and then back at her and she felt his tacit disapproval.

"It is not for me to say, *memsahib*," he said finally. "Come—we will remove *sahib's* cloak, and that, with your tunic, should make a pallet strong enough to carry him."

They struggled through the tunnel to the steps, and there, they hauled him upright and got him up the stairs; and then over the drop, and they were careful to take the time to replace the stone at the entrance to the grotto along the way.

With all that, it took two hours before they set him down at the opening of the crawlway to the first tunnel.

"It will be cold tonight, *memsahib*. We will make a fire, and guard the entrance until daylight."

She unwrapped the tunic from under Con's listless body and tucked it around him. She was shaking with fear again. They'd come down to the valley with so little; they'd expected so much. And they'd gotten more than they'd bargained for.

She didn't know how they were going to last the night.

She huddled close to the meager campfire that Sidhu had made, the lump that was *The Eye of God* pressed between her breast and her knees, and the only warmth she felt emanating from the proximity of Con's body.

But the fire and the two lanterns gave this outer cave at least some semblance of safety, and she was grateful for Sidhu's calm presence and his assurances that Con would recover.

Recover what? she wondered as she stared at the fire. *And how much had he already lost?*

"Beware of useless dreams, *memsahib*. They come back to haunt you."

"What if he doesn't awaken?"

"All will be well, *memsahib*. Sidhu assures you."

Sidhu had brought some food into the Valley with them, and he was stirring up a pot of tea on the makeshift campfire. "You will warm yourself with tea. You will turn your thoughts to the future. For good and evil, you carry *The Eye of God, memsahib*. That alone should bless you."

He poured the tea into a tin cup and handed it to her, and then took one for himself.

"Why did you come?" she asked him. "I thought you were not permitted within."

Sidhu shrugged. "Who knows by what method we are called to do anything, *memsahib?*" He handed her a biscuit. "I heard the call to come."

And what had she heard? The call to greed.

"And before—did you assist him?"

Sidhu nodded. "And I owe *sahib* my life."

She bit into the biscuit. It was stale. Dry. It tasted like manna. They were blessed, alive, and removed from the grotto, and all that remained was to get through the night.

"*Memsahib* should sleep."

"I'll keep watch with you."

"No one will find us."

"But the ropes—"

"No, *memsahib*—" He looked at her kindly, the beggar with wise eyes, and said, "—you can rest easy. The enemy has gone."

Or the enemy was herself.

She cradled *The Eye of God* between her breasts and wondered if she should lie. When Con awakened—*if* Con awakened . . .

The tunnel was blocked now; he wouldn't be able to go back. She could just tell him—it would be so tempting to tell him—that both of the diamonds were gone.

A manipulative slicing up of the truth . . . and not the first time she'd ever done it. The stone was so warm between her breasts, so tantalizing . . . as seductive as a lover.

She never heard Con stir.

She would have sworn she hadn't slept.

And she was shocked to find him kneeling beside her, ruthlessly stripping away her clothes.

"What the hell do you think you're doing?" she gasped, batting his hands away. She reared up, half naked, and lunged at him.

"You're a clever bitch, Darcie." He wrestled her back down to the ground again. "Sidhu told me, you thieving hellcat." He pinned her arms mercilessly. "And yes, I can see."

* * *

She sat resentfully across the campfire from him, eyeing him warily as he cradled *The Eye of God* in his hands.

His gaze was no longer blank; it was sharp, perceptive, keen. He was a different Con Pengellis from the man she had saved. Everything about him now was focused and contained and she, conversely, felt uncertain and constrained.

She didn't like it. It was like the power between them had shifted and she was standing in quicksand and sinking fast.

And she hated the way he looked at her across the campfire.

"And what happened to the *black* diamond, did you say?" Even his voice was different, with a tone of confidence and command.

"He had to have taken it." This was the third time she had told him and he still didn't believe her. But then, he thought she'd tried to steal *The Eye of God;* Sidhu told him she'd taken it, and then left her at his mercy to gather wood for the campfire, not betraying by a glance or a muscle any astonishment at the fact that Con had regained his sight.

"He cleaved it into two pieces. And when I awoke, it was gone."

"So convenient," he murmured, turning the diamond this way and that in his hands. All he had done, all he had suffered to come to this moment, to hold *The Eye of God* in his grasp, and to see in its depths the power and the possibilities. "The entity took it. I wonder why I don't believe you."

He was sharp as a knife now, she thought, and deft at slicing to the quick. This was the Con Pengellis of the portrait, only more mature, honed to an edge, and fully in control.

"And I wonder why you never mentioned it," she

retorted. "All that mystical mumbo-jumbo about upsetting the balance and the stones neutralizing each other . . ."

He looked at her then, a scathing glance that would have frozen stone. "How can we know, Darcie? What do we know, after all? Well, we know how avid you are to possess this stone."

She didn't know *him*—now. He wasn't in the dark anymore. *She* felt unbalanced and out of control, and like she'd been the one who'd been blind.

"We know," he went on inexorably, "you don't scruple to lie. And we surely know you'll do anything to get what you want."

In the dark.

But now he was in the light, and he didn't like what he saw.

She felt raw, slashed, as if he had drawn blood.

"We wouldn't be here if it weren't for me," she shot back. "I think some gratitude is in order."

"Where is the black diamond?" His voice was calm, neutral and laced with steel.

"He took it." *He took everything, in the name of Samael. And she would never get it back.* She remembered the slivers of black stone, tucked in the pouch at her breast. "Look." She unpinned the pouch. "Hold out your hand." *Oh, his hand . . .* She spilled the five remaining small diamonds and the shards of crystal into his palm. "That was all that was left."

"A careless cut," he murmured, pushing aside the diamonds, and picking up one long shard. He held it to the waning campfire light, staring at it for a long time. "But then—maybe it didn't matter." He gave it back to her. "Put it away."

She was pinning the pouch just as Sidhu returned with an armful of wood.

"Dawn approaches, *sahib,*" he said, as he knelt to replenish the fire.

"Good. There's just enough time. Get up, Darcie. We're going down to the grotto."

She got slowly to her feet. He still didn't believe her. He picked up a lantern, grasped her arm and propelled her back into the tunnel.

"What a pleasure to be able to see such treacherous footings."

She wrenched her arm away. "And who got you safely through?"

"Who had her own agenda?"

"We are both still in danger," she said grittily.

"So you say. It occurs to me, Miss Darcie, that yours is the only story we know. For example, *I* don't know that it was Lavinia or Roger who imprisoned me. I don't even know that you were married to Roger. I only have your word for it—watch the drop—" as she almost stepped over it and into oblivion, "and we know how good you are at spinning tales."

"I see," she said angrily. "We're going to backtrack over everything that's happened, and then we're going to call me a liar."

"How about a fabricator of truth?"

"How nice you can see that—now."

"I think I was in the dark about a lot of things, Darcie."

"It's a bargain you'll regret."

"Or you will."

They were at the steps then, and he flashed the lantern downward. "You first, Scheherazade. I can't wait to hear what tale you'll tell."

"I'm not going to say a word. You didn't see the thing. You can't know. You made a devil's bargain with an apparition from hell."

"Or maybe, Scheherazade, that was *you.*"

She descended the steps furiously, aware that he thought her perfectly capable of sending him over the edge, and he followed her, holding the lantern low to light the way.

And then to the right, and into the anteroom, through the stone columns and into the grotto. And nowhere was there any overwhelming sense of lurking doom.

Nor was there that blessed light to warm and welcome them. The grotto was cold and soulless. A pagan altar, eons old.

He stepped up to it, holding the lantern over the ledge. There was nothing to indicate that balanced there had been two mythic diamonds. Only the scorch mark, round, deep, black as a hole.

"He couldn't remove *The Eye of the God,*" Con said, examining the ledge. "There are chisel marks in the stone. He tried to prise it up, and he couldn't move it. Not all the powers of Samael could move it. And yet you were able to pick it up without resistance, without any invocation."

He turned to look at her, an odd look, an assessing look. He hardly wanted to think about it—about her, the Darcie of the dark, the Darcie of the lies, the Darcie of his dreams.

None of that mattered now because, in spite of his plans and regardless of her schemes, they had been deliberately brought to this place, and *she* had been given the benediction of *The Eye of God.*

And he had to live with that. Darcie's dream. Darcie's will. Darcie's desire. And he had no choice but to use her.

He swirled the light around the grotto. "Sidhu said we were unconscious for a day and a night."

"That's what he said."

"What did it look like?"

They were in the right place for ghost stories, she thought. And he would say she was weaving still another tale because it was so unbelievable.

"He looked like a corpse," she told him, shuddering as she remembered the horrific way it formed from the fog. "He looked like a corpse; bony, gray, burning eyes, wearing a long robe like a monk."

"Yes."

He knew this. She saw by his face, by his all-seeing, knowledgeable eyes. He knew all about this, and the unspeakable evil encased in that stone.

"We have to recover that diamond."

"We?" Now she wanted no part of it. She wanted her share of *The Eye of God*—no more, no less. He could pursue his demons on his own.

"We," he said furiously. "We have to stop him."

"Stop . . . ?"

"Lazarin. That's what he called himself, yes?" His eyes hardened. "He has to be stopped, and we have to reclaim the diamond."

"Oh no. Not me. I'll just take my little piece of *The Eye of God*, and go back where I came from."

He ignored her. "We'll be able to move faster this time. We can do more this time. And we'll have to leave soon—he's already had too much of a start."

"Con—you're not listening," she said desperately. "You don't even know where it's gone."

"No—you're the one who doesn't hear. *We* have to do this." He swiped the lantern over the ledge once more but he saw nothing more. "You know, if I had some dynamite, I would blast this place to kingdom come."

He took her arm, and pushed her toward the ante-room. "You don't understand. You have to do this because you've been anointed, Darcie. *You* are the one sanctified by *The Eye of God.*"

"She is blessed."

"So I perceived," Sidhu said. "All is in readiness for departure."

"This place must be destroyed."

"It will be my holy duty to do this for the *chowkidar sahib.*"

"I will be a watchman no more."

"It will be as you wish. Fate has been kind that you could watch over this place even as you were blind." Sidhu bowed. "We must go now."

Con had stamped out the fire, packed the lanterns and removed all traces of their presence there. It only remained to move the stone over the portal to the catacomb of his rebirth, and then they would be ready to make the ascent from the Valley.

They started out in the late morning.

Sidhu shimmied up the rope first.

Darcie watched how he did it, digging his feet into crevices in the wall, scaling his way up hand over hand, cleft by cleft.

I can't do that. I could barely get down.

"I'll go next," Con said, shielding his eyes so he could watch Sidhu's agile body. "And then Sidhu and I will pull you up. I'm going to tie the rope around your waist now, you'll wear the gloves, and you just let us do the work. It will be faster that way."

She didn't think so; she was terrified already of the idea of swinging on the rope with only his ability to tie a knot to protect her. It was a solid knot, though, thick, tight and seemingly secure. She would hold the rope, she would try to get a foothold now and again, and she would be up at the ridge before she knew it.

She watched him doubtfully as he grasped the rope and began to climb. Simple as that, when you could see. You could see everything for a thousand miles, even your destiny.

He disappeared from view, and a moment later, he tugged the rope, the signal that he was about to pull.

She grasped it just at face level and girded herself as she felt herself being lifted off the ground. Like a circus performer, up up up, into the rafters.

She closed her eyes; she couldn't look. To the Top of the World, like an angel. In the dark, like a man who couldn't see . . .

She reached for an outcropping of rock as she neared the top, and braced her leg against it. She reached for Con, as he lay on the edge of the cliff above her, extending his hands to her.

She looked into his dark unfathomable *seeing* eyes and wondered if he would grasp her hands and then just let her go. She saw herself falling down the valley wall, a conspirator who knew too much, and had to be subdued.

She closed her eyes as he took her hands, pulled her up, and swung her onto the ridge.

They stood there, buffeted by the raw mountain wind, at the Top of the World, silhouetted against the sun.

"You don't understand, Darcie," he murmured. "You have all the protection, all the power. *You* are the one."

"I don't want to be any one. I want to go home."

"You said it yourself. Until this thing is done, we can't go home."

"No—I said until we claimed *The Eye of God* . . ."

"You claimed it."

And she carried it still. And she felt the weight of the burden of it.

"We're not selling it, are we? You won't cleave it. What good is it?"

"The good is that we have it, and Lazarin does not. And Lavinia—" he paused, thinking about it a moment; his family hadn't entered anywhere into his calculations to this point, except for the tantalizing feeling that he was missing something about Lavinia.

But his family had nothing to do with their pursuit of the black diamond. And there was no time to consider anything else.

"At this point," he said, "Lavinia doesn't count."

Sixteen

They returned to the houseboat on the Nagin Lake in Srinagar. They came out of the cold harsh mountains from the Top of the World and into the warmth of a hill country spring, where the servants questioned nothing and always were waiting.

"They could be waiting for you in Srinagar," Darcie protested. "They could have followed us this far. They could have followed us to the valley."

She didn't know why she felt so frenzied and unsure. But she really did. It was because she was no longer in command. It was because Con had taken control of everything. Con with his eyes, with his memories, with his past. He was treading on solid ground now; he would make no missteps the way she had while she fought every inch of the way to come this far.

And now she felt as if she had toppled off a mountain. She didn't like it. *She hated it.*

"They caught me in Srinagar all those years ago," Con said casually, as he divested himself of his sheepskins, his *aba,* and his boots.

It was a revelation that unnerved her.

"Then why are we here?"

"Because we have lodgings, we need some time, and we have a friend."

He rang for the *khansamer* who appeared as silently as air. "Have a bath drawn, will you?" he ordered in Hindi, and translated for her. "And dinner at eight, please."

Dinner. What a lovely word. Not beans, or skewered meat that was raw inside. Real dinner. With Con. Who could see to cut his meat and eat his dessert.

This was a whole different Con. He would never hold onto her again. Never be dependent. Never turn to her in the dark . . .

She shook herself.

She should know better than this. She was a gambler, and one thing always held true: sometimes the rules of the game changed. And sometimes the stakes. And if everything went to hell, you bluffed your way through.

But what did you do when all the boundaries got turned inside out?

You make new ones, she thought. *And you don't let him overrun them and take control.*

She felt him looking at her, as she paced the large front room of the houseboat, and she wondered what he saw under the tunic and cloak and the headdress, and under the henna dye.

She felt uncomfortable suddenly; Con Pengellis knew her too well—in the dark. You couldn't hide from a man when you were naked in the dark.

In the dark, there were no barriers, and no boundaries.

And she saw he remembered that too.

"Lavinia will not rest until she finds you," she said to distract him—no, distract herself. "Wouldn't this be the logical place for her to start?"

He looked so different without his headdress and his paint. Astonishingly different with his eyes. The light in them changed the whole aspect of his face. Made him look hawk-eyed, sharp-sighted, vigilant, keen.

"Maybe. Probably." His gaze swept her, head to toe, missing nothing.

For the first time, she felt the edginess of their enforced togetherness. This was not the same as her taking charge, directing the quest, and fueling it with her hunger and her greed.

In the blink of an eye, everything had passed out of her hands and into his.

At the mercy of Samael.

It was now his jewel. His dream. *His* quest.

She turned her back on him and stalked to the window. It was just coming on twilight, the orange sun sinking into the horizon and reflecting off of the lapping river.

This was a place people came to find calm. To escape the heat.

But the heat was building up behind her, seeping into her pores, stroking her skin.

She whirled to face him. And wished she hadn't. Those eyes grazed her eyes, her mouth, her breasts.

"How can you be so calm?" she demanded.

Those eyes devoured her; those eyes could *see*.

"I can't worry about Lavinia now," he said. "They will not find the grotto. Sidhu will attend to that. They will never have the diamond; it's in your possession now—"

"I hate this," she said fiercely. "I don't want to do this."

"But you've done it, Darcie. You spun your tales, you saved a sinner, and you vanquished a villain. What did you expect?"

"Stop talking like that!"

"Why is that, Scheherazade?"

"It's too mixed up. I don't understand it, and I don't understand you."

He smiled faintly, devastating now that he could see. She could barely stand to look at him. *Only in the dark. God, she couldn't deal with this, she couldn't. Or maybe it was the repercussions of the unbelievable things she had seen.*

"The only way Lavinia can get to me now is if *you* were the one giving her the lead," he said, his tone gentle, his expression hard.

She felt like slapping him. "Oh! It's just inconceivable you could think that."

"Anything is possible."

Anything. Like Roger might not be dead. And that she was his enemy and no one else. And a white diamond balanced the evil in the world, and Lazarin existed.

"But," he said, "that's not important now—"

"No," she interrupted snidely. "You're going to have us chasing a corpse."

"We *must* recover the black diamond." There was no brooking that tone of voice.

"You must. You can. We're going around in circles."

"Because you're tired; you need a bath. And dinner."

"And sanity," she said stonily.

"And rest."

"Unless Lavinia kills us first."

Lavinia—what about Lavinia kept bothering him? The murderous Lavinia avid for a child—why did it sound so familiar?

"Darcie . . ." he said warningly.

"Con—" she said, imitating his tone.

"Sahib . . ." The *khansamer* at the parlor door.

"He says the bath is ready. Go, Darcie. Relax. I'll watch out for Lavinia."

The bastard. "This is *not* a game."

"I never thought it was. You'll give me the two pouches, Darcie. They should never be out of either of our hands from now on."

"And how do I know you won't sneak away with *The Eye of God?*" Oh, she liked saying that; she liked turning the tables on those knowing eyes.

"The stone wouldn't let me."

"Dear God, don't start that."

He held out his hand. "I won't even pursue that. Go to your bath, Darcie. The stone will be here when you get back."

Darcie . . .

Darcie, Darcie, Darcie . . .

What to make of Darcie . . . the Darcie of his dreams?

He knew her intimately and he knew her not at all. He knew the heat of her body, her sinuous curves, the shape of her breasts, her hot greedy mouth . . . and the reality of her was nothing like what he knew of her at all.

She was tall and slender and strong as tempered steel. And the thick silky hair in which he'd dug his hands was as glistening black as a raven's wing.

But it was her eyes that were utterly unexpected: they flashed bolt-blue in her heart-shaped face, smudgy, expressive, derisive, a mirror of her soul. And that mouth— when he looked at that mouth he dreamt of kisses and lies and the succulent moments when it had fully encompassed him.

It was a mouth made for kissing and tasting and passion, wide and full and endlessly fascinating.

Darcie's mouth. Telling tales, weaving lies, enchanting the stone . . .

Maybe she was an enchantress. He was already under her spell. And now, she was possessed of the white diamond; all she'd had to do was take it—and he would never know if it would have come to him.

What had he done?

Tempted fate. Played with destiny. Provoked the gods.

Made his life's work a mythical white diamond—and got Darcie Boulton instead.

And he didn't know—he still didn't know where she fit in the story. But he knew where he was going to keep her: in his bed, under his body, and—for as long as it took—by his side.

She had no clothes. She was immersed in the bath before it occurred to her: everything had been sacrificed for their journey to India. Clothes. Toiletries except a comb and a bar of soap. Maybe if she wished on that blasted diamond, it would provide those things for her.

Nothing seemed real. The whole adventure from England to the desert seemed like a dream. She couldn't believe now, in retrospect, she had done the things she'd done, and with Con's blindness as an impediment.

But they'd done it—they'd recovered the diamond—and he'd known all along that it would have a mystical claim on whoever found it.

She didn't want any part of it. There had to have been something in that grotto that precipitated that nightmare. Entities didn't disappear in a fog; phantasms weren't born out of smoke. It was a magician's trick, engineered somehow by Con, and probably all in aid of keeping *The Eye of God* for himself.

What if his blindness had been a ruse?

A wave of heat washed her body. *All the things she'd done—in the dark . . .*

What was illusion—what was real?

The Eye of God was real. Disappointing, but real. And when they got it back to civilization, where it could be properly cleaved and polished, it would provide her with riches for a lifetime.

That was all she wanted. *All.*

The rest was all a bunch of hocus-pocus, that probably any spiritualist in London could have conjured up.

Exactly. Atmosphere was everything. And where better to perform a mystical sleight-of-hand than in an isolated grotto in the depths of an impenetrable valley?

She was a gullible fool.

It was all about the diamond and its value.

And that was all.

They were going back to England.

And that was that.

She climbed out of the bath and found a towel. It was the kind of seasonal rental that provided those things; so that was good. But something to wear—that was a problem, and the shirt and trousers she'd worn under her tunic for the last month would just have to do.

The *khansamer,* she discovered, had cleaned them as best he could without having the luxury of washing them. That was good too. She began to feel less like an animal rooting in the wild.

She tore a piece of leather from her headdress to bind up her hair, and she shoved her bare feet back into the thick walking boots.

She marched back into the parlor, prepared to do battle.

Which battle—lust or greed? Or were they inextricably entangled?

She found him lounging on a cushioned wicker chair before a table set for dinner. He'd called for a barber; he'd gotten a shave and a haircut while she bathed, and he sat back now, watching her come in, seeing *everything* with those *eyes.*

He looked more like himself now—too much like himself. Like the Con of the portrait. The Con that she'd saved. This Con unnerved her and she didn't know what to say.

"You might want to wash," she said waspishly, pulling up a straight backed chair.

"I've already done so. Gat is waiting to serve us."

Thank goodness. She wouldn't need to talk. She wouldn't need to look at those eyes and wonder yet again how he was seeing her.

He snapped his fingers and the *khansamer* appeared, along with the kitchen boy, and set out the tomato soup which was followed by spiced beef and fried potatoes served with chutney and a red pepper conserve.

She'd never felt so hungry in her life. There couldn't be enough food to fill the void. And Con intently watched her devour every bite.

Her only recourse was a frontal assault.

"So when can we leave for London?"

"We're not going back to England yet." There was infinite patience in his tone.

"Well then, I'll tell you what. Why don't you give me one or two of the remaining Pengellis diamonds, and *I'll* go back to England, and you can go off chasing ghosts."

He ignored that suggestion. "I gave Sidhu another diamond to sell. We're going to need more equipment, and to pay the servants. Clothes. Transportation—"

"Transportation—where?" she demanded suspiciously.

"I think I know where he went."

"He? *He?* That was *not* a *he.* That was an *it,* and I don't care where it went. I care where *I* want to go."

His eyes gleamed. "The stone won't let you go. Don't you understand? Only when the black diamond is recovered will the balance be restored. Now listen. I think it draws its power from the diamond, and that's why it was taken. But since the stone was split, the power must be diminished. So I believe it will seek a diamond field from which to draw and stay at a certain level of energy. I don't think it will go to South Africa. Nor do I think it will stay in India. I believe it will unleash its evil among the furthest known diamond fields in the world."

"The furthest . . ." she said faintly.

"On the Nizmennost Plains of Siberia."

"Oh my God." She closed her eyes. The man was mad. "We—*you're*—going to the most isolated part of Russia on the strength of a hunch?"

"An educated hunch. An educated deduction. Fewer people. A lot of opportunity to wreak havoc. And an untapped supply of diamonds underground."

"Hocus pocus," she muttered. "I'm going home."

"But I have the diamonds," he said gently. "And—as much as you hate it, Scheherazade—I'm in command."

How stupid was she, not to have stolen one of those diamonds as a hedge against this lunacy? She couldn't believe her gullibility. The best she could hope for now was opportunity to rectify that mistake.

She was never going to sleep again. There was only one bedroom in the houseboat, where she'd had her bath. One bed, enshrouded in mosquito netting. One armoire. One washstand. One, one, one.

And two pairs of eyes.

In the dark. What did he see?

She gnawed on the question, as birds as big as vultures swooped outside the bedroom windows and the boat rocked gently against the midnight tide and cradled them in sleep.

He slept. She thought he slept. Or maybe his all-seeing eyes were busy conjuring up illusions.

She was finished playing. She had to find where he

had hidden the last of the diamonds they had removed from their settings. By her reckoning, there should be four left. One would suffice.

She lay stiffly beside him on the bed, having removed only the heavy boots. *In the dark.*

The godawful unholy dark . . .

He couldn't see in the dark—

Unless he was a blasted phantasm himself.

And maybe she'd once thought he was, back when she'd fallen in love with a portrait. She'd thought he was a god, and because he was dead, she could worship him forever.

The reality . . . ah, the delicious reality—when she'd been in control . . .

She most definitely didn't like not being in control.

She had *to find those diamonds . . .*

She moved experimentally to check if he were asleep. Not a movement beside her. Deep breathing. Deep dark.

She couldn't trust the man. In the dark.

She needed to emulate his thinking. Where would a sorcerer conceal his apparatus? One thought occurred—and she pushed it resolutely out of her mind. But maybe, she thought a moment later, it was not such a far-fetched idea after all.

But it meant she would have to put her hands on him, seduce him and leave herself at the mercy of those eyes.

In the dark.

It didn't matter; it was different, wholly different, because of those eyes. She didn't feel so free now in the dark. Everything had changed and she hated it.

Nevertheless, the objective was the thing.

She was not going to chase a ghoul across two continents just on his whim. She'd had enough of deserts and camps and sultry foreign air.

She moved restively against him. The diamonds

might be in his pockets or in his boots. For all she knew, they were woven in his hair.

What if she just touched him? Just gently grazed his thigh, by his left trouser pocket. She'd be able to tell if there were a bump or bulge. It was just a matter of lightly brushing her fingers . . . there, there—and gently *there*—

She was breathless, suddenly, as her fingers wafted over the firm hard contour of his leg. *Oh God, she wasn't after that . . . not now, not with those eyes.*

Maybe. Maybe . . .

In the dark.

In the dark, he caught her hand and pinned it against her side.

"Darcie, Darcie, Darcie . . ." he murmured, turning and shifting his weight over her. "I was just waiting for you to make a move."

But now—he could see . . .

"You're making more of it than it was," she muttered.

"Ah, Darcie. And you made life so bearable in the dark."

Always the dark—she couldn't get away from it. She couldn't get away from him.

Did she want to ?

He was poised above her, on his elbows and knees; she was surrounded by him, enveloped by his scent, his heat, his desire.

His lips unerringly touched hers; she shook him away.

"Darcie—" a whisper against her mouth. A flick of his tongue against her lips. A questing taste. A further foray, and she didn't resist. He kissed like he remembered her mouth; like he was still without sight and wanted to explore every inch, with hunger, with knowledge, with taste.

No part of his body touched her, only his mouth, yet

the sense of him above her pressed against her; she squirmed beneath him, seeking his weight.

He gave her nothing, except his kiss. He took her with his mouth, thrusting ferociously into the heat and wet of hers.

"Oh God, I missed this . . ."

That firm carved mouth all over, all inside of hers. That long strong body caging hers. Connected to him solely by the lush hard thrust of his tongue.

"Darcie . . ." Breathless, seeking, devouring kisses— in the dark.

It was still the same, in the dark.

He was so strong, so forceful, in the dark. He wouldn't let her go.

"Con . . ."

"No . . . no—"

Swooping down on her again, like those birds out the window, never caressing her, never touching her except by the fierce greedy seduction of his tongue.

He meant to make her crazy; he wanted to make her come by the sheer erotic force of his volcanic kisses.

She felt wet, wild, consumed with wanting him. She couldn't wait to strip off her clothes.

She reached for him, and he shimmied away from her questing hands.

"No fair, Darcie . . ."

"I don't care—"

She slipped both hands between his legs and cupped him. His resolve faltered as he placed himself in her hands.

"Take me," he whispered, and slipped into her mouth.

She tore at his clothes, arching up toward him as he sprang into her hands. She grasped him hungrily, sliding her hands down his jutting length to his scrotum, and under, to the sweet erotic stroke of skin beneath.

There, just there, holding him tightly in one hand and massaging him gently, sensuously between his legs. Just . . . *there.*

And then—

"Don't stop." His voice was shaky, barely above a breath.

". . . couldn't . . ." she sighed, as she alternated the stroking of her fingers with rolling the taut sacs of his scrotum between her hands.

She was avid for him, all of him, devouring the essence of him with her greedy hands.

He held his body away from her still; all she had was the hard jutting length of him and his voraciously demanding mouth, and the erotic sense of his containing her with his body.

All she wanted of him was the hot cream of his desire—and she knew exactly where.

With one hand, she tore open her shirt, and pulled away her camisole to expose her breasts. "I want you here," she whispered. "Come to me here."

He shuddered in her hands. She felt him quicken in her hands.

"I want it on my breasts."

He shoved himself against her encircling hand.

"I want it coating my nipples."

He made a deep animal sound and thrust harder against her fingers. She levered herself up against him, holding one breast against the smooth underside of his throbbing length.

He could feel the hot tight point of her nipple rubbing against him, and the firm massaging of the fingers of her free hand. She was over and under him, writhing against him, massaging him, coaxing him, squeezing and stroking him.

And he held himself back. He wanted to give her what she craved . . . without spending himself on her. And he felt himself coming. That part of him wanted to give her a fountain of cream. Wanted her to swim in it, bathe in it, absorb it into her body. Wanted her never to go anywhere without wearing his scent on her body.

It spurted out of him involuntarily, the magma of the volcano.

She swiped it off of him and spread it on her breasts, covering each hard pointed nipple with his luscious essence.

"Like that," she whispered. "And that," as she stroked the essence of him onto her body. "It feels so good . . . You're so powerful . . ."

He didn't let her finish. He swooped down on her mouth and crushed it, pulling himself away from her hands. If she had so much as moved those hands one fraction, he would have spewed over her, and he wanted to save himself for better things.

He felt her hands reaching for him; shuddered at the tremulous begging moan against his lips, "Don't. Let me . . ."

"You got what you wanted," he growled.

"I love it—I want more . . ."

"No . . . now you wait until *I* want to give it to you."

"You're ready now. I can feel it: if I touch you, you'll come."

"Want to try?"

"I always want to touch you." She reached out her avid hands and caught him hard between them. "Oh God, you're so hot and hard. Let me . . ." She started stroking him, rubbing her fingers along his turgid length.

"You're not getting any more of me."

"I want it. I love it. I'll suck it out of you."

The image of her hot greedy mouth surrounding him shot to his very vitals. He felt himself quickening, rearing back to give her the shot, aching to put himself at the mercy of her succulent tongue and greedy mouth.

He pulled away roughly.

"You can't have it."

"I need more. I want more." Her body undulated beneath him, taunting him, goading him. "You're all ready for it. You're bursting with it. Let me have more. Let me just . . . lick all that deliciousness from right—*there*—" She grabbed for him, and caught him right at the head. "You're an absolute rock," she whispered, as she rubbed her thumb just at the tip.

She felt a drop of it pulse at her fingertip, and she levered herself up and licked it, and then she pulled him into her mouth.

He jerked away abruptly. "I told you—you can't have it."

"Why—?" A cry of pure lust and need, and he loved hearing it.

"Because you want it so much."

"So do you," she whispered.

"But I love making you beg for it—"

"Except you're the one on your knees to me," she taunted him.

"Not for long." With one shocking motion, he pushed her onto her stomach, and his arm snaked under it and lifted her onto her knees so that her bottom canted against his hips. "That's better. Now—" He ripped her trousers away from her buttocks and tore off the thin cotton drawers and exposed her derrière.

She felt him cover her, balancing himself on one hand, and his knees, so that the ramrod length of him rubbed enticingly against her buttocks' crease.

That felt good, and the sense of him enveloping her, but it wasn't nearly as delicious as owning him with her hands. She felt his fingers slip between her legs, feeling for her opening, slipping easily into her wet. Almost . . . he was pushing against her buttocks and probing her with his hand. Almost . . . she was breathless with excitement. Soon . . . she felt the surge of anticipation, the swell of desire.

She pushed against him demandingly.

"What's your problem?"

"Give it to me." Her tone was as imperious as a queen.

"When *I'm* ready."

She felt his one hand on her hip, positioning her. And then his probing fingers slipped away, leaving her empty.

Almost . . .

She wasn't going to beg. She licked her lips, she undulated against him, she pushed against his rock hard length, demanding him. She bit her lips so she wouldn't beg.

She couldn't stand knowing he was behind her, throbbing, naked, ready to explode, and she couldn't have what she most desired.

She broke. *"Do it."*

"You want it that bad." He had to know.

"I want it any way you want to give it to me."

"Good," he murmured in satisfaction, and he reared back and he poised himself just at the apex of her cleft, and slowly, inch by inch, he penetrated her, pushing into her forcefully, a little of his length at a time.

He wanted her to feel it—his length, his strength, his potency. And he wanted to embed himself into her so deeply and powerfully that she would never want it from any other man.

He was getting there. He was loving it, connecting with her solely by the hard jutting length of him furrowing into her. He was almost there, almost buried in her to the root, hip to bottom, his rough pubic hair grazing her tender buttocks, as she bowed on her knees to his virile possession of her.

For a long lustful moment, he let her feel his power and his might, and he slowly withdrew himself from her with the same slow incremental stroke.

And then into her again, slowly, giving it to her so slowly, so lusciously, so forcefully—his stroke measured against her whimpers and moans as he possessed her.

He touched her nowhere else. He took her solely with his penis, methodically and deliberately, giving it to her in short emphatic piston-like strokes that bound her to him as surely as love and kisses.

She wanted this, this rough raw coupling, she wanted his sex, and his power, and he wanted her, and he would use her need as surely as she used his. It was enough.

He wanted to give her everything she demanded. But for now, he was going slow, excruciatingly, heatedly, throbbingly slow, pushing in, in, in; pulling out, out, out. Pushing in to the hilt. Pulling out to the very tip, his penis pulsating to her moans, aching for release, determined to drive her to the very edge so she would never crave another man's sex.

He pushed himself against her buttocks so she could feel his strength.

She moaned against the pillows, begging to feel his length. He was so long and strong, and *there*. He filled her. He lived in her. She'd never known she wanted it like this. She couldn't get enough of him.

He wouldn't stay long enough for her to get enough of him.

His short thrusting strokes drove her wild. She didn't

know what to do to entice him. She wanted to seduce him, to make him stay.

If she could only make him come, he would be hers forever.

He was thrusting into her again when she felt it, fracturing from that sweet spot above her pubis, a spangling glissade of sensation spiralling downward and exploding, with his last throbbing lunge, between her legs.

He buried himself in her, he couldn't get deep enough, tight enough, hard enough for her. And he stayed that way, embedded in her, until the spasms of her climax eddied away.

She couldn't move. All she felt, all she knew was *him*— the pulsating throbbing hard part of him. She had never felt such a vibrant connection before, never felt such a lust to possess anyone. No other man had a penis like this. No one but he knew how to play.

She was aroused by the sheer feeling of his focused force rammed into her like that. She wanted him all over again, and she didn't hesitate to let him know it. She wriggled against him enticingly. She shimmied her buttocks hard against his pulsating length and his churning hips. She arched herself up to him, inviting him like a cat to stroke her and stoke her.

He couldn't refuse her blatantly voluptuous plea. She still hadn't had enough of him. He flexed inside her, girding himself, feeling as potent as a bull, as mighty as a tree.

He took her remorselessly, giving her what she wanted—his long strong pummelling strokes pounding into her, and grinding into her as he finally came, swamping her, drenching her, filling her to the hilt.

Seventeen

She wanted more.

He didn't need words to tell him: her naked body moved voluptuously against his, restive and hot to the core.

He could take her now, he thought, but it was better to wait. Let her need stoke her appetite; let her seethe and writhe and moan. He relished the longing in her that burned with lust for him.

Anticipation was everything. And memory. And the body's hunger to replicate the exhausting, pounding pleasure of their coupling.

And the sheer carnality of her nakedness pressed against his body excited him, and aroused him to a fever pitch, hard as a bone and ready to plow.

But he wouldn't give in to her, not even if she were Eve. Not even if she used all of her erotic wiles.

He loved this moment, in the dark, where he was master and the instrument, and she was the wanton slave of her own desire.

Her body rippled against him, teasing him, torturing him.

His erection elongated still more, thrusting stiffly into the air.

She made a little sound as she felt his covert movement. He grabbed her hand before she could reach for him and immobilized it.

And waited.

She hated him. Why, when he was stone hard and hot to rut in her, was he making her wait?

She wriggled her hips, hoping to entice him.

He held himself tight as a drum as his body betrayed him with an aching, longing surge.

He got it ruthlessly under control. And he waited.

She wedged herself tightly against him, hip to hip, leg to leg, so he could feel the alluring brush of her pubic hair against his rock hard thigh.

She couldn't tempt him.

And he waited.

Aching. Rigid. Towering. Burning to drive himself into her hot tight sheath.

And he waited. He wanted the tension at a fever pitch and her voluptuous need for *him* stoking her as white hot as her greed.

It was unbearable. She lay next to him squirming with lust for him, hot and wet for him, her nipples tight hard points for him.

She didn't understand why she couldn't just climb onto him and ram his desire home.

He was playing some strange game with her. Making her wait like this. Getting her crazy wild and feeding on her hunger for him.

She forced his hand between her legs, and he jerked it away.

"Oh no. No," he growled. "You'll wait until I'm ready."

She went breathless. "I'm waiting."

"Good."

Her body went tight at the sensual implication of that word.

"How good?" she whispered.

"As good as you'll ever get it."

She writhed against his restraining hand. There had to be some way to break him. Some way to make him come. She inched her leg over his, straining closer to his heated body.

Closer still, winding her foot around his ankle and rubbing his skin. And she felt the faintest flex of his body.

Yes.

He waited.

She lifted her foot and stroked his leg. He reacted violently, his hips convulsing at the touch of her toes.

Good. She loved the word. She loved his involuntary response.

She waited, as he mercilessly clamped down on his rampant need.

And she waited, because now she was in control, and she understood about the waiting and the heightening of desire.

Now he was squirming with hunger for her.

Good. That was how you turned the tables. And now—

She lifted her leg and inserted her foot between his legs against the taut sacs of his scrotum. He stopped her there. He kept her there. Her toes flexed against him and his hips moved involuntarily.

"Don't. Do. That." Her voice, ragged and raw. "I want you. *Now.*"

He moved her foot and stroked her toes against the underside of his erection, and then he rubbed the hard throbbing length against her foot.

"There's a part of me that wants your foot, Scheherazade."

"You want *me,*" she groaned.

"Let's see. Since you couldn't stand to wait, let's see what it will take to make me come."

He moved her foot to the base of his penis where it jutted away from his body, and he rubbed her foot up up the length of it. "Ummm. That feels good."

Good . . . as good as—

She yanked her foot away, and he caught it back, and stroked himself again. "I like your toes caressing me," he murmured. "The pressure is just right."

"Why are you doing this?" she moaned, frantic with wanting him, willing to take him any way she could get him now. Even with her toes.

"Because you wouldn't wait. I told you it would be good. Better than before because of the waiting. You're hot, juicy, soaking wet; just ripe and ready for me."

"Then take me," she begged.

"Tell me you want me more than your toes."

"I want you."

"Good." *That word, that luscious meaningful, self-satisfied word.*

As good as . . .

He rolled over so that he was poised above her. He grasped her hands and pinned them above her head. She hooked her legs around his thighs, and waited breathlessly for him to mount her.

With erotic precision, he breached her, in one hard soul-shattering lunge, as hard, hot and deep as he could go.

"Yes," she whispered. "Yes." How unbelievably hard he was; how tightly he filled her. She wanted him to stay there forever.

He rocked against her gently, to maintain his fierce control.

"Never, ever . . ." she breathed.

"I know."

"Don't move."

"I couldn't. Not yet."

"The waiting," she murmured.

"I can't move."

"I want you to come. For me. In me."

"Not yet. *Not . . . yet*—"

"Kiss me."

"Not even that. I'm too close."

"Then do it. I want you to do it." She undulated her hips against him, testing him, tormenting him, sensing he was on the edge of his iron control.

Big mistake.

"Tell me a story, Scheherazade."

She made a little sound at the back of her throat. "The story is," she gasped, as she shimmied desperately against him, "I'm . . . going . . . to co-ome—" She broke as her body seized up, spasmed, and began the soft melting slide into oblivion down his long stiff pole.

She toppled into a churning, foaming silence. And then she was complete.

And he waited. Waited. Holding her. Surging incrementally against her hips. Waiting. Sensing. Needing. Needing . . . needing—

He blew. He barely gyrated his hips, and his whole body gathered, he pushed, and he erupted violently into her with one sweet cradling move.

This was a different man, in the dark, now that he had his eyes.

And by daylight—Darcie knelt beside the bed and studied him in the dim dawn light. He was just as she remembered him that first night: long and strong and tempting to touch.

He watched her through hooded eyes as she climbed up onto the bed and buried her face between his legs, rooting for him with her mouth.

"Ah, Darcie . . ."

"I need you again," she whispered, pulling at him, sucking on him until he stiffened in her mouth.

"I have something else for you," he murmured, easing himself away from her. The test was now. The test of his prowess and her need.

"All I want is you," she said, rocking back on her heels.

He leaned over the bed and swiped up his trousers. "But you don't want to go with me."

Her expression changed. "Maybe I do."

He dug into a pocket and handed something to her.

She closed her hand tightly around it: one of the remaining Pengellis diamonds.

"It's yours."

"For services rendered?" she asked, bitterness lacing her tone.

"You're free to make a choice now, Scheherazade." He tossed his trousers to the floor and leaned back with his hands behind his head.

She looked at him, at his long lean body fully displayed for her pleasure. At his thick towering manhood already hard and yearning for her.

And she looked at the diamond.

She got off the bed and took it to the window, holding it to catch the sun to reflect its rainbow light.

"I don't understand."

"Stay or go—that diamond is yours."

"Do you want me to stay?" she asked carefully. It was such a soul-sapping conversation, with both of them naked and ready for other things.

"Don't play games, Darcie. If you stay, there are rules."

"In the dark, there weren't any rules," she said.

"But in the dark, I didn't have any power."

"You had power," she countered.

"I had you."

"Now you don't need me."

He chose not to answer that. "Make up your mind, Darcie. *You* were the one who wanted to go back home."

She vaguely remembered that she had; could barely remember the reasons why: last night had blasted all of that right out of her head.

Oh yes, she'd been rooting around for the diamonds. A stake to get her back home. And now she had it, with no repercussions, in the palm of her hand.

But she wouldn't have *him*. She wouldn't have that body, those kisses, his penis, that lover. And after last night, she couldn't let that go.

"Do you want *me?*"

He gave her a crooked smile and gestured to his body. "Do I, Darcie? I've been in a perpetual state of arousal since you rescued me. And seeing you just makes me hotter and harder for you. Is that what you want to hear? That I'm constantly hard for you? I am. I want to jam myself into you every way I can think of. Every day. Every hour. Every minute. That's your power, Darcie. Your nakedness incites that kind of lust. I'm always rock hard and ready for you. Any time. Anywhere. So you tell me, Scheherazade, what are you going to do?"

She loved that kind of power. She adored his admission that he was always hard for her. She wanted him, and she wanted no one else to have him. And she didn't care how high the price.

It probably started at one Pengellis diamond. She put it on the washstand and sat down on the bed. "I'll go with you."

His eyes kindled. Beautiful, sensual Darcie. He hadn't been sure. He hadn't known if his sex was enough. If she'd said no, he had no idea what he would have done. He'd gambled—and this time he won.

"Good," he said.

Good . . . as good as—in the dark . . .

"Tell me the rules," she murmured, sliding her hands up his hair-rough thighs. "I know one—if you want to wait, we wait."

"Good." He watched her hands and he let her . . . *let her* . . . grasp his throbbing length. "So good." And he let himself—*let himself*—discharge a drop of his essence onto her hand.

She held his eyes as she rubbed it on her breasts. It was so erotic, he almost came; he didn't know which was more powerful: imagining it or watching her do it, and he almost didn't care.

"I want to coat myself like this every morning," she whispered. "That's my rule."

"If you play with me much longer, you'll be able to swim in it," he growled, pulling back from her greedy hands.

She smiled faintly, as mysterious as Eve, reaching for him again. "Tell me your rules."

He envisioned her drowning in his essence, and he spurted again.

"You will never deny me. You will always be naked and willing for me just as I am always hard and ready for you. I could spend my seed on any woman but I'm hard for you. Will you accept those rules, Scheherazade; do you want it that much too?"

Her hands on him had been quiescent as he spoke. But now she stroked him purposefully as she considered his rules.

He wanted her always wet and hot and ready for him. He wanted to give it only to her when he was hard and he wanted it. And that was her power—his lust for her, his need to spend himself only on her.

And she wanted that. She would deny him nothing. She wanted it every bit as much as he did—more. She wanted it now and she would want it ten minutes from now. And this afternoon. And tonight and tomorrow.

Whatever they had done before was nothing compared to the luscious games and the sumptuous couplings of the previous night. What woman would deny herself that? Or the reverberating pleasure of holding him, possessing him, and knowing he was hers?

"I accept the terms," she whispered.

"You want it." It wasn't a question.

She rubbed the thick ridged tip of him. "I want it."

"Take it."

She climbed up on the bed and straddled him, her eyes shrouded in mystery. "Now?"

"Now."

She rose to her knees, and poised herself over him, and then slowly, agonizingly ground her way down to seat herself on him.

And now he was at her mercy. He must wait. She held herself still, her excitement escalating to an impossible pitch, as she watched his face.

But she couldn't help the slight rocking motion. How could anyone keep still when his gorgeous male root was centered in her? She wanted to feel it as completely and fully as possible. She was thrilled that for the first time he could see whose body brought him to this pleasure.

That he could see *her.*

She arched her back against the all-consuming orgasmic sensation of his penetration. It wouldn't take much to send her over the edge. And she could see that he was playing a game: he wanted to wait as much as she.

Just sitting astride him made her hot. The sheer nakedness of her body straddling him like that. Her breasts bare, firm and taut. Her hair, wild and free. She lifted it slowly from her shoulders as he flexed himself inside her.

"No, no, no," she said coyly, wagging her finger at him. "We're going to wait. I'm just going to sit here and feel you so hard and hot inside me and know you're just yearning to explode, and we'll wait. You *do* love to wait, don't you?"

"You'll have to wait too, Scheherazade."

"I'm learning to like it. I get more of you for a longer time between my legs, and I do love that. So—be still. Let me enjoy how hard you are, how stiff you feel."

"What if I can't wait?"

"But I have you rather at a disadvantage. What can you do?"

"Let me show you."

He pressed down on the bed to give himself some leverage to thrust. Immediately, she ground down on him, and smacked him lightly on the thigh.

"That was bad of you—and good for me. Now I've got you even deeper inside me."

"I can't wait, Scheherazade."

"Oh, I see. You wait if it's excruciating for me. And you can't if it's hard for you."

"I can't wait because it's hard for you."

She wriggled tauntingly against him. "You're so right."

"Darcie—" This time there was no playfulness in his tone.

"Yes, Con—?" Her voice was light as air.

"If you push down one more time, I'm going to come."

She smiled, that elusive smile. "Really? You can't wait—? I can't believe it. A man with your rules, your appetites—" She knew it wouldn't take much; she could see in his face that he was struggling to maintain discipline.

It was the last thing she wanted him to do. She began rocking on his erection, slowly, imperceptibly at first, and then with a sensual gyration of her hips that sent him spinning out of control.

He grabbed her hips and pushed her; she bent over him, her hair a curtain around them, as she deliberately plunged back and forth on his shaft.

She looked into his eyes, and it was that knowing, mysterious look of hers that sent him over the edge. He clutched her hips tightly and in one violent convulsive movement, he jammed himself into her and pitched headfirst over the brink.

She was swimming in it. Loving it. Didn't want to move away from it. Loved watching him slide down the tower of his ecstasy to pure soul-sapping completion. It was all she wanted: to be the only one who could bring him to this.

She relinquished him only when his energy and desire were finally manageable and at his command. But until then, she had him, nestled between her legs, fully extended, ridden to exhaustion, and deliciously *there*.

And she refused to let him console her with his hand.

"I'll wait," she said placidly. "I can wait. I'm not the one who couldn't abide by the rules. I'll be waiting for you. And you'll know, all day, that I'm wet and ripe and just on the crest of all that pleasure. So we'll see who really knows how to wait."

"You'll drive me crazy."

"I hope so," she murmured coyly. She wandered around the room, picking up clothes. "I hardly have anything to wear."

"You don't have to dress."

"You're right. One of the rules." She tossed him his clothes. "What about breakfast? I'm starving."

"I'll ring for the house steward. He'll serve it in here."

"And Sidhu is coming today?"

He eased himself up and swung his legs over the side of the bed. "This afternoon."

"Oh good. *Lots* of time to wait."

"Darcie . . ." he said warningly.

"Naked and willing—that's what you said . . . and *ready* . . ."

She watched him as he struggled into his trousers.

"Oh . . ." she pouted. "Not ready."

Depleted was more like it. Drained to the core. Enervated—but feeling his juices slowly heating up again as she sashayed naked around the room, and settled on the bed where she had just lain with her legs splayed.

"Stupid rules," she said, infusing a sulky note into her voice as she wriggled around pretending to try to get comfortable. "But you'll just have to wait."

His body leapt to attention instantly.

"No, no. You promised me breakfast, and I'm perfectly willing to wait."

"You will pay for this little rebellion, Scheherazade."

"I'm looking forward to it, Con."

He sent her a sizzling glance as he closed the door filly behind him and went in search of breakfast.

She turned over and buried her head in the sheets, seeking his sex and his scent.

She had never felt so aroused in her life. She felt like she was riding on it, swamped by it, surrounded by it in a sensual haze that must be obvious to all.

She didn't care. She didn't need love. She didn't need marriage. Those things were not important. All she craved was his unrelenting lust for her body, which bound her to him more securely than any wedding ring.

Already she had turned the tables on his little sensual fantasy. It had already cost her something—but the reward was worth it, even though her body still clamored for release.

She could wait. She wanted him thinking about her all day long, about how she had rejected her pleasure, and forced him to capitulate to his. She wanted him thinking about her naked body still hot and unfulfilled.

And she wanted him stiff as a poker, and bursting for relief. And then she would cuddle him and caress him and tell him to wait.

By the time he returned with a tray, she was somewhat composed.

But he was not. He was furious with her for seducing him and making him wait. He set the tray down on the table with a bang, and roughly pulled the chairs over to it.

"Breakfast, *madame,*" he said curtly.

"I *am* hungry," Darcie said. She sat down opposite him, extending her legs. "Ah—tea. So revivifying. Would you like some? And eggs. Fruit. Biscuits. A nice simple meal."

"Quick, at any rate." He took one of the boiled eggs on his place. "I know what I really want for breakfast."

"What's that, Con?"

"Your nipples."

She felt the twinge through her whole body. "Not on the menu, Con." She smiled at him and bit into a biscuit. "I guess you'll have to wait."

Sidhu arrived at tiffin, by which time Con was in a cataclysmic state of arousal, and couldn't have cared less what he brought and what they had to do.

It was Darcie on his mind as she dressed behind closed doors. Darcie, whipping up his fantasies of her waiting for him, ripe, hot and yearning for him to her core.

Darcie, dressing to entice him . . .

"You will go by wagon, *sahib,*" Sidhu was saying, "up through Tashkent and north to Omsk. I have procured money, supplies, clothing for several weeks. You may not be able to track the godless one until you reach Siberia. It is a long trip, *sahib.*"

He spread out the map that Sidhu brought, and marked his way. Through the mountain passes they had already traveled and over two borders. It felt like a lifetime away.

He could barely concentrate as Darcie sauntered into the parlor, dressed in a lightweight shirtwaist and skirt, her hair pulled back in a knot at her neck.

"Memsahib." Sidhu bowed.

She nodded in turn, and sat down at the table. "Let them serve now."

Con clapped his hands—mainly to keep them off of her, and the house steward set out the meal. There was lamb, this time, and vegetables, and the inevitable tea.

And Darcie sitting so composed; she must be squirming in her seat. Waiting, all this time . . . how could she stand it?

Unless . . .

. . . someone else?

In his place. That place. Embedded there, buried there—

He would kill whoever it was . . .

He clenched his hands, dismissing this insane, untenable thought. She was driving him crazy with wanting her, thinking about her. He couldn't wait for Sidhu to depart.

He left just at sundown, after going over every detail of their upcoming journey with a thoroughness that made Con clench his teeth because he wasn't listening.

"Don't get any ideas," Darcie told him as she moved around the room, extinguishing the lights. She was so excited she could hardly stand it, but that was not for him to know. Yet.

"I've got a hundred ideas. Get in the bedroom and take off your clothes."

"No. We have to wait."

He was already ripping off his clothes. "Never deny me."

"That seems contradictory to waiting, Con," she murmured as she watched him. "You can't have both."

"I can have you," he said, pacing toward her. "I'll destroy those clothes if you don't strip now."

"You have to learn to wait, Con," she said chidingly. "A man has to control his urges."

"I'm going to control you," he growled, and he grabbed her; he ripped away the tissue material of her shirt, her skirt, everything, he tore to shreds, and then he pulled everything from the dining table onto the floor. "Now, I feast on you . . ."

And he lifted her onto the table and pushed her on her back, and pulled her toward him so that her pulsating femininity just grazed his penis head. He waited, so that she could feel the jutting force of him poised to take her on.

She pushed up on her elbows to see it, and he held her eyes as he thrust himself into her inch by delicious inch. She almost came then, watching how her body devoured him, how he rotated his hips to push into her, and how deep and far she could take him until he was stuffed to the hilt.

"I've waited all day for this," she breathed, shuddering with excitement. "Don't move." She loved looking at it, the connection between them, solely and wholly to his hard hot sex. But she couldn't stop herself from writhing against it with hot frantic little movements that didn't escape him.

"Beg me for it, you tease."

She groaned. "You know I'm aching for it."

"No one would ever know it."

"You've been thinking about it all day," she accused him, her voice hoarse with need.

"I think I'll let *you* wait."

"Oh, no, don't," she moaned, "don't . . ."

He gyrated his hips. "Like that?"

"Oh yes."

He made a little grinding movement. "Like that?"

"Yes, more—more—"

He drew back an inch and rammed into her. "Like that?"

"Just like that," she whispered.

He drew back again a little further, and drove hard again.

"Yes . . ." she moaned, grasping onto the edge of the table.

He touched her nowhere else. He wanted nothing else, just this erotic connection, her moans, her need, her sex.

He reared back, and took her again.

She arched up violently. "Yes . . . !"

And again.

"Oh God . . . yes . . ."

And again—and again and again in a frenzy of possession, again, like a piston, again, in and out of her again and again, couldn't get enough, not enough, not enough, not her cries not her moans not her spasms not her groans not enough not enough enough . . .

He came . . . like lightning bolting through him, breaking him open sending him skyward like a shooting star . . .

. . . not enough—

They lay languidly entwined in bed. Already he was hot as a poker and thick as a tree and all he could think of was plowing her again. *"Darcie."*

"Ummm."

"Feel me."

"Umm?" She obediently put out her hand. He bulged upward, stabbing the air. "Oh." *Yum.* She smiled to herself. "What do you want me to do about it?"

"I could think of a few interesting things."

"Name one."

"Getting between your legs."

"Oh. That."

"Darcie—"

"I know. The rules." As if she were bored, barely interested when she was trying to suppress her rising excitement. "Do we have to?"

"Never deny me."

"Oh right. That." She put her hand out again. How did he do it, how could he be so rampantly ready two hours later? She stroked him lightly, pausing to play with his head. She loved feeling him elongate in her hand.

"Tease. All you have to do is spread your legs."

"That's the *best* part," she murmured. "And you do all the work."

"I'm ready to work you over right now."

"I think we'll wait," she said. "Somebody once told me something about the heightening of pleasure that comes from waiting."

"You are a witch. You've already kept me waiting too long."

"Let me see." She swooped her hand up the long length of him. "Ooo—you *are* ready." She fondled the bulbous tip, thumbing the ridge. Driving him crazy.

"Who wouldn't want to be possessed by this wondrous thing?"

"Let me guess."

She liked this game, and she loved playing coy.

"How about if I just play with you?"

"I'm not in the mood for games."

She rubbed him lightly, tip to root. "Couldn't I just rub you and stroke you?"

"How about if I rub and stroke you?"

"All you think about is sex," she said, pouting, as she kept her hands extra busy rubbing his length.

"So do you."

"How can I help it? I get to have you between my legs."

"Let me be there now."

"Hmmm . . . I'll think about it." She smiled to herself as he thrust himself into the circle of her caressing fingers. She had him anxious, fuming, and she loved it. "How can I deny you?"

Her tone was getting to him, even in the game. He felt deadly serious as he rolled onto her and poised himself to enter her. He never wanted her to feel lukewarm about their sex and he didn't care if it were a game.

He stabbed himself against her. "Open yourself to me."

He felt her body give—she reached down and guided him, and he surged into her. And into her. Endlessly endlessly into her, as if he'd been waiting to be enfolded by her heat before he gave in to his need and spumed.

The rocking of the boat lulled them into a state approaching sleep, in the dark. Outside the window, they heard the caw of a passing bird. The lap of the water. A mellifluous bell.

"We leave tomorrow," Con said. "Sidhu says there have been questions about us. You were right again. They have come back to look for me in Srinagar. We have to go."

She swallowed. It wasn't for her to protest, when she had agreed to come with him. But oh, she didn't want to go. She wanted to stay here with him and spend their days and nights spending his sex.

He touched her there, as if he knew what she was thinking.

"*This* doesn't end. It's only begun."

"But it's such a long journey, and you don't even know where to look."

"You look where evil dwells and people are afraid."

"What about your bargain? How can you trust this blessing will last?"

"Truthfully? You can trust nothing, Darcie, not even me."

And who could he trust? He walked on air, with nothing beneath him to cushion his death. They were coming for him. They knew where to find him. No, she knew they would come.

She—sapping his life force as methodically as his enemy. She said there was a child, and there was nothing. She spoke with a different tone, a demoness in his dreams . . .

What?

Demons—surrounding him, tossing him on the ground . . . shifting memories and nothing—until he was found.

Burying himself in her—

Dead dying never see the sun . . .

Evil, black evil, sundered in two . . .

Lavinia, holding in her hand the last stone of the broken necklace. What have you done?

He spiralled downward toward the truth. Lavinia. Roger. The child that never was. Survival. Lust. Dreams. The stuff of myths and death. Somewhere in there truth lies sleeping . . .

Darcie!

He awoke with a start, his head whirling with the imagery of his dream, and the faint apprehension that nothing around him was what it seemed.

Eighteen

Their caravan climbed to the Top of the World and beyond.

Nowhere, on those snow-crested ridges, could they see any trace of the valley or the stone that marked the place.

Sidhu had buried it forever.

"The legend was that the valley was impenetrable," he told her, "and that the diamonds were scattered all over the valley floor. And the only way to recover them was to throw down a slaughtered animal; it was said that the diamonds would adhere to the flesh, and the eagles that nested in the valley would fly the carcasses out and into the waiting hands of the deserving. One of a thousand and one tales, Scheherazade."

But it didn't sound like any tale she could invent, and she infinitely preferred the sensual stories they acted out with each other, in the warmth and in the dark.

On this trip, it was bone-jarring cold and it snowed in the mountains as they headed toward Gilgit and Tashkent. Periodically, there were little cabins, crow's nests they called them, where they could take their rest from the relentless weather.

Sidhu had provided well: maps, directions, the proper

clothes. Provisions. A guide who was known to him and trustworthy.

They had divided the last of the diamonds they had brought with them.

Who can you trust?

She carried two of the remaining diamonds in the pouch, with the shards of *The Stone of Samael*. He had the other two, and *The Eye of God* besides.

She wondered if it were enough. If the quest were worth the reward. If going after the entity was even sane. If she even cared.

"We've let ourselves forget about Lavinia," he said. *Something about Lavinia—or was it Darcie, in his dream . . .* "She took some time to send her operatives to Srinagar, but now they're there. The threat is real, just as you've always said."

But she didn't like being so right and knowing Lavinia so well. And now it would be reported back to her that Con had an accomplice as well—

Her time at Goole Abbey seemed a lifetime ago.

And where he thought the danger was real, she was beginning to believe she had imagined it. Things had changed so drastically. And nothing that had happened to them could possibly be connected to Lavinia.

Except that Lavinia was avid to get her hands on *The Eye of God*.

It was getting complicated again, just when it had become simple. They could have had each other forever instead of a mystical diamond; they could have stayed in that carnal sanctuary in Srinagar forever.

Instead, he had rooted her up so early in the morning, it was obscene, and they had dressed, packed, eaten a rushed breakfast, taken care of the servants, and gone to the house of the guide prearranged by Sidhu.

She hated Sidhu for stressing the urgency of leaving at the early hour.

It was too early up in the snowy mountains they climbed by mule road as they pressed on toward Gilgit. A day and a half later, they camped outside the outpost, and spent the night there.

Their guide, whose name was Naib, arranged a wagon, called a *tarantass,* to take them on to Tashkent.

Nor was there any comfort there; it was a perch and a flat bed on wheels and nothing to cushion the ride. At best, they didn't have to walk or ride the mules. At worst, they didn't have to carry their things. And it was a long journey over weather-rutted roads besides.

A fool's chase . . . and broken dreams.

They came to Tashkent through a large stone gate, and into a city of minarets, walled houses, tree-lined streets and garden greenery. There was a hotel, but it offered no amenities. They took a room anyway, spending the night on an uncomfortable bed before exploring the town.

It was a place that was Eastern and Russian both, with an unexpected level of sophistication. There were long avenues of villas and an old town with a grand bazaar. There was the English Club with a tolerable restaurant, and a reading room attached, that offered books from home and current periodicals.

There was heat and dust and flies, and the ubiquitous women in veils.

"If you don't count the women, it could be a city someplace in America," Darcie said in awe. "It's so much more *green* than I thought it would be, and warmer."

"And English," Con said. "With churches. But probably no one comes here unless they have to. Look at Naib. He's taken the wagon and gone already, even though I offered him a place for the night. I think we'll stay a day—maybe two—and see what we can find out."

But that put them in the position of being outsiders, and they were going to need help. They decided to have dinner at the English Club and see what they could find out.

Con bribed the hotel manager, and they got a bath—lukewarm water in a very small copper tub, but clean water nonetheless, and set before a roaring fire in their room.

Luxury, after a week tramping up and down mountains.

"Imagine squeezing in there," Con murmured, eyeing the tub with real interest.

She slipped her hand between his thighs. "Imagine squeezing *there*," she countered lightly.

"Why don't we?"

"Don't we have to wait?"

"Isn't five days enough? I've been crazy not being able to have you in this cold."

"It's warm now, Con."

"And I'm damned hot."

"You are stoked like a furnace."

"What are you going to do about it?"

"I'm going to take you in my mouth and make you roar."

She knelt down and began undressing him. God—five days—in the desensitizing cold, as they huddled under sheepskins and flimsy tents, their sensual hunger had been dormant. It was enough to manage to keep warm.

So the minute she unleashed him, she felt her own desire blaze up like wind whipping the embers of a dead fire.

She wanted to devour him, right there, right then.

He had never looked more luscious, more succulent. Their enforced abstinence only made her lust after him the more. She wanted to stuff the whole of him in her mouth, but he was so huge, so long, and he was on the brink of erupting, and she wanted—and she didn't want—to bring him there.

He was ripping off the clothes that he could get to. He hauled her up and away from the taste of him and backed her against the wall. "I can't wait. I want you now."

She held him as he tore away every impediment, and when she was naked, she eased his way. He was meant to be there; he was perfectly shaped and curved to take her standing this way—or lying down, turned over, backwards, forwards, in her mouth, in her hand . . .

She didn't care where, or what he did, only that *he* belonged to *her*, and that he was always aware.

She wrapped her arms and one leg around his hips as he began to thrust—oh, and just the way she liked it: those short hard little thrusts that she felt so sharply. He knew just how to do it, just how to keep himself hard and cocked within her while priming her there.

She felt their coupling keenly, she envisioned it as he drove himself as relentlessly as a piston, hard, hard, hard. Perfect emphatic strokes. Inexorable and strong. Hard, hard, hard. Thick and long. Didn't want it to end. On and on. Breathless and insensate, and climaxing on a moan—long and strong in undulating glistening waves, hot as the sun—until they broke violently over the rock of his erection—and she was alone.

He caught her—he came in her backwash as she rode him home as mercilessly as he had taken her, and still joined, he lifted her in a radiant kiss and brought her finally to bed.

He never broke the kiss. The kiss was the aftermath

that was never going to end. A week's worth of kisses he had to expend. Hot writhing kisses, arousing kisses . . .

And whispers: "I want you again . . ."

Wait . . .

Unending kisses, no beginning, no end. Hours of kisses . . .

"I can't wait . . ."

More kisses, were there ever such kisses . . . ?

"No touching—or I'll explode . . ."

She had to touch. He was rampantly there, demanding her caresses.

He grabbed her hands and pinned them. "You do enough, just with your tongue."

"It's not enough—I need your body."

"Oh, believe me, I know you do . . . but *I'll* say when."

"I don't want to wait."

"Shut up, Darcie," and he covered her mouth again.

She lost track of everything in those lush consuming kisses. He held her hands prisoner so that only her body could move.

Ineffectual body; he didn't want it: he wanted her kisses.

She was soaking wet, her nipples pointed and hard, she was hot for him, aching for him, moaning for him, and all he gave her were those hot luscious kisses.

And a steaming awareness of *him*. Of his heat, his body, his need. His tension and his power. The mastery of his kisses. His red-hot desire. His granite hard erection. His iron control.

She writhed her body, seeking him. He was so close, almost there.

"Please . . ."

"I want to—but not yet."

"I hate you."

"But you love my kisses." He came at her again, stoking her mouth with the same fury he took her body.

She was going to melt from his kisses. She was so hot, she thought she would explode. Or he would. All his delicious essence, all over her.

Yes . . . yes, yes—

He seethed with his lust to possess her. And he loved the waiting. Always he thought he could never get bigger or harder or crave her more. And every time, waiting made everything more explosive.

And he thought, he could insert himself just at the delicious opening between her legs—just there, just the rigid ridged tip of him . . . into her hot velvet just so she was aware . . . He pearled up just envisioning it.

He wanted it. Just the tip coated now with the evidence of his desire.

Still pinning her hands, he straddled her, caging her as before, nudging her, seeking her as she parted her legs to welcome him.

"Please—yes—"

Yes—he found her, yes, he put himself there just as he'd envisioned. Just the tip. Just . . . *there* . . .

She caught her breath. "Oh God—Con-n . . ."

"You like that."

Did she like that? She contracted her muscles in a carnal caress. Just *there*.

Just breaching her, letting her feel him so intensely she thought she'd scream. Rocking slightly against her, letting her know how much more there was to come.

This was enough. If this was all he wanted to give her, she would take just this much. It was all she needed. She undulated against the power of his luscious tip. She was so ripe, so ready; she knew just how to cant her body against him to make the most of him.

It was so erotic, him holding her like that. She arched her back, bearing down on the tip, and riding it high and hard at her center, rotating her hips violently, and gyrating him in turn.

It wasn't quite the same as his full-bore possession of her; it was different—a slow sweet shuddering kiss of a climax as she called out his name.

She slid down into delicious silence. He didn't move. He remained inside her, looking at her with skepticism and disgust.

Seeing eyes—what was he seeing? This was not in the dark, and he could see her now for what she really was: a woman full of sexual tricks and unlimited guile.

She should not have done that. What woman would?

"Well, well, well," he murmured. "You do know some interesting things . . ."

She felt a wave of heat wash over her. "You'd be surprised what those London society ladies have up their sleeves. I was with a very fast crowd that first year."

"But you found me in a brothel, Darcie. It does give me pause."

"It doesn't change anything."

"But it explains a lot."

"Con—don't do this."

"Oh—I won't. I like the idea that you're a whore. It makes everything—simpler somehow."

"Don't—" the word stuck in her throat. "I'm not."

"If you say so." He pulled away from her, still rampant and hard. "I don't have to finish now, Darcie. This time, I'll wait."

"If you feel that way, you should send me home," she said stringently as they awaited the service of the first course at the English Club.

"Let's just say I need a little time to get used to it."

She didn't know what to do. Or what to say. He'd never asked one question about her marriage to Roger or the tenor of their relationship. He'd never been curious even about whether they'd had sex. Never spoke again about the baby that wasn't.

"I loved it," she said finally. "I love it with you."

"You say that to all the men who poke you, Darcie."

She turned her face away. Con with his eyes was as formidable a man as she'd ever met. You couldn't hide a thing from those eyes. Or that body or that mouth. And there were too many things left unsaid. And secrets she'd kept.

"Send me back to England then."

He shook his head. "No."

She decided to be bold; what did she have to lose? "I won't go on if I can't have you."

He sent her a malicious smile. "Oh, you can have me. I wouldn't deny either of us that."

He paused as the waiter served the soup. Good hot thick pea soup, edible with a fork. He felt like smearing it all over her body and licking it off.

He didn't know what he was so annoyed about. Nothing had changed. She was a sexual temptress with an enormous appetite for sex. It should have given him a clue, but instead, he had let himself become immersed in his unending lust for her.

And he meant it: he wasn't going to give that up.

"I had sex with Roger for the first year of the marriage before he went off to the pigs," she said suddenly. "At least he had the decency to wait six months after my father died to publicly rut in the streets. I wanted to know—what did they know that I didn't? What did they do that I couldn't? Why was copulating with a trollop more satisfying than with me?"

"This is a good story, Scheherazade." He motioned to the waiter to remove the soup. "Go on. I'm fascinated."

"We were still living in London. I went to his friends. You know, all those Ladies and Honorables. The ones who, behind their philandering husbands' backs, funded Madame's brothel so that they too could have a place to sport. It was eye-opening. But it didn't answer the question. Because there was nothing I saw there I wouldn't have tried in order to please Roger."

"Well known there, were you?"

"I went a half dozen times with several ladies with whom I would assume you're acquainted. You would not want to know who they are. It would be a terrible disappointment for you to know their lecherous vices."

"And you joined in them, of course."

Her voice went husky. "I watched." She took a deep breath. "A peculiar sort of morality for someone like me. I just wanted to *know*. Not that it helped. In any event, I do know Madame recognized me when I came to her door the night I found you."

He clapped lightly. "That's very good, Sheherazade. Excellent, in fact. The confused and yearning newlywed wife. The horrible husband. The remedy, in fiction, if not life. This is some damned story."

"Any more insane than your accepting your sight and then babbling about the powers of *The Eye of God*?" she shot back. "I thought you'd gone crazy."

"And I have my sight."

"At what cost?" she retorted.

"We don't know yet," he answered quietly. "That's the gamble I took. But you know all about risks like that, don't you, Darcie?"

She stared at him, stony-faced. "Yes, I do."

"We *are* a pair. Today was just a little reminder that this is not a journey to heaven, and you're no angel."

"No," she hissed. "I'm just the woman you have sex with."

"Then I hope we both get what we deserve," he said mockingly, and he motioned for their hovering waiter to serve.

She lost her appetite over that, but she managed to eat some meat and drink some tea, while he devoured everything on his plate.

After, they wandered into the reading room and he struck up a conversation with one of the military men who was looking at *her* with undisguised interest.

He was in his early forties, a veteran of this kind of outpost duty; he was well-fed and had a fleshy face and sharp pale blue eyes.

He introduced himself as Colonel Giles and happy to be of service. And what on earth was a beautiful woman like Madame Boulton doing in Tashkent?

That was blunt and to the point, and the point with the colonel *was* women and sex and nothing else.

"You're looking for *what?*" he asked finally, disbelievingly after the third brandy. "You're wasting all the time of this trip with this adorable woman chasing after who?"

"He's a monk I believe. He might have come this way. I'm looking for someone to translate for us so I can find out."

"Oh hell, you'll always find someone here who wants to earn a few quid. All they have to do is gamble and drink anyway. I'll do it myself, if you don't mind. Can always use a pint and a pound. So tell me about this monk."

"I just want to know if he passed through."

"Is he a criminal?" He gave Darcie a long speculative look up and down. "He hurt Madame Boulton here?"

"No." Con made an instant decision on the basis of his instant dislike of the man *and* the way he was looking at Darcie. "He's a thief. He took something from my family."

"A monk, eh?"

"On the estate," Con lied blandly. "Goole Abbey, in Croxfordshire."

"I see." Giles stroked his chin and looked at Darcie. "Certainly, I'll help you. You want to ask at the church?"

"That's where I'd start."

"All right. These Sarts aren't much for talking anyway. Father Licasi would probably know."

"Is he available now?"

"You're sure in a hurry."

"Tomorrow morning then?"

"He does a seven o'clock mass."

"I'll meet you there."

"Will do," Giles agreed, picking up his snifter and sauntering away. "See you tomorrow. Nice to meet you—both."

"I've never seen you in action before, Darcie. What a treat." He thrust open their hotel door with the force of a bear.

"He's a pig. You'd better go see this Father Licasi without him."

"I appreciate the advice. I know that in your profession you have to be an excellent judge of character."

"Oh you are something, Con Pengellis," she seethed, balling her fists to keep herself from killing him. "The only thing you can hold against me is my making a very bad error in judgment—namely rescuing *you*."

"Ah, Scheherazade—he was just ogling you."

"But you're the one who spun him that fairy tale."

"Nonsense. I told him all of the truth he needed to know."

"And the rest of it just skirted the edges of being pure fiction. And better than anything I ever made up. Stole something from your family—ha! Diamonds out of a fairy tale . . ."

She swirled around the room furiously because she didn't know what else to do. She felt as if he had left both of them hanging. And he wasn't going to couple with her tonight. She was so annoyed she felt like taking the venal Colonel Giles in his stead.

Just to see what Con would do if he found someone else in her bed.

She ruminated on that satisfying little scenario for a moment. But it wasn't worth the trouble. Once they started on the journey again, there would be no time for all that heat and desire.

But until then—ah! She felt that involuntary sensual twinge. No. No. Not now. But already, she was thinking of the moment he penetrated her earlier that afternoon. All those luscious kisses leading up to that one ravishing crowning of her body.

She had to stop thinking about it.

Suspended by it, dependent on it, yearning for it, out of her mind for it . . . a bare inch of his hard length could make her come . . .

He was right: she was as dissolute as any whore.

They should have separate rooms. Separate lives. She should have left him alone.

"Get undressed, Darcie," he said behind her. "Go to bed."

She undressed behind a screen. That, along with the

bed, a washstand, an overstuffed chair and an armoire, was the only furniture in the room.

And she had very little clothing left; he'd ripped it all to shreds.

I have to stop this. She did have something to wear to bed: an oversized shirt of she'd appropriated from Con. She slipped it on, at once annoyed and aroused by the need for propriety.

Sometimes something covering your body was the most sensual thing of all, she thought, as she crawled into bed. But he wouldn't even give her the pleasure of watching him undress. He waited until he'd lowered the lights, and she knew he was done when his side of the bed depressed.

But he was naked. That was good. And definitely deliciously hard. That was better.

Now she'd just have to make him respond.

"That Colonel Giles *was* very interested in me," she murmured. "English women must be few and far between out here. But surely the men have places they can go to spend themselves. There must be women here who are willing to accommodate a man's lust. Maybe a harem full of women who do it for a price."

Oh yes—this is working. He's steaming already, I just have to pour it on . . .

"Every man must be different, the way he takes a woman. I wonder how a man like the colonel does it. He's a big man. It makes me wonder how big the *best* part of his body is. That's always a sign of a man's potency, don't you think? How big he gets when he's having *social* intercourse with a woman . . ."

She paused coyly, knowing he was seething, knowing she was detonating a bomb. But she wanted it—blasting ferociously deep into her core. And she wasn't averse to lighting the match to send the fire raging out of control.

"I'm trying to remember if I noticed. I mean, why speculate? Of course, I've been concentrating so much on only one man lately. But I'm thinking that I must have noticed *something* . . ."

She felt him lever himself up and climb over her. He grasped her hair and pulled her head back. *Oh yes* . . .

". . . since I can't stop talking about *his* . . ."

He yanked her hair.

"Goddamn you, I'll stuff your mouth if you don't shut up . . ."

"Good," she whispered. "I can't wait."

He felt the primitive roar of absolute dominance explode in his body. Her eyes were his—she'd offered them for life. And her orgiastic body—she would never deny him. And that mouth, that wet, wild, succulently sucking mouth, to live in and die, a thousand little deaths—he wanted it *now*.

With a guttural sound, he came into her mouth, into the wet, the heat, the avid hungry haven of her sucking mouth, her greedy hands, her worship and adoration of the most male part of himself.

She took him, inch by inch, laving and loving him, stroking and caressing the strength and length of him. Pulling everything from him with her lips and her tongue, until he could control it no more, and he spent, in her mouth, all his power.

Nineteen

In the dark, she owned his power and his passion. In the dark, where he couldn't see.

She unbuttoned her shirt and lovingly rubbed the residue of his essence on her skin.

He reached out a languid hand to touch her. "Don't ever do that to me again."

"Do what? Devour you?"

"Bitch. Talk about another man."

"I'm not a whore."

"That remains to be seen."

"Then I guess all observations are fair in this game, Con, if that's what you want me to be."

"At least you don't claim I made you," he murmured, turning on his belly.

"Oh no—" she pushed him. "You don't hide from me. If you're awake and hard, I get to look at you. And if you're asleep and hard—I get to look at you."

"And if *you're* asleep and I'm hard . . . ?"

"Wake me up and take me," she said insolently.

"And if we're having *social* intercourse, and I'm hard?"

She looked at him from under hooded eyes with that elusive, knowing smile as he hardened up before her eyes. "I just know you'll find a way to spend yourself in me."

"You *are* a bitch. I told you I'm hard for you all the time. If you want it, beg for it; I'll stuff you to the hilt, but don't ever *ever* moan and groan about another man's sex to my face."

"Can I moan and groan about *your* sex?" It was thunderously huge now, flexing with all its might, enticing her almost of its own volition.

"No . . . after what you pulled tonight, you have to get on your knees and plead for it."

He rolled over onto his back so that he was poking stiffly into the air.

"At least I can look," she murmured, easing back onto her elbow. "I really *love* looking."

She reached out her hand and stroked him, and he pushed her away.

"Don't try to stoke me, miss bitch. I'll live with my erections. But if you want the colonel, you can't have me."

"There's only one man I want."

He wouldn't be mollified. "You *talked about* his."

She put out a finger and rubbed the underside of his erection. "I don't *want* his."

He caught her finger in his hand. "But you *looked* . . ."

"Maybe," she temporized. "I said maybe I thought I might have . . ." Knowing it was driving him crazy now, and he'd never know if she did or not.

Good. Maybe it would keep him as off balance as she felt.

"You just like looking, don't you? I should just get dressed and never be hard for you again."

"You won't do that. You're about to burst from wanting me. If you just touch me, you'll come like a firecracker. That's how much you want me. You don't care how much I look at you—or any other man—just as long as you're the one in bed with me. You'll probably give

Giles all the details tomorrow so he can salivate over the fact that you're the lucky one. Isn't that what you want? Isn't it?"

"No," he growled, his control slipping. *"You* do—"

All it took were her words . . . and the iron will that held him taut and erect as a pole wavered, and there a drop of his essence pearled up on his luscious tip.

She rubbed it lightly over his head, and brushed her finger over her lower lip. "Take me."

He wasn't giving in.

"Beg me."

"Your body is begging. It wants to come."

His iron will slipped again, and another drop of ejaculate appeared.

"Don't waste it," she cautioned coquettishly. "I need it."

He levered himself up to a sitting position.

"And now you're going to get it. I'm finished playing with you. I'm hard. You're ripe. It doesn't matter where I spend myself. Get off the bed. I want you facedown over the arm of that chair."

She bent over the arm, quivering with excitement. The angle of the arm elevated her bottom and she could feel his length against her crease.

Oh yes . . . yes—all the games and words all to come to this . . . what they hungered for . . . the endless surcease of coupling their bodies . . . yes—

She was canted perfectly to receive him. She clutched the cushion in anticipation as she felt him nudge her just *there*. There was no impediment to his possession. He stood behind, naked, erect, and holding her buttocks to position her, he entered, slowly, slowly, slowly, his body shuddering on contact with her heated wet cleft.

Don't waste it . . .

I need it . . .

He almost blew.

I must have noticed it since I'm talking about it—

His resolve stiffened like a rock.

He would make her forget other men altogether.

He worked his shaft into her an inch at a time. He felt her shivering with anticipation, and wriggling against him, pushing her bottom to accept him, acclimate him and bring him in all the way to the bone.

Don't waste it . . .

The secrets of Eve . . . she knew them all, courtesan that she was. She'd take it any way he gave it, and he wasn't coming till cock crow, and he had pounded her home.

Don't waste it . . .

She was so eager and so wet. She shimmied against him, enticing his thrusts. He gave them to her, hot, hard, emphatic; the same piston-like strokes that she loved, that she begged for. Long steady constant thrusts, in out, in out, holding her hips, in out, absorbing her cries, in out, the center of her world, in out, the core of her being, in out, till she spiralled away, in out, he wouldn't let her go, in out, and she tried to get away, in out, wrenching her body, in out, relinquish his grip, in out, one more thick thrust, in out, pitching them into a storm of sensation impossible to control.

It rammed her dead center, unexpected, unrelenting, pounding her like a hurricane, breaking over her like a dam; he swooped after her and willingly followed her over, and pitched headlong into his wrenching spuming release.

And into silence. That lapping soul-sapping silence, that moment they died the little death.

The only movement, his subtle withdrawal, and they collapsed together on the bed and into the deep swooning silence where nothing needed to be said.

* * *

"I can see Father Licasi alone," Con said the next morning as he sat at the edge of the bed. "There's no need for you to get up."

She stretched luxuriously and reached for him. "I can think of one reason." She struggled to sit up. "In fact . . ." She slipped onto her knees in front of him, and grasped his jutting length in her hand. "I can think of two."

"We don't have much time."

"Then let me coat my nipples with your cream. That's the only thing I want this morning. You can give me that—" She circled his head and began to pump, arching her back to give him an unobstructed view of her breasts. "There—" as he spurted. "There—" as she anointed her breasts, and she took him home.

He left her a half hour later, lolling in bed. She felt pagan, primitive. Curiously sated. She wanted to lie in bed naked all day long, waiting for him. Impossibly, she wanted him again.

Tomorrow, they would start the next leg of the journey, north toward Omsk. Days and days of travel, with no time to give in to their desire. Of course, she wanted to have as much as possible of him now.

She wouldn't let him leave the bed when he returned, she thought. She wouldn't even get dressed. Or pack. She wished she were certain he was thinking about her, that he wanted her.

But there was something in him that enabled him to put all these things into different compartments to be examined one at a time. He could just remove himself from *her*, relegating her to the compartment marked *satisfied for now*.

And now, he followed Lazarin's trail.

When he returned, she would make him forget all that. They had one more day . . .

She awakened to the sound of a knock on the door—and she jumped out of bed. She didn't know how long she'd slept, but maybe that was good because he was back already, and sooner than if she'd spent all that time waiting.

Stark naked, she pulled open the door and jumped back in shock.

"Colonel Giles!"

"Aren't you eager," he said, closing the door behind him as she flew behind the dressing screen. "I love it when a woman is eager."

"What do you want? Why are you here?" She had no clothes; nothing to wear. Frantically, she pulled on the wreck of a shirt and her skirt.

"Don't hide from me, you little tart. I read the invitation in your eyes. I know what you want. I made sure to get your paramour out of the way. We have—oh—fifteen minutes, a half hour at the most." He tossed away the screen. "How much do you want?"

"Are you crazy?" she shrieked. "Get out of here!" She dove across the bed and scrambled to her feet just as he pulled a short fat riding crop out of his boot.

He's insane. Living with this deprivation . . .

He smacked the crop against the bed. "Don't play coy, whore. Looking at me like that. Name your price, I'll pay it."

"He'll be back sooner than that." She needed a story. She was Scheherazade, wasn't she? "He never leaves me alone for long. I swear to you, he'll kill you if he finds you here. If he says a half hour, you can be sure he'll return in ten minutes. He *owns* me."

"Well, I'm going to possess you too, you little hot-tailed tart. Wriggling your bottom at me like you want it." He struck the bed again. "What do you expect a man to do? I can pay for it. But I'd love to force you. It's your choice."

She stood shivering by the window, thinking that throwing herself out and landing on Con's head was easier than trying to reason with him.

And that riding crop was scary. And he *looked* like he loved to use it.

"Colonel, if you just leave this minute, I'll never tell anyone you came."

"You're very very good at this, my lovely, just the right amount of indignation and outrage. Is that your act in bed? But—we're getting nowhere, and obviously—" he paced around to the foot of the bed, "you like it rough." He struck the footboard.

She jumped onto the bed, putting the footboard between them. But that was worse, cat and mouse. Either way she went, he could corner her, and she didn't see anything she could use as a weapon at hand.

"Eager little piece, aren't you? Just lay down and relax, you strumpet, and I'll give you what you want."

She eyed him warily; he just stood there, smacking the crop against his hand, waiting for her move. One way or the other . . . she couldn't just hold him there until Con returned.

She made a feinting move toward the window side of the bed, and he took two steps around to grab her.

She popped off the bed toward the door, reaching to pick up the screen. Anything, anything—too heavy— maybe she could jab him with it.

He vaulted over the bed after her, and she lifted it, with difficulty, and swung it over his head.

Wham! He collapsed on the mattress. *Wham!* To make sure he was unconscious. *Wham!* Her temper got the best of her. She dropped the screen on the floor and knelt beside the bed.

It was a lump of soggy manhood. She debated a moment about whether to search him before she dragged his sorry carcass out of the room.

Why not? He had no business being here. He was supposed to have met Con at the church to interpret for him with this Father Licasi.

She rolled him over, and tapped her hands over his uniform; nothing obvious there. She unbuttoned his tunic, and folded it back to the inside pocket.

Ah! Everything here.

Just not what she expected. No military identification. No letters of commission. Nothing, except a passport in the name of Percival Giles—from a village in Croxfordshire.

Oh, this was getting crazy. They had relaxed their guard too much, never counting on Lavinia's arm reaching *this* far.

They had to have been followed from Srinagar.

But how? Sidhu had made the strictest arrangements. Had buried the grotto. Destroyed the clues.

Had he?

She didn't know what to think. She didn't have time to think. The only decision she had to make was whether to leave him for Con to see.

And that was taken out of her hands moments later, when he appeared at the door.

"Well, well, well Scheherazade; are you telling him bedtime stories too?"

She wheeled around, startled. Thought fast. Didn't want him asking what Giles was doing here in the first place, but that was inevitable. But maybe she could detract from his questions by what she'd found.

"It's worse than that, Con. He lied."

"Oh, he did. He never showed up, and look where he is."

"Listen to me. No more fun and games. He is *not* military." She thrust the passport in his hand.

He scanned it quickly. "Oh Jesus." He tossed it on the bed. "Damnation. It gets worse. Father Licasi speaks English."

"And?" She was pulling out their suitcases as he spoke.

"He probably thought he'd seduce the thing out of you—" Con muttered. "I'll kill him."

"Father Licasi?" she asked, grabbing whatever clothing she found to hand and folding it haphazardly into the suitcase.

"This piece of cow dung." He nudged the body with the toe of his boot. "Not so alluring now, is it? I think it's dead."

She ignored that. There was no time for games. This was serious. "What did Father Licasi say?"

"Father said all Russians are messengers of Death. And many itinerant priests have come through Tashkent because of its direct route to Omsk and the Trans-Siberian railroad. He remembers this one, particularly because he was not travelling to St. Petersburg or Moscow. He didn't know his name. But he told the Father his calling was the Siberian village of Nadyl on the Nizmennost Plains of Siberia."

She felt chilled down to her toes. The diamond was the key. And a sparsely populated area in which Lazarin could unleash its evil powers.

"We can go by wagon and coach to Omsk. But it's a three-day journey. And probably that and more to Nadyl, by wagon or sled."

"But he was here, Lazarin was here. And now Lavinia is in pursuit, sending this piece of offal, her agent."

"Which means—"

"They were in Srinagar," Darcie finished for him. "And they know we're together."

Worse and worse if that were true. She hadn't even considered that aspect, that Lavinia must see them as the guardians of two treasures to confiscate.

She should leave him, she thought. They should separate. He could move so much better, so much faster without her. And there would only be one life and one thing of value on the line.

Her hands trembled as she threw the last of their meager possessions into the suitcases.

"I could . . ."

Con closed the suitcase emphatically. "We go together, and leave him here. You saved me the trouble of killing him. We are in service of the diamond. You are the chosen; when the time comes, you must be at hand."

"It's a lot of nonsense, mumbo-jumbo," she whispered. "Too much to risk when your life is at stake. And I'm scared to death of what the consequences will be of your covenant with Lazarin."

"A devil's bargain," he said, shrugging. "He does give us what we want, but it *was* a gift."

"Or maybe—" a thought suddenly struck her that was the most terrifying of all, "it was the only way for Lazarin to get possession of *The Eye of God.*"

Lazarin had orchestrated the whole thing.

They set off to Omsk with that awful conclusion hovering over them. Everything, from the entity Karun in his original guise as the deckhand, to the moment when they breached the tunnel and entered the grotto, it all had been planned and designed so that Con would come and liberate the stone.

"We could ruminate on this for the whole three hundred miles of this trip," Con said. "There's nothing rational about these events."

"But now it starts to make some eerie kind of sense. You said yourself he couldn't move it. And he gave you back your sight. Why? Because he knew you understood his magic and that it had to be stopped. And how? By the power of the stone that only you could move."

"But now you're in the equation, Darcie. And that's the thing that throws it off."

"And Lavinia." She looked at the desolate landscape without seeing it. "But apart from her desperation to possess the stone and have an heir, where does Lavinia fit?"

"Lavinia wants the stone and wants an heir. And maybe it's as clear cut as that."

"But still—the cruelty toward you . . ."

"I was an arrogant beast, Darcie. But seven years in a dungeon makes a self-centered man angry, hungry, vengeful and mature."

"She'd kill you in a minute, and maybe that was Giles' mandate today," she said thoughtfully. "But how—no, I won't think it . . ."

"I've considered it. How did he get here before us?"

"If Lavinia knows, then she has made a pact with that devil too."

"Or," Con said, thinking the unthinkable, "it was Sidhu."

They stayed overnight at a road inn in Karazhal, one of several way stations on the journey to Omsk, where they shared a sleeping dormitory with a dozen strangers.

In the morning, they were given a breakfast of tea and cakes, and a coach accommodating six arrived there at eight. It left within the hour, and within two, they were acquainted with their fellow travellers: a doctor, an English governess on her way to St. Petersburg after touring the Mediterranean; a banker; and an importer of Russian artifacts, jewelry and gemstones.

Darcie clutched Con's arm. *Dear God—he wasn't saying it but what he meant was—diamonds . . .*

They were everywhere—

But not by word or action did the gentleman betray anything suspicious, and Darcie thought that within such close quarters for so many hours, he would have let slip something.

Maybe it was a coincidence. Maybe they were looking for demons where there weren't any.

It was snowing when the coach rumbled into Omsk down the slushy main street in the center of the city. Here and everywhere, broomsmen worked, sweeping the snow from the sidewalks, dodging sleds and wagons, and passersby. They passed block after block of shops, restaurants and a theater square.

Beyond this was the railway station and a block of hotels, and the coach pulled in front of these.

"Did you arrange your accommodations?" the import merchant inquired. "I can recommend one if you're going to stay a while."

"Are you?" Darcie said. "Staying, I mean."

"Oh no. No." He was a funny little man, plump, stylish and very precise. "I'm heading north in three days' time to the diamond fields of the Nizmennost Plains of Siberia." He leaned toward them confidentially. "I make my best deals with the *natives,* man to man, you understand. My little secret, so I trust you won't tell. But if you're not remaining in Omsk, you'd be just as comfortable at the Hotel Vyatka at the end of the block. I'm staying there myself. Good luck!"

And he was off.

"I don't think we can afford *not* to stay there," Con muttered. "I've got to find out who that man is, and why he's going north to Nizmennost."

And there were other arrangements to be made: money to be converted; registering at the hotel; clothes for the icy climate; the rental of a *drozhky;* horses, furs, a driver who would take them as far as Okrug.

The hotel cost two rubles a night for the most utilitarian room. The transportation, more than a hundred times that.

"It's worth it," Con said.

"I'm impressed at your knowledge of Russian," Darcie murmured.

"Enough to get by."

They went to a nearby restaurant for dinner, tramping in their warm mountain garments through the packed snow. No one looked askance. There were so many travellers passing through Omsk.

And they needed to talk where they couldn't be overheard.

They took a table very far in the back near the kitchen with no one else near, and ordered a simple menu of soup, roast pork, potatoes and tea.

"We don't even know what that man's name was," Darcie fretted.

"I'll find him," Con said grimly, "and I'll find out what he's up to."

"I'm scared."

"We do *not* have a choice. That diamond is already split in two. The best we can hope is that we can recover both pieces."

And he was deadly serious.

"We have no plan."

"Maybe things work better *without* a plan. How could you plan for the appearance of a Lazarin?"

"We must be running out of money."

"We will have to sell another stone fairly soon."

"Perhaps to our friend the importer?" Darcie suggested.

"You mean—as a test? I think he'd call the authorities in the blink of an eye. He's someone who very well might know the Pengellis diamonds. No, *I*—yes, *I'm* going to get into his room and find out who he is, and if he's a threat. And yes, I'll have the revolver, so just keep quiet, Darcie, and eat your soup."

"I have to do *something*," she grumbled later as they finished their tea.

He sent her a scorching look. "Wait up for me."

Their room was small, with the chimney of a central heating stove radiating a fair amount of warmth. There were hooks on the door for clothes, a wash basin and stand. Two kerosene lamps. A small table and one sagging chair.

It would do. Only she was the one waiting, and there was no room to pace. She sat at the table wearily and waited.

Con and his waiting. A person could die waiting.

She jumped up impatiently. It was a coincidence. It had to be.

Lavinia just couldn't move that fast. *Couldn't.*

And yet—

Time crept by. Con had left her on their return from dinner, and she had no idea how long ago that was. And the room was in the back of the hotel, on an upper floor, and all she could see was rooftops and the sky.

And an occasional light dimming, and finally going out.

How late could it be?

And then, she imagined something happened to Con. The merchant had caught him, abducted him, killed him. Or called the authorities. Or something.

Why wasn't he here yet?

She threw herself across the bed. Better to sleep than make up scenarios that had no basis in reality.

Wait up for me . . .

She thought she would.

She slept.

And felt a hand on her arm, shaking her awake.

She bolted upright. "Con!"

"Shhh."

"What? Tell me!" she demanded in a whisper.

"His name is Kleist, according to the coachman. But he's not registered at the Vyatka. Or either of the two other hotels. Or any of the rooming houses that I found when I was searching out the driver. That precious little man has disappeared into thin air."

Nor could they find any trace of him the following morning. And as far as they could tell, he hadn't rented a driver and sled.

"This is too eerie," Darcie said.

Snow was falling again, and they had come out early to scour the shops for woollen clothing and furs.

"I feel as if we imagined him."

"Or else he's biding his time, waiting until we leave." Con was spending rubles like they were wheat. Two fur blankets; a little heater for coals; sheepskin boots and coats for both of them, and a fur throw.

"You're insane."

"It's cold." He bought woollen underwear and suits for each of them, and mittens, socks and gloves. And some dried fruit and beef; canteens for tea and water and—"I think that's enough."

They needed a wagon to bring it all back to the hotel, but there seemed always to be an *izvozchik* waiting for a fare.

Dinner out again in the hotel restaurant, their table tucked in a far corner where they could talk.

Still, Darcie felt so far removed from the world they were about to breach. She could almost pretend that they were on holiday—or a honeymoon. Oh, but that thought was best left buried.

Especially when Con told her the precautions he'd taken.

"We'll have with us two revolvers and a knife. And I found a small lead-lined container for our trust, which you must wear fastened around your waist. We can't lose it. Or the remaining stones. I plan to sell the next one tomorrow in the market. And then we'll each have one, in case anything happens."

"Nothing will happen," Darcie said, her voice tight.

"We're travelling relatively light so we can move fast and get things done."

"You call that mountain of fur and wool *light*?"

"For the lower reaches of Siberia—yes. You'll be ready to move out as soon as tomorrow morning, as soon as I return."

"And until then?" she whispered.

He sent her a heated glance. "You'll move for me tonight, because, Scheherezade, I'm hot and ready and burning for you."

Twenty

A night of secret pleasures, told in the dark.

Always in the dark. Began in the dark, ended in the dark, by touch, by word, by feel. Naked in the dark, your sex open in the dark, with a hunger you yearn to feed.

That way, in the dark, upside down, cradling his sex while he worships your crown.

The dark passion devours you; you resist, then you come, in the dark, on his tongue, till he finally sucks you away . . .

He left for the market at dawn, having called for tea, and bundling himself in the new underwear, suit, coat and gloves.

She felt leisurely this morning, replete from sex, and removed from the idea of any threats. She could drink some tea, pack—it seemed like she was always packing—and they would get a late morning start.

It was still snowing, and it had drifted up against the rooftops and the back of the buildings that she could see. And she heard the unmistakable sound of a cow mooing in the distance.

Just for this moment, things felt right.

And then she picked up the case in which she would carry *The Eye of God*—and the feeling dissipated.

She took the diamond in her hands, and held it to the light, and for the life her, she couldn't understand why men risked their lives to possess this large dull stone.

She wrapped it in coarse cotton and tucked it into the case. Then she threaded a belt through an attached loop, and wound it around her waist.

She pinned the pouch with the Pengellis diamond on her camisole between her breasts. Now, she thought, she was ready to get dressed.

She waited a long time—too long—for him to return, pottering around the room; filling the canteen with the remaining tea, rearranging everything in the suitcases—anything to fill the time and ease her fears.

But when he came, the news wasn't good.

"Kleist is still in Omsk. He was at the market, waiting—"

"Oh my God . . ."

"Following me . . . shadowing me—there was nowhere to make a deal."

"What are we going to do?"

"I think I outwitted him for the moment. Our driver is waiting. We're leaving—*now.*"

"Oh God—Con . . ."

"Shhh . . . everything is taken care of. Grab your suit and coat and let's *go.*"

They left by a back staircase, slipping out a side door, into an alleyway. Con took the risk and summoned the driver to pull up there.

She threw everything onto the floor and tumbled into the backseat.

Their driver snapped his whip, the sled lurched forward, and in a matter of minutes, they were one of dozens of conveyances plying the streets of Omsk, until they passed over the train tracks, and down broad avenues to the outskirts of the town, and they were gone.

* * *

She wasn't reassured that they had gotten a head start on Kleist.

"He's coming after us, and not the other way around."

"Probably," Con said. "It's still another chance we have to take." He had tented the blankets over their heads both to protect them from the steadily falling snow, and to give them some anonymity.

"Dmitri, our driver, says he's done it many times," Con said. "One wonders."

"And what if Kleist got to him? What if he's waiting somewhere down the line?"

"We'll do what we have to do. All I care about is if you're warm."

"I'm warm."

"It's damned cold. Your nose is red. Bury it in that fur for a while."

"God, I can't believe we're doing this. All for that stone. Every time I look at it, I see a big colorless rock."

"And yet—" he started to say, and he caught himself. "Maybe not yet. This isn't the time to extol the properties of the stone."

"When will that be? When Lazarin is about to kill us?"

"That *would* be a good time, yes."

"Con—"

"Shhhh. We're going forward, Darcie. That's all we have to know."

But they didn't go swiftly. Several hours into the trip, they stopped to change horses, and replenish their tea and coals. By nightfall, they were ready to stop, and they found a hostel.

Again, they slept in a barracks, wrapped in fur and

heat, among a half dozen travellers who had also sought
shelter for the price of ten kopecks.

They were off again in the morning, through a landscape dotted with huts, rivers and mansions, seen
through a curtain of diminishing snow.

"Dmitri says—another day, maybe two if the weather
keeps up."

"I'm hungry. I *hate* this place."

"We'll find something to eat."

She'd never seen such a bleak landscape. The snow
was intermittent and ongoing, constant and white.

Another change of horses at another way station
Dmitri knew, and they were able to get breakfast: eggs,
meat, tea, water. It was enough. But the lower reaches
of Siberia were endless, a horizon that stretched into
the night.

They pulled in once again to a barracks for the night.

Dmitri negotiated the price and took off the horses,
and she and Con went inside. There were a dozen travellers in the bunks in various stages of sleep.

"Darcie!" Con reached out and held her back.
"Kleist . . ."

She gasped. Kleist here, in the wilds of Okrug when
Con had outwitted him two days before in the Omsk
grand market.

God, there was no end.

They backed out of the room, and into the vestibule.

"I'll get Dmitri." Even he was shaken. He was back
in several moments. "Come."

They slipped out into the snow and into the side yard
where the sleighs and animals were corralled.

"We have to go *now*," he said, as they approached
Dmitri. But he'd already told him that.

"The horses are ragged out."

"I don't care." What was he doing, arguing with a peasant driver?

"You go at your peril," Dmitri said, and then he started laughing loudly, contemptuously, taunting them with his laughter as he transformed himself, before their very eyes into the plump body and plummy tones of Kleist. Laughing at them, mocking them as if to say he was invincible, and they'd never get away from him.

He couldn't reach a gun; he couldn't pull the knife.

He grabbed Darcie and they ran, ducking behind the sledges and horses, and out of sight of their nemesis.

His laughter echoed into the night.

"I hope . . . I pray," Con muttered, "another traveller comes in here tonight."

They merged with the shadows, burdened with their bags. They moved slowly, cautiously, Kleist's laughter following them.

"He can't be everywhere, dammit," Con swore, digging for a weapon. His fingers grasped the knife. "Good enough to immobilize Karun. Good enough to undercut Kleist. Can you see him?"

"I don't think he's moved," Darcie whispered.

"Let's get closer, from his back."

The laughter was impossible, high-pitched, not quite sane.

They crawled noiselessly toward him on the snow.

"It won't work, you know," Kleist called out. "I know where you are. Just give me the woman. And the stone."

Con gestured for Darcie to stay still. They were within feet of Kleist whose laughter echoed into the trees.

"Come out, we'll talk, perhaps we'll make a trade. You've already accepted a gift from Samael—" and he laughed again.

Con crept closer. Closer still.

Aim at the head.

He poised the knife on the tip of his fingers. He gauged the distance to the entity's head. He aimed.

Kleist laughed hysterically, horribly.

He snapped his wrist and released the knife.

It hit Kleist with a sickening thud, and he dropped like a stone.

"Darcie—!" He reached behind him to grab her. "I have to make sure."

Darcie covered her eyes. "I don't want to see."

He inched forward toward the body; it had fallen forward, the shaft of the knife buried in its neck. Blood spewed from the wound, a shocking pool of red on a white ground.

"It's not moving. It's bleeding."

"How much time?"

"I don't know. And I don't know if we should go or stay."

"We can't move anywhere in this snow."

"You're probably right. I'm going to drag him into the trees and cover up the blood. You go inside and get us two bunks."

"I don't want to leave you."

"You're better inside."

"I've never been so scared."

"I'll be in soon." He watched her reluctantly go, and he looked down at the bloody entity. Immobilized for maybe a day.

Or maybe a bloodthirsty man could do something about that.

Silently, with only the snow as witness, he pulled the thing into the shadows, and made sure it was dead.

And now he had blood on his hands, in the name of *The Eye of God.*

He took the reins of the sled the next morning, and they forged ahead; blindly, snow blown, determined, they pressed on toward Okrug in tandem with two other travellers who were going that way.

Blessed be . . .

They could have been attacked by their enemy.

They could have died in the snow.

The power of the stone . . . ?

Buried in the snow, what remained of Kleist, never to be found until the snow thawed . . .

In the name of . . . ?

They raced on through the storm, the whole of their world a white vista before them. Stopping for maps, food, change of horses, sleep.

Through Strezhvoy, Nizhne, Tarko-Selo, pausing only to ask had people seen him, did they know him, the tall ascetic monk with the burning eyes.

They knew of him, they said; they'd never seen him. And it was said he lived in the village of Nadyl on the Nizmennost Plains of Siberia.

And it was there they headed in those final hours, deep on the plain in the near north reaches of Siberia.

The place of diamonds and death.

It was a village of thatched log huts lining either side of the snow-slick road. And then a church, a school-house, a cemetery dressed in white. An abandoned wagon, a lone braying cow, fenced-in yards. And a knot of a half dozen children racing alongside them, throwing snowballs, and calling out questions.

"Where is your village priest?" Con asked them, and they pointed to a large house next to the church. "Where are your fathers?"

They said, "Down in the mines."

"Whom can I talk to?"

"Father Vasili."

They drove into the church courtyard, surrounded by the children.

"We're a novelty," Con said, as he helped Darcie from under the tent of furs in which she'd been wrapped the entire journey. "The priest will welcome us, hopefully he'll feed us, and tell us what we need to know."

He was tall, Father Vasili, and dark, dressed in his robes, and he appeared immediately at the door of the presbytery with a welcoming smile, shooing the children away all the while.

"My son, my daughter—come. There's tea and cakes. Come, get warm."

They removed their coats and their boots in the vestibule, and followed him into the large well-lit room where he motioned them to a table that was set at a right angle to the window, and on either side of which were comfortable upholstered chairs and a sofa.

"Sit on the sofa, do. Manya will bring food. I know you're from far away. Tell me your names."

Con told him, filling him in as best he could with limited language on why they had come.

Father Vasili nodded from time to time and then: "Ah! Here's Manya. Let us warm ourselves before we speak."

They drank, they ate a leisurely meal, by the end of which Darcie was itching to get some answers.

Con sensed her mood and opened the discussion, translating for Darcie as his questions were answered.

"Father, we've come from India seeking some answers. What can you tell us?"

"My son, my daughter, you've come such a long way on your quest. I can tell you, it ends here. Whether it is what you want to know—well . . . it is for you to tell me."

"We have heard, along the road and in the villages, that the man we seek is known by many to live among the people here in Nadyl. He is said to be a monk, a man of purpose. He is said to carry a divine stone."

"Ah, the stone. Yes, he is our holy man, blessed is he. But you mistake, my children; he has been among us for years."

They looked at each other in shock.

"Oh, yes, he came among us with his talisman stone. He blessed it to our community; sanctified it to the blood of Our Father by dipping it in goat's blood; and in the name of his divine Lord, he cleaved it. A piece of that stone reposes in the church, and we believe implicitly in its powers."

"And the other piece?" Con asked shakily.

"Our holy man has taken it to St. Petersburg to gift a part of this miraculous stone to our beloved Father Russia with the prayer that it will guide his rule and the country will prosper."

"Oh, dear God," Darcie breathed. "No . . ."

"So . . ." Con went on, pushing aside his shock, "he is gone."

"But for two weeks, maybe three."

"And a piece of this stone remains in your church?"

"Indeed. Would you like to see it?"

"We would."

"We shall. There is a walkway to the church. I will take you."

They put on the coats and boots and went out into the swirling snow.

"So white the landscape," the priest murmured. "So black the holy stone. This is," he added, as he pulled open a thick wooden door, "the incantation of our holy man. And in a moment, you shall see why."

He led them from the outer passage into the sanctuary, a simple church for a plain people. Stark white walls, wooden pews, a simple altar, a heavy pine wooden cross over it.

And there, to the side of the altar, displayed in an elaborate sarcophagus, was a faceted piece of *The Stone of Samael.*

"And your holy man, Lazarin, he consecrated this stone to your church?" Con asked, appalled.

"Oh no . . . no. Indeed, the stone was blessed to our church. But our holy man—his name is Rasputin."

They were given a guest room on the first floor of the presbytery. Father Vasili did not want them travelling any further.

They had dinner with him, and pleasant conversation, and then he left them alone.

"What are we going to do?" Darcie whispered.

"We have to steal that stone. Sneak in when the priest is sleeping. And then we've got to get to St. Petersburg, and see what we can find there."

"God, I hate this. I was shocked when he said he's always been among them."

"Power of suggestion, enhanced by the stone. They have no idea what's in that sanctuary."

"I have a feeling they don't care."

"I think you're right."

"I hope we can do this," she fretted. "I didn't expect this, did you?"

"I thought he'd be here," Con said. "But nothing has happened the way I thought."

And they waited. The clock in the presbytery parlor tolled midnight. One. Two.

Darcie took the candlestick and got their boots and coats. And then, like ghosts, they slipped out of the side door and into the snowy night.

The sky was as dark as a tomb. Not a star, not the moon, nothing to light their way but one flickering candle.

"God, this is eerie . . ." Darcie whispered, cupping the flame to shield it from the wind.

"Keep walking."

Their boots made such a loud crunch in the snow, loud enough to wake the dead. All around them, a matte, flat silence. They pushed forward, in the dark.

"We're almost there."

She held up the candle as they reached the doors.

"They always leave them open."

They slipped inside.

"Don't talk; the sound echoes."

Into the sanctuary, the candle flame casting long ghostly shadows in front of them.

Down the aisle they went and up onto the altar, to the shrine where the sarcophagus was kept, closed at night when supplicants were sleeping.

Darcie stood beside him, holding the candle aloft, as Con eased open the cover of the casket. The stone was nestled there, opaque, pitch black, evil incarnate on a pillow of tapestry depicting a biblical scene.

"Now . . ." He took it in both hands.

It didn't move.

"Oh my God . . ."

He tried to prise it up.

It didn't move.

"Darcie . . ."

She set the candle down and together they tried to heave it.

It didn't budge.

"Only Lazarin can move it," Darcie whispered. "Just like he couldn't remove *The Eye of God.*"

"You have it?"

"Yes."

"Take it out."

She saw he was desperate, leeching on to the one thing that had any connection with the stone so far away from its cave of origin.

She tumbled open her coat and pulled open the case. Handed him the wrapped oval of the stone. Grabbed the candle, and then stood back, terrified of what she would see.

He pulled away the protective cotton, and the stone began sparkling all over, radiating like the sun. And then suddenly it shot a fiery lance straight into the heart of the black diamond.

The air crackled above it, lightning bolts shot in the air. Before their horrified eyes, the diamond disintegrated, in the casket, and Con watched, his face impassive, until it was nothing more than a handful of black dust.

"Like a scorch mark," Darcie whispered.

He closed the lid of the sarcophagus. "It is done."

"We should take the casket with us."

He shook his head. "There is no need. Its terrible power is destroyed."

He took one step off of the dais, and stopped. *"Who's there?"*

Darcie slowly lifted the candle, her heart pounding, her whole body shaking in abject terror.

A shadow loomed menacingly at the door, long, lean,

filling the threshold and the whole of the sanctuary with the odor of corruption.

It raised its hand in conviction. Its voice echoed in the darkness, deep, eerie, otherworldly as it paced toward them.

"In the name of Samael," it thundered, *"so shall you be judged . . ."*

And then it vanished into a wisp of smoke that trailed the foul stench of walking death.

They laid everything they had out on the bed: the diamond, now wrapped and in its case; the Pengellis stones, of which there were three; the remaining rubles—of which too little would remain once they gave alms to Father Vasili for the church.

"It was Lazarin," Darcie said. "He is everywhere. We'll never outrun him."

"He is in St. Petersburg, cutting up the rest of that damned stone. And we have to get out of here before the good Father discovers our deceit."

"I think that priest knows everything."

"Anything is possible," he muttered, counting the rubles. "We'll need at least one change of horses as we go through—at least till we reach a place I can barter the diamond."

"This is so crazy." She still felt it—the horror, the terror, the panic. Her hands shook; her heart pounded as if she thought he were standing right outside their door.

Boom boom—at the door—heavy knocking, like doom.

She jumped. Con was more forethinking: he swept their stash into the case with *The Eye of God,* and thrust it under a pillow.

"Open the door."

She swallowed her foreboding, and slowly opened the door.

"Good morning, my children."

Father Vasili.

She let out her breath. "Father."

"Breakfast is served. Already it's dawn. I have a feeling you wish to be on your way."

"As soon as we can, Father."

"So it will be," he murmured, and left them.

Darcie closed the door. "That was odd. He can't have discovered it gone already."

Con stared at the door. "Can't he? We've got to get out of here. Come *on.*"

It took them fifteen minutes to wash, dress and get together their things, and then they joined Father Vasili in the parlor.

"I have had our cook put together some food for you. It's a long journey to St. Petersburg."

That stopped them cold. *How did he know?* Darcie started to ask, but Con shook his head.

"Thank you, Father. You are indeed perceptive in all things."

They sat at the table and ate: coffee, fresh bread and cheese.

"We are indebted to you for your kindness," Con said, as they donned their coats and boots in the outer room.

"Perhaps it is I who must thank you," Father Vasili said.

Con pressed a handful of rubles in his hand. "For your trouble."

The priest nodded. "So it shall be, my son. Your sled awaits you. I have packed the basket inside."

He walked them out into the sun bright morning,

and helped Darcie into the seat. Con spread the blankets, and throw and positioned himself beside her.

"Godspeed, my son," Father Vasili said, making a sign over them and Darcie saw his lips move as if in prayer.

In the name of Samael . . . judge of the dead—

No, no—she didn't see that . . .

Con snapped the whip and the horses took off.

"Con—"

"Shhh . . ." He urged the team faster.

She swallowed her words and, her heart pounding wildly, she turned around.

Lazarin stood at the presbytery door, laughing.

Twenty-one

They were travelling too fast, too long, working the horses beyond endurance, and themselves too. They stopped, first at Nizhne just for the night, and finally, at Tobolsk, the next near-sized city to Omsk.

They had travelled a day and night by then, as fast as if the furies were after them, and they hadn't even touched the basket of food.

Or maybe, Darcie thought, still trembling at the memory of Lazarin watching them depart from the church in Nadyl, they had decided by mute consent, they had better not. That if they opened whatever was packed inside that basket, they might release an unholy host.

"We haven't come nearly far enough," she murmured, as they unhitched the horses in the dooryard of an inn they had come upon just outside the city.

"Far enough for tonight," Con said, heaving up their suitcases, basket of food, and the furs. "We can make one more night on the money we have. Tomorrow, I'll sell whatever I can—even the furs. We won't need them once we reach Samara; we can get the train there."

"It *was* Lazarin in the presbytery courtyard," Darcie said. "What if he turns up, like that awful Kleist, here?"

"I'll kill him again," Con said, with not a trace of

emotion in his voice. "And as many times as it takes to destroy him."

"And if he never dies?"

"He's still not holy enough to redeem the world."

He was dreaming again, on a deep blue sea. Ships, and storms, and diamonds in the rough, and Lavinia, where she shouldn't be . . .

Conscripted—anonymous . . . how he'd come . . . Three months at sea for a cut of the sell. And then something, at docking swung high and struck. All he remembered—but it was enough . . .

Lazarin, laughing . . . and vision gone—

He jerked awake in the dimly lit room to find himself sleeping on a chair, and Darcie curled up on the bed.

Lazarin—everywhere . . .

He'd had an accident on the docks on some voyage over. He couldn't remember it, not what, nor where. Only the sense of injury, and his body falling, almost as if they had disposed of him there.

And then what? Madame came calling, looking for prospects?

"Darcie." He shook her awake.

"Umm. What?"

"It was an accident. The blindness. I don't know where or when. But it was an accident. And they left me for dead."

"So glad you remembered," she muttered and turned back to sleep.

It answered some questions at least. And he could infer the rest. The ship had docked in London, for one thing. And he *had* managed to elude his captors. And he would've gotten home.

Lazarin . . .

On one side, shrouding the powers of The Stone of Samael. *And Lavinia, on the other, so desperate to find* The Eye of God *she would kill.*

Why? Why?

Why?

Lazarin, knowing he was powerless to move The Eye of God.

Lavinia, searching the four corners of the world for it—to learn its secrets, to deplete its power?

And Darcie, in the middle of it all, with a baby that didn't exist, and Lavinia avid to possess it.

It was as bizarre as anything he'd ever experienced, and he wouldn't have believed it if he hadn't seen for himself.

And he knew it wasn't over yet.

"We're not taking the basket."

Darcie dropped it onto the bed. "We're not. All right. Maybe we should look through it?"

He stared at it, an innocent wooden basket with a towel laid neatly over foodstuffs for a trip, packed by a conscientious peasant cook who worked for the village priest. What could be in there that wasn't blessed? Breads, cheeses, a bottle of milk? Some cold meat, fish, eggs and fruit.

Darcie had seen Lazarin in the dooryard.

"You're right. We should see what's in there."

Darcie pulled away the napkin. The basket was crammed with shapes wrapped in paper and cloth.

In the name of . . .

"I'll do it," Con said. "I'm the one." He took out the first of the shapes and unwrapped it. A loaf of bread. Then, a block of cheese. The next: a bag of apples. Pieces of cold roast chicken. A jug of milk, slightly sour.

And on the bottom, a piece of paper, folded into a

packet and sealed with a wax stamp marked with an indistinguishable sign.

And writing on the back: "Open in Samara," Con translated.

They looked at each other.

"I didn't even know we were going there," Con said slowly. "How did he?"

"Which *he?*"Darcie murmured, a chill coursing down her spine.

Con rubbed his grizzled face, his tired eyes and made the decision. "All right. We leave everything here."

"Not that," Darcie said slowly. "We have to open that. We have to know what it is."

"Especially that," Con countered. "And I don't want to know."

"I have a better idea. What if we open it on the way?"

"Let's open it now." He held her eyes. "Or do you think for some mystical reason, we have to comply."

He moved to the window without waiting for her reply, and pulled at the seal; the paper ripped and he unfolded it carefully.

She peered over his arm to see what it contained.

A handful of black dust, against the white parchment. Overriding evil, wafting into the air.

"Fold it up!" Darcie cried. "Hurry. Hurry." She grabbed the packet from his hand and threw it into the embers in the fireplace grate.

They flamed up instantly, roaring up the chimney, crackling like a witch's laughter, howling like an animal in pain.

The fire reached out, threatening to consume them.

She grabbed the jar of milk and poured it on. It hissed and spit like a tiger as it burned into the air.

She threw in the bread, the chicken, and it devoured all of that.

And then she laid on the cheese, and it slowly melted over the popping, snapping flames until they diminished and finally went out.

"We would have brought that with us to Samara," she said, her voice suffused with horror. "We would have unleashed the unspeakable evil of Samael in Samara."

He had no answers. "How did you know what to do?"

"I don't know. I just knew."

They looked at each other. No words needed to be said. She wore *The Eye of God,* and she was blessed.

Three days later, they were travelling west toward St. Petersburg on the Trans-Siberian railway. Here, as in the pullman cars of the Orient Express, they had a private compartment with pull-down berths, a folding table, a washroom, and closet. Attendants to make up the beds, and a dining car with luncheon served at eleven, tea at four, and light edibles available into the late hours, and even delivered, if you wished, to your car.

It was pure luxury after everything they'd been through, and Darcie sank into it with a hedonistic sigh. There wasn't enough food to fill her, or water to bathe.

There wasn't enough Con either. He sat silent as a grave.

"Come, eat. We're safe for the moment."

"I'm not so sure." He rubbed his eyes wearily. "I don't even know what we can accomplish in St. Petersburg."

"We can find Lazarin. We can destroy what's left of the stone. Surely that's not so impossible."

He smiled blearily. "It's a huge city, Darcie."

"Someone will know him," she said confidently.

Spoken like the adventuress she was. Nothing was impossible for Darcie. She'd hauled him over continents, found the diamond, foiled the villains. She was heroine for a pulp novel, just as he'd always thought.

The strange thing was having his sight back and participating in the adventure. He wasn't in the dark any longer. And yet, everything was as blank as could be.

"What will you do when we return to England?" she asked idly as she poured him some coffee.

"I haven't thought that far ahead."

"You *must* go back to Pengellis-Becarre."

"Must I?" Even he didn't know, and Darcie, watching him, felt a tremor of foreboding. Once they vanquished Lavinia, the story would be over. What would happen to Scheherazade then?

"We don't need to talk about it now . . ." she started to say and he interrupted her.

"Can we talk about any of it? This far from Srinagar and Nadyl, do you believe *any* of what we've seen?"

"I believe you found the diamond and that Lavinia still wants to kill you," she said gently, worriedly. This kind of thinking wasn't like him; he was usually so sure. "Isn't that real enough?"

Lavinia, he thought. It all came back to Lavinia. All about Lavinia.

And him. He was the source—the connection to everything.

But what was Darcie? Did he truly believe that Lavinia was desperate to get an heir from Darcie? What about that story still didn't fit?

Or was she always meant to be the instrument of The Eye of God?

The questions haunted him as the train bowled down the snow-shrouded tracks, and Darcie set out their afternoon snack just as if she were serving tea at the palace.

That night, they slept on the fur throw on the rolling floor of the car, coupling blindly, heatedly to the rhythm of the wheels on the tracks, rocking together on soft radiant waves until they simultaneously climaxed.

And even then, he didn't let her go. He rode her until morning, cradled between her legs, matching the pulse of the wheels, the cadence of the track.

"It doesn't matter where I am," he murmured in her ear, "I love being inside you."

She shimmied against him, enticing him slowly. "And I love it when you are." She felt the delicious spurt as he hardened still again.

"You are so wet, so responsive." He nuzzled her neck.

"I can't get enough," she whispered. Stiffer and stiffer. One more time again. "I love when you take me."

He rocked against her, feeling the expansion of his power. There was nothing like the dark wet mystery of her. Everything else receded beside it. He wanted to live in it forever.

He wanted her now.

He shoved against her experimentally. "Like that?"

"Ummm," she sighed.

Harder. "Is that better?"

"Ah."

A long hard stroke deep into her core.

"Perfect," she breathed, and begged for more.

He pumped her in tight hard steady thrusts, just the way she wanted it, just the way she craved it. Perfect. Tight. Hard. Gone. She convulsed beneath him and around him, and took him along.

They saw Moscow from beside the bridge that crossed the river, under the threat of snow. It was still another city of contrasts, ancient and new, its dwellings clustered near the river that divided the city, and the spires of its numerous churches soaring against the lowering sky.

Here, Nicholas II's coronation procession down the Tverskaya just a year and a half before. There, the walls of the Kremlin and the vista of Red Square. Market stalls in the Upper Bazaar, and Kuznetsky Street for shopping. They took it all in during the brief two-hour layover, whirling through the city in one of the dozens of cabs that waited at the station.

And then on their way again in the early evening, with the snow lightly falling.

And another night, wrapped in fur and passion and fury, laying on the floor.

They arrived at the Nikolaevski Station in St. Petersburg the following night, and were transferred immediately to the Great Northern Hotel across the way.

The next morning, they were going to scour the churches again as a starting point. The stone could be anywhere.

And, as Con pointed out, maybe not even there.

"No. I don't believe that. It's here, somewhere— probably in some church."

She was determined, fired up. She inquired of the concierge the location of the nearest church, and he directed them down the Ekaterinski Canal to Resurrection Church.

It was a cold day, the snow had abated, but she was thankful for her wool and furs. They hurried down the long residential street divided by the canal, the church in the distance rising up like a benediction.

"We'll find some answers here," Darcie whispered. "It has to be here."

They mounted the steps to the entrance and pulled open the door.

This was a vast church, as different from the plain country church in Nadyl as night from day. The ceilings soared, picked out in gold, with murals and icons all along the walls. Velvet drapes at the sanctuary, and at the doors, and two porcelain stoves heating the nave. The scent of incense permeated the air.

And a feeling of majesty and reverence unlike anything Darcie had ever experienced.

"Have you come for a blessing?"

They whirled at the voice behind them, a young acolyte, dressed in robes.

Con translated and answered, "We come to speak with your priest."

"Father Cyril prays."

"May we wait?"

The acolyte nodded. "I will tell him you are here."

Darcie sank into a pew and just stared. "He cannot corrupt this."

"He corrupts everything," Con said. "And he is everywhere."

"We will find him here."

She jumped to her feet, and began pacing restively.

"My children . . ."

Oh no . . . no—no—

The voice of Father Vasili greeted them as he stepped into the aisle.

"So—you have eluded death and come this far," he murmured as Con translated. "Blessings on you, clever ones. I will tell you what you need to know."

"Ask him—" Darcie prodded. "Where is the stone?"

"Listen to me, foolish ones," he answered in response. "There is nothing more you can do."

"I don't believe it," Darcie said adamantly.

"He has been here since the Neva froze over," Father Vasili said. "He has accomplished much. And there is still more for him to do."

"What has he done?" Darcie demanded. "What is he going to do?"

"So impatient," Father Vasili murmured. "But that is the way of the chosen. Only, there is nothing she can do."

"Tell us then," Con said, motioning for Darcie to contain herself.

"He has mastered the stone. Samael be with you, as he will be with our little Father the Tsar."

They froze.

"What does he mean? What *can* he mean?" Darcie cried.

"He cut the stone," Con surmised.

Father Vasili nodded. "Our wise and holy man did indeed cleave the stone—into three beautifully faceted pieces."

"No . . ." Darcie moaned.

"And through the auspices of a well-known jeweler, and in the name of Samael, he has presented those valuable stones to our little Father to mark the occasion of the birth of his daughter. One for his sceptre. One for his crown. And one for the Empress to wear on her brow."

"Oh God—"

"And now, he whom you call Lazarin, will make his home in St. Petersburg. He will mingle with all strata of society, he will become a man of holy destiny, as he draws ever closer to the Crown."

"Con—" Darcie said beseechingly, and he shook his head.

Father Vasili went on: "The time is not right, not yet. But soon, soon. This is the judgment of Samael: that Mother Russia shall come into the holy hands of the monk Rasputin."

He looked deeply into Con's eyes. "And so it shall be. All your effort has come to nothing. This is the judgment of Samael: there will be no mercy in any quarter. And *The Eye of God* cannot protect thee. So saith Samael, and so it shall be."

"We can do nothing more here," Con said.

"Kill him," Darcie whispered fiercely. "Take vengeance on him, at least."

Father Vasili looked at her, almost as if he were reading her mind, and he raised his hand. *"No* mercy. This is the judgment of Samael."

And he lowered his hand slowly. "So it shall be," he intoned, and when his hand dropped to his side, he disappeared.

"Oh my God—" Darcie breathed. "Oh my God . . . Where is he? Where did he go?"

"I believe him," Con said. There wasn't any point wasting time on trying to define what you didn't know.

"We have to make sure," Darcie said frantically. "We have to check it out."

"You don't believe it? Believe it. The stone is gone, and there's nothing we can do now. The evil is loose and it goes with the Tsar everywhere he goes. It infects his family. The people. The land. It's too late, Darcie. We got one little piece of it. And it's not enough to stem the rising tide. Rasputin—Lazarin—whatever they will call him—*he* will be in control."

"How can you know that?" she whispered.

"I know. How many times have we faced him, and he hasn't died? You think Kleist is dead and buried a hundred miles from here in the snow. No, by now he's resurrected just like Karun, and he lives in Rasputin's body, and he still goes on. Nor can *The Eye of God* destroy him, or it would have, just like the stone."

"What do we do now?" she whispered.

He gave her a sardonic smile. "Damned if I know."

* * *

It's over. The grand adventure is over. It only remains to return to England so he can reclaim his life.

She didn't want it to be over. Not ever.

How could she tell him? What was she but an opportunist of the worst kind? She'd gotten out of it exactly what she desired. *The Eye of God* entrusted to her like a baby, and nestled between her breasts.

And Con. *Mustn't forget Con.*

And one of the famous Pengellis diamonds. Oh, she'd made out like a thief this time. Sex and money too. She could live like a queen forever, just as she had planned.

They walked down to the frozen Neva River, near the Winter Palace, and watched streetworkers breaking the ice, and over to the Academy of Art, with the two Egyptian sphinxes guarding the front. And across the broad avenue of Nevsky Prospect, and to the Fortress of Saints Peter and Paul.

And nowhere was there any trace of Lazarin. It was as if he had disappeared into thin air. Or it had been he, transmogrified into Father Vasili, just Darcie had seen Lazarin at the presbytery.

And finally, three futile days later, Con told her: "It is time to go home."

They travelled again by the railway, this time going south, from St. Petersburg, to Moscow, Tula, Kursk, Kharkov to the terminus in Sevastopol and, to him, the familiar sight of steamers plowing the Black Sea.

He expended his last diamond in Sevastopol for expenses and passage home. They sailed across to Varna, and it was the last thing he saw.

By the time they reached Bucharest, he was blind again.

Twenty-two

"I don't understand, I just *don't* understand," Darcie fumed as she paced the confines of their sleeping car. They were stranded someplace outside of Bucharest for the moment, the snow being too high and thick for the train to push through.

And here was Con, his eyesight utterly gone, for reasons that she refused to believe.

"The judgment of Samael! Honestly, Con."

"You don't believe it?" Did he? He didn't know quite when he began to notice it: the tired eyes. The blurring. The weariness he just didn't see. *After* their encounter with Father Vasili? Or before?

"You do? I think you're falling for all that flummery far too easily."

"No mercy in *any* quarter," he quoted mordantly. "What do you think happens when you try to destroy a god?"

"That's funny. Why didn't Father Vasili just kill you?"

"For the same reason I didn't kill him, I suppose. You don't kill the messenger."

But there *was* something else. It tickled the edge of his consciousness like a spell. Something he knew. Something he'd even said.

"They used to," she countered acidly. She should

have done it, she thought. She *could* have done it, with the power of *The Eye of God*.

If only she'd taken it seriously, if only she'd really understood that it was hers all along.

And now, he was in the dark again.

"It's ironic," he said. "We begin and end exactly the same."

"No. We don't," she said sharply. "We *don't*. We've crossed continents. We've climbed mountains. We have the diamond. And—" She stopped short. *And?*

The problem was, there wasn't any end. Not until he confronted Lavinia, and took back his life.

"It's *not* the same," she finished firmly. "And we have to figure out why this happened."

"The gift was taken back. It's as simple as that. Penance must be paid."

Yes, he thought, that was familiar too; he'd thought that before, what seemed like a hundred years ago.

She hated the fatalistic tone in his voice. "I'm not going to let you think that way. There *has* to be an answer."

He thought that too, but as with everything else in his life, he'd gambled and lost.

"Darcie, the whole thing was a big vainglorious self-aggrandizing risk. Do you understand that? *I* gave up Pengellis. *I* let Roger just walk in and take it up while I went on my wild-goose chase. I was so convincing everyone thought it was real."

"Well, it was," she interpolated.

"I didn't *really* know that then. I was going to be a hero, all that fame, all that lovely money to be had from splitting a legendary diamond; and that over and above all the other money we made in London and South Africa. Tell me, Darcie, when does a man get smart? How much does he really need?"

She knew the answer to that. "When he makes his final strike."

"Well, we did that, didn't we? And look at the cost. We haven't moved one foot from where we started. And we haven't gained a thing."

"Except the diamond," she said. *And each other, she didn't say.*

"We haven't gained a thing," he repeated. "But we *have* unleashed something unspeakable on the world. *The balance must be kept.* I knew that. And I arrogantly walked in and changed it. You don't think that calls for a cosmic punishment, Darcie?"

"I think something's going on that's closer to home."

"You're so practical. So sensuous and beautiful. How lucky I am you found me." But his tone was bitter. Mocking—and she didn't know if he were ridiculing her or himself.

Neither was acceptable.

"Sometimes you can't choose, "she said. "Sometimes things are meant to be." But that sounded fantastic, and fatalistic too, and it wasn't quite what she meant to say.

"Well, there you go," he murmured derisively. "It is the judgment of Samael: that he shall from this time forth walk in darkness. And so it has been."

She wouldn't let it be, she thought fiercely. She would not let him believe in the vengeance of an entity that didn't exist.

"I wish we had kept the dust," she said suddenly. "Maybe it could have worked for you like what you said about Lazarin—his drawing his power from the diamond fields . . . Maybe if you still had a part of the stone . . ."

Yes . . . that shocked him into awareness. She had defined his elusive thought: but not the dust—the shards. The slivers of black diamond he'd carried with him from the Valley to Tobolsk. Where he'd sold the second to last diamond, and discarded the pouch.

Where they'd burned the dust.

"Jesus, Darcie . . ." His possession of the shards had preserved his sight, and not the capitulation of his soul.

She wasn't aware of them in Budapest, but she was certain by the time they reached Vienna, Lavinia's agents were after them. Almost as if she had blanketed every train station of every possible route.

They were at every stop where crowds swarmed, and they were passengers on the train. They ate in the dining car, and paced past their door, and there was no way to escape.

She cursed fate that they were burdened by his sightlessness. How did you save a blind man from disaster when it surrounded you like air?

It was coming, as surely as the dawn. Lavinia hadn't given up on claiming her treasures. Or killing Con.

This was just a different kind of evil. Maybe one from which they could run. They might even have a chance— in Paris—if she could keep them at bay.

She didn't tell him, at first, but she was so tense, and so unresponsive, he prised it out of her.

"Lavinia's people are on the train."

He thought that was interesting. Everywhere she'd seen Lavinia's *people*, he'd had only her word. And now, when he was doubly dependent on her, they were all around again.

Darcie had the diamond . . .

Darcie had the answers.

Surround him with the enemy, and kill him with what he couldn't see . . .

Was *that* what it was really all about?

Whom did *you* trust, when a fabulous diamond was at stake?

And how much was spit and fairy tales to take advantage of his dependence?

He felt like he was falling in the dark. It rose up to meet him, slamming him in the eyes.

Darcie the trojan horse.

Darcie's allegiance to—who?

The body that launched a thousand mile quest had seduced him royally. He had fallen like a shooting star.

And all to return to the crux of the matter, except that Darcie had accomplished exactly what she'd set out to do.

The last big strike.

And he'd handed it to her too.

. . . dear God—

Lavinia was just the diversion so he wouldn't perceive what was going on. And just like any other man, he'd let Darcie subjugate him with his heart.

Goddamn, damn, damn—

"Con? I'm scared."

Was she?

He girded himself to amplify the deception, remembering the journey out. What was real, what was the lie. "You're not scared of a thing, Scheherazade."

She looked at his stone carved face, his blank eyes. *I'm scared of you.*

"We might be able to elude them in Paris."

"Why?"

"More ways to escape; more routes we can take. We know the city. You know the language."

"You're right," he murmured, "that does make sense." She was masterful, he thought. He had named her exactly right. "But for now, what do you want to do?"

She'd be a stranger in a strange land, so she wouldn't

leave him now. But in Paris—she had the means, the motive—she'd abandon him like a sack of rotten wheat.

"We have to keep to the car. I'll get our food—"

"Just like last time," he murmured. Was she that clever she thought she could replay the same scenario and he would still bite? "But you shouldn't be carrying the diamond—if the threat is that pervasive."

"And you can't see our enemies," she retorted. "We're some fine pair. I think I'm better off holding it."

"And if they attack you—?"

She didn't like saying it. "It's gone."

Very good, he applauded silently. Just the right tone. "I can think of maybe one place no one would think to look. Do you want to risk it after all we've been through?"

"But I can *see* the danger," she argued.

"Not from behind. And not if they grab you from both sides. Not if they immobilize you."

"All right—all *right.* You have a point. Maybe the thing is, we can't protect it to the extent we should right now. We can only do what we can do."

"Well then—you must leave it here when you see to our meals. We'll have a password or something and I won't unlock the door unless I hear it."

He thought that sounded reasonable, and not as if he were suspicious of her at all. A compromise of sorts that for the moment he could live with.

"All right. I won't gamble with it. Choose your password."

"Why don't you?" he said.

"Our enemies know everything about us," she muttered.

"Then let me suggest—they can't know this—*penance must be paid.*"

* * *

He held *The Eye of God* in his hands—in the dark. A rough eight-sided stone that felt and looked like less than it was.

Yet men had killed for it; women had lied.

And because they had taken it, the balance had tipped to the other side.

It wasn't easy to hide either. Darcie had drawn the shade on the door window, and doused the lights since he sat in the dark anyway.

He ruminated on her cleverness.

Probably this would be the only time he'd get his hands on the diamond. Probably, she'd never let it out of her sight from now on.

Probably. And she'd look for somewhere neat to kill him, like that attendant she'd thrown off the train.

Oh my good goddamn. All the things Darcie had done in the name of protecting him and sustaining their quest. It made him queasy, remembering.

For all he knew, she was a professional thief and this was an elaborate hoax solely to get possession of the diamond. She wouldn't scruple to kill him then. And blame it all on Lavinia.

And there! The other thing that niggled at him: the woman Darcie described was not the mother he'd known.

Lavinia was a hard-headed businesswoman, pure and simple. She coveted The Eye of God *because of its value split into individual stones, and what it would add to the bottom line. And the public notice it would bring to the firm. Lavinia had known just how to merchandise those things.*

If she couldn't have the diamond, she'd publicize the quest.

And she had been a damn sight better at it than he had been. And a gentle mother when he was young . . .

There was a knock at the door, two short raps, then one, repeated twice, as prearranged. He pocketed the diamond and moved to the door.

"Who's there?"

"Con—it's me. *Penance must be paid.*"

He slipped the locks and she eased in.

"I guess that worked," she murmured, "but you have to pull down the table so I can see to the lights."

He knew his way around the car by then, and he got the table, she groped for it, and set down the tray, and then she turned up the lights and locked the door.

"We'll leave on the lights next time," she said, slipping onto her bench. "Well, it's chicken again. The usual accompaniments. I hope you're hungry."

She didn't say a word about the diamond as she arranged his plate, and they ate in silence, as they usually did. And then she would leave the tray outside by the door.

"Con—I should hold the diamond. That only makes sense."

He knew he couldn't stop her, except by force. And he weighed, in that split second, where that would leave him. Give her the diamond, and she could abscond forever. Keep it himself, and he might have to hurt her.

Either way, he could be left dependent on strangers, with no way to know who was an enemy or a friend.

Blast the power that had taken his eyes!

"Maybe not," he temporized. "Especially if you'll be going in and out two or three times a day just to feed us. Maybe it makes more sense in my hands."

"There's something weird going on here," she said suspiciously.

"No, we're just being supremely cautious. Now that Lavinia's after us, I mean."

He heard the rattle of the china as she cleared the table. Pulled the locks. Opened and closed the door and locked it again. Like she was using motion to cover her frustration, her anger, her dismay.

Or else she was planning her next move.

Either way, he was keeping the diamond.

He heard her fold up the table, and pull down her berth. They'd agreed that no attendants would make up the beds.

"Have it your way," she said finally, and there was a shrug in her tone.

"It makes sense," he said, and he too lay down.

She lay angry and seething in the dark.

He was acting so odd, like he didn't trust her. After everything that had happened, and all they'd been through. She felt like shaking him.

But as she lay sleepless across the room from him, she understood that things were very different this trip. Now they had the diamond. And he had again lost his sight.

What man wouldn't be bitter alone in the dark?

She wondered why she thought they had forged any bond. She'd been nothing to him but a whore, in the dark.

Now his attitude finally made sense. She already had her tithe and he was finished with her. When he claimed Pengellis-Becarre, he'd take a *worthy* bride, and *The Eye of God* would be the centerpiece of his return.

And he wasn't giving it up, even to save his life.

She couldn't believe everything she'd done for him, but that was the risk an adventuress took. Had she thought he'd be dependent on her forever? Or fall in love with her unceasingly demanding body?

She didn't know what she had thought, except that she couldn't bear the idea that the thing was over—in every way.

But not yet. They still had to get to Paris. Make their escape. Return to England and successfully make their claim.

His claim.
Damn. Damn. Damn.
Blessed be . . .
There was still that—and what it might mean.
And they'd yet to confront Lavinia.
She took a deep steadying breath.
One thing at a time.
The story still wasn't over.

The train passed through Munich, with a brief stop. Darcie reconnoitered the dining car and brought back lunch. She felt like a servant, a waitress. Less than her worth.

Like the stone, with its hidden power that she'd seen. Maybe she too had covert powers she hadn't yet tested.

She felt the evil eyes of their enemy watching them. "Con . . . ?"

He was looking at the window, seeing nothing. She felt an abject wave of sorrow wash over her. What *would* he do, once they returned to London? He'd *have* to give over the running of the company to someone else. He could still be the hero, the figurehead. The blind Con Pengellis who'd once been a god.

How did a man fall so far from grace? This was such unjust punishment. It wasn't fair. And it couldn't be fought on any terms that made them equals.

She was the daughter of an itinerant miner, and he was the son of a wealthy diamond merchant, and a honorable to boot.

Damn. Those discrepancies didn't matter in a desert. They mattered on a train going back to civilization. *His* civilization. She had been an interloper there.

Oh, God—it was so complicated. The truth of it all

was she'd been nothing more than a camp follower trying to get rich quick.

And while she supposed she had rights as Roger's wife, Con probably wouldn't want her anywhere near him when they returned.

"Con?" she tried again. She hated these silences. This was not a man on a mission. It was a man who was thinking too hard and making assessments she was not going to want to hear.

"Yes, Darcie?" Polite. Calm. Raging inside probably at this awful turn of fate.

"It will be all right, when we get to England," she said. She didn't know what to say; he was such a stranger and now she walked in a strange land. And there was nothing she could say to crack his impassive mein.

"You'll be safe," she added, hearing the desperation in her tone. "I'll make sure we're safe there."

He smiled faintly, and she didn't like that smile. "I'm sure you will."

Paris!
A half hour to arrival at Le Gare du Nord.
The conductor's voice echoed all up and down the sleeping cars.
Make ready, all who will depart at the station . . .
She was the one who packed. She felt his helplessness, his fury. And something else contained that she couldn't define.

This was it, the moment. "I think we should get out as far from this car as we can."

"You lead the way."

He was too agreeable, too amenable.

He didn't believe her—

No! There was too much at stake. He *had* to believe her.

She had two valises, wrapped in the fur and strapped together, so she could manage them with one hand.

And she had him.

"Do you need help, madame?" She jumped. An attendant? Or an enemy?

"Non, merci." She needed it desperately. She held Con's hand as they shuffled to the next car, squeezing by irate passengers trying to debark.

"Go on, Darcie, it doesn't matter."

"I *hate* this new sensibility of yours. Why aren't you fighting? Why don't you believe me?"

He supposed he shouldn't have been shocked. What could he hide from the Darcie of the dark who knew him so well?

"Don't you *dare* not fight—" she said fiercely. *For this—for us, she didn't say.*

"I feel like we can't escape it. I feel like I cheated fate and now—penance must be paid. What do you feel, Darcie? Triumph? That you've won?"

"I just feel like getting out of here before they get us."

"Right—*they* . . ."

He didn't believe her. He didn't *believe her!*

She pulled him violently down the passage, not caring who he slammed into in her haste. Damn him. Damn him, damn him, damn him.

She managed to get them three cars away from where watchers would expect them to emerge.

Managed that, with all his reluctance and the passenger herd.

And then the train whistle blew, and they had to get out.

She stepped down warily at the next exit, peering out from the protection of the train.

"Oh my God," she breathed. "Oh dear God—Con . . ."

They were waiting for them. They were right in front of the car she had chosen to exit.

And, she thought, she shouldn't have been surprised. Anything was possible. Con had said so, all those months ago, and they'd seen it time and again in the succeeding months.

Anything was possible, and so there they were: Roger and her *father*—the living dead.

"Welcome, my dear," Roger said. "Do hand over the diamond—or I will shoot you dead."

Twenty-three

The train whistle wailed. The engine started up in a huge cloud of steam.

"*Run* . . . *!*" Darcie screamed, dropping everything and pulling his hand.

"Jesus, Darcie . . ."

"*Shut up* . . . *!*" Even though she knew it was futile, they ran, knocking into passengers, tripping over baggage.

Roger was right behind them; her father pawing through their luggage.

They just might make it, they just might . . . if only Con had his eyes.

She felt him fall behind her, heavily, pulling her down flat on her back.

Roger had tackled him, and now he stood, covering them with his gun.

"Resourceful, Darcie. You were ever that. Get to your feet, both of you. We won't make a scene."

She had gambled on the fact he wouldn't. She scrambled to her feet.

"Con? Are you all right?"

"Yes." *And humiliated. And a fool.*

Roger.

And his accomplices.

Including Darcie.

It made such sense. And Darcie had the diamond.

And she told such wonderful stories, even the one about pretending to try to escape from Roger.

So good. Good as it gets . . .

He wanted to kill them all.

"My father is here," Darcie whispered.

"How neat," he murmured. It just tidied things right up. They'd used him, all of them; he was the dupe, the gull, the tool.

They were all going to share in the cut from the diamond.

Darcie too.

By God . . . penance was being paid—

"Come now," Roger said. "Lavinia awaits us."

"It was all an elaborate hoax, wasn't it?" Con said. "From the moment I escaped, you had the thing planned."

"More or less," Roger said. "Of course, Darcie's father conveniently *died* to give her an urgent motive to seek the diamond. There's nothing like greed. We had you covered on all fronts, until you escaped. And then of course, I had to *die*. We thought that might get you back to Goole. But in any event, things have worked out. You have the diamond, and we'll just cleave it tidily and sell it at a profit."

"And Lavinia?"

"Ah . . . Lavinia. She's getting old, Con. She's a little dotty. Keeps talking about its powers. Nothing worth listening to. A few million pounds ought to quiet her down. Then of course, we do have the birth of the child to look forward to. Except"—he took Darcie by the elbow and turned her around— "I don't see any evidence of it, do I Darcie? There never was a baby, was there?"

He shoved her away from him and she fell against Con.

"Aren't you the sharp-witted bitch, my darling. Mother bought it, whole cloth. She'll be so disappointed. I don't *think* there's anything else. So that should answer your questions for now."

She hated him. She despised Roger with a killing fury. A man who looked so much like Con and who was such a liar and a cheat.

"What happens now?" she asked, barely able to contain her rage.

"Why, we'll go back to Goole, my dear. And we'll sort out our lives."

It rose up before them in the twilight, stark and eerie, a pile of stone and secrets, shrouded in silence.

The trip had been excruciating. She had to face her father, face her own sins. The man she depended on, loved, cared for and carried, had been seduced by the stone.

His big strike. She was to have been his foil. Hadn't he hammered it into her, the legend of the stone: And made her feel responsible for getting his share?

Oh yes, he'd primed her well for the task. She'd had everything at her disposal: he'd bought her entree to the castle, outlined the quest, and gave her the mission. And then he'd perished, to enhance her mandate to carry out the task.

Treacherous! Such a betrayal—of her love, her belief in him, in them—as partners, as a team.

Her whole life was a lie, she thought, beginning to end.

Or maybe her life had begun the day she rescued Con.

She had no other allegiances here.

"You will give up the diamond," Roger kept telling her. "It will be mine."

"Ours," Leonard Boulton added. "Such a clever Darcie, finding Con, and getting him there."

Her heart was stone; he couldn't touch her anymore. She did not know this man he had become.

"My dear," he chided. "There's no difference between this and what we did to gain possession of the Colorado mines."

She turned her head away. That was a long time ago. A long long time ago. It was the deal that had given him the wherewithal to come to England and instigate this plan.

An uncut diamond worth a fortune in gold . . .

She didn't want to think about it—any of it—or her part in it.

She hadn't thought about it at all from the day they'd left Colorado; she'd never looked back.

The mark of a gambler, depending on luck.

"I know Darcie has the diamond," Roger went on conversationally. "There was never any doubt once we knew you two were together. She's very good at what she does, isn't she, Con?"

"Most excellent," he said dryly. *And oh, what she does . . .*

He felt the impotence of a man abandoned by fate. He'd lost everything. He couldn't defend against Roger and Darcie, who still had their eyes.

Such a clever Darcie . . .

And he hadn't believed in the danger.

He just hadn't thought it would come from his heart.

"Are we there yet?"

"We're in the park," Roger said. "You remember the park?"

And all the dead trees, their branches begging heaven . . .

"Almost there. Mother will be waiting."

Ah yes, Lavinia, the other part of the equation.

What about Lavinia?

The carriage lurched to a stop.

Coming home again, blind. Always blind to what was around him, even when he could see.

Hands helping him out. Not Darcie.

Roger's rough hands, pushing him. And the distinctive scent of the air, dry as dead leaves. Goole was dead. He'd never seen it, but it had always been so.

"Clever of you to have brought him to Goole after you found him," Roger murmured to Darcie. "I'm utterly taken by your ingenuity. I had a treasure beyond price and I never knew it."

"You should have stayed dead," she spat.

Good, Darcie. Good. That sounded so protective, so combative. Darcie to his defense, white knight to a man immured in an endless night.

The air changed as they entered the hall.

Thick, stuffy, redolent of spices, bringing back the moments and memories. The portrait—that everlasting blasted portrait that made Darcie fall in love—it was in front of him, over the stairs, haunting him, the ghost of his former life, because he knew it was there.

He heard footsteps. And then the starchy tones of the butler, as he took their coats.

And then he heard a lighter step running along the balcony above him.

And *her* voice: "Where is it? Where's the diamond?"

Roger, speaking first. "Mother—"

"I don't give a damn about anything else. *Where is that stone?*"

And finally, a puzzle solved. He couldn't see, but he knew, and he wouldn't pretend, so he said it boldly, out loud.

"That's not my mother's voice."

* * *

They froze.

Darcie plucked his sleeve. "Con, that's your mother."

"That isn't she."

"Roger, where is *The Eye of God?*" Lavinia was tired of games, tired of waiting. Darcie could see it in her face, in her eyes. The lines were deeper, the cruelty more apparent. She was a woman on the edge of a precipice, struggling not to fall over.

"*She* has it." Roger gestured to Darcie.

"Give it up, girl. Grab her, Roger."

Immediately, he clamped his hands across her shoulders, pulling her tightly against him. She kicked him, bit him, stomped on his foot.

"Oh, she's a one. Look at her—fighting like an animal. She's wreaked enough havoc on this family. I'm tired of her. She took damned long to get the thing. And now—it's *mine . . .*"

Lavinia reached for her, her fingers clawed; Con jumped, toward the sound of the voice and the threat to Darcie, and knocked her down.

"*Who are you?*" he demanded, his hands at her throat.

She choked, fighting him with what seemed like superhuman strength.

Boulton wrenched him off of her, and held him back.

She made a guttural sound. "This is no son of mine. Roger—tear off her clothes if you have to. *I want that stone.*"

She backed up against the staircase to watch the melee.

Right under Con's portrait, Darcie noted with one part of her consciousness, as she wrestled with Roger. There was nothing she could use as a weapon. This was a sparsely furnished hallway. Rugs. Paintings. A trestle table covered with a tapestry. A suit of armor. An ax.

"Darcie . . . !" He was on the floor with her father. ". . . don't . . ."

"I . . . won't . . ." she panted as she shoved Roger, hard, and wrenched away. She ran down the length of the reception hall to the pedestal with the suit of armor.

"No you don't—" Roger, two steps after her.

Frantically, she pulled and twisted the long handle of the ax, forcing it free.

"Stay back!" she commanded, brandishing the thing in his face.

"Darcie . . ." Roger, conciliatory now.

She took a quick glance over his shoulder; her father had gotten Con down and he was sitting on him.

Damn them all.

"Back up, Roger, or I'll take off your head."

He raised his hands and stepped backward.

"If you know anything about our little adventure," she continued conversationally, following him down from the pedestal, "you know I've done a fair amount of . . . interesting . . . shall we say? things along the journey. I won't scruple to do what I have to now. So—" she turned to her father in a vicious movement, "get off of Con, or I'll slice you to pieces."

"Ah, that's my Darcie," her father said, climbing to his feet.

"Over to the stairs," she ordered, as Con got to his knees. "You traitor. I know which part of *him* I'd butcher. Are you all right, Con?"

He nodded. "Are you?"

"I found a nice medieval weapon just down the hall, Con. Not quite as efficient as a knife, but I see a few parts I could hack off with ease."

"For God's sake," Lavinia spat. "The thing's as dull

as a dish." She advanced toward Darcie. "I want that stone."

Darcie held her eyes as she swung. Rounded, dark, vicious eyes like an owl. The Lavinia she had known—and not.

"Who *are* you? Why are you so desperate? What do you really want—a baby or the diamond?"

"I'll have both," Lavinia sneered.

Darcie shook her head. "Neither. There was no baby . . ."

Lavinia's face changed, transformed into something evil and beyond human. "You lie!" she shrieked, charging toward Darcie.

Darcie swung, and nicked her shoulder.

Lavinia howled: "Leonard—she's your daughter. *Get her . . . !* Roger—*kill her . . . !*"

They started toward her menacingly, and she swung with all her might. One by one they dropped to the floor.

"Darcie . . ." Con behind her, listening to the chaos. "You have to cleave the diamond."

"Oh my God, are you crazy?" She poked the ax at Lavinia who made a movement toward her.

"Don't touch that diamond," Lavinia screamed.

"You're the only one. You have to do it. It's the only way to stop them. She is *not* my mother."

She swallowed hard, swinging the ax again as her father approached.

"Don't do it, daughter. What do you know about cutting gems? You'll destroy it, the legend of a lifetime."

"Darcie . . . you have the power. It's the only way."

"Why, Con, why? Who are they?"

"They are acolytes of Samael, possessed by the evil. We cannot give them the diamond."

She groaned. "Con . . . I can't. I won't destroy the diamond."

"You have to, Darcie. It was meant to be."

"Don't listen, don't do it!" her father shrieked.

"We have to defeat him. We have to destroy *her,* she is the most dangerous of them all. We must right the balance, Darcie. Penance must be paid."

"Yes—" she whispered.

"NOOOOOO . . . !" Lavinia screamed.

"Yes!" Con decreed. "This woman—this *thing*—the shell of the woman I called mother. She is possessed, her body inhabited by the entity Lilith who walks the earth in the company of Samael, whose stone we destroyed.

"Lilith, the first wife of Adam, who was condemned for her disobedience, and for her voracious appetite for children and men. It is said, because of this, when she went to heaven to beg for the oil of mercy, she was turned away, and that only when she finds a body to inhabit may she try again. No wonder she was avid for your child, Darcie. The love of a child begs mercy.

"But now we know: Samael is among us, seeking the diamond. You *must* cleave it and destroy *her* forever."

"DON'T LISTEN TO HIM!"

Her father, this time—or maybe not . . . who knew what entities were among them—and she couldn't take the chance.

"I will—I'll destroy it—"

"Better than this wickedness . . . I'm *telling* you— even though you know her as my mother . . . it is *not* she—and it *must* be done . . ."

She backed up toward the table, and they followed her, almost as one body—her father, Roger, Lavinia.

"He's lying," Lavinia said, reaching out her hand.

Whoosh. Lavinia jumped back.

Tears streamed down Darcie's face. "Are you *sure,* Con?"

"It was my dream, my quest. I knew there was something—something about Lavinia, and I'm telling you now—you have the power . . . kill the evil—*cut the damned diamond!*"

Whoosh—another warning, as Roger lunged toward her.

Con heard it all, and he couldn't do a thing. Darcie had to believe him. She had to keep them at bay. And she had to achieve a cut.

God, he would kill to have his eyes back . . .

Darcie felt his anguish; she had to be strong, for both of them. They were watching her—those eyes, those flaming dark, looking into pools of hell eyes . . .

Con was right. She *had* to do it.

She slipped the stone out of the leather pocket and set it on the table.

"That's it . . . ohhhh—that's it . . ." Lavinia whispered, reaching out her hand.

Whoosh . . . the blade sliced the air, just nicking her hand.

"Bitch," Lavinia screeched.

"Oh God. That's it," Boulton muttered. "Like dross before it becomes gold . . ."

Whoosh—she'd kill him too if she had to . . .

Whoosh—Roger jumped backward as she sliced at him.

She held their eyes. She watched them. They were all looking for the moment, the chance when one—or all of them—could dive for the diamond.

She had one chance, one choice, no niceties. She didn't have to understand angles or fractures. All she had to know was if Lavinia possessed the diamond, everyone's life would rupture.

She poised herself, swinging the ax toward them, aiming at their necks. Their necks were good—tender, vulnerable, pulsing with lifeblood.

And they knew it. They weren't going to rush her. She could do serious harm.

But it was just in that moment, when she lifted her arm upward, and before she sliced down—

And it could pop out from under the pressure of the blade, she thought.

Then they might get to her . . . and pull her down.

"I'll hold it," Con said calmly, as he sensed her frenzy.

Oh God, worse and worse. Con could be killed.

"Angle it over the table, and I'll stand on one side."

"You're crazy," she muttered.

"Do it."

Do it. She'd been doing it, one way or another, her whole life.

"All right. Take the stone and position it where you feel comfortable."

He groped his way to where she was standing. "You don't want your back to them."

"A good point."

Whoosh—as they saw this conversation as an opportunity to move.

Now he was at the head of the table, between them and the stone.

"That's good, Con."

He balanced it on the tapestry cloth. "I'm ready."

I'm not . . .

She couldn't swing from full high—they'd get her first. It had to be a short, sharp, emphatic swing, right to its heart.

Her hands were icy cold, her heart pounding. She poked at her father as he started to move.

"You know, maybe I ought to practice this—get a little twist in there where I could kill someone who tries to get in my way."

Her father froze.

"That's better—*daddy.*"

Now . . .

She chewed her lip. Con stood there like a statue, his hand balancing the stone. One chance. One swing.

She held out the ax so that the blade touched the stone. Thank God the thing was big.

She turned to look at them. They cursed her to hell.

She lifted the instrument and chopped it down on the biggest, most legendary diamond in the world—

Lavinia screamed as the blade connected—

And she cracked it—

Roger roared—

And she pounded it—

Her father moaned.

And she split it in two . . .

Liquid spumed out—great globs of thick clear liquid—she heard Lavinia scream, and she looked at Con, and the liquid was all over his face, and the way he was staring at her, and she could tell—he could see.

And Lavinia howling . . . shrivelling before their very eyes into a sharp-beaked gull, and then transforming into an owl, a vulture—swooping up into the air suddenly to attack Roger.

Roger! Pushing at the thing, beating it away, and it flapping its wings, shrieking, screaming, biting him with its beak and suddenly, there was an explosion and— nothingness.

And both of them—gone.

Everyone else—frozen in place.

Con, dumbfounded; Darcie, transfixed. Her father, utterly bewildered.

And then her father moved. He leapt for the table and grabbed one piece of the diamond. And then he sprinted for the door.

He never made it. The liquid enveloped him like lava,

foaming out from the center of the diamond, and adhering to his skin.

He died on the spot.

Darcie couldn't look. She looked at Con. *Con with his merciful eyes.*

Blessed be . . . meant to be—

Alone with the diamond and all it had wrought.

It looked like two halves of a broken stone. No luster. No sparkle. Nothing to distinguish it from a rock on the sand.

And this had been *The Eye of God.* And now that it was sundered, the balance would be maintained.

"How did you know—all of that, about the possession, and *the oil of mercy*?"

"The oil of mercy is legendary; I've studied the lore of every culture in search of clues to the whereabouts of the diamond. There had to be a link to Samael to explain why she was so desperate for the diamond. It meant something for her. Not just the riches from splitting it up. Something deeper.

"Some property of the diamond was essential to her. And then something about her obsessiveness about the child struck a chord. I remembered the legend of Lilith's demand at heaven's gate. And the old story about Samael accompanying her. We *had* to know what was contained in the diamond, Darcie. We had to make things right."

"Your eyes are healed. Nothing could be more right," she said.

He nodded. "And the enemy vanquished. The judgment is: from this day forth, he who had been blind, now can he see. And that which must be done, will be done. The power *was* yours, Darcie. The evil is dispersed, but now there can be remedy. We will split *The*

Eye of God, into as many pieces as we can, and we'll gift it where its power will counteract the evil. Penance *must* be paid, Darcie. That is *all* we can do."

After all that, she thought. And in the end, the cost was too great. The diamond would be cleaved because penance must be paid.

And greed and cupidity rebuked and given into the service of good.

Epilogue

Kisses. All he could think about was kisses.

Darcie's kisses.

And diamonds. He was drowning in diamonds since he had taken back Pengellis-Becarre. His return caused a sensation. Everybody wanted to see, to touch, to hear Con Pengellis who had returned from the dead.

Con, who only wanted to see, touch and hear Darcie. God, he wanted Darcie. There wasn't a waking moment he wasn't thinking about Darcie, and the quest, and all the luxurious hours of their lovemaking.

Darcie!

And where was Darcie? Darcie was living the life of a profligate wealthy widow in the Mayfair Hotel.

Darcie said, they had to wait. How would it look, if he were living with his brother's widow?

Very biblical of Darcie. It tied right in with everything. He *really* appreciated her concern for his character and morals.

He *really* did.

Was there ever a woman like Darcie?

He sat at his desk and looked over papers, and budgets, and drawings of new faceted cuts, and all he wanted to do was deck Darcie from head to foot in diamonds. He wanted to deck Darcie altogether.

He played the perfectly proper suitor, willing to wait.

He *hated* waiting, and he cursed the day he ever made Darcie wait. She knew just how to use it like a club and he had taught her how.

Of course, that didn't stop her from attending a whirlwind of events. He read about them now and again in the gossip columns because *he* wasn't allowed within a block of her. *Not* good form, said Darcie, pursuing your dead brother's wife in public.

He wanted to pursue something else, but even that was denied to him. He couldn't make the rules now. She could—and did—deny him *everything*.

And he wasn't sure how long he would put up with it, but it did add spice to things—for now.

And in the meantime, while he was *waiting,* he put his time to excellent use—when he wasn't daydreaming about Darcie. He was planning their wedding—although she didn't know about that part yet. He was designing her ring—but she didn't know about that either.

And he was constructing their life—but he hadn't gotten around to mentioning it.

He planned to inundate her with diamonds. It was the only proper gift for a heroine.

But he was annoyed to see he was not the only one who thought that about her. There was Darcie, her photograph in the paper, the lovely widow Pengellis, the story said, enjoying the races on the arm of the Earl of Fotherington.

That got his juices up.

He called on Darcie the next day.

"Con, you *cannot* visit me like this. It's not good form. I've been learning *all* about good form. There are *rules,* you know."

"I remember rules," he muttered. "I'm coming in."

"This isn't right," she fumed. "I'm trying very hard to live down all those stories that circulated about me after you announced your return and Roger's death. I have the Pengellis name to maintain now."

"And you're doing a right and proper job of it too, Darcie. At the theater last week. At the races Saturday. Church on Sunday. And all on the arms of three different men. My brother, if he hadn't been such a swine, would be turning in his grave. Besides which, I'm tired of waiting."

"Oh, but Con—people just won't understand about your brother's wife. Those are the *rules.*"

"I'm sick to death of rules and waiting."

She considered this for a moment. "Oh. Well. All right. Was there anything else you wanted to tell me?"

"Who the hell is the Earl of Fotherington?"

"A *very* nice man," she said earnestly. "He'd love to get married and set up his nursery . . ."

"Oh? Is he lined up behind your other paramours? Or are you keeping them all *waiting*?"

"Of course he doesn't have to *wait*. He's not my brother-in-law."

"Darcie—I swear . . ."

"But Con, I don't understand why you're so annoyed. What do you have to do with the Earl, or anyone else? I mean, you know I can take care of myself. And now there's money, and time, and . . ." her voice trailed off.

He looked into her deep blue eyes, and he saw the eyes of a gambler who knew when to cut her losses. And that was just what she had been doing with him, and it struck him like a blow to the gut.

This was no game.

"Are you jealous, Con?" she asked.

"I will kill the man who gets hard because of you. How about that, Darcie?"

"How about you?" she asked challengingly.

"Why don't you see?"

She held his eyes and bit her lip. She didn't know what he wanted from her now. She had thought that now he had reclaimed his life, he would want to stay as far away as possible from the Darcie who had destroyed his family. He wouldn't want an adventuress who was out for what she could get. He wouldn't want someone he knew too well.

Now that he was the Honorable Connack Pegellis, Bart., he would want a *lady*, born to his social set.

And then she had thought if she made herself into the kind of woman he would pursue, he might come for her—eventually.

The problem was, it had taken too damned long, and she had just been on the cusp of giving up on him altogether.

She wanted him so badly. If she touched him, she would set off a conflagration. She'd go to a place from which she'd never come back.

It was a moment to weigh the risks. She would either come away with what she wanted; or take home a different pot.

She almost thought it was worth it and that her ploy to keep him dangling was working.

"What's in it for me?"

His expression set. "Me."

"That's tempting, Con."

"I rather thought it was."

Arrogant beast. "But of course the Earl . . ."

"You've been *noticing* the Earl, have you?"

"Well, really Con—I'm free to *notice* whomever I want. We're not in the middle of the desert, you know."

This was getting ridiculous. "Darcie, come kiss me."

"I can't do that either, Con. You know where that will lead."

He was tired of this game. And it *was* a game. He liked their other games better. And he wanted her. He swept her into his arms and crushed her mouth under his.

"Darcie, dammit . . ."

"Very romantic," she whispered against his lips. Oh, how she'd missed his lips. "More."

That was better. That was Darcie.

Kisses and diamonds . . .

Proper dresses—proper hair . . . he pulled at them as he kissed her—Darcie in diamonds, Darcie bare . . .

Darcie's hands slipping in and cupping him between his legs.

The feel of her fingers, explosive *there*.

"Hurry." Darcie's voice, breathless with need.

"God, Darcie—all this *stuff.*"

"I know." Her voice was tremulous. "I hate it."

"Don't wear it." He had off her shift, her corset, her camisole. "Always be naked for me."

Her eyes closed and her knees went weak. "Always be hard for me."

"Am I not? I've been hard for weeks waiting for you to finish playing merry widow. God, Darcie . . ."

They sank to the floor naked.

"Oh, Con—let me see you." She grasped him tightly, and all her intentions went out the window. Whether she would be a brother's widow or his whore, she wanted him. She needed him. And she wasn't too proud to beg.

"Take me."

She kissed him there, on the tip, the head, up and down the shaft. Kneeling to him, worshipping him, never enough of him—*there*.

"Darcie—" he murmured, pushing her to the floor almost too late.

He opened his hand, and diamond dust swirled all around her, all over her body, glittering like paint.

"Let me adore you."

His hands all over her then, all over, and she felt him press something against her skin.

She lifted her head to look, and she saw he had set a diamond in her navel.

"Con . . . !"

"We cut the diamond, Darcie. We made a dozen stones. Two of them will be set among the Crown jewels for the protection of the King. And we will present them in court, you and I, at the end of the month."

Balance. It was all about balance.

And there was only one more thing he had to do for balance to be restored.

He spread his hand over her belly. "Isn't there something biblical about a man cleaving to his brother's widowed wife?"

"Is there?" she asked barely above a whisper.

"And that it's a blessing if he marries her?" He touched the stone in her navel. "This is a fragment I cut and shaped for you. Let it be your engagement stone."

She caught her breath. "Yes."

"You'll marry me."

"Yes. But only because it's a blessing."

"No waiting."

"I promise."

"No rules."

She smiled. "Only if you make them."

"Forever?"

"More," she promised, she asked.

He kissed her deeply, in token of *his* promise, and

then he lifted the stone to the light and rainbows shot out, striping her bare body in liquid color.

"And in honor of our love," he murmured, setting it again reverently in the hollow of her navel, "this diamond shall be known forever more as the Eye of Heaven."

Darcie levered herself up on one arm and touched it. She felt a trembling deep inside her, a quickening just beneath the stone, and she looked at him with wondrous eyes.

He held her gaze as he shifted his weight so that he was over her, and poised for the moment of possession. "This is the judgment of the stone," he whispered. "You are *my* chosen one, Darcie. You are my heaven," and with a triumphant thrust, he brought them both home.